For Pat
(also known as Patricia)
and Andrew
(also known as 'Monster Boy')

One need not be a Chamber – to be haunted –
One need not be a House –
The Brain has Corridors – surpassing
Material Place –

Emily Dickinson

DARK CORNERS

DARK CORNERS

STEPHEN VOLK

DARK CORNERS

First published in 2006 by Gray Friar Press.
19 Ruffield Side, Delph Hill, Wyke, Bradford,
West Yorkshire, BD12 8DP, England.

Email: g.fry@blueyonder.co.uk
www.grayfriarpress.com

www.benbaldwin.co.uk

Typesetting by Gary Fry and Simon Strantzas

ISBN: 0-9550922-4-8 hardback
(Limited to 100 copies worldwide)
ISBN: 0-9550922-3-X paperback

CONTENTS

No More Hidden Things –
An introduction to Steve Volk's Dark Corners

Tim Lebbon

Dark Corners are generally where you find things you've lost. Hidden there under a pile of dust, dead spiders and brittle leaves, you'll discover objects you haven't seen for some time, artefacts of your life that have perhaps even faded from memory, existing now as echoes of dreams or rumours of something else. They're swept there by time and neglect, or perhaps placed there on purpose by people who should know better (because *everyone* knows that dark corners are the first place you should look when something is lost…if you've got the guts).

However, I believe that Steve Volk *likes* these places. Steve's Dark Corners are places for revelations, and revelling in words. He likes to visit them and go searching, because he *wants* to find those long-lost things, and he *needs* to see what has been hidden away. He even has the skill and audacity to create them himself, just to see what may be there.

He goes looking where many people would not. And I'll tell you why:

Steve is a screenwriter. Check out the Author Biography elsewhere in this volume and you'll see an impressive list of credits. His creation *Ghostwatch* can be talked about in the same breath as Machen's 'The Bowmen' and Welles's *War of the Worlds* broadcast, both of which managed to turn disbelief to belief amongst their intended audience (intentional or not). He also wrote the recent ITV series *Afterlife*, one of the spookiest programmes on TV for many years. So, with these and other credits you'd have figured by now that Steve certainly has admirable horror credentials. But screenwriting is a whole world away from writing novels and short stories, both in technique…and the business side of things. What horror novelist can claim that "I knew I was in Hollywood when I went to a party and, at three in the morning, Jack Nicholson sauntered in wearing sunglasses." Ahhh, that's *showbiz* folks, not writing whilst subsisting on cold baked beans and trying to protect your computer from those roof leaks that won't go away, no matter how many pairs of holed socks you stick in them.

So what's a screenwriter doing writing a whole collection of short stories? For the money? Er...I don't think so. One screenplay sale will pay for a lifetime of short stories. For the fame or infamy? Please. Go and apply to appear on *Big Brother*.

For the art? Now there's a truly refreshing idea ...

Although Steve has never told me this, I know why he writes short stories: it's for love. He loves words, loves imagery, revels in language and wallows in tone and voice, and you can sense this with every story of his you read. And maybe being a screenwriter – one-line pitches, sparse language, nothing too flowery or indulgent – means that the short story is the perfect place for him to feed this addiction.

It also happens that he's fucking good at it.

A little about the stories. This is an Introduction to the collection, not a review, so to preserve your enjoyment I won't delve into each story in detail. I wouldn't want to spoil them for you. These dark corners will remain hidden until you discover them for yourself. But I can at least hint at what they're hiding.

Some of the stories here are inspired and linked by an obvious love of older horror tales. You know the sort I mean: a character – usually a seeker of arcane mysteries, Steve's version of whom is Mr Venables – meets a wise old man in a gentleman's club in Chelsea, they sit comfortably in the company of brandy and fine cigars, and then the old man grows stern as he starts to relay one of many strange stories he collected during his travels. It's a story within a story style that people like Machen and Blackwood used so well. There's something safe about it – you know that the narrator of the tale survived, however terrible the tale may be – but there's also a sinister side to things here, a realisation that things are not what they seem. The safety of cigars and brandy and high-backed chairs in front of a roaring fire seem pitiful when faced with the tale's final lines. Venables, whilst actively seeking such tales and mysteries, cannot help being affected by their menace.

You will also find crime stories here, plumbing deep into the minds of criminals and painting unexpected psychological profiles that would surprise Clarice Starling. The best of these, for me, is 'Indicator', a beautifully observed parable of guilt, responsibility and power that left me musing upon it for days. 'Time Capsule' is a daring and brilliant study of a delicate subject, while 'Blitzenstein' uses dark humour and horror to stunning effect.

My favourite story of the collection – and indeed, I'll say hand-on-heart that it's one of my favourite stories of all time – is 'Three Fingers, One Thumb'. I don't want to say too much because I'd hate to spoil your reading experience...but read this without crying. I dare you. Can't be done.

I could go on in depth about the surrealism of 'Curious Green Colours Sleep Furiously', the spookiness of 'The Latin Master', or the disturbing psychological games of 'No Harm Done'. I could, but as I said before, this isn't a review. So it's far better for you to discover Steve's stories for yourself.

I have an admission to make. I've known Steve for about ten years. We meet regularly for a meal and a catch-up, chatting about current work and future aspirations. And in all that time I've thought of him as a screenwriter. I've seen the occasional short story from him – I think the first was 'Blitzenstein' in *Hideous Progeny* – but they were few and far between, and though I liked them I thought he was just having a bit of fun. Cleansing the literary palette between screenplays. Taking a rest.

I was wrong. Steve isn't a screenwriter, he's a *writer*. He knows the power of words, and he wields that power as effectively as some of the very best short story writers around. He knows people, and he understands them, and he can put the reader comfortably into the mind of a wide array of characters, both good and repugnant. His fiction is mature and insightful, compelling and powerful, and he's not afraid of digging deep.

Most of all, he knows what those dark corners hide.

So turn the page and find out for yourself.

Tim Lebbon
Goytre
January 2006

No. Don't want to go back to that place. No way. No how.

Cut to:

September 12, 2002.

Ruth Baumgarten telephoned me with the BBC's idea. She didn't want anything to do with it, but she felt duty bound to pass on the request to me, just in case. I hadn't heard from her in eight years or so and when she hung up I knew I wouldn't hear from her again.

There are certain TV producers with diaries marked in green and yellow highlighter pen, the better to anticipate upcoming anniversaries in which to cash – the fiftieth anniversary of World War One, the twenty-fifth anniversary of Kennedy's assassination – but Ruth, the producer of *Ghostwatch* and once a close friend, I can safely say, is not one of them.

We had all agreed long ago that GW was a one-off, never to be revisited. We should be so lucky. As if anyone would listen to us, the mere creators of the programme.

In the wolfish hunger for so-called reality TV after three mega-successful series of *Big Brother*, it wasn't difficult to see where the Powers-that-BBC was coming from, in its Dyke-driven quest for ratings.

The proposal was a simple one. Put forward, no doubt over a lunch at Groucho's by a producer I'd never heard of, who had been twelve at the time of the original broadcast, and who now, at twenty-two, was inexperienced enough to embody the yoof audience BBC1 desperately wanted to attract. At that stage yours truly, the humble writer, of course, was not deemed necessary to consult, even though technically the concept was still legally my property, though the rights in the programme itself rested with the Beeb. Nevertheless at this meeting, otherwise known as a lunch, the produceress, in designer glasses way more trendy than Parky's in his 1992 Specsavers commercials, evidently pitched a sequel: *Ghostwatch 2, Return to Studio One.* And they clapped till their hands bled. Or at least didn't say no.

My own reaction to the proposal was predictable.

1

My body went into spasm.

I didn't jump at the idea. I didn't rise to the occasion, or the bait, in writing, by phone call, by e-mail. Pleading, moaning, cajoling, didn't shift me one iota. I don't know what did, in the end.

I think the fact that fear, real palpable terror bubbling up from inside – a pure, physical, ectoplasmic surge in my gut – said, *Aha! I have you!* And I wanted to prove it wrong. I wasn't afraid. Not now.

Not ten years later, for God's sake.

FLASHBACK

Almost all of the people involved in *Ghostwatch* I had lost contact with, for obvious reasons.

The aftermath of the original live programme from the haunted house in Northolt is well-known and well-documented. The outrage caused ripples in Parliament as well as the hallowed halls of BBC management. The horror caused by the innocuously named "Mr Pipes" – the malevolent ghost of cross-dressing paedophile Raymond Tunstall (or was it the older, more demonic Victorian bogey-woman Mrs Seddons?) – had held the nation in a stranglehold that Halloween night, 1992, and had given our Great British credulity and preconceptions a good old shaking.

I don't mean to sound flip. I have taken to using this kind of language. It is the equivalent of the black humour used by paramedics and policemen.

It protects me from the truth.

Michael Parkinson never now talks about the events of 31st October 1992. His agent circulated the quotes used in the newspapers the following week, in which Parkinson countered attacks of irresponsibility with the remark that "some people believe the wrestling." In fact during this time, the unflappable talk-show host was recovering in a private clinic in Buckinghamshire away from the glare of publicity, his mind and memory seared by what had happened to him in that television studio, staring into space, repeating over and over, "Round and round the garden, like a teddy bear..." Within weeks, ostensibly fully recovered, he re-entered public life, but in the intervening years he never sought to re-experience those ninety minutes of Hell via therapy or indeed via videotape, and to this day the mere mention of the word "Ghostwatch" is banned in his presence. The entire event is a blank, and if it ever existed in his memory, it has been recorded over, possibly eradicated forever. You only need to watch him these days to know that is true.

Pamela and Kim Early moved to the USA in a strategy no less secretive than the FBI witness protection scheme. Kim is now twenty and, under a different name and with a Mid-western accent, studying towards a career in biological sciences. Pamela, her mother, died in a household fire in 1995. She had since re-married, in a paradox worthy of the pages of *Fortean Times*, a fireman. It is reported that she visited many psychotherapists over the years and indeed studied and became one herself, specialising in helping people with "spiritual intrusion problems." She was in the process of writing a book about guardian angels.

The fates of both Suzanne and Sarah Greene are unknown.

It is now well-known that Sarah's transmission on Children's BBC a few days after the fateful broadcast, reassuring younger viewers that she hadn't disappeared, or died, horribly, inside the Glory Hole, was of course recorded by a look-alike, as were a number of subsequent TV appearances on holiday programmes and the like.

In actual fact, when the Northolt police forcibly broke into the house in Foxhill Drive and pulled the door off the Glory Hole under the stairs into which Sarah had ventured to rescue a sobbing Suzanne, they found it empty except for the smell of cats and developing fluid. And a thorough search of the house from top to bottom, to the extent of near-demolition, revealed nothing of either person's whereabouts.

Studio One at BBC TV Centre was immediately closed down. The power was cut during the poltergeist-induced chaos and the doors sealed pending an internal investigation which, predictably, drew no conclusions. The paranormal rarely does –- maybe that is its purpose and its essential nature. In the ensuing weeks, superstition was rife. Broadcasting House had proven itself a haunted house. People refused to work there. Certainly people refused to work in Studio One. It was declared out of bounds. A few tabloid photographers had tried to get inside, to no avail. They tried to write a bogus story, but the BBC lawyers clamped down on them, and they were gagged. It was, after all, an episode of public

Stephen Volk

service broadcasting that Auntie would prefer to forget had ever happened – and wished to God it never had.

Cut to: Ten years later.

Now they wanted me, the poor writer, Stephen Volk, to accompany six other selected special guests and go into that studio – boarded up and unused for ten years – on Halloween night, 2002, at 9.30pm. The exact anniversary, to the minute, of the transmission of the notorious *Ghostwatch*. And do it again.

GREEN ROOM

31 October 2002 – 2pm – BBC TV Centre, Wood Lane

"There's no such thing as ghosts," says the PA, Pippa, cheerily. Everyone just looks up at her. She blushes. "Sorry."

Cigarettes stub out in quick succession.

"All I know is," I say as the Make-up Girl powders my billiard-ball shaved head, "I want that bloody auto-cue out of there."

We sign our release forms, whatever they are. To whom it may concern, blah blah. Pact with the Devil. *I promise to pay the bearer...*my soul? Maybe we'd done that already. Some of us.

4pm

Alan Demescu's beard looks a lot greyer now and he has the look of a gaunt Bosnian refugee about him, as we clammily shake hands. *Somebody for God's sake smile,* I think, almost out loud.

These are the other participants in this fandango.

Emma Stableford. Remember her? The viewer who first phoned in having alerted the audience – if not the studio team – to the presence of "Pipes" standing next to the curtains in the girls' bedroom in Foxhill Drive.

Emilio Sylvestri, the CSICOP arch-sceptic whose acerbic appearance on GW by satellite link from NYC boosted his fame and arse-holiness no end, making him the doyen of chat shows in the US as well as a regular on *So Graham Norton*. Sylvestri, who had made the most of his involvement in the *Ghostwatch* tragedy (or fiasco) in his catch-all debunkfest *Tales from the Script* (Prometheus Press, 1993), greeted me with a bonhomie that presumed I could ignore his past record of cheap jibes and castigations against the production team.

Wrong.

Mike Smith declined the tactless request for him to take part. As did Uri Geller, an early short-listee who was nixed after his lack of longevity on ITV's *I'm a Celebrity Get Me Out Of Here*. Jade Goody apparently had been approached, but said she had been "scared shitless" by the original *Ghostwatch* in 1992, having watched all but the last 10 minutes when her mother switched off the TV set.

At the time of transmission, the BBC phone lines were jammed with calls, many of them from angry and terrified viewers. One such call came from the Reverend Edmund Edward Gryffin of Brynmawr, who berated the BBC for "tampering with Satanic forces," for raising demons beyond its control and for being in league with the Devil, no less. In the intervening years he had become no less vitriolic in his convictions, and today, joining us as spiritual guide (yes, exactly) few of us were going to argue with him – on a metaphorical level, at least.

During the original broadcast, according to the BBC duty log, three pregnant women were so shocked that they went into labour. The good old BBC had traced one of these women, Berenice Gannon of North Berwick, Scotland, whose daughter Louise was born at 10.30 that Halloween night, at precisely the moment of *Ghostwatch's* final fade to black. Apparently, with the slamming of the Glory Hole door, baby Louise took her first intake of breath. Louise – or as she preferred to be called, by her second name, decided months prior to her birth – *Suzanne*.

I decide I'm going to call her Louise.

"All right, Louise?"

She says, "Look what I've got. Remember him?" A BBC props buyer has given her a cuddly toy rabbit, exactly the kind Kimmy had in the original *Ghostwatch* house. The one whose pin-button eyes she, or Pipes, or Mrs Seddons, had mysteriously plucked out before drowning said toy rabbit in the kitchen sink.

Shit. Whose bright idea was that, I wonder. "Bubby wanted to come back, didn't you, Bubby?" she says, matter-of-factly.

"What the hell…" I mumble, knocking back my orange juice in the Green Room. *I'm only the writer.*

STAND BY

9.25 - *Five minutes to lift off.*

I can imagine those deliberately hokey graphics, those ghost-white swimming letters, being lined up on the video playback. "Roll VT." They say in my ear-piece. "All systems go."

Dr Lin Pascoe is in there, looking at the bank of TV screens as the director cuts between them.

TX

9.32

Flashlight beams cut through the dark. So far, so *X-Files*. Unbelievably hokey. *Hey, kettle, pot, black, who am I to talk about cliché?*

Divers in the wreck of the 'Titanic,' the six of us walk inside. There are three brave (short-straw?) cameramen at three studio cameras, and now the cameras raise their heads like cows in a field to look at us, framing us up as we enter.

Over to the left the phone-in alcove has a layer of cobwebs over it and I am unsure whether they are genuine or a thoughtful embellishment of the design department. My flashlight scans. *Please.* It finds the bedsheet-ghost image, the painting by Gottfried Helnwein I saw many years ago in a Vienna gallery and recommended to the designer, in its frame over the Addams Family fireplace. Then, as now, fat pumpkins glowing orangely either side of the mantelpiece. Grinning skulls, eagerly, mischievously welcoming us back for round two.

We hear the Control Room in our ear-pieces. "Cue SFX."

The Studio One door slams with sarcophagus finality. Real or pre-recorded.

"Take two, Mr Volk," Emilio Sylvestri drawls. "This time with feeling."

"Shut the fuck up," says Alan Demescu under his breath.

I say: "That'll be bleeped for a start."

"Language," says the director in the headphones, disembodied, invisible. "Luckily we're not gone live yet. Still rolling the intro." *Language, always the BBC's priority over sex and violence. Language. The writer's domain. Bad language. Good. Evil.*

Demescu murmurs "Sorry" to Louise Gannon, the little girl.

Louise says, "I've heard a lot worse than that. A *lot* worse!" She wears red Kicker-type shoes and a rucksack in the form of a fluffy white seal cub. Her blonde hair has a few dreadlocks in coloured strands and she has talked mostly so far about Gareth Gates and Britney Spears.

"What happens now?" asks Emma Stableford.

"Who knows?" says Alan Demescu.

"Mr Pipes, perhaps," says Sylvestri, with a sneering intonation the equal of Ned Sherrin, fluttering his fingers in the air and rolling his eyes mock-spookily.

"Be careful what you wish for, it might just happen," says the Reverend EEG. "That was the moral of the original, Stephen. Correct?"

"Only fiction can have a moral," I say. "Something that really happens can't. Fact can't. Correct?"

"Correct," says Alan Demescu, the scientist in the baggy pullover.

"Are we on yet?" asks Louise.

I study the cameras. One has a red light in the dark. I remember the red eye of Raymond Tunstall, of Pipes. Of Kimmy's drawing. "Oh yes. We're on." Says Emma Stableford. "It's *Stars in Their Eyes*, Loo-loo. Who are you playing?"

Louise laughs. It echoes. *Christ, it echoes.*

"You know," she says, grinning, her thumb nail twisting against her teeth and jiggling her hips from side to side, childishly bashfully but not bashful at all. Acting bashful. Bashful like bashful is what we want her to be.

9.43

It is so silent it makes you want to shout. But we don't. None of us do. We whisper. Why are we whispering?

I ask: "Why are we whispering? This isn't a church."

"It is," says Louise. *Echoing.*

Giggling, like it's a joke. Not understanding what jokes are yet. Ten years old. Exactly ten years old, I realise. *Her birthday, of course it is. That's the whole point. That's why she's here.*

Children understand what jokes are at ten years old, don't they? Children understand good and bad, right and wrong, don't they? Do we? Now? What are we doing? Do we even know? Ever?

9.47

Then it comes.

Then I hear it.

The words.

I knew they would come and I knew they'd come from the child.

"When's Pipes coming?"

Quiet in the Control Room. I'm thinking, they love it.

They're not speaking because they love it. This is peeing in the shower. This is getting drunk and falling over. This is Jade's tears. This is "*minging.*"

"I think we should pray," says EEG.

Of us all, he is the one playing (praying?) to the cameras. He's the one who is really in church now. The one who protests about obscenity is more obscene than any of us.

He kneels in the middle of the television studio with tightly clasped Christian hands, corny as a Mickey Rooney movie.

He is the first, then Louise kneels down beside him. Then so does Emma Stableford and so do I. The only one who remains on his feet is Emilio Sylvestri – the sceptic.

And he loves it.

9.59

One thing in common with 1992: nothing happens. Hardly anything happening at all, for a long time.

Why are people watching?
Why are they interested?
Why are they looking at us?
What do they want to see?

Now it is campfire-like. Emma Stableford is telling a story from her childhood about something eerie on the Yorkshire Moors. Very friend-of-a-friend. Very *Fortean Times*. I eye Emilio Sylvestri and he eyes me.

Alan Demescu and I talk about *Ghostwatch*, the pre-production, the myth, the actuality, the aftermath: really re-playing the many Q&A session we have all done over the years, ad infinitum.

All Q and very few A's at the end of the day.

10.07

The sentinel pumpkins grin like a gummy audience. One inter-cranial candle flickers as if flecked by the demonic thoughts swirling therein, and goes out. The vicar re-lights it with a lighter in the shape of a woman.

We are playing cards now. Strip Jack Naked. And the ten year old thrashing us every time. Is this game supposed to be based on chance? If so, the laws of chance are staying away tonight. Maybe they don't like Halloween. Maybe Halloween doesn't like them.

We switch to Snap and, every time, Louise gets excited and yells SNAP and grabs the cards, irrespective of whether she is right or wrong, and laughs uproariously.

Till she says: "Oops, I think I've wet myself."

I smile. "I don't think that's allowed on BBC1."

"What's a baby farmer?" she asks me. "Do they plant babies in the ground and watch them grow? Is it like test tube babies and Dolly the sheep? We've got a sheep in school and he's called Dolly."

"*He's* called Dolly?" says Alan Demescu, raising a bushy eyebrow.

"It's just a word. Two words," I tell Louise. "It doesn't mean anything."

"Everything means something," Louise says, shuffling the cards, the wisdom hanging in the air. "When is Pipes coming?"

When is Pipes coming?

10.10

"Scooby Scooby do, where are you?" sings Emilio Sylvestri to the sea of darkness we're swimming in.

I say: "God's sake, I think we've come on a little way from that, don't you?"

"I was trying to lighten the proceedings."

"Please do," says Emma Stableford, the housewife.

"I'm c-cold," says Louise Gannon. "Are you? Is anybody else cold? I'm f-freezing."

"Oh," says Sylvestri, with a mock-sympathetic dip in his voice. "Fasten your psychic safety belts, folks, I think we're in for a bumpy ride."

"What is your problem?" snaps Alan Demescu, eyes flaring but voice staying calm. His lips pull tight like elastic bands. "What do you think, that we all made it up in 1992, that it was all fake? That it's all some massive hoax like the moon landings? What *do* you believe, Sylvestri?"

"Only that people experienced some delusion on a grand scale. On a scale of eleven million viewers, to be precise. But just because David Copperfield makes the Statue of Liberty disappear on ABC doesn't mean it isn't still there when you look the next morning." Sylvestri was always good with the one-liners.

"And what about Sarah?" I say. "What about Suzanne? Are they part of the hoax too? Where have they been for the last ten years? Just lying low to make the most of a good joke?"

"People have reasons to disappear," says Sylvestri. "People disappear for no reason at all. It doesn't mean we have to call Mulder and Scully. It doesn't mean we scuttle into the little funk hole in the desert with the sign saying IRRATIONAL BELIEF – PLEASE HIDE HERE TILL IT'S SAFE. There's a rational explanation for everything, strange as it may seem."

"God save us from rational explanations," says Alan Demescu, turning away and shaking his head as he walks into the shadows.

"God save us from God, for that matter," says Sylvestri, pleased with himself disproportionately.

He walks to the centre of the space, to the big reel-to-reel Revox tape recorder and presses "PLAY." Its wheels turn and we hear the guttural, encaphemous voice we all heard, to chilling effect, during the original *Ghostwatch* broadcast.

"Switch that off," says Demescu. "Switch that damned thing..."

I beat him to the OFF switch. The echo, the reverb, the memory or trace of that voice continues, I'm sure, for a second or two after the tape spools stop turning.

"Roll VT," says someone in my ear-piece. "That was great, well done." Not telling us what was great, or what was well done.

I rub the back of my neck, staring at the ceiling, the nothing, the night sky of the meagre lighting rig.

What time is it? How far are we into this? I have no idea. I listen, they talk, I don't hear. What the hell is happening out there? Jesus, when is this going to end?

Jesus – I look at them. Jesus – are the rest of them as afraid as me?

10.13

"One minute more of VT. Stand by," said the voice in the ear-piece. "When we're back on air just keep the conversation going, as naturally as possible."

Naturally. I almost laugh. What the fuck is natural*?*

This from the director who had pep-talked us with: "Don't worry about content. There is no content, just character. Just talk, and atmosphere, and the audience. A la B.B., get it?" I took a second to decipher. She meant don't do anything, they'll watch anyway. Just like *Big Brother*. Geddit?

We are back for about forty non-eventful seconds, then they go to the compilation VT segment, as per the script.

Viewers have been voting for a week for their favourite top ten *Ghostwatch* moments, and now they are playing clips 5 to 3 in reverse order. The Welsh bloke whose sandwich did a nose dive off the arm of his chair gets a look in. They interview him, a sound-bite, ten years later. This interspersed with clips of contributors recounting what they were doing, where they were and what they thought, on the night GW went out. Sara Cox, Johnny Vegas, Linda Robson, Ross Kemp, Christine and Neil Hamilton, John Simpson, Paul Daniels, Rolf Harris, Dr Susan Blackmore, Dr Raj Persaud, and Marjorie Wallace, chairperson of the mental health charity SANE.

10.19

There is no monitor in Studio One, and the six of us deep-sea videonauts hermetically are deliberately, we realise, without swapping this observation, sealed off from the outside world.

"When is Pipes coming?" asks Louise, again.

When is Pipes coming? When is Pipes coming?

Silence, and none of us likes it, so one of us fills it. I divert the question that hangs in the air by asking Louise what she wants to be when she grows up.

"An adult," she answers.

With which it's very difficult to argue. I laugh a sigh, sigh a laugh, whatever the phrase is.

Silence again, and nobody likes it, but this time nobody speaks and the silence wins.

I walk over and press the thin membrane separating the phone-in area from the studio proper, onto which the corny, ghostly *Ghostwatch* logo had been projected then eerily dissolved away into the ether at the top of the show. The thin veil between fact and fiction, sanity and insanity, this world and the next.

You have a way with words, mate. You ought to be a writer.

In the silence of the haunted studio I think of the endless Media Studies dissertations that *Ghostwatch* has spawned over the years. I had been told by one professor at Aberystwyth that every year without fail one of his students would put it forward as a thesis subject. Pages and pages, books upon books of analysis, observation, libraries of it. It's hard to imagine. Like the last shot of *Raiders of the Lost Ark*. My favourite, predictably Freudian, interpretation of *Ghostwatch* came from the student who made the connection that *"Pipes"* when translated into French slang, meant *"Blow jobs."* The female adolescents were therefore appealing to the TV audience for blow jobs, and this, on an unconscious level, was what the masculine-centric audience was demanding to see.

Give that girl a first, with honours.

10.21

Louise looks down at the cards, plain playing cards, laid out in front of her on the studio floor.

"Happy Families." Ironic.

She shuffles them and deals them out in a line as if she is playing some improvised form of Solitaire. I watch her, knowing that her mother Berenice is somewhere, out in the control box, sitting next to Dr Lyn Pascoe, watching all this. A mother who leaves her child in a haunted house with five strangers. What kind of mother is that?

Mother. Mother Seddons. Mother Seddons will get you.

"I know what this spells," she says, looking at the row of playing cards. "S-A-R-A-H... Sarah..."

"All right, very funny," I say.

"Yes it is very funny," she says.

"No it isn't."

"Yes it *is*. *He* says it is. *Pipes* says it is." She holds up a card. "Pipes is the King with one eye. Pipes is Camera One."

"Out of the mouths of babes and sucklings," mumbles Sylvestri.

Wait – then the banging starts. Banging – there's another little Freudian double-entendre. And wait – it isn't just *similar* to the banging in the Foxhill Drive on Halloween 1992 — it is the *exact same* banging. It's like someone has switched on a tape recording and it's the *same noise* coming amplified from some great big stadium sized speakers in the dark.

Emma Stableford immediately holds her ears and screams like an infant and starts shaking. Everybody goes rigid, looking at each other without moving.

It's the producers, I'm about to say, *it's a joke, like Craig Charles jumping out of the kitchen cabinet in the original. It's not happening. Not really.*

"Control Room, please, stop messing around, there's a child in here," Demescu says to the air. "Stop playing silly buggers."

"What's wrong?" shouts Dr Lin Pascoe in the ear-piece. Too close too the microphone.

"The noise, stop it, turn it off, now. It's not funny!"

A hair of a pause from Pascoe. "Noise, what noise? We can't hear anything. What can you hear? Tell me exactly what you can hear. Can you hear me? Can you hear what I'm saying?"

"Silly buggers," laughs Louise. "Silly buggers!"

Then bingo. *The cards spray up into the air, like a fountain,* Alice in Wonderland fashion. One spins sideways – changing direction in mid-air – hitting Emilio Sylvestri in the face. It cuts him like the slash of a mugger's razor blade. He bleats more in puzzlement than horror, probably just feeling the warmth, but when he looks at his trembling fingertips he instinctively raises to his cheek, they are stained with blood – his own.

"*Silly buggers, silly buggers, silly buggers...*" crackles in the air, not matching Louise's mouth any more. The lip sync going wrong. The lip synch going wrong *in real life.*

"Jesus she did it Jesus how Jesus sleight of hand," Demescu is gabbling, grabbing Louise by her stick-like arms, shaking her madly, twisting her wrists behind her back like a rough LA cop. "She palmed one with an edge did you see did anybody see she she she – "

"*Pipes is here, Pipes is coming! He's coming! He's coming! He's here NOW!*"

Emma Stableford is standing rigidly, hyperventilating, with outstretched hands like a blind person trying to find her way, pointing into the dark.

"*There! There!*" she is yelling. "*There! There! I see him! I can see him!*"

The banging again, sonorous as thrashing drums, from the pipes, from Pipes, from everywhere, from inside our heads.

"*I can see him again!*"

I look into the dark place and I see the shape of things not there. I see nothing and the nothing walks out. And the nothing is wearing a long black coat like a Catholic priest's soutane, paedophiles all of them like life imitating art, God help us, everywhere now, demons flying out of every tabloid. And *here*, behold. Watch, watch with Mother, Mother Seddons. Bald head, skull. Bitten and sucked face, the carrion of cats, but no longer the face of Keith Ferrari the actor who played Mr Pipes in our programme, whose first appearance was silhouetted and computer-enhanced in the folds of the children's curtains. This face with its one bloody eye, clawed out by hungry felines in the Glory Hole, is different. This face with its staring sky blue eyes – *is Sarah Greene's.*

"It's what you wanted, isn't it? *Isn't it?*" screams Louise, in the voice of Suzanne Early. Missing Suzanne Early. Dead Suzanne Early.

And Pipes swims towards me in the dark as if dangling from a mobile gibbet, his drippy eye becoming like a ghoulish maw. The other eye Sarah Greene's piercing blue of a lost, lost soul, fixed on mine. And her voice, in a sing-songy lilt like a lullaby, direct to me and only me:

"Round and round the garden...like a teddy bear..."

The words my Grandmother used to sing to me before tickling me, as Pipes takes the open palm of my hand and runs his skeletal finger round its perimeter. Now it is in my ear-piece too: a MILLION – how many MILLION? – nine MILLION – ten MILLION – eleven MILLION voices chanting:

Round and round the garden
Like a teddy bear
One step
Two step
Tickle under there!

I feel the fingers take a double leap onto my forearm then elbow, then they bury deep into my ribs, into my heart. The muscles contract and spasm as some iron hook turns and churns and guts me out, spinning my insides like they're entwined on wire and the wire connected to a lathe and the lathe switched on.

The pain explodes in my eye. A billion cats' claws tear through my brain. Every inch of my body shakes. I feel blood filling my left eye, I try to blink it away but only feel its warm piss-feel on my cheek.

Opening my eyes I can only see – nothing. Pipes is gone. Vanished.

There is only us. The six of us, participants in primetime madness. Emilio Sylvestri backing into the dark with his hand over his mouth. Emma Stableford shaking and shrieking in terror. EEG with his eyes tightly shut, going Our Father who are in heaven hallowed be thy name. Alan Demescu waving his arms in cross-like shapes into the cameras, *switch off switch off switch off.* And Louise Gannon, the ten year old child born of *Ghostwatch*, born of my creation, ten years old, staring at me, and pointing at me, *directly at me* – and as I grabbed her and shook her to stop, stop, stop saying it, stop, until she did stop – pointing at me, screaming: "It's him, it's him, It's Pipes! He's here! He's *here!*"

The Best In The Business

Gus Beatty didn't need it. He'd spent his lunch break, a sub sandwich at the best of times, yelling down the phone at a dumb-ass writer in Seattle to re-fax his page 112 which had been mysteriously lost by Gus's pre-menstrual assistant between Talent and the Mail Room, and the schmuck with the Remington was pissed they'd screwed his chance of HBO liking the first draft. "You only get one chance for a first read, man!" he'd moaned, probably over his falafel and lentils. By the time Gus had waded through two hundred stacked-up e-mails, his laptop was doing ooga-booga with his eyeballs, and by the time he drove at reckless high speed to a meeting at Le Dôme at seven, staring at Lou Giordano's coke-spiked eyes and monumentally expensive dentistry, listening for five hours to the sub-Brando drawl from that penis with ears and pretending he was enjoying it, the day was just beautiful. And it wasn't even over. At midnight, the gorilla decided it wanted to party, and decided it wanted company. Gus went along, feeling like a Republican at Woodstock: "This is my new agent manager. Why do we have to have actors taking 85% of our fucking fee, right Gus?" Guffaws over the Perrier glasses. Gus smiled incessantly, occasionally worried it looked like a rictus of boredom. At three a.m. he made his apologies and slunk away, the asshole action star reassuring him with an O.K. circle of forefinger and thumb that his representation was in the bag. Secretly, at that point, Gus couldn't give a flying fornication. He still had the headache, no longer the mother of one but the whole damned family, going back generations, like fucking *Roots*. All the way home, the taxi driver asked what line he was in, hoping he was a producer (like most of them, he was a hopeless, hopeful actor). Off the top of his head Gus said sure, he'd made *Batman Begins*, and didn't give him a tip. He told him the rubber schlong they designed to go inside the bat-suit cost half a million dollars. (For all he knew, it had.) So it was a bat-fuck of a day and all Gus Beatty wanted when he reached his Malibu home was, mainly, for it to be over.

And now – this.

"Honey, honey…" he kept saying, trying to calm her down. Her voice had never seemed so abnormally strident, rising in pitch as he started the 'honeys'.

He didn't really listen to what she was saying at first. He presumed it was the usual string of reprimands about waiting up late, why didn't you call, feel like a paid servant, no consideration, yada yada. He guessed he'd take it on the chin, wait for the customary gap and, if absolutely necessary, go into his 'who's-the-breadwinner, anytime-you-want-to-throw-away-this-lifestyle' routine, but he didn't get the chance.

"Look, just *look* at it!" said Holly, his wife, eyes toxic and inflammable. She had the look of a woman who'd been mugged or accused of shoplifting. Her eyes seemed to have gotten bigger in twelve years of marriage, he thought. He must have smiled inwardly at that because he heard: "This is beyond a joke, Gus! I'm not kidding! You have to *do* something about it!"

"Uh?"

He peered into the kitchen cabinet as she opened the swing-door. All he saw was the pasta jars, packs of Jell-O, decaf, and the massed ranks of fennel, fruit and camomile tea.

"What's the big deal?"

"Look!"

She stubbed her finger at the dirty marks on the white surface, accusingly.

"Yeah. Dirt. So fire the maid. Don't give me a hard time about it," he said.

"*Footprints!*"

"What?" Gus stared at the tightness of her lips. His eyes crinkled into a pained expression, the nearest he could get to a laugh. "Hon, what are you talking about, 'footprints'?"

"All right, paw-prints, claw-prints, whatever the damn hell you call them!"

He groaned like a ghost. "Come *on*. Are you sure?"

"*Look* at them. You can virtually see what size Nikes the son of a bitch is wearing!"

Gus bent over, squinted.

"What – a mouse, you reckon?"

"Well not a fucking Tibetan panda, Gus!"

"OK, OK, calm down, you're the amateur naturalist all of a sudden. Look, hey, I'm real interested, my sweet, but it's – Jesus Christ – four o'clock in the morning. D'you think Mickey and his pals might just wait till tomorrow?"

"I don't think it'll look any different tomorrow," said Gus's wife. Her arms were folded across her breasts, and she was bristling for thirteen rounds.

"Well, maybe it will. Let's see. I'm tired," said Gus. "And in the great scheme of things, frankly..." He took a bottle of Tylenol and a glass of water up the stairs with him. "Goodnight." He needed sleep, not a fight.

Like a big, black dawn, the hangover came. The irony was, he hadn't even been drinking. Gus's head felt like a coal-cellar, a great rock impossible to lift from the pillow. Maybe it was a virus. When he did rouse, he could feel his brain sloshing around turbulently inside his cranial cavity as he staggered to the bathroom. For once, there was no line, the rest of the family were up and about. From the bedroom he phoned the office and put on a pert, authoritative voice to say he'd be catching up on reading scripts at home. The way he reckoned, he was due some slack for what he'd endured chaperoning Giordano.

Breakfast was brittle after the testiness the night before. Gus tried to keep a low profile, spooning milky bran slowly towards an increasingly inaccessible mouth. The maid drifted round elsewhere, knowing what was good for her, but not before she'd served the kids waffles, fruit and maple syrup.

Chris, the eldest at twelve, was in her ecology phase, so relinquished the cholesterol but would probably get a chocolate bar from the vending machines in school. Gus sighed. He wondered if she was getting the health education she should be. She was reading a leaflet about AIDS, avidly, and Gus wondered, weirdly, if he should, or could, disapprove.

Max was more of a concern. Vietnamese by birth. Adopted, in that Benetton poster-kids social-conscience phase L.A. went through in the nineties (and lasted about five seconds). If Chris was twelve going on twenty-five, Max was eight going on – well, eight. Introverted to the point of surliness, he disliked his school, or school, period. He had an incredible competitive streak, which was good, but everything he did, sport, games, chess, X-box, he was determined to win at. There was no enjoyment in it for him. He was robotic. Driven. At times, Gus thought he was going to grow into a screwed-up adult. Or Bill Gates. He and Holly blamed themselves, but sometimes it's the luck of the draw. For all your efforts to bring up good, kind, balanced, wonderful human beings, you forget they have their own personalities and there's not a whole lot you can do about that.

The twins, Allie and Tommo, five, tucked into the waffles – Allie always resembling her Mom so spookily, and Tommo who resembled Allie almost exactly: head twisted to get his daily fix of the breakfast-time cartoons. The two of them were arguing over something about some transformative superhero-monster that was far too esoteric for Gus. He took the Tylenol from beside his plate, and knocked it back with the scummy dregs of his coffee cup.

The gurgling came from Matthew, the new addition – unplanned – who sat in his highchair like a despot, waiting uneasily for his gooey feed. The children, except for Max, who hid his jealousy shallowly, doted on the newcomer, astonishingly. Once Gus had caught Allie bending over the buggy, giving her brother an impromptu kiss, tucking him up like a doll. Tears had prickled in his eyes. He thought it was probably one of the nicest memories of his life. Needless to say, a blissful contrast to his working world of egos the size of small African countries – a world that he occasionally loathed, but it was the water he swam in. Plenty did, and he did it well. And there was no crime in earning a good living for your wife and children in the best way you could.

Holly placed a glass of cold tropical fruit juice, banana orange and lime, in front of her husband.

Beside it, on his plate, she put a rectangle of cheese with a semicircle gnawed out of one corner. Gus looked at it and sighed, bracing his throbbing head with his arms propped on the breakfast table.

"Mickey?"

Holly placed a packet of sugar on the table, too. White sandy grains poured neatly from a small, round hole, making a mound that reminded Gus of the coke he'd gazed at abstemiously on the glass coffee table the night before.

"Mickey."

He avoiding saying 'Shit' in front of the children. It was the beginning of Let's Persecute Gus Beatty Week.

After three days, realising that pleading and downright anger were futile, Gus exploded that he'd heard ENOUGH about GODDAM MOUSE-CRAP! Day four, Holly's silent glances became more and more accusatory. Day five, there was an invisible '*Do* Something' balloon hovering above her persistent and un-fetching scowl.

At breakfast each morning she would produce more ravages from the closets, hoping that the catalogue of horrors would erode Gus's complacency. Gus, however, clung stubbornly to his 'I've got bigger and more important things to worry about' standpoint, but soon Holly punctured that one: "What about the health of your children? Isn't that important to you? Do you know what *germs* that thing must be spreading?"

"It'll go," he said. But it hadn't.

Holly's attitude to the little visitor became more than a little obsessive, Gus thought, soon into week two. He'd come home to find her on her knees, rearranging storage jars, inspecting for droppings. Her uncovering of the evidence became almost gleeful.

She'd lie awake at night, little dots reflected in her eyes as she listened intently for tell-tale noises. The tension spread to the body next to her. Gus would wake in the morning feeling as though he'd been a homeless guy sleeping on a park bench.

Then, Allie came down one morning in tears, holding a doll whose leg displayed a horrid wound from which the fibrous stuffing was fluffing out. The poor thing was ruined. Holly worked out, (like fucking *C.S.I.*), that the mouse was mutilating Allie's doll collection to make its nest – which made her daughter burst out crying again. Holly looked at Gus as if he'd smacked her with his hand.

Next day, Pili the maid was heard shrieking Hispanically, her grandmotherly tits jiggling, and claimed something furry was staring at her from the sink. From the sound she made Gus had thought it was at least the Zodiac Killer. She was incomprehensible but the gist of it was she wanted him to do something or she was out of there. Pronto, Tonto.

Weirdly, that seemed to have more effect than Holly's days of huffy protestation and anxiety.

And so, finally, the agent-manager whose usual idea of manual labour was lifting a paper clip, went into some mythic phone booth and became Practical Man. And it wasn't a pretty sight.

Gus laid traps. Regular metal traps that the guy in the local hardware store said would do the job, no problem, in three days. But Gus suspected he was an Iranian and didn't have a complete grasp of English. Three weeks later, the traps were sprung, the bait was eaten, and the mouse was still at large. But Gus felt he'd done his bit, albeit unsuccessfully. What more could he do?

He hoped, in time, the pest and Holly's worry over it would fade away in unison.

Wrong.

The droppings came back.

The droppings didn't go away.

The droppings increased.

"You know what?" said Holly over a supposedly romantic dinner on their anniversary, leaning closer conspiratorially: "I think there's *more* of them. A *nest*. Dozens, maybe more..."

That night, when he had harbored the hope of gratuitous, if predictable, sex, his amorous intentions were scuppered by Holly suddenly going rigid with terror at the sound of a fervent scuffling and scratching above her head. She lay back open-mouthed as he felt his penis melt away to nothing. He wanted so say "Jesus Christ, Holly," but didn't. They lay awake, together but apart, listening to the clear sound of rummaging rodents on the attic floor above.

And when sexual intercourse entered the equation, Gus could avoid the issue no longer. The stresses and power play of the agency now paled into insignificance. This was war. This would not stand. This was not negotiable. And, as far as his marriage was concerned, this was a deal-breaker.

He looked in the phone book under Pest Control, and went for the first reasonably-sized ad on the assumption that if someone can afford a big ad they must be successful at what they do. He arranged an appointment for what the guy on the cell phone called a 'site visit' for nine the next morning. And hung up with a feeling of deep satisfaction.

At ten he was still waiting, his fingertips drumming the breakfast table. He pondered whether to ring the Pest Control number, or ring his assistant at the agency to say he was delayed. He had a breakfast at Hamburger Hamlet with an African-American MTV director he'd had to cancel but he was pencilled for a 10.30 with the boss and it was Bad Karma if he was late for that. He gave a string of curses, and decided to ring the pest people and give them hell.

Just then the phone rang and he picked it up.

"Yes?"

"Hello. Mr Beatty?"

"Yes."

"Ace Pest Control here." The voice was a redneck drawl, real South, and Gus hated it instantly. Country damn bumpkin, Jesus Christ. "Real sorry I'm late, sir. We had a major infestation in Sherman Oaks and the traffic's real bad."

"Oh yeah?" Gus looked at his watch. "It would be. It wasn't half an hour ago. Look, where are you?"

"I'm here."

Jesus God help us. "No. I mean, *where*?"

"Here!"

Gus ground his teeth.

The Southern voice said: "Go to your front door."

Gus placed down the phone, gave his wife a brief, perplexed look, went to the door and opened it.

A white Toyota pick-up sat in the driveway. On the door was a transfer depicting a dead rat, in the style of a No Smoking logo. It reminded Gus of *Ghostbusters*. Up from the logo, a face leered at him out of the window, a cell phone to his ear: the man from 'Ace Pest Control' was ten feet from his own front step.

"Marvels of modern science," chuckled the man.

"Wow. All the latest technology," said Gus, but the man didn't pick up on his sarcasm.

"Yep. You betcha."

Without being invited, the man entered the house, looking at the Mexican tiled floor and designer furniture as if he'd entered the Taj Mahal. Whether he thought the abstract was a poor imitation of Kiefer (Anselm, not Sutherland), Guy doubted. He was more likely adding up the dollar signs for his brother-in-law to ram-raid the place in a week's time.

"My, you an art collector. Yeah?"

"No," said Gus, almost adding: "Just rich."

"You got taste," said the man, who wore his hair back in a pony-tail from a red, weather-beaten face. His cheeks and eyebrows looked like they were conspiring to hide his eyes.

He walked through to the kitchen.

Holly, who stood in a tight white T-shirt making bread, smiled at the porky little man – he was one of those characters you say are five feet in any direction – and he returned a nod, rubbing his hands.

"Mrs Beatty. See you're having a cup of coffee."

"Oh," said Holly. "Would you like one?"

"That's real kind. Don't mind if I do. White, three sugars. Much obliged." He pulled out a stool from under the breakfast bar and made himself comfortable. Gus had left a copy of *Time* magazine on the table which the man opened and began to flick through. "Good strong cup of coffee. Brings the bodily system up to speed. Focuses the energies. Then to work."

While the man drank in no perceptible hurry, Gus phoned work, irritably stabbing the buttons, to say he was unavoidably detained. When he returned to the kitchen, the man was on his second cup and discussing interior design with his wife. Seeing Gus's impatience, he smiled a gap-toothed smile, put the half-cup in the microwave and said he'd have it later. He gave Holly a wink, and patted her ass.

Holly's eyes were laser beams at Gus, in case he didn't notice. Gus pretended he hadn't.

"This way."

Gus led him upstairs.

Halfway up the man paused, sniffing the air. He opened the door to the bathroom and sniffed again.

Gus took him to the twins' bedroom and showed him the gnawed doll, which the man examined meticulously, putting on a pair of incredibly dusty spectacles.

He climbed onto the bed and examined the ceiling beams, plucking mouse-droppings and sniffing them periodically.

Then he got down. He was a good foot shorter than Gus. "I don't want to alarm you, Mr Beatty, I really don't. But in my considered opinion, I think you have a very sizeable infestation in this domicile."

"Oh, I don't think it's as serious as that."

Gus knew instantly he'd said the wrong thing.

The man looked at him. "Let me tell you one thing before we start, Mr Beatty. I'm well known in these parts. I've got rid of rodents for some very famous clients in this city. Did you know that Elton John has had a substantial infestation?" Gus shook his head. "Mr Isaac Hayes had a rat in his basement the size of a damn coyote. Mr Tom Jones had a similar problem. Jamie Foxx. Steven Spielberg's ex-wife over in Laurel Canyon. Who did they turn to?"

Gus thought *Ghostbusters* again. "I apologise. I didn't mean to impugn your reputation..."

"Damn right you don't do that, sir. I don't think you know

who you're speaking with."

"That's right. I don't. I'm sorry. Could we just get on with the job, please? It's having a very adverse effect on our lives. I don't know why we didn't call a rat catcher weeks ago."

The man looked deeply offended and stopped up short. "Pest Control Executive."

"I'm sorry," said Gus. "Pest Control Executive."

"What I am, Mr Beatty, is the best in the business. I offer comprehensive advice, service, and back-up, all without the overheads of the larger companies. But I tell you this, when I give advice, I expect it to be taken. After all – what's the saying? You don't employ a dog and go barking in the street yourself, ain't that right?"

"It is. Indeed. I'm sorry."

"This is my profession, sir, and I do know what I'm doing."

"Of course."

"And I do think you have a major infestation."

"OK. All right. If you say so."

"Now – how do I get into the attic?"

Gus took him along the landing and showed him the ceiling hatch. He pulled down the retractable ladder which Gus had never used since buying the place, and the fat man in his white overalls struggled up the steps and peered into the dark cavity above.

"I don't want to alarm you, Mr Beatty…"

"Yes?"

"You have a hornet nest up here."

"Yes. It's an old one, isn't it?"

"Matter of fact, you have seven hornet nests up here."

"Jesus Christ. Are they all active?"

"Well to tell you the truth," said the man, descending, "damned if I'm going to find out."

He smiled at Gus and Gus realised the worst. He'd suspected it ever since seeing the man's big round belly plugging the small, square hatch, and thinking to himself: that fat bastard is never going to get through that hole. No way. He, Gus, on the other hand, was six-foot – and a skinny-assed Jewboy from Pittsburg.

"Come with me,' said the Pest Control man, and led Gus outside to his pick-up truck. He took out a full-length beekeeper's costume, gauntlets, boots and visored helmet and handed it to him. By now Gus just wanted the whole thing to be over and for the guy to go away. But he didn't even argue. There was nothing to argue about. Thinking 'why am I doing this?' he found himself obediently donning the ridiculous suit – feeling like a cross between Darth Vader and Neil Armstrong, and the man led him clunkingly back upstairs to the hatch. Holly glimpsed her husband from the hall, said, "Oh my God," and shut the kitchen door.

This was one small step for a mouse.

Gus went up the attic, his breath misting the plastic mask, and the man from Ace Pest Control handed him a thing like a fire extinguisher, which Gus proceeded to use to douse the massive wasps' nests that hung from the eaves. Occasionally he'd hear barked orders from behind: "Left a bit. That's the fella. Right a bit. Now don't forget to cover it real good! And be careful, those suckers can still bite ya, even in that suit!" – and he'd turn to see through the hot mist of his own breath the man's chubby face, in a gas mask, watching intently from the hatch. "Saw a man once died of hornet stings once. Horrible. Puffed up like a balloon, like an elephant. Poison got all the way to his heart. Didn't die though. Paralysed from the neck down. You know how many thousand stings you can get from seven hornet nests, on average?"

On average. No. He didn't. Nor did Gus care, frankly. He was wondering why in hell a guy who had negotiated a seven-figure play-or-pay first-time director's deal two days ago was now choking on bug-killer in an atmosphere that would make David Blaine's glass coffin desirable. What was the answer to that, he wondered, and why didn't that obese son of a bitch go on the G.I. diet before advertising his fucking services?

It took thirty minutes and by the end Gus wanted to throw up. Once down the ladder, he tore off the headgear, coughed and rubbed his lips.

"Won't get any more trouble from them," said the Pest Control man, non-plussed. "Now your rats."

"*Rats!* I thought they were *mice!*"

"No sir. Rats," the man pronounced determinedly.

"Sorry, you're the expert. As you keep reminding me."

The man said, yes, he was, and took a number of packets from his tool box. He held them up one by one for Gus's deliberation: "This is an acute poison."

"Good."

"Not so good. Don't like using it. If you've got pets around.

And, trouble is, some rats get poison-shy. They try it and if they don't like it, don't go back to it. Waste of damn money.' He held up the second pack. 'Anti-coagulant rodenticide."

"Great."

"Not so great. It's weak, you need repeat feeding, you might find they get resistant to it, you start to breed a super-rat. Then you'll never get rid of the things."

"OK. So what do you recommend?"

"This one," said the man, taking a blue cube from its pack. "Comes in wax blocks. Rats like the taste, and they only need one feed to take a lethal dose. Then it works like magic, like an edible time-bomb, between four to eight days. Dead. Even the most resistant strains."

"Terrific."

The Pest Control man went back up the ladder and, from what Gus could make out, liberally flung the wax blocks across the attic floor until the pack was empty. Then he came down, took off his rubber gloves with two resounding twangs, and asked for his cup of coffee.

Sitting down in the breakfast room, he told Gus to check the attic in a week and clear it of the dead rats, burn them in the garden or (he joked) let your cat or dog play with them a while. Holly wasn't amused. The man noticed. 'Sorry to be a bit disgusting, Mrs Beatty. " 'Course you *could* eat 'em. They do in Malaysia. Rat pie's a real delicacy out the chinko countries. They gobble 'em up plenty of places, they get desperate enough."

He laughed loudly and Holly left the room. "You want to tell your wife there I just eradicated her problem. She don't seem too appreciative."

"Holly hasn't got much of a sense of humour."

"No. That's for sure." He sipped his micro-waved coffee thinly through his teeth. "She ought to have been in Eye Rack." It took a second for Gus to realize he meant Iraq. "The grunts there used to run bets: who could bite the heads off more rats. I won. I won every single time…"

Gus didn't believe him. He hoped it was a joke.

"Yes, er…" Gus changed the subject rapidly. "What do I owe you for this, Mr…?"

Ace Pest Control swung back in his chair, the chair Gus yelled at the children for swinging back on. 'Well, let's see here.'

He took out a pocket calculator. The buttons were miniscule and fragile under his sausage-like fingers. "Site visit, fifty dollars standard charge. The poison, twenty dollars. The wasp nests fifteen dollars each – what's that? Fifteen times seven?" He blew air. "A hundred and five." He squinted. "Hundred and five plus twenty, plus fifty. That comes to, grand total, here, one seven five."

"That's," Gus froze, speechless, had to summon the words carefully, now: "A hundred and seventy five *dollars*?" Jesus Christ!

"That sounds about right."

Gus laughed. "About *right*?"

"Uhuh. Make the check payable to Ace Pest Control. I don't take Mastercard. Mastercard rip the pants off your hide and still come back for the rump-hairs." The Pest Control man grinned broadly and stole a chocolate chip cookie from the bowl on the table. The sausagey fingers were starting to make Gus feel sick.

But he just wanted to get him out of there. He took out his bank book and laboriously wrote the check, seething, but keeping his anger dampened down, thinking: I only get angry when I'm being paid for it. This fucker is not even worth it. Not by a million miles.

He handed him it. The man held it up to the light.

Jesus fucking Christ!

The Pest Control man's eyes twinkled. He was joking again. Gus was losing his sense of humour by the second. He shook Gus's hand vigorously. Like he was saying goodbye to Martin Luther King. Like this had been a real pleasure – which it hadn't. The whole time his eyeballs never left Gus's. "And remember, if you have any further problems at all, please don't hesitate to call. At all."

"I won't," said Gus ambiguously, and shut the front door on him with a grateful finality.

Holly appeared from the study, asking if he'd gone.

Gus said yes, and that he needed a drink. She made him a Virgin Mary, and said if it was a choice between that guy and the rats, maybe they should have stuck with the rats. Gus laughed, in fact they both laughed – for the first time in weeks. He couldn't remember how long, and that was bad.

In fact the following week was the best week for both of them, in ages. Holly had another commission for children's book illustrations, actually for an annual report for a charity that gave computers to autistic children. Chris's moods had been diagnosed as a hormonal imbalance that was easily put right. Max was suddenly enjoying school, and little Matthew was an unbridled joy. And, most important of all – no rodent droppings. No scratchings. No holes in the food.

No rats.

Gus gave it a full ten days before venturing up to the roof space. Ace Pest's (that was Holly's new name for their Who You Gonna Call? Rat Catcher To The Stars) – Ace Pest's horror stories about the hornets still lingered in Gus's memory, producing a notably yellow streak up his back. But when he did go up, he found the rodents all right. Dead as door knockers. Twenty of them.

By way of celebration, Holly decided on a trip to her beauty salon in Westwood for a Botox, tummy-tuck and nails, while Gus piled the corpses in the garden, got a can of kerosene and made a bonfire out of them.

The next week there were four or five more. Equally, and incontrovertibly, dead.

The week after that, none.

Zero.

Gus made a final inspection optimistically, the evening after getting home from nailing a particularly antsy deal memo to everybody's satisfaction, including his client's, and, more importantly, the studio's. The boss was euphoric and he felt, as he did occasionally: yes, I can do this shit. Holly had made a delicious meal, veal and salad, and Gus had showered her with praise. He needed to. He wanted to. He also said he loved her, which he hadn't in a while, inexcusably. It made her blush, which made him sad, and made him remember her the first time they'd met, at a pre-awards season Writer's Guild screening they both wanted to get the hell out of.

The attic was bare. The kids were playing noisily round in the swimming pool. The sun was going down. They were alone.

It was an excuse to open the Moet that the boss had brought over at Thanksgiving. He poured some for her. He was recovering, so it was water, but fizzy at least. It wasn't so much that booze had been his problem, but dope, and you kick one addiction, you got to kick them all, as his mentor said. One day at a time, sweet Whoever. The cork popped and he allowed himself to enjoy the guilty pleasure of smelling it.

"So it was worth the money after all," said Holly, girlishly happy, knees up, tight Armani jeans discarded on the Santa Fe rug, his hand on her bare ankle, sitting across her husband on the sofa, later.

"What money?" he said, after she kissed him.

She giggled, tipsy. "Duh! The hundred and seventy-five *dollars*?"

He sipped his water. "What hundred and seventy five dollars?"

"C'mon. Ace *Pest's* hundred and..."

"Oh, Ace *Pest's* hundred and seventy five dollars!" he took another mouthful of limey Perrier. "What about it?"

"It was worth it."

"Yeah, sure," he said, disgorging the ice cube he'd taken into his mouth back into his glass. "Everything's worth it if it's free, right?" He wasn't exactly grinning, but the word smug might have come to mind.

Holly thought a moment, then sat up quickly, taking her long legs off his lap. "Free?" She said it like an altogether different four letter word. Outraged.

He said, "Gimme a break, Hol. You think I'm going to pay thirty dollars for him to fling pellets round my attic? And *twenty* dollars *apiece* for hornet nests that *I* have to go up and spray? You're kidding! At risk to my frigging life and health, up there? No way! That ovoid cracker-barrel fucking jerk-off must have thought there's a sucker born every minute, well I've got news for him – I ain't one of them! Not a chance!" In his anger he picked up her glass by mistake and slammed it down. It splashed and the champagne fizzed as he dabbed it up with his hand. "Fuck." Then gave up, picked up his own drink, then put that down too. He stood up and turned away from her.

His wife was shocked. Gus's underhand tactics in business never shocked her that much, it was the name of the game and everyone in the biz did it or were done by it. Screw or be screwed. But this was different. Getting one over on mega-rich producers, or a percentage point off millionaires was one thing. But a blue-collar guy trying to make a living? When did he last look at the seven bedroom hunk of real estate they were living in? When did he last look in the *mirror*? What's going on, and why didn't she *know* about this?

"So what *did* you pay him?"

He rattled the ice in the glass, proudly. "I paid him zip, honey. Plus tax. Plus commission."

"Nothing?"

"Nothing."

She realized it was a victory to him. That was the thing. It was a *victory*. "How?"

"Easy. I wrote the check from our old bank account, the one that doesn't exist anymore."

"You did it right here? Before he left, you did that? It'll bounce. They'll write to him. You won't get rid of him. You don't. He'll be in contact. He'll be on the telephone."

"He has been. Mr Ace Pest Control…"

Now Holly was really shocked. She took another slug of Moet. Then, quickly, another. "What did you *say*? God, Gus – have you got any idea how embarrassing this is?"

"Embarrassing? No. Not to me it isn't. Holly, for Pete's sake, before you get on your high Democrat horse, take a reality check. He's a nothing. Guy like that doesn't even register on the radar – any radar," said Gus, cracking more ice with his back teeth. "He phoned and said the twenty eight days were up, and I told the fat fuck he was crazy if he thought I was about to pay for a job I'd done myself. Anyway it was way overpriced, he didn't give an estimate, I suspect his car wasn't taxed, or *he* wasn't, and if he wanted to argue I'd see him in court. Which I will. I'd wipe the floor with the creep. Anyway, I never heard back so I guess he's written it off. So don't worry about it. End of story."

"Thank God."

"I win."

She looked up. "You call that winning, Gus?"

He grinned broadly. "Of course. Don't you?"

She looked away.

"Now," said Gus, seeing that beautiful dark promise in the sheeny V of her pantyhose. God, she was sexy. "The kids are keeping each other quiet for once. Let's be naughty and go to bed before they do."

A chill rose gooseflesh on Holly's arms. He was right. The children *were* quiet.

"No. Phone him."

"Jesus."

The gooseflesh tingled.

"Phone him! Now!"

She ran past him and flung open the windows to the garden and pool, running out in her bare feet. Gus moved to catch her, but hadn't. What was going on? He followed her, quickly, not knowing why he was doing it. Some deep imperative took over. Against the warm blackness of night she seemed ghostly, sylph-like in the silky top. Her long hair gusted like a banner. Her eyes were wide and terrified as she clawed it from her face as she did a quick circuit of the deserted pool area. Her breasts rose and fell as she panted for breath and suddenly it wasn't sex he was thinking about at all.

She was calling out their names: "Max! Chris! Allie! Tommo!"

Gus looked across to the balcony, where Matthew's high chair stood empty. Toys were left unattended on the floor.

The swimming pool was like a flat turquoise carpet, eerily aglow with the underwater lighting. Holly was far away now – and running to and fro, hysterically, still calling the names of his children.

Soon she was screaming.

Gus staggered back into the living room and picked up the phone, not understanding why he was doing that, either. He took the business card from his wallet, dialled the number, and it was only as the recorded voice began telling him, in that flat synthetic tone, he must have dialled incorrectly, please try again, that he first read what was on the card between his finger and thumb:

ACE PEST CONTROL
P. Piper
Complete Professional Service – Guaranteed

The Latin Master

The last time I met Bairstowe was at ten o'clock on New Year's Eve, ten years ago, in the library of the Ludlow Club in Chelsea, then as now frequented almost exclusively by authors and artists or varying degrees of repute, and talent. Only now, writing this up on a dreary Sunday evening, has it occurred to me that I never saw Bairstowe *but* in the Ludlow Club. As far as I know, he ate, drank and slept there, as if it were a self-imposed prison, which perhaps it was – I shall let the story he told speak for itself.

After a notable supper of goose in the crackling warmth of the log fire, about six of us unbuttoned our waistcoats and retired to the library, initially to prove or disprove a man called Ibbotson's claim to have been at Eton with Harry Yeats, the fast-bowler for Yorkshire. The evidence was there, sure enough, but before too long, as the cigars were offered and the port was passed, the talk mellowed into schooldays in general, and public schools in particular, of which we were all products – or so I had foolishly presumed.

It was myself, as I recall, the old Harrovian, who put his foot in it. "I say, Bairstowe, you're keeping quiet. Where did you go? Some dreadful Northern prep?"

Bairstowe at first did not seem to hear, as if he were remembering rather than listening. Then he perked up. Among the ruddy faces in the firelight, his alone seemed pale as candlewax. "You fellows make beastly assumptions. I'm nothing but a Grammar School lad. Heave over the decanter, Sutton."

I felt embarrassed for making him feel uneasy and, I thought, suddenly rather sickly-looking. "I really am most awfully sorry, old boy. But there's no need to feel so bad about it."

"Oh, I don't feel bad about it, Venables," said Bairstowe. "It was a good school. I got a scholarship to Cambridge. It set me on the road to success, and I'll put myself up to any of you, intellectually or otherwise."

"Hear, hear," someone muttered.

"No, it's not that. It's not the school. It's something that happened *at* the school. But that's all a long time ago..."

"Look here," said Caldwell, anxious to make up for my lack of tact. "No need to dredge up the past and all that!"

Bairstowe looked into the fire absently. "The past..." he repeated gently.

"Would you like to tell us?" I asked.

"Yes. Yes I would. Very much. If someone will top up my glass. I think I'll need it, and so might you. Unless you'll call me barmy and call for the men in white coats!" We laughed aloud, but Bairstowe did not.

I admit at this point I took out a sharpened pencil habitually carried in my breast pocket, and some club notepaper, and thus the following narration was committed, verbatim, to shorthand:

'If you do not know the Old Priory School at Monkford in Wiltshire, and there is no reason why you should, I can describe it as the sort of monolith in Bath-stone that gives so much character to that part of the Avon valley. In spite of its architectural grandeur, however, it was shabby rather than daunting, with beech trees standing abreast of the long drive like sentries, and thick privet hedges walling the playing fields. The paint needed a lick even then – goodness knows what state it might be in nowadays, if they haven't pulled it down altogether. I shouldn't grieve too much if they have.

'My family had moved to the district from Muswell Hill. My father retired with a disability pension from the railways and bought a post office in Monkford Village. Hence I entered the Grammar School in the fourth year, a gangly and rather self-opinionated young man, keen to study but easily bored, enthusiastic for sport but congenitally weak, eager for learning but thinking he knew it all. My vocation at the time was to be a keeper of sea-lions at the zoo, as I felt I had the necessary qualifications to throw fish, and there seemed very little more to the job than that. This having been decided – alas, it was never to be – school seemed a peculiar waste of time and energy.

'Watkinson agreed with me. He was as cantankerous, if not more so, than I. More mischievous, certainly. He boasted that he'd felt the Head's cane more than half a dozen times, which I thought a strange thing to boast about, representing as it did either a love of pain or extreme idiocy, but Wat was such a laugh, always messing around and pulling stunts, he made the dreariest of lessons endurable. I say that with the notable exception of Latin.

'Now I'm no Latin buff. "*Caesar aderat forte – sic ubet.*" is about my limit. You chaps can probably *amo, amas, amat* till the cows come home, and good luck to you. I'd rather study the form at Chepstow than the Gallic Wars any time of day. The truth is, I was always hopeless at it, and as I wasn't prone to burning the midnight oil, I was slipping steadily behind. Ever more miserable marks for tests charted my insalubrious decline. There was only one consolation – Watkinson was worse than me.

'Our teacher in the subject was a man called Guy Layburn-Allan, which made matters worse. He ruled the class with a steady glare. There wasn't a disciplinarian in the school to match him. Even Watkinson, who used to tease and rib the worst sticklers, shut up when the bell for Latin sounded. Layburn-Allan was a dry old stick, exceedingly tall and thin and like a bat sweeping the corridors in his black schoolmaster's gown. He cut quite an intimidating figure, like a predatory bird. I once drew a caricature of him, on one of my copy-book covers – it was never discovered, thank goodness – but the hooked nose, deep-set eyes and lined forehead sloping into the bald dome of a head was a gift to any budding Gillray or Cruikshank, which I was, did I but know it.

'To be truthful, I felt ill at ease from the very first moment I stepped into Layburn-Allan's class at Priory. I can't explain it, but it was little comfort to learn that my form-mates all had similar, inexplicable, misgivings. Look at my hands right now, wet with perspiration at the very mention of him! Who is it says the child is father of the man, that our school days make us? I believe him! All our hopes and fears are kindled there. My fear was kindled at the Old Priory School, and I shall tell you exactly how.

'The first incident, I am almost certain, occurred in the spring term. That's right, because Purbright had had his birthday that same week. It was a strange sort of spring, cold, as if winter were hanging on like grim death to the spindles of trees. Thompson, a small boy, the son of a baker, a very wealthy baker too, was allowed to keep his scarf around his neck – that gives the nature of the season.

'The classroom, as ever, was ice cold, though that was nothing to do with the weather. It was to do with Layburn-Allan.

'Let me say at the outset, that I never saw him do or threaten anything to inspire this fear. He never so much as raised a hand to any boy to my knowledge – or even his voice for that matter. It remained, even at times of intense stress or agitation, as school boys are wont to instill in the most unshakable of tutors, quite calm, monotonously flat and invariably quiet. In fact, it was more a whisper than anything. Nevertheless, for all this, the man unmistakably imparted an air of – no, perhaps not of menace – but of pervading gloom.

'Watkinson was standing, a copy of Horace's *Carminum, Vol. I* in his hands like a prayerbook. I remember the quotation he was on as well as I remember my own name. It ran: *"Quae saga, quis te soluere Thessalis / Magus uenenis, quis poterit deus?"* But poor Watkinson stuttered to and fro through the damnable verse, see-sawing the words without making head nor tail of them. The more he read them, the more confused his ideas, the more hot and flustered he became as Layburn-Allan refused him even the dignity of an admonishing glance. The teacher's pallid face remained downward-facing at his own copy of the ancient text, as the boy floundered and squirmed: "Can any saga... Can any story...with all its Thessaly *soluere*..." It was torture to watch, but the torture was all Watkinson's.

'Layburn-Allan finally took mercy. *"Thessaliam ex negotio petebam"*, he intoned drily, attempting to guide the hapless youth through the semantic minefield in which he had become lost. *"I had occasion to visit Thessaly on business."* Thessaly is not a person or a thing. Thessaly is a place. A land of mystery and magic and marvel... Go on...

' "Can any saga..." muttered the boy.

' *"Saga!* No, boy! Can any sage, or *witch*..." corrected the master.

' "Can any sage or witch..." repeated Watkinson.

' *"Quis te soluere Thessalis?"*

' "With all the sol – sol – solutions in..."

'Layburn-Allan's voice cut through the air. *"Can any witch, can any mage, for all his Thessalian charms and potions, nay, can heaven itself free thee from the spell of love?"*

' "Yes, that's it," said Watkinson curtly, as if he had known it all the time. He tossed his book down and sat back at his desk, arms tightly folded. "Bother this!"

'Now Layburn-Allan raised his head. It moved like a weight on a pulley, like a puppet head at the end of a string. His eyes stared from the expanse of unblemished, parchment-coloured skin that stretched over his skull-like features, and he blinked his wrinkled eyes like a turtle. "Bother this?" he whispered, then a little louder. "*Bother* this?"

'Watkinson swallowed. "Well, sir," he pleaded, clearing his throat. "What's the good of all this? What's the point? I mean, sir – Latin, is it really a necessity?"

'Layburn-Allan's eyes narrowed to a squint. "A necessity? It's a luxury, boy, a *luxury!*"

' "But the Romans, sir. It's all gone, all that. It's not even history, it's *ancient* history. It doesn't matter to us. Nobody speaks it any more. It's just in old books that other people have translated anyway. It's just a dead language, sir."

'Layburn-Allan made no movement at all. His body did not show any sign of anger, either at the content or the manner in which the pupil delivered his opinion. I do not think he even blinked, he just said very quietly, "The Roman Empire, Watkinson, was the most powerful cultural and military force in the history of the world. The Romans brought intelligence and sensitivity and peace to heather backwaters and pagan dirt-piles. They gave cave-dwelling savages the dignity of language, art, commerce, the law, transport, water, health – of civilisation, boy – and you say Rome is dead? Rome is alive. In the roads we tread, in the laws that hold our society together, in the books we read. And if this small, pathetic island has any pride, any history, any power, any wealth, any future, it is because of that day a certain Julius Caesar set foot upon this shore and said – Bairstowe?"

'A finger singled me out. I reacted. *"Veni, vidi, vici*, sir..."

' "Which means, Clark?"

' "I came, I saw, I conquered, sir."

' *"Veni, vidi, vici*," Layburn-Allan repeated slowly, glaring back at Watkinson. He had a pencil gripped in his hands, as if ready to snap it. I could see the fear in Wat's eyes. I knew he thought he was for the stick, without a doubt. And Layburn-Allan seemed to hold him there almost hypnotically, riveting him to the spot, for what seemed endless minutes but must have been mere seconds.

'Anyhow, as fortune had it, he was saved by the bell. It rang in the corridor, and seemed to wake the class from a sort of dream the strangeness of which was only fully realised in the events that were to follow.

'Our next lesson was games, and we filed out gratefully for the rescue of the cricket pitch. The hubbub seemed to dissipate the awful silence and stillness of Layburn-Allan's glare.

'In the showers after the match, Wat came to me and asked me if I'd heard Layburn-Allan mutter anything as the two of us had passed his desk to leave. I said I hadn't. I was sure he hadn't uttered a word. Wat insisted he heard it quite clearly, something in Latin. And considering his ineptitude in Latin he remembered it quite clearly: "*Somnia, terrores magicos, miracula, sagas... Nocturnos lemures portentaque Thessala rides...*"

'I have no idea what it means. Perhaps one of you fellows can have a guess.

'The term progressed, but my Latin prowess did not. My desire to become a zoo attendant was usurped by the notion of life as an artist. I wasn't bad at art, and here I am today making a living at it, so it wasn't such a bad decision. Watkinson wasn't making plans at all, though: he was increasingly preoccupied about Layburn-Allan. The humiliation of that terrible lesson had clearly cut into his normal *laissez-faire*; in fact the boy began to seem positively peaky with worry. "Why does he think he knows best, just because he's older? He might not – I don't see why, necessarily. As for Latin, I still think it's rot and he won't convince me otherwise." We used to give L-A the most vicious nicknames – Dracula was the most popular one; The Claw, because of his slightly arthritic right hand; Beak, because of his nose. We used to say he slept at night in a coffin, hence he was so pale. We even hung garlic over the classroom door at one time – Godfrey Underhill had six strokes for that, and we put him up to it, poor lad.

'The School Journey came around May, as a welcome respite from pre-examination cramming, and that year – and I strongly suspect every year – the trip was to the city of Bath.

'We arrived there on a blissfully sunny day when the place was thronging with tourists, but not too crowded to accommodate a party of fifty or so schoolboys, escorted as we were by Mr Evans (Geography), Mr Vernon (History and Divinity), and Mr Layburn-Allan (Latin). Most of us were looking forward more to the gift shop and a cream tea in the Pump Rooms than a rummage in our illustrious past, still we had enough boyhood imagination to retain the appeal of Rome in the form of chariots, gladiators, and Christians-to-the-lions.

'The guide was a small woman in tweeds with a very loud voice, who kept referring to "we" as if she had helped dig out the remains personally, which perhaps she had. She told us that, of course, the whole thing virtually, as we see it now, is Victorian – only to eye-level is it actually Roman, the columns and statues on top being comparatively recent additions. We were told how this was one of the most important meeting places in Northern Europe where senators and businessmen (but not women) met to discuss trade and swap gossip, jumping into hot then cold baths, and having their armpits plucked and their bodies massaged and perfumed. It was a spa long before the Romans discovered it, however, and the ancient Britons in the area long revered the water's properties for enhancing good health – though we schoolboys were not allowed to drink it, as it had not been treated and was full of minerals and deposits, among them arsenic. The water itself, apparently, owes its heat to the fact that it travels down towards the earth's core before rising at pressure, though the process takes some several millions of years to complete. However, the dipped fingers of several eager little boys attested to the pleasant temperature of the pool.

'During this talk, I happened to glance away from the guide, and saw Mr Layburn-Allan, in his long raincoat, hat in hand, looking down at his own reflection in the steamy, lichen-green waters of the Great Roman Bath.

'I broke away from the party as it moved under the colonnade, and to my surprise I saw that the teacher I approached seemed quite overcome with emotion, like a mourner at a funeral. As soon as he heard me approaching he quickly stiffened, turned away and placed his hat firmly on his head.

' "Sir?" I ventured. "Is anything the matter?"

'There was silence for a moment. Bubbles rose from the warm and sickly broth.

' "Roman lead, do you see, boy?" he slowly pointed down into the water, at the floor of the bath. "Roman lead from the Mendip Hills." He knelt, and dropped his hand into the water, letting it float for a moment, then raised it dripping. Then he began to tremble.

' "Sir?"

'His fingers bagan to shake like leaves. He stood, gasping for air, trying to calm himself. Then his voice spat out, tremulous with tears. "Go, go away, boy! Go! This will be over soon! This hell on earth is coming to its end! *Go, I said!*" and this he cried with such vigour I felt myself physically shoved backwards away from him, and gratefully hurried back to the crowd.

'Layburn-Allan, I observed, staggered weakly to the exit from Aquae Sulis, and we did not see him again that afternoon until we returned to the train station for our journey home.

'The most interesting part of the guided tour, our Latin master missed entirely. Our guide confided that she would show us, exclusively, some work that was currently being done to excavate a basement under an adjacent row of shops. She took us, in torchlight, down some narrow steps to an even narrower passageway into a dank and pungent cellar.

'Some finds were arranged on a wooden table, a horse's head simplified into little more than a flowing linear design in bronze, and a few coins with weathered but distinct human heads – clearly Celtic. But also present were Roman artefacts, notably a short sword and a hammer. Through a partition at the end of the tunnel we were shown an almost-unearthed grave, in which a rude stone coffin lay containing what seemed at first to be strips of leather tied to indiscriminate pieces of stained wood, but was in fact the corpse of a British chieftain – or what remained of him. His skull was cleft in two and the archaeologists had deduced that the blow had come from the Roman sword found in the same catacomb. The rest of the boys and I stared in wonder at this age-old corpse with a mixture of fascination and dread. Thompson stuck up his hand, he had a question. "Please, Miss, what are those things in his hands?" The question was duly answered, though I wish in many ways it had not been. The guide told us that they were wooden nails used to pin the body's hands to the coffin, ensuring that he would not return to haunt his murderer. On that cheerful note, fifty pale schoolboys filed eagerly towards the daylight.

'Some weeks later, we were plunged into the horrors of our exams. My parents were strict enough, and I was always made to work for a good few hours each night before having my cup of cocoa and bed. I don't regret that they did.

'But I remember all too clearly one night. I had been swatting history and drifted to sleep with my brain full of Henry VIII and his six wives – nothing of which, I hasten to add, has been the slightest use to me since. I was woken from my sleep by a rapping, a very clear and methodical, urgent tapping on my bedroom window. I sprang up with a start, wondering who on earth it could be. I asked who was there. "Me," said a voice; it was Watkinson. "For Pity's sake, Bairstowe, let me in!"

'As my bedroom was on the ground floor and next to the kitchen, I crept to the back door in my pyjamas and carefully clicked the latch. The face that greeted me almost drew a scream from my throat. I had never seen Watkinson so agitated. He was like a madman. His hands flew to my lapels. He hugged himself to me, his eyes wide with terror and his lips drawn back from his teeth. "Don't tell anybody!" he was blubbering insanely. "Don't tell anyone!"

'I reassured him that I wouldn't, and sat him at the kitchen table. I asked him if he wanted some milk, or a cup of tea. He asked if I had anything stronger. I looked shocked, and he laughed but there was no humour in it. I crept into the sitting room and stole a tot of father's brandy. No sooner had I sat it in front of my schoolfriend than it was gone. He let out a long, quavering breath and arched his head back, staring at the ceiling.

' "What on earth has happened?" I asked.

' "Happened?" he stammered, and ran off a dictionary of expletives. "I am going mad," he said at the end of it.

'I asked if he wanted another brandy.

'He said nothing.

' "Tell me, please," I implored. He must have seen the earnest sense of horror in my eyes, because he began at last to tell me what he had done that night.

' "You know we had Latin today. Well, it was a disaster for me. It probably was for you. I just stared at the d——d thing. I wrote my name at the top, the date, and that was about all. I tell you, Bairstowe, I couldn't do a word of it – not a word. Not a blessed word!'

'I put a hand on his shoulder to calm him.

' "Don't let it upset you so much…"

' "Well, it's all right for you. Your parents are good about it all, they understand. More than mine ever would. They've got it in mind that I'm something I'm not, somebody great. They don't know I'm a clown. And if it weren't for this d——d Latin I wouldn't *be* a clown. So you see, that's why I wanted to do it. Just once. I know it's bad, but…'

' "Do what?" I interjected.

'Watkinson looked very sheepish all of a sudden. "I'll tell you straight, Bairstowe. I wanted to get into the school and swap my papers. I went through the questions with the textbook earlier, and copied out the stuff – leaving a few mistakes, not to be too suspicious. So I thought if I could sneak into school, just take my old blank papers and substitute the new ones, I'd save my skin and my parents – and Dracula – would be none the wiser."

'I was aghast at his cheekiness. "Did you do it?"

' "I got in, no problem there. You know the hole in the fence next to the changing rooms? That path past the shed is ill-lit at the best of times, and I found a window by the chemistry lab off its latch. The whole place was in complete darkness, and that was eerie after going there every day in daylight with a noisy rabble filling the classrooms and corridors. I wasted no time and headed past the Head's office to the annex, and up the stairs. My heart was beating so loud I was sure someone might hear me coming. I was petrified with fear, I don't mind admitting, but I'd gone too far to turn back now, even though I'd have given a king's ransom to have been able to.

' "Layburn-Allan's office was about ten yards ahead of me when I reached the top of the stairs. The door was shut, but a thin yellow outline betrayed that a flickering light burned inside. I stepped closer, cursing each treacherous creak of the old floorboards, and pressed my ear to the closed door.

' "My ears tried desperately to detect any movement from within the room – although I prayed that there would be none, and that I would discover only that an oil lamp had been accidentally left burning. I realised quickly that my hopes were to be dashed. I could hear the distinct rustling of papers, the flicking of copy books, and the scratching of a fountain-pen indicating its brutal crosses, ticks, and crossings-out. With mounting apprehension I came to the unavoidable conclusion that, even at this late hour, this incredibly late hour of eleven o'clock, Layburn-Allan was still in school, and, worst of all, marking the very examination papers I sought to sabotage. My heart sank. At first I decided to cut my losses and run. But something stopped me.

' "I heard Layburn-Allan's voice inside his room. It came from his creaking captain's chair, as if he sat in it agitatedly. The words were clipped, garbled, and very very nervous. I heard him throw down the fountain-pen, and he was on his feet, pacing the room. With a change of emphasis, his words – though I still couldn't understand them – seemed conciliatory, pleading, almost tearful, and then becoming just a series of short sobbing noises. This was followed by a few moments silence, and he spoke again. I caught only the odd word – *sunt, lemures, manes, spectris* – and then of course it dawned on me and my flesh bagan to creep as I realized – *omnis et humanis lustrata* – Layburn-Allan was speaking Latin as fluently and freely as English."

'Watkinson saw my expression, and caught my arm.

' "It's true! Absolutely true – and that's not the end of it. For then I began to hear a second voice, deeper, gruffer by far than his. A man's but a large man's, as if it came from a barrel of a chest and yet was croaky as if with some breathing difficulty – you know like Tom's father whose lungs gave in after twenty years in the mine, but even worse than that. And it was this other voice, this loathsome other voice, who said: '...*Saga et diuina, potens caelum deponere, terram suspendere, fontes durare, montes diluere, manes sublimare, deos infimare!*' "

' "They were conversing..." I began to say.

' "Conversing in Latin," Watkinson completed on my behalf. His eyes were even wilder now and I had the uneasy feeling that the worst was yet come.

' "What did you do?"

' "I had an idea that here were two Latin teachers discussing the examination. What else could it be? So I would hide in the corridor, there was a convenient locker of sufficient size to accommodate me, and I would wait until they left, as soon they must. I secreted myself in the cupboard and simply waited. As soon as I shut the door, of course, all sounds of the conversation were cut out. I gave it perhaps five, ten, a maximum of fifteen minutes before coming out again, and when I did I was delighted to hear that the talking had stopped and the lamplight was extinguished. I breathed a sigh of relief. The schoolmasters had gone home. Now I could get to work.

' "I crept towards the door and pushed it open gently. It swung inwards, revealing the small room which I knew to be a dungeon packed with shelves of books – in fact with barely an inch of wall or floor given to anything else. The place was covered in shadow, only the tall windows of the bay showing the blueness of the night sky and moonlight beyond. I noticed, first of all, that one of the windows was open, and swung in the wind, allowing the rain to splatter both the window-sill – which seemed for a moment to gleam with a slimy sheen – and the drapes that hung framing the leaded, stained-glass windowpanes.

' "I walked in, very slowly. If they were still about, I didn't want the masters bursting in on me when I'd come this far. The dastardly deed was almost done. I could see the mound of exam papers on the desk. The pen sat beside them, its ink bleeding into a blotting-pad. With a dry mouth and tightened throat, I approached the pile with arms outstretched, ready to substitute my meagre submission for a fuller one.

' "I touched the top sheet, and thumbed downwards. If it was in alphabetical order, I'd be near the bottom, so he wouldn't have reached me yet. This thought was just going through my mind when, as I tugged one of the sheets of paper, suddenly a hand sprawled across the sheets, pen and desk. But not a hand. A hand would not have stuck a great ball of air in my gullet, wouldn't have slapped me dumbstruck until the very moment you opened the door to me, Bairstowe. Bairstowe, listen to me. It was a fleshless hand, a caked green-brown hand, it was the hand of a skeleton."

'I stared incredulously. I couldn't believe him, but seeing his face neither could I disbelieve him. I was simply overcome with the certain knowledge that whatever the explanation – praise God these would *be* an explanation – this was something, well, out of the normal order of things, to say the very least.

' "Now tell me, Bairstowe, because I need it said to me. Tell me this is some jape pulled on Layburn-Allan by some schoolboy. Tell me someone scuttered up the roof and into the window with the express purpose to leave the skeleton from the biology lab at his desk, and give him the fright of his life next morning. Tell me, Bairstowe, that is the only natural explanation..."

'I said it was.

'But I neglected to say I thought it was probably not, however, the truth.

'With that we stared at each other a long while, talked around it all, vaguely – I don't remember what we said exactly. I offered Watkinson another brandy, and joined him in one, let him out, firmly shut the back door, and bolted it which people in the country rarely do; then I went back to bed.

'Suffice it to say I have had better nights' sleep.

'I woke, and hoped at least part of it was a dream. Sadly, not so. In class, Watkinson was ashen. Neither of us were much good at first lesson, maths, and grabbed each other in the corridor immediately afterwards before RI.

‘ "Have you heard?' asked Watkinson frantically. I said I hadn't. He gabbled that they had found the skeleton in Layburn-Allan's room, slumped over the desk. The Head initiated an inquiry – his first reaction conformed to Watkinson's hurried theory, a joke involving the skeleton from the biology department. However on inspection, the biology skeleton proved to be in its usual place, hanging quite untouched. Of course, had it even been missing, the explanation could not have accounted for the deposit of dry mould and congealed substances over the skeleton in Layburn-Allen's room. Nor could it have offered any comfort concerning a resemblance the skull offered to a certain person we all knew.

‘Layburn-Allan disappeared. He was never seen again. Rumour was manufactured that he had fled an affair with a schoolmistress, but it was neither in his character to have an affair nor to flee it. However, for those that needed answers, it was one.

‘Nothing ever happened to explain the events I have described, whilst Watkinson and I attended the Old Priory School. We took a little more interest in Latin, though. In particular certain words. *Spectrum*, meaning ghost was of interest to us. Also, *manes*, according to Festus the grammarian meaning someone fearfully deformed or hideous.

‘S. Augustine tells us, *De Ciuitate Dei, IX, xi*, "Apuleius says also that men's souls are *daemones*, and become *lares* if their merits be good; if evil, *lemures*, goblins; if uncertain, *manes*." For those who are interested, Ovid gives a full description of Lemuria, *Fasti, V, 419—486*.

‘I left school in the fullness of time, studied art, travelled and lived in Paris and in New York, achieved some sort of reputation for political cartoons, et cetera. I lost contact with old Wat completely, until I bumped into another schoolfriend in Piccadilly ten years later and was told that he had contracted a nervous disease, had been committed to a hospital for the insane, and had died.

‘Soon afterwards, in some sort of mourning, I found myself returning to Aquae Sulis-Minerva. Much had been restored, some of it badly, the general presentation of the place had improved and the dig had advanced somewhat. I joined the tour and heard much the same as I had those many years before. I lingered afterwards, staring into the Great Bath where the melancholy schoolmaster had dipped his scrawny hand.

'The guide – the same guide, fortunately – came over to me. I introduced myself, and she was glad I could recall my school visit here with such detail. I could not of course tell her why.

'We conversed a while, and she offered to show me how much more of the British chieftain's tomb had been uncovered since my boyhood visit. We stared through the glass into the pit which was the noble figure's last resting place. The guide explained that from pathological evidence, they had discovered that the man had been murdered – probably by the Romans when they overthrew the original settlement. He had been buried and ritually nailed to the floor as a symbol that the subjugated natives were no longer able to rise.

'I asked if the nails had ever been removed. She said, yes, briefly, when they made their examination of the semi-mummified body. "A strange thing, that night," she said. "We had left it lying on a trestle table to one side of the cavern. When we returned in the morning, this glass partition was hanging off its hinges, and the body lay in its grave again – the ground was spoilt by footprints." The only explanation she could give was that vandals had intended to kidnap the half-decayed figure and had been disturbed, thus depositing it quickly in the hole for which it had been intended.

'I did not need to ask her if this had been the same night as that of Watkinson's nocturnal visit to the old Grammar School.

'I was about to go, when she turned to me and said, "Wait, here's something that might interest you. We've only recently had it translated – there are only two experts in the world that could do it, and they've argued the toss for five years now – but they've come to an agreement as to the basic gist of the thing.

' "You see this thing that looks like a letterbox? Here the Romans visiting the spa used to feed in their wellwishes and offerings to the goddess, asking for good luck and so on – coins, brooches, that sort of thing. But we've also found the odd curse: 'May my enemy have sleepless nights and no children and no lovers and finally die' is one rather blunt example. Then, more recently, we unearthed this – scratched in Celtic characters on bronze, and sealed. A curse, again, obviously – but deposited here by an enterprising Briton, obviously.

' "It reads: 'He who has slain the king of the Celts shall never have this land. Not even six feet of it to call his grave. Nor shall he cross the water to his own nation and escape this curse. This island shall be (this man's) prison until he (the king) is free (freed?) to take revenge. Even if it be ten thousand years or ten times ten thousand years. His touch shall bring those years upon his murderer whose name is Caius Labienus Aelian, Roman centurion.' "

'In those words I finally understood, in silence, who had been Guy Layburn-Allan's mysterious visitor that night, why they had conversed in that long-dead-tongue, and how he had far from disappeared, but faced the ghastly revenge of the man he murdered, so many centuries ago.

'And, though I could never tell a soul this story until tonight, I gathered some tiny pleasure from the knowledge that the evidence for it all was there plainly to be seen, in the strange "woad-like" pigment that my archaeologist friend was so perplexed to identify on the British chieftain's chest and arms, which was, in fact, all too recognisable to me as navy-blue ink: the kind used by schoolmasters.

'Caius Labienus Aelian, *requiescat in pace.*'

Three Fingers, One Thumb

Frankly, I wasn't taken in by the castle. It looked fake. But of course, that was what it was all about. Fairytales. Make believe. *Fake.* Of course, it didn't matter. Our five year old, Elize, was completely spellbound, and that was what counted. This was her world. *Their* world. Children.

Stupid grown-ups, a thousand lollipop-lickers were thinking, rightly. *What do they know?*

It was the holiday we had promised ourselves for years, ever since Elize was born. The first year, Val seemed to be post-natally ill or morose most of the time and I was overworked or depressed – which was increasingly normal in my line of business. The second year, we were in the same stressful lethargy. By the time Elize was three, the idea of a holiday had evaporated – we'd got lazy with our lives. Then we both realised it was all part of the drawn-out grief which was sucking us down. Elize didn't save us from it, as we'd prayed, but buried us in it. Now was the time to get our lives in order, shake ourselves up. Or else.

I was head-hunted by a firm in Swindon, a goodish leap in salary. It meant Val could stop part-timing and study something afresh – which she needed to do badly. Something self-expressive, to let out that pernicious anger I could see burning inside her. Crass as ever, I decided that what we needed was a holiday before I started the new job. I booked four weeks in the States, with an Avis hire car we picked up in that microwave oven they call New Orleans, (or rather, *Noo ORRlins*).

A year before Elize came on the scene, we had lost our first child. I had seen and heard him inside my wife's body, but he had only a fleeting glimpse of our world. After nine months in darkness, in a sea of vague, dimly-grasped sensations, Christopher died the first night he spent at home.

We'd worked so hard for him. As Val bulged and bloomed, our love for each other became almost uncontainable. Painting the nursery ready for the new arrival was an unbridled joy. We chose bright pom-pom circus colours, and that wallpaper with the endlessly repeated cartoon animal, big ears and black olive-shaped nose, trail of stars striping from a white gloved hand. We heard our kiddie's laughter in our mind as we smelled the drying paint, but it was never to be. Not in real life.

It was a dark house afterwards. The non-eye contact of friends begged with us to try again. We were in two bubbles of horror and emptiness. The little we talked, we bandied self-accusations and guilt. All we saw in each other was a mirror screaming back at us the memory of that tiny being, lost from the moment it breathed air. We never said it, but we wished we could kill each other and say, "There. All gone. All over." I think the only thing that stopped us was Elize.

Elize was born, perfect, beautiful. She arrived like Pinocchio. Like we'd made a wish. She saved us, God bless her.

Val and I felt a natural trepidation bringing her home to that room. It was unchanged, of course. We couldn't even bear to repaint the furniture pink instead of blue. I don't think we had even touched the door handle since the doctor came and knelt beside the cot that morning. I remember he joked about his cold stethoscope and I laughed. God above, how could I have laughed?

That night I dreamed of Christopher sleeping in the next bedroom. His inadequate breathing coming through the baby listening device.

When Elize awoke, crying, I went in and cuddled her to my chest. She stared around her wide-eyed at the cartoon animal, the animator-created buck teeth, bow tie, happy whiskered cheeks, duplicated on the wallpaper like some kind of saccharine but sinister modern-day hieroglyphics. I wondered what was going on behind my daughter's gleaming, bewildered, tear-filled eyes. I kissed her roasting cheeks.

The same cartoon animal stood there, in the flesh now, in sunlight, gloved hand raised and waving good-naturedly in big trousers. The fixed upturned snout, the clown shoes. He gave me the creeps, the way only images of enforced happiness always do: clowns, dolls. Who was inside? Was anybody inside? He held hands with the crowd. They loved him.

America the beautiful.

Land of make-believe. Where you can be anything – even sane. *Noo ORRlins.*

I bought a Diet Coke. I was dry as a rock.

Children chuckled and roared all round me. I took Elize on a ride and she clung to my body, terrified and screaming with pleasure. Fear and laughter beamed from her face and she was eager for more. But did she know real fear? Could she? She felt so fragile, like a trembling leaf.

Elf-like minions ran around ensuring the enchanted realm was litter-free. Fairies and frog princes paraded comically under the beating sun, half a world away from the Brothers Grimm. But for all its staggering banality, I found myself enjoying the place – the force-fed feelgood factor, the unembarrassed kitsch, the simple born-again faith in Goodness. It was forbidden here to be unhappy. Depression did not compute in Fairy Land. It didn't *exist*.

How could you fail to have a good time, when dragons in dungarees were dancing and playing banjos?

Val came back from the Haunted Wood to find me sitting on a large concrete ladybird. Before she stopped striding she was saying, "Where is she?" I couldn't see her eyes behind the Ray-bans. The sun had reddened her nose. She said Elize had run ahead to meet me while she, Val, searched for the Ladies. I looked round stupidly. Val's head darted like a chicken's, she must be around somewhere, she can't be *far*, for God's *sake*. "She's not here," I said. She looked at me.

The earth, this pit, opened up.

Trying not to panic, we retraced Val's steps. The crowd was thicker. There were hundreds of kids like Elize – God, why didn't we dress her in polka-dots or a hat with great orange plumes or something instead of bloody blue jeans and a white fucking T-shirt? The heat and sudden activity started to slosh nausea – *NOR-sha* – round the pan of my skull, like someone panhandling for sense. I shoved Val in the direction of one of the elves, to get an announcement over the speakers. *Quickly*! Anything.

Oh, Jesus.

I ran after the parade, following the kazoo music. I trod on heels, side-stepped pigtails. I fought against the rapids of people. My eyes lost focus.

Maybe it was a mirage in the heat haze. I saw a familiar shape in the crowd, towering higher than the little kids – the enormous ears, black in silhouette, the round nose, the whiskers. A girl at his side. The cartoon-red lips in a fixed grin. I thought of the wallpaper in the house we'd long sold – the wallpaper peeling, faded, rotten, decayed.

"Elize!" I screamed, clawing through the crowd in pursuit. I tore at the jungle of T-shirts and Nikons, sun tans and shades.

But when I reached the merry-go-round, its bongo-drumming beating against my forehead – nobody was there.

Her name piped over the speakers. I ran to every ride we'd been on, every shop. I pulled little girls by the shoulder – never the right one. They were alarmed when they saw the tears running down my face.

I elbowed past Rumpelstiltskin. I smacked the head off a Dodo. I crossed rainbow bridge after rainbow bridge. The children's universe closed in on me with pirate parrots and Nutcracker toy soldiers and the Woman Who Lived in a Shoe.

Christopher, no! I was gibbering inside. *We loved you – we did love you! We will always love you!* I began calling for Elize again. The sound of her name seemed abstract now.

Dusk fell violently red. The crowd thinned. I wandered aimlessly. I lost all sense of time.

When it was dark, the elves swept the streets and *Make Three Wishes* played as some bulbous American cops arrived and my wife wept in my arms.

At 3 a.m., the cops wept too, when they found Elize, curled up like a foetus in the trash behind a pink-and-white striped cotton candy stall. The smell of burnt sugar was sickly in the air.

Now Val and I are dead again. We're walking and breathing but we're dead. Christopher knows that. He knows that there'll never be another child now, to take his jealously guarded place in our memories. And he knows that, when I identified my daughter's little broken body, though I'll never – *could* never – tell my wife, I saw the bruises on her poor, small neck.

Of three fingers, and one thumb.

The Anamorph of Hans Baldung Grien

It has long been the contention of those with the knowledge and sensitivity to pronounce upon such things, that Art is in effect a reflecting mirror, not of the actual world, but the inner world of the seer. They say that even the most seemingly representational of paintings, to be successful, must reveal and betray the mind of the artist-observer: every portrait, therefore, is a portrait of the artist as much as the sitter. Why are we drawn to a certain picture in a crowded gallery, in preference to another? Unless because we detect – non-intellectually, but instinctively, on the purest level of the most *occult* emotions – a like mind, a same-shaded eye, a viewpoint we are suddenly so eager to explore, for no other reason than the desperate, greedy reassurance that our souls are, in some tiny way, not alone in this world...that the reflection we see is our own.

Some time ago, I had experience of such a painting, though its effect, let us say for now, could hardly have been anticipated. At the time, to fund my return to Academia, I earned pin-money by way of bookkeeping for a printer's works off the Gray's Inn Road. I completed their figures monthly, and it was my habit, because of the almighty din of the place, to take to the streets at noon to straighten my back, treat my eyes to sunlight, and wash my ears with the barrow-boy bartering amongst the nearby market stalls – resembling a Cockney version of the Souk in Tangiers – that lined Lamb's Causeway all the way down to High Holborn.

On one such day, the prospect of returning to the works being somehow even less compelling than usual, I began to browse the several antique shops in the vicinity. In one such place, no more remarkable than the rest (in fact, the details of its appearance and even its name escape me), my eyes alighted upon a picture which, amongst the mounds of *objets d'art* from watercolours to moth-eaten taxiderms to brass candlesticks, had that queer *magnetic* quality upon which I have already attempted to theorise.

Let me describe it, if I can. I have no fear I can do at least a reasonable job, since the very vision of it hovers before me, the dull glaze crisscrossed with a pattern of hairline sutures evidential of its age – even to a less-than-able connoisseur such as myself.

The painting resembled, at first sight, a skull. At a distance of ten feet or so, standing across a crowded junk room, that is *exactly* what the painting seemed to me, its yellow dome set gloomily in a dark russet, almost black, background. The strength of that image was riveting: in spite of the fact that the frame was barely a foot square, it dominated the room. But – this was the hook that caught and slowly reeled me closer – I noticed, to my astonishment, as I came nearer, that the composition was not a skull at all, but that of a fifteenth century maiden, her back to the viewer, facing her reflection in an oval mirror, her hand extending along a row of Pharmacie jars or perfumeries. At a distance, the woman's hair and the corresponding oval mirror became the dark orbits of a death's-head; a drape became the nose; the row of bottles, the teeth; her pale arm, the line of that porcelain jaw.

The perfection of the illusion was uncanny. I almost laughed with delight at the discovery of it, like a child gloriously deceived by a magic trick.

"Can I be of assistance?"

I turned to see an old man in a Dickensian cardigan and half-moon glasses. His bald pate seemed as comically premeditated as the tonsure of a monk, emphasised by the hedge-like wildness of white hair like a fallen halo behind his ears.

"Just browsing," I said. I looked around the shop, but my gaze could not resist falling back upon the curious work of art, one moment seeing the Skull, the next, the Maiden. The old man could tell where my interest lay.

"Extraordinary," I said. "Do you know anything about its background?"

The old man hardly looked up, and said that he did not. His terse reaction upset me, and I left, but I found that, try as I might, the image of the optical illusion would not leave my mind.

Next evening I visited a friend with some interest in painting, who lived in Kensington. It is a credit to him that he did not turn me away, since I had not looked him up for over six months, but instead embraced me and treated me to a hearty supper. His home was cluttered by paintings which would not have been out of place in the Royal Academy, which reassured me of his expertise – his love. Over cigars, I described the uncanny portrait to him, and he had no hesitation in recognising the type.

The thing was obviously what is termed an 'anamorphosis': a picture of one thing that conceals another. There is a painting by

Hans Holbein the Younger, 'Ambassadors Jean de Dinterville and Georges de Selve,' in which a curious shape across the bottom of the painting becomes, when viewed from a certain angle, a human skull. Another famous anamorphosis, of the English School, is the death's-head painting of Charles I, which, under a correcting mirror, becomes a portrait of the living king.

My friend elaborated that this manner of skull-picture was the vogue at the turn of the century, in Germany and Paris – the decadence and erotica of beauty and Death was certainly evident. "And I daresay that's when your picture dates from, but it was very much a tradition born out of the late middle ages – representing a kind of modern awakening, as a matter of fact. It's very interesting, actually! You see, previously images of Death invited the viewer to repent or be damned. Now, in juxtaposition, in the form of an enigma, life and death were intertwined – Blossom and Decay, as it were, vanity and nothingness – the message is clear, death is all around us, and within us."

I resolved in that moment to possess the portrait, and to return to the antique shop at the earliest opportunity the next day.

Sunlight had barely begun to cast its silvery light on the ice and scales of the fishmongers' stalls next morning, as I approached the shop. I did my best to conceal my excitement with an air of indifference which I was sure could only be painfully transparent. The old man watched me intently, and I knew he could easily read my thoughts. The game was up.

"What's the best price you can do for me? The Renaissance Woman – the, er – the skull, there?"

He let out a long, troubled sigh. "Ah, you don't want that, sir…" He spoke with the croaky whisper of a Spitalfields Shylock.

"What do you mean?"

The old man's manner was spiky and inhospitable. "I mean I am not sure I want to sell it, to tell the truth. It is a horrible thing. I don't like it, personally. I only keep it here because the owner, she wanted me to repair it. You see that cut there? That tear in the canvas? No, it's not ready yet. It needs repairing and… No, I think it's better not to – "

"Then can I leave a deposit? I'm really desperate that no one else buys it. I'll pay you for the repair, as well, if you put it aside in my name. It's Venables. I've never seen anything like it." I left him in no doubt that I was very interested indeed.

"Let me put it to you like this," said the old man carefully. "I'm not sure you'd so much want it, if you knew what happened to it..."

I was taken aback for a moment. "Look, I've really had enough of this playing around. Either you want to sell it, or not. If you do, I want to buy it. I don't see what there can be to complicate the matter!"

The man took off his spectacles and peered myopically at the small painting. I detected a kind of derision in the expression that puckered his face. He then turned away from it, as one might turn away from a person one is about to besmirch with a whisper. "A woman brought it here, some three months ago. She was very upset. She had purchased the painting some time ago and it had occupied a position of some...sentimental value in her household, since her late husband, he acquired it abroad; but when she came here with it she said she found its very presence loathsome and unbearable, and she had to part with it. She could not bear it in her house a moment longer. What caused her to feel so strongly, it was very plain..."

"Go on," I urged him.

"Her son had returned from ten years with the Merchant Navy. He had been the apple of her eye before he ran away to sea, and she greeted him like the prodigal son. However, the joy of the widow-woman was, aye – short-lived. Her son, he had suffered the sun-stroke in some equatorial country, and had suffered fever of the brain, it took him close to death. Of course she knew none of this until he began to show signs that the balance of his mind had been disrupted. He would curl up in his room for days on end. He would fly into violent furies. He would disappear, sometimes for days, and complain of fearful burning *voices* in his head. Most terrifying of all – in the depths of his delirium, he imagined that the Death's Head of the picture was looking out, controlling him and forcing him over the brink, urging him on to unmentionable evil. Finally the son's madness exploded, and he attacked his mother with a knife, with the intention to murder her.

"Thank the Lord, she was not badly hurt, but in the struggle, the blade tore the painting." His voice trailed off for a moment, and when it returned it was the barest whisper. "And so the son is in Bethlem Hospital, and the painting, it is here..."

His expression became so mournful that I became

embarrassed by my very presence.

"It clearly upsets you," I said. "And I can understand why. But I have no personal relationship with these people – it doesn't frighten me that it has some sordid story behind it. All the better for me to take it off your hands, surely?"

He laughed and shook his head. "I am sorry."

"I'll give you twenty pounds."

"I am sorry."

"Thirty."

He propped his head on his forearms, making a triangle with his elbows and rubbing his head as if suddenly beset by lice.

"Fifty. Name your price. I'm sorry, I'm not leaving this shop until you do."

After some thought, he looked me in the eye. "You can have it," he pronounced gravely. "But I'll not take a penny for it."

I began to protest but he interrupted me.

"You can take it with you now. Live with it, if you can. Look at it, sleep on it, overnight. Hang it on your wall. And if you still want it hanging there tomorrow, consider it yours."

I left the shop with the painting, wrapped in brown paper, under my arm, excited and bewildered. "I will see you tomorrow," the old man said quietly, and with disarming certainty.

That night I was beside myself with delight as I unveiled my new acquisition to my friend, the Collector. Chuckling, I spouted out an abbreviated version of the story told me by the old man, but when I turned to look at him, my friend was staring at the painting, the winter rosiness of his cheeks drained white as chalk. I asked him what the devil was wrong.

He apologised, seemed suddenly flustered and uncertain, and took a seat with his back to the picture. "This is really nothing, *nothing* like I imagined," he stammered. As I watched, he twisted, almost as if against his will, to stare at the anamorph that hung on the wall of my room. We sat and ate the unostentatious meal I had prepared, and periodically as we leafed through the art history books he had brought along he would shoot yet another glance over his shoulder, with the appearance of somebody suddenly aware of being watched.

It was approaching eleven o'clock, and outside the harsh wind warned of a harsher frost – the mildness of the summer had ill prepared us for a relentless winter – when we successfully identified the artist of the portrait, from a scrawled signature in one corner.

My friend had referred to a sixteenth century painting, 'The Young Woman and Death', in which the naked, almond-eyed maiden whose eyes encounter the viewer bore a striking resemblance to the woman in my painting: the same waxen complexion, the strange ornamentation shackling the neck, the air of innocence – yet knowingness. The strange distorted-looking foetus, blindfolded, in her arms, was also echoed in a tiny shape within the alchemical jars, and the skeleton leering over her shoulder with a grin like broken bark bore a certain resemblance to the overall, forest-like background to the composition.

The author of this weird pseudo-portrait was Hans Baldung Grien, born in Gmund, Swabia in 1485. Baldung Grien was one of the few German artists of the time to push beyond the limits of the Gothic mould, with bold sensuality and a dark drama missing in most of his contemporaries. Unlike them, he came from the elevated middle class rather than a family of craftsmen, so possibly a classical education tainted his subjects. He underwent his training in Strasbourg and in 1503 entered the studio of the great Albrecht Durer in Nuremberg as an apprentice.

Early in 1509 he returned to Strasbourg to acquire both his own studio and a new wife, Margaretha Herlin. From then on, his work encompassed both the ecclesiastical and the secular, with altarpieces like 'St Sebastian' and 'Three Kings' giving way to portraiture such as that of 'Baron von Morsperg' (1525), and finally, in 1529, a series of gloomy, almost demonic narrative paintings like 'Two Witches' and the 'Death of Lucretia.' It is for these scenes of witches and death dances, together with his frankly erotic portrayal of female nudes in conjunction with a melancholy longing for death, that Baldung Grien is best known.

"Well, so much for you expertise, my friend!" I said with a laugh. "Clearly this painting is worth a pretty penny more than you imagined! Turn of the century be dashed! Mass-produced, eh? What do you say now?"

"I say, get rid of it," my friend answered coldly.

"Not a chance! I knew you'd try to get me to part with it. Not for all the tea in China!" I lounged back, basking in my glory.

"I'm serious, man. It's hateful."

"The eye of the beholder!" I suggested.

"It's vile!"

"I like it."

"For Pity's sake, take it down. I can't bear the thing in the same room as me!" he said, springing up and pacing like a man awaiting a birth – or an execution. A muscle in his cheek was trembling nervously.

"Good heavens, steady on," I said. "If I didn't know a good deal better, I'd say that old wives' tale the shopkeeper spun me is having its effect. Obviously he's a good salesman! I wonder what price he'll slap on it tomorrow, eh?"

"I'm *serious*. There's something unnatural in it. Don't you see?"

"No, I'm afraid I don't."

"Well look, damn it!"

He extended a bony finger behind him, refusing to turn to face the painting on the wall. I walked closer and peered at it through my cigar smoke.

"The woman wears an orange and black dress, am I right?"

"Correct," I replied.

"The vanity mirror, look at it closely. I don't know if you know about these things, but it's indisputably Louis XIV style. The necklace, the scarab, is clearly Art Nouveau, *unmistakably* Art Nouveau! And – no, don't interrupt me, just look! – in the oval mirror, look at the reflection – you see the reversed writing – the tiny writing on a calendar? It's a date – do you see it now? The date is 1904…and Baldung Grien died in 1545!"

"Well observed. Capital. So you've unveiled it as a fake. A pretty feeble one, too. Rather a giveaway, those mistakes, what? As if the artist is having a joke at our expense, don't you think? Ah well, a hoax after all – but never mind. I like it anyway."

"But the paint… I know the difference between egg tempera and a Sunday watercolour. Believe me, Venables, *the paint is four hundred years old*," he said in a whisper.

'Then the faker is cleverer than we thought!' I laughed.

My friend the Collector did not. Without a word he made across the room and retrieved his hat and coat. Despite my entreaties not to part on bad terms, he left immediately, without a backward glance.

*

I read, as was my habit, until midnight, when my landlady's husband returned from his nightly visit to the local public house. The invariable contretemps with the sober members of his family soon died down, with the kicking of his dog, or his wife, or both.

The wine lulled me into a deceptively mellow sleep, and I began to think about my friend's misgivings. Slumber, however, more often embellishes and compounds worries than resolves them, and soon I found it impossible to rest peacefully. Neither did I have the concentration to return to my books. My thoughts and my gaze instead turned to the anamorphic painting, which hung on the wall in a window-shaped patch of moonlight which turned the skull from its faded parchment-colour to a vivid ivory.

Again, I turned over and tried to sleep, but the thought of a face looking out – the thought of *being looked at* – crept over me like a tangible force, to the extent that I tucked my blanket under my chin like a five-year-old afraid of the dark.

I tried to shut out the sounds of the night, the creaking of the old house, the unpleasantness of the weather, the darkness that surrounded me like a pool, a darkness so welcome – yet –

I opened an eye.

The rectangle of the canvas hung on the wall, the maiden and the cadaver battling for predominance.

It stared and it stared back. I sat up, cross-legged on my bed. I shook myself awake and alert and said to myself, "Come along! Pull yourself together. It is paint on canvas, nothing more. Your friend is over-excited, perhaps even ill. There is no reason – no reason on earth – to lose sleep over this painting because a funny old man told you so!"

I finished the half-glass of wine that was at my bedside. It tasted uncomfortably sour.

I went to the window, opened it, and took in some of the night air. I needed to cleanse my lungs. The rush of oxygen brought me back to reality, and, turning back into the dingy room, I saw the picture for what it was once again: an elaborate puzzle, a joke, a fake.

I toasted her with the empty glass, the Nameless Maiden, as anonymous as La Giaconda with her small, enigmatically smiling lips, the velvet beret with its ostrich-feathers, the waxen complexion, the almond-shaped eyes – no blemishes, no eyebrows. No name.

At her throat she wore a bejewelled ribbon which matched the orange-and-black medieval tracery that patterned her bodice, whilst over her shoulders was draped a heavy gown. The orange seemed to match both the peach of her bud-like lips and the gleam of strangeness in her half-shut, knowing eyes. Her face seemed both classical and timeless, at once both Botticellian and Pre-Raphaelite, ageless and eerily familiar, even to the gentle coil of a hairband...a hairband – was I mistaken? – that had not been there a moment before...

I stepped closer.

It was there, as clear as day, the hairband I had not noticed before, and it was as much a part of the portrait as the orange collar – the orange collar which now, remarkably, incredibly, had become a white Elizabethan ruff...

I could not believe my eyes, but neither could I look away. The enigma held me. The almond eyes held me.

The once-black gown was a sleeve, slashed in the seventeenth century manner, tied in bows over the bare flesh of her arm. The robe puckered, *changed.* The hair, once high and hidden, now grew long and flowing in cascading ringlets.

I stood frozen, my eyes unable to turn away, as surely as if my lids were nailed back to my head. I felt I was the unwilling catalyst, the victim and perpetrator; but of what action, of what vile deed?

Now the medieval tracery had become the plainness of a Victorian blouse, the collar, once a ruff, now a ruby-red brooch, and the hair – the hair – now lifted, as a comic character might feign terror: up and looping round into a neat coiffure, while the waxen face stared on, and out at me.

My eyes saw that the perfume bottles, whose contents were once indistinguishable, now contained innumerable loathsome objects. A foetus with a single, cyclopean eye, a toad with four arms and four legs, a deformed and webbed human hand. And I saw in the reflection within the oval mirror in the painting – as if reflecting my own body now crouched in terror on the bed – the body of an old man, contorted in agony, clawing at his abdomen, and yet screaming curse upon curse in some Germanic tongue, while the smite of his demented wife lingered on amongst her poisons.

60

The witch.

The witch Margaretha Herlin had slowly killed her husband, Hans Baldung Grien, and he had cursed her; cursed her in his hatred in every brushstroke of his last, undiscovered work: 'My Wife and Death.' And now I knew her madness lived on in the sickly colours and cracked patina of the anamorph.

Suddenly the maiden vanished, and vividly in focus the skull broke the boundaries of the frame, leaping towards me like a demonic Jack-in-the-Box, its dome touching the roof of the attic, its chattering jaws engulfing the bedposts, like the Great White Whale intent on devouring its Ahab.

I hurled the wine bottle. I ran out of the house and hammered on the door of a bed and breakfast place in Holborn. They took pity, thinking my delusions to be those of a drunkard, and assuring themselves I could first pay my way. There I spent a fitful and sleepless night, until dawn broke.

I returned to my lodgings to find the house in some minor uproar. My landlady, a normally genial sort, was irritable in the extreme, which she excused as being due to lack of sleep. The children were wailing and she apologised on their behalf, saying that they had been complaining all night of strange noises, and that the house was haunted, Lord love us!

I said nothing.

I went upstairs and found the painting, face-down, as I had left it. Without looking at it, I wrapped it in its brown paper and tied it with string. My wine had given the peeling wallpaper a blood-like stain.

Without regard for my slovenly dress and the fact that I had not shaved and looked abominable, I strode off immediately for the antique shop in Lamb's Causeway.

The street was deserted of the usual market stalls. A few stray cats lurked suspiciously in the gutters. I was relieved to find the shop open. The bell tinkled when I entered – a bell I had not noticed before.

A woman of middle age sat reading a small book which she politely closed as I entered. She gave a smile. She wore a faded, floral-patterned dress and a Puritan-style bonnet over grey hair. Her face had the scrubbed beatitude of a nun.

"This…" I began to say, tearing the paper off the painting. I

Stephen Volk

found that no more words were forthcoming. My agitation took my tongue.

"Very nice," she said demurely. "Quite an unusual piece, sir, I must say. Very unusual, I should say. All the rage at the turn of the century, of course. How much did you want for it, sir?"

"No, no. You don't understand. The old man, is he here? He'll remember all about it."

"Man?"

"Is he here? An old man, bald head. He was here yesterday. Strange little man. Thick accent."

"No, sir," she said, shaking her head with genuine regret. "I think you must be mistaken. This is my shop, nobody works here but me."

"But yesterday…"

"Yesterday we were closed, sir. In fact, we've been closed for a week. You see, my son, he's returned from a long time abroad. Merchant Navy. He's been a little poorly, so we took the train to Brighton to get some fresh air. He seems so much better now. The sea air is such a good healer, don't you think? Now, how much shall we say? I think at least ten pounds, don't you? All right, then, sir, fifteen. Sir?"

To my eternal regret, I said nothing, and left the shop, and have not had the courage to return since, either the next day, the next year, or the many years that followed, for fear that what I might discover might be worse even than what I knew already.

I have no knowledge of the whereabouts of my poisoner, my Giaconda of the Dark, or where her tiny peach-coloured smile now lingers.

Perhaps Art is a reflection of Life. And Life is nothing but a puzzle which, when viewed in a certain way, amid a certain light, reveals only that great and unavoidable truth which even the greatest of artists cannot distort or disguise – our mortality…

Blitzenstein

Cliff Salvat was an American, and if he hadn't been there we wouldn't have done it, not on our own. Cliff Salvat had different trousers. For a start he called them pants, which made us chuckle. Pants were what you wore underneath. And they were long, to his ankles, like a grown-up's. In fact he looked like a grown-up in his shirt, bow tie, and jacket. My Dad used to call him the midget. Where's the midget? Or, where's the Yank? Where's Buffalo Bill, then?

Cliff Salvat used to say Hey when we said Oi, Hi there instead of Wotcher, and automobile instead of car. He taught my baby sister to say automobile in her pram. Say it. Go on. Automobile. He used to ask her to say words like transmitter, or eucalyptus, or Venezuela. He used to come to our house for tea and we'd play with tin racing cars and skittles in the back yard. But he was never my friend, not really.

He never said please or thank you, just, Hey give me that, or Do this. And when my Mum asked, What do you say? he'd go Huh? She said he was a sad little boy.

He arrived in our school one day halfway through the war and no-one would talk to him, so we did. Our gang was me, George from next door, Arthur his little brother, Cyril with the glasses, and Esme. Cliff Salvat looked rich (compared to us) so we thought he would have toys and tell us what cowboys were like. We thought he must have lived on a ranch, but he didn't. He came from Minnesota.

Somebody told us that his father had been killed in the war. Shot. A US marine. But I never saw him cry about it. There was never a tear in his eye. I looked, every day, and I never saw one. Not one.

He knew good games though, and told us what to do, and that's how he got into our gang, really. We made an African mask once, and a Flash Gordon rocket out of tea chests and bicycle wheels, and a toboggan we painted green, and we used to tie rope around our toy soldiers and dangle them over the wall as if they were mountain climbers.

When a doodlebug came over, Dad said, Right you lot, down in the ground, that's where we'll all be one day, look sharpish. And we'd waddle off into the air raid shelter like a line of ducks with gas masks on. When the noise of the doodlebug stops, that's the worrying bit, because it means it's dropping. Like when your mother gave birth to you, Dad said to me. When she stopped whining, that's when our trouble really started, eh, Glo? Then, when the all clear sounded, we'd go out and have a gander. London still intact, Dad used to say, No thanks to you, Gerry Bastards! Sometimes there would be bricks and stones all over the yard and bits of broken things, like it had rained them, like the world had been turned upside down and given a good old shake.

When she was one year old, my sister got a dolly for her birthday. My Mum put it in her cot and went, Ahhh. I asked her why little girls have dolls and little boys don't. She said little girls have to get used to holding babies and little boys don't, they have soldiers instead. But the dolly opened and closed its big blue eyes and you could turn its arms and legs and pretend it was walking. It was pink and had clothes, like a real thing. Like a tiny friend. I tried to pull it off her, just to play with for a minute, but she cried and I had to give it her back. The next day after a bombing raid, we'd go exploring. Sometimes we'd see a house was missing, or a street. Sometimes we'd see somebody sitting on the pavement with a coat wrapped round them, looking like they had a headache, or lost something. Once we saw a policeman with his arm around somebody. Once we saw a boy with no clothes on. Once we saw a dead baby in the rubble, and some bodies being carried on stretchers: one of their hands dangled down and the ambulance man kept picking it up. Once we found some ladies knickers and a dead cat. Once we saw a house with only one wall left, and a candle in a candle-stick, still alight. If the ARP warden saw us we'd run, because if he got hold of us, we'd be for it. We were more afraid of them than we were of the Germans.

One day George said, You'll never guess what I found. He ran off with us following, down the alley behind the sweet shop, through the allotments. A few of the houses had been flattened in the night and the vegetable patches looked as though a hand had squashed them, like a baby playing with its food. Beckoned by George's stubby finger, we squeezed through a wire fence to face a pile of bonfiery wood, the shipwreck remains of a garden shed, at which he was pointing in between wiping his hands in his shorts. In amongst the scattered planks was a foot, and belonging to the foot was a leg and a body, none of them moving.

Is he dead? asked Arthur.

'Course he's dead, said Cliff Salvat. What else would he be? He's not moving. What is he, *faking* it? Dope.

Esme went over and poked the foot with her own. It didn't move. She backed away, cuddling her doll.

The rest of us went closer. I moved a bit of wood and I saw some blackish hair and a bloody ear underneath. Relax, said Cliff Salvat and started moving the debris aside. It was the dead body of a man. He was naked except for a dressing gown belted with a red and white rope with tassels. One leg was bare, with a hairy, veined ankle and the other foot was wearing a red slipper twisted at an impossible angle. His chest looked flat and skinny but he had a roll of fat under his chin where there was grey stubble mixed with black and his teeth were yellowy. He had obviously been in the shed when the bomb fell, and the blast had torn him apart but also half-buried him, that was how come the ARP wardens and firemen hadn't found him and taken him away with the other bodies.

He's got grey stuffing coming out of his tummy, said Esme, Like my teddy, look!

That's not stuffing, you twit.

What is it then?

Shut up!

Cliff Salvat broke a stick off a nearby bush and started to prod the dead body with it. Nobody said anything. He prodded harder. It cut the skin and made a mark. Something brown oozed out.

I said, Don't.

He said, Why not?

You might wake him up, said Esme.

Cliff Salvat pulled more of the wood aside, noisily. His head's missing, he said. His brains have all come out. And one arm is blown away, there's all just strandy bits hanging down. And that leg underneath, there's just bone at the top. And all his insides are missing. There's only half of him left. Look.

We ought to tell somebody, I said.

Who? said Cliff Salvat.

We'll get in trouble, said George. I'll get in *big* trouble!

Can't we shut up about it and just go? asked Cyril. Before somebody catches us?

Nobody'll catch us, moron, said Cliff Salvat. Nobody knows. There's only us. He's ours. He's our baby. Isn't he great? Isn't he fantastic? Our own body. Our own dead body. Us.

I crouched down like he was and looked at the small, perfect ear dabbed with crusty, blackening blood. What should we do? I said. Do we bury him? What?

Cliff Salvat looked down with a funny expression in his eyes, like when we made a fire for the first time, with matches. He said, We should put him together again.

What?

We should put him together and bring him back to life, he said, a bit louder.

Blimey, said Cyril.

People don't come back, I said. Dead is dead.

That's what you think, said Cliff Salvat, looking up at the distant drone of an invisible aircraft, its engine giving a bad imitation of thunder. Don't you think they keep secrets from us, he said, Grown-ups? They don't want us to know the truth because it's too horrible.

What secrets? asked Esme.

That Germans can come back from the dead, that's what.

Don't listen to him, I said. Then to Cliff Salvat, You're scaring her.

Am I? So what? It's time she knew. It's time we all knew. They don't die. They can't, that's why they're winning the war, we knock them down, they jump back up, all sewn up, all more horrible, just coming on, and on, mad, evil, not feeling any pain, nothing. Scars, and bullet holes, and...

How do you know? asked Georgie, his voice too quavery with fear to be truly sceptical.

Cliff Salvat walked over to the shade of a brick wall and crouched with his back against it. We huddled round, on our knees, perching on stones, and he passed around bubble gum. He said, My Dad took me to the movie theatre back home. The lady at the ticket booth said, Mister, that kid's too young for this kinda stuff, you know? My Dad said, Hey don't worry, he's a big boy, he can take it, you ain't scared, are ya, Cliffo? And I said, No sir, and he laughed real loud and slapped my back, and she said, OK soldier, and winked and jerked her head and we went on in. Well. When I saw it, I tell ya, I *was* scared, and I hid behind the seat. You wouldn't believe it. I'm not kidding. On the screen there was this big, big guy in black and white with his eyes pulled down, and a big iron block of a head, with scars and hinges, and he was put together with parts from dead bodies, and they cut his head open like a boiled egg and put a brain in, and put electricity through him and brought him back to life.

And it's true, I know it's true, because the word NEWS came up big, with a rooster standing there and a voice talking about Germany and the war, and I saw soldiers in black and white smiling and smoking cigarettes. And then the monster ten feet tall lifted up a little girl and threw her in the river. And I remember there were thousands of them, Germans, millions, all in rows doing the straight-arm salute and shouting, It's Alive! It's Alive! It's Alive!

And then, and then men and women doing athletics, perfect people who could never die. And soldiers with lightning bolts on their collars. And their boss up there, facing them, mad and shouting that they were the Gods now.

Cliff Salvat looked at our faces one by one. Have you heard of the name Frankenstein?

We all shook our heads.

That's their boss. That's the mad scientist who stitches them back together and says the whole country will live forever.

We were quiet.

Cliff Salvat poked at the dirt with the toe of his shoe. Boris Karloff, he was the first one. That's a German name isn't it? Boris. And Karloff! How much more German can you get than that? I've been thinking about it... A lot... Why they have those steel helmets shaped like that. It's to cover their flat heads. The heads where the brains have been put in. And that's why they don't feel any emotions or pain or feelings, nothing. Then he said, If we put him together, he'll come alive and he'll have to be our slave and play with us. He'll be like our Dad. Forever.

And so we went about creating our man. It wasn't too different from building a Guy Fawkes in preparation for bonfire night, except of course instead of balls of paper and rolls of cloth we had to find real organs and pieces of meat. You couldn't bring somebody back to life filled with paper.

We visited the allotments whenever we could, mostly when all of us were together but sometimes in groups of two or three. The first time, we pulled the corpse from under the wooden planks and put him in the garden shed; it became our laboratory. Each of us stole knives or forks or string from our parents' houses – nails, needles, scissors, anything that looked medically useful, when our Mums or Dads were looking the other way.

We cleaned the blood from him, tip to toe, scrubbed him like our Mums did our faces when we got smeared with chocolate. We scraped off the hard black chunks of burned flesh with bits of slate and tried to cover the stains and discoloration with paint from a Christmas paint box. Then we set about getting the Bits and Pieces.

For the following days and weeks we were on the look-out. We'd seen all sorts of things in the bombed-out houses, and now we had a need for them. Cyril found a leg behind the station yard. It was a lady's leg, but never mind. We took the shoe and stocking off and tied it onto the burned stump of the dead man's body. Esme said she'd learned from her Mum how to sew, and she licked her needle, frowning seriously in the torchlight, and we cut stretchy patches of skin with scissors from the limb to the joint like we were darning a sock.

George got a bull's eye from his uncle the butcher, saying he needed it for Biology, but we put it in the big hole on the side of the dead body's head. It jiggled and bulged when we did it but in the end it was a good fit.

Arthur found an arm. It belonged to a black man. It was lying next to a stretcher and nobody noticed it in all the commotion. He just nipped in and nipped out again with it wrapped in the *Daily Mirror*.

Cliff Salvat said do this, do that. He seemed to know everything, and we didn't question him. We didn't mind.

When we had something new to add on, Esme would put her dolly on the shelf and set to work with her needle and thread while we, and the dolly, looked on. There were some fingers missing so I stole one of my Dad's woolly gloves and put sausages in to make it look right. Sausages were meat so they were OK, Cliff Salvat said. Sometimes Cyril brought some milk and digestives and we'd stop and have a snack and think to ourselves proudly how good our Man was looking, half-lying, half-sitting there, half in shadow and half in sunlight as Esme tied a knot in her thread and bit off the rest, and patted his chest and said, There there sweetheart, like her mother said to her.

It was exciting.

It was better than making a Guy Fawkes. Much better. We

couldn't wait to go there, every day. We couldn't wait for him to be *alive*!

In a few days he smelled a bit, so we used to wear our gas masks when we operated. We put up little hooks and hung our tools round the walls. We made a list of what he would eat: fruit, meat, nuts, eggs, spuds, tomatoes. We went shopping and mashed it all up and put it in a bag and filled his empty belly. The maggots fizzled away and the centipedes burrowed off into the earth. It squelched and we had to use my snake-buckle belt to hold his newly-restored gutsy bits inside.

One day George and Arthur found a dead dog and brought it in a wheelbarrow. Its eyes were staring and its tongue was grey and long. We hit its skull with a hammer till the bone cracked and we put its brain into our man, in a broken saucepan to protect it, with a lid on.

Cliff Salvat said, he needs bolts here and here. For the electricity. So we took apart my bike and rammed the handlebars through his neck, in one side and out the other, and put big wing-nuts on either end with a wrench. It looked smashing.

Rummaging the bombed-out husks of houses, we collected about twenty-five shoes, all sorts of colours and sizes. Cliff walked up the line and did the choosing. One was a soldier's and the other was a shiny one, like Sunday Best. We took a shirt from somebody's washing line and some grey flannel trousers – pants – from somebody's bottom drawer. We'd argue sometimes about what we wanted him to wear, and sometimes we'd vote for it, and sometimes we'd draw straws. Our parents wondered where we got to all day but we didn't tell them. It was our secret.

After a while our man, our German didn't stink any more. He smelled as sweet as Parma violets. We loved him.

Esme brought some lipstick and put it on his lips. Sometimes she'd lie next to him, looking like she wanted to sleep there, cuddle up in his lolling arms, but Cliff Salvat would get angry and tell her to get off him, he's not a toy, he's a Human Being.

Why? Why can't I? she'd say. He's not *yours*.

Yes he is, I said. He belongs to all of us. We *made* him. We made him and he's going to *live*. He's going to walk, you'll see.

Walk and talk, said Esme. Walk and talk.

Bloody hell, said Arthur. What's he going to *say*? Will he be angry?

Will he talk German? asked Esme.

No, said Cliff Salvat. He'll be real happy. You'll see. We'll teach him words. Any words we like.

Suddenly we heard someone outside giggling and we all went quiet and ducked down, away from the window, terrified anybody would see or hear us. They got closer. We heard them chatting and lighting cigarettes. A man and woman. We heard him ask her to lie down on his raincoat and they started doing things and groaning and gasping breath. Esme started crying and Cliff Salvat hissed at her to shut up. We didn't move an inch till it got dark and the man and woman kissed again and talked and went away.

What if they find him? asked Esme.

They won't, I said. Nobody's going to find him. We won't let them. He's our property. He's our friend.

If they see him, they'll all want one, said George.

Look at him, said Cliff Salvat, his eyes sparkling like broken glass. He's wonderful. He's magnificent. He's almost ready. Almost. Ready.

He grinned and so did I.

The air raid siren sang and we scattered home. As I closed the door, looking for the peg on a string to lock it, I glanced back in, seeing the moonlight sloping down onto the slumped, improvised scrawl of life we had built from a jigsaw of dead flesh and the indiscriminate salvage of war. A Pinocchio of the perverse, a train-set of humanity, a monstrous concoction of childhood wishes and fears, waiting to wake up, and yawn, and beat its breast, like Tarzan.

And that's what I wanted – what we all wanted – more than anything in the world.

That night I lay awake, too excited to sleep, too immersed in my thoughts to notice at first the sound that came from the sky like the bass drum of a military parade. But then I *did* hear it. I ducked behind the blackout and peered out through the crucifixes of sticky tape that protected our window panes. The sky was clear and the colour of a pearl. There was no siren but the sky was lit up in flashes as a violent thunderstorm thrashed the clouds. Blinding spikes stabbed down at the dark, sleeping city.

Mum!

What is it?

Mum!

Go back to bed. What are you doing down here?

I have to go…I have to! I have to!

After my Dad hurried me back to my bed and put off the light, I rushed back to the window, my heart pounding.

No. No…

Suddenly a zed of light arrowed down beyond the back-to-backs and was gone. Seconds later thunder cracked in my head. I held my breath. I was sure the lightning bolt had struck in the exact location of the allotments. A second, more jerky and serrated burst fell, but gap between it and the thunderclap that followed, even now, was longer – as the storm lumbered away, almost as if it knew its job was done.

The following day was bright and cloudless, and the pavements were bone dry. When our gang gathered at the allotments I noticed for the first time that the grass was beginning to poke through the ash and dirt, and a couple of cheerful sparrows hopped on the half-ruined fence.

Cliff Salvat was already inside the shed when we shoved the door open wider. When we followed him in, somehow we knew what we would find: the dingy, ramshackle hut was empty. Our Man, our Boris, our Lazarus, our Dad – was gone.

Poor human, said Esme.

They must… George began, hesitating. They must have found him. I mean the firemen, the ARP wardens, whoever. They must have come here and found the body and...

Cliff Salvat was not listening. He was staring at the space where our handsome creature used to be, and for a moment I thought he was going to cry. His shoulders began to shake, but he was laughing. The rest of us looked at each other and Esme cuddled and kissed her doll. Cyril took off his glasses and cleaned the lenses in his grubby shirt. Cliff Salvat was laughing till tears ran down his cheeks. We did it, he said. We did it. We did it! It's alive! IT'S ALIVE!

He threw his head back, yelling it so hard I thought the roof would cave in, so unashamedly, deliriously happy it frightened us, and we left him, scurrying back to our burrows, not wanting to share his happiness any more than we'd wanted to know his unhappiness – with that singular and spectacular callousness unique to children, and monsters.

Now nobody talks about the war. There have been too many wars, or pseudo-wars, since. If not with countries, then with diseases. Now it's my profession. My vocation. It's what I'm good at. I put them all together, stitch them up, as best I can, ship them out. Now, the dead walk every day. I only have to look around me. Cancer, cysts – if in doubt, cut them out. Amputations, new limbs, donor cards, hearts harvested all over the country, farmers with their severed hands packed in picnic baskets of ice.

I see it every day across my Harley Street desk. Everybody wants to live for ever. We conquer death every day, every day we wake up, but we can't conquer the fear of it. Perhaps the fear of it is what makes us human.

Poor human.

We drifted apart after that glorious summer. No other games held our fascination, nor, curiously, did we hold fascination for each other.

After the war, when we went our separate ways, I heard only dribs and drabs about their subsequent lives, fed from parent to proud parent. Esme became a costume designer for the RSC, then opted out and went to live in a commune in the Orkneys. George and Arthur took over their father's greengrocery business, never moving more than a street away from where they were born and brought up. Cyril, a British Bill Gates, wrote software for the City, was married and had five kids and a house in Spain. And Cliff Salvat went back to the Bible Belt of his birth and became a Pentecostal minister: a new flock, a new gang, a new Father, at last.

Our lives are ordered now, and we are, for our sins, successful. The war was a long time ago, and yet it's only yesterday. For some of us it doesn't die.

I look down at my wrists and I see the scar tissue there, the stitch marks. I remember the lightning that seared through my brain to make me better, and lo, hallelujah, awakened me, and let me live again.

The Chapel of Unrest

There is a man frequenting a certain public house in Yorkshire, who, for the price of as many pints as it takes to tell, will share with you this story:

There is one question I cannot answer. Given the choice, would I have chosen a different profession? The business was my father's, and his before him. Mine was the name above the door, and somehow I knew that from infancy my destiny was to be fulfilled therein. By the time I was old enough to question, I was too old to change my ways, and there it is.

The profession of funeral preparation necessarily separates its acolytes from everyday society. Apart from the solitary nature of the work, there is some suspicion on the part of a public satiated by centuries of folklore, that such a practitioner may somehow be privy to some dark knowledge best left alone, some arcane sensitivity merely by dint of his contact with the dead. It is a view one must grow accustomed to tolerating. People brand us as carriers of melancholy and gloom merely because our station requires a modicum of dignity and respect. I became used to being treated as an outsider, as everyone in my trade must. I also became used to my own company, for the same reason. I have only had three friends in my life, and two are dead. I buried them both. The third will bury me, I suspect.

But we are needed. Why? Because people fear the dead. It is a dirty job, and people do not wish to do it themselves – they would rather entrust their dearest ones to a stranger. It is peculiar, and I will never understand it, but it is true.

People imagine a corpse to retain something of the nature of the living being that preceded it. However, in my experience, there is no such ambiguity. The dead are sad objects. Their souls have passed on. We deal only with the husks, and it is our function therefore, not to attend to the needs of the deceased so much, but the living – by providing sympathetic services to help the process of grieving. That is our function, and no more.

One thing changed my mind. One thing happened to make me question all the certainties I have just expressed. One thing made me begin to approach my job with increasing – unease. Even, yes –

caution.

It was a day in April. I remember because one of the boys made a joke about April showers. The sun shone brightly on pavements like glass. It was a miserable day. I had stayed in my office all night, pondering my accounts. My father had died seriously in debt, and however I juggled the figures, it always came out the same – I owed his creditors several hundred pounds. I could not even afford to pay them pennies. The resolution that greeted me with the dawn was the only possible one: with a heavy heart I decided to sell the business.

These thoughts were foremost in my mind as I received a message from Dr Frith that a death had occurred up at the Big House to the west of town. (It had been called 'The Big House' since my childhood, though its true, unremarkable name was Pryne Hall.) In a miserable mood, I took the hearse whence I was bidden, and found myself ushered into a death-bed tableau no different from dozens of others at which I had been present over the years I had been an undertaker.

The owner of the house was a tall, thin man with a stooped back, and a jutting chin supported by a wiry neck. His eyes were pale and clear for one of such advanced age, and his head was adorned with white hair as insubstantial as melting snow. He gestured with the cordiality of a nobleman, and spoke, which he did infrequently, with the merest hint of an accent, though his English was barely short of impeccable.

He sat immobile in a cushioned chair as the doctor and I conversed, all the while his eyes fixed with a kind of deep suffering upon the pitiful figure in the bed. Occasionally his eyes darted sidelong, nervously, or he would blink, or twitch, but always his eyes would return to rest on the deceased.

She was his daughter, a woman of some forty years of age. She lay as peacefully in death as if she had been arranged there, like the composition of a Pre-Raphaelite painting. Her hair was dark and lustrous, and lay thickly on the white waves of the pillow. Yet I saw no tears in her father's eyes, merely numb and staring eyes set in a wan and haggard countenance. But grief takes many forms, and I thought no more of it.

The doctor signed the death certificate and I transported the cadaver to my Chapel of Rest. At the door the old man hesitated, as if to say something, then declined, and shut the door. Only upon leaving, and hearing the bolts thrown from inside, did I notice that every one of the windows of Pryne Hall was barred like a prison.

Preoccupied by my troubles, I could do no more work that day. Instead, I confined myself to my office. I even drew the drapes to block out the mocking happiness of sunlight. Once more I pored over the books, and once more could only come to one conclusion: sell the business. I paced, stamped, cursed. I prayed to God: give me a way out of this mess! There was no answer.

I had just taken my coat from the peg to go for a brisk walk to work off my frustration, when a visitor was announced. I had him shown in, though I was in no mood for company.

It was the old man I had met earlier in the day. His name, I had learned, was Gaetano Prelati. He wore a heavy coat and had his hands stuffed firmly in the pockets. Against the darkness of the material, his pallor seemed almost grey. He refused my handshake and as he sat his head sank into his collar, bird-like.

"I have come," he said in his almost-perfect English, "to discuss" – he hesitated – "*arrangements.*"

"Very well," I said. "Have you spoken to the vicar, sir, or would you like me to take care of everything? Naturally, you will want things taken care of as soon as possible. Perhaps we should strive for a Friday funeral? I'm sorry – I have not asked if you are – er – Church of England, Roman Catholic...?" His unemotive manner was flustering me.

He shook his head. "Whichever."

I coughed. "I see. Well, we have a rising scale of prices; perhaps you would like to see that?"

"No."

"There is a wide range of caskets available: oak, mahogany, satin black – plain, velvet-lined – with gold furniture or bronze. Let me see if..."

"I am not interested in the quality of the coffin," said Mr Prelati.

"Then what have you come to discuss, sir?" I enquired with what politeness I could muster.

"The preparation of the dead."

"You would want our full treatment, sir? Yes, we can do that. Naturally, we can do that. The normal health and hygiene processes..." I used the usual euphemism for embalming, of course.

His pale eyes were unblinking as he produced an envelope

from his pocket and placed it in front of me. "I wish my own treatment. I realise my request is unusual, and when you read it, you may well have extreme reluctance to carry it out. I can only say, however, that my daughter's *condition* necessitates such action, and if you will not comply, I shall find another who shall."

I held the envelope in my hands, and let out a light laugh. This all seemed over-dramatic: why didn't the old man merely *tell* me his instructions? Why the secrecy? Why the warning? What could be so – *objectionable*? I was soon to learn, and as I read the enclosure my fingers began to tremble, and a cold sweat rose up my body.

After reading it, I flung it down. I stared at him.

"In the name of God, man!"

My first instinct was to throw the fellow out. Had he not been so old and frail I may have dealt him a blow. As it was I just stared, and he stared back at me with limpid blue eyes.

"There is no purpose in explanation," he said. "I could tell you the truth or I could give you one of many lies, but I have no intention of either. You accept the work, or not, as your feelings see fit."

"What kind of monster are you?" I blurted, able to keep my silence no longer. "This goes against every law of God and Man. It is the foulest of all deeds to abuse the sanctity of the dead!"

He sneered with awful bitterness. "You do not need to lecture me about the sanctity of the dead. I have my reasons. Religious, philosophical, call them what you will. I need your co-operation, and for the use of an hour of your time, and your guilt, I am prepared to pay – let us say – substantially."

I looked at the paper again. "Nothing can pay for – this! This – abomination! Good God, she was your daughter: does that mean nothing to you?"

"It means *everything* to me," he said quietly. He took out a cheque and laid it on the desk before me. Upon it was my name. He said, "One thousand pounds. In your pocket – or another's. Nobody will ever know. The grave cannot speak."

I was struck dumb. My thoughts spun, my head swam, no longer with disgust but with – interest. The rest of the conversation I cannot, will not, remember.

I poured myself a brandy, and to my horror found that I had poured two, and before I realised it we had raised the glasses and made a toast for which, to my eternal horror, I was, in that moment, eternally grateful.

Time was the monster.

I lay on my bed, fully clothed. The clock in the room ticked like the workings of an infernal machine, each passing minute reminding me of the first two words of Gaetano Prelati's abhorrent instructions.

Before sunset.

I turned on my side, closed my eyes to block out the room, but could not block out the thoughts. I felt unclean. I felt as if I had been complicit in a Faustian bargain. My body churned inside – my professional ethics flung asunder, my soul felt like a sacrificial lamb, terrified, bleating, yet unable to escape. To do this – to succumb – for greed. Where was the dignity of death? Where was the dignity of life? Would I ever have it? Could I ever truly *live*? Oh God – help me.

Before sunset...

It was madness. My humanity does not have a price. There are more important things. No. I shall not do it. I shall resist. I respect the dead.

Why?

What are they? What is it? A husk of flesh and bone. It isn't alive. It's a thing. It can help me. If it knew what I needed, perhaps she would have said in life – yes, do it. Do it if you need the money. Do what he wants you to do! Who are more important, the living or the dead?

Before sunset.

No. I can't. I have to resist.

Yes. Do it! Now, quickly. Don't be weak, have strength for once in your life. Do it and build the business again, or if you don't you'll go under, you'll be destroyed, *you'll* die.

Suddenly in an instant I became aware of the lengthening shadows in the room. The sun was setting over the far rooftops. I sat up, rigid. I took in a deep breath of air. Even so, I swayed giddily, heady with the responsibility of a decision I had now to make in a moment.

Why?

Why before dark? What nonsense was this? Bugaboo tales? Would an hour make such a difference? Does it have to be *now*?

Couldn't I have an hour, a minute, to think, to ponder, to *decide.* I laughed, but the air was chill. I was cold. Evil, feverish cold fell over me, and I shivered till my teeth chattered.

Obey them to the letter, he had said.

Before sunset.

I stood, determinedly. I went to the telephone. I rang Prelati's number. But before it began to ring, my mind had begun to think of the money again. The madness was mine: what did it matter *why*? Ask no questions. This is no murder, no one will come to harm. Why am I even questioning it?

It goes against God. But where is God in *my* hour of need?

I took up the paper again, and read it.

Before sunset...

Yes, yes. I picked up the box on top of the wardrobe which contained all the equipment I needed. It had not been taken down since my mother had died. It seemed faintly sacrilegious even to touch it – but I dispelled my fears. I took the crucifix from the wall above the 'Home Sweet Home' emblem.

The shadows were like a thick wash of seaweed at a shoreline as I waded along the landing and, in the silence now, not even comforted by the ticking of the clock, I descended to set about my grim task. Moonlight imbued the passage downstairs with a church-like serenity, filtering as it did through the stained-glass of the front door. For once I wished that my profession did not regale in the trappings of Christianity. The Christ portrait stared with accusing, watchful eyes as I entered the Chapel of Rest.

My hand twisted the handle of the door.

In the ante-chamber, coffins were stacked in rows, one on its end, its lid half-open. I used one arm to part the scarlet drapes that led into the Chapel itself, and the candle-lamp that I had brought from upstairs lit my path with a flickering, beeswax glow.

The Chapel was not a catacomb. It was not shadowy, nor sepulchral, nor even eerie. But the silence of the place seemed designed to catch any whisper – even the unsaid whisper of a guilty mind. I was afraid even to breathe.

The coffin lay on its bier, without a lid. I paused for a moment, looking down at the pallid figure of Alba Prelati. I thought it must have been the intensity of my emotions, or the ambiguity of the candlelight, but for an instant I would swear she had the face not of a forty-year-old woman, but of a girl of less than twenty summers,

I could not shy away now. I had come too far. Then it must be done without faltering, quickly.

Holding my breath, I placed the crucifix from my bedroom wall in the corpse's limp right hand, closing the fingers tightly around it. Strangely, they were not yet stiff with rigor mortis. In fact they were curiously warm, and clammy. Hastily removing a second crucifix which I wore around my neck, I placed this one in the palm of her left hand.

Place a crucifix within each of her hands.

I turned and went to fetch the large, leather-bound Bible from the lectern that faced the pews. I placed it upon the dead woman's breast, the cross embossed on its black leather covering her heart.

And a Bible upon her heart, the Trinity to bind her to the place, the weight of the Lord's might to hold her down... And in penance for her Sins, in Hell for all eternity.

I opened my mother's sewing-box. You cannot imagine how long it took for me to thread the needle with thick black twine. The perspiration more than once blinded me. I licked the end of the cotton a hundred times into a tiny point, but still it would not thread.

Before sunset...

The needle finally threaded, I leaned over the beautiful face beneath me. The beauty of the dead had not been lost on me, the sadness of a perfect child, the pity of beholding the full bloom of womanhood cut off in its prime: but here was something altogether different. Something inexplicably different about the upturned nose, the full lips, the almond-shaped eyes.

I touched her lips. They were dry as parchment. I puckered them together between my forefinger and thumb and began to sew. I had seen my mother sewing the Christmas turkey, pricking the pale flesh with the needle, forcing it through, pulling, stitching again, yanking the twine until the whole was a tight, immovable scar.

...the mouth must feed no more, and let her hunger...

The twine criss-crossed the mouth, pulling it shut, dragging the entire face into a grimace, drawing hideous wrinkles across the once-perfect cheeks. With the black outlines, it seemed she had the grinning teeth of a skull. I bent down and bit off the twine, and knotted it.

And now. My breath was tremulous, but echoed around the Chapel loudly. The stone angel stared with unseeing eyes, blind but all-knowing. Oh God. I must finish. Finish and go.

...and let her eyes not open...

I took the needle to her left eye, and beginning at the inside edge, I inserted it just under the tear-duct, and through the inside of the upper lid, out, and in through the lower lid again. I made in all seven stitches to seal her eyelids together before beginning on the other eye.

Suddenly it opened.

Like a glistening pearl it shone in the darkness, with the same steely blue as her father's. But staring, bulging, terrified, darting to and fro.

With a scream wrenched out of my intestines I fell back, spewing the contents of the sewing-box over the tiled floor of the Chapel, needles and cotton-reels and buttons tinkering in all directions.

In an instant I was out of the place, falling against the staircase, using my arms desperately to claw my way up the carpet, rebounding along the walls to the sanctuary of my room. I flung myself on the bed, at once rising to lock the door, and place a chair against it, and for an hour sat on the bed, shivering and gibbering like a lunatic, my eyes never leaving the door-handle.

I woke at two in the morning, as if from a nightmare. I prayed it was. A brandy bottle lay upended on the floorboards. My head was throbbing. The chair was propped against the door.

Wearily, I forced myself downstairs, one hand gripping the staircase as if for dear life.

I entered the Chapel of Rest to find that the coffin was empty.

"Dear God!" I said to myself, almost collapsing with horror. Within minutes I was in Pryne Hall, screaming my horror at the perpetrator of the crime himself. "Dear God!" I cried, pacing so that it shook the house. "You are *evil* as well as perverted! You deceived me! You lied to me! That you wanted to do this – this disgusting ritual – was bad enough, to a dead body! But she was *not* dead! I saw her, she looked at me! Dear God! May God have mercy on you! She was *alive!*"

Gaetano Prelati said nothing for a long while. He seemed in a dark reverie, a prisoner in the book-lined library in which we confronted each other. Beside him was a side-table on which a pair of wooden glove-stands sat in an attitude of prayer.

"Your daughter is alive!" I screamed again.

"No," he said, and for the first time his voice quivered with emotion. "Alba is dead. She died fifty years ago."

I was overcome with rage and for a second time wished to attack him, but found myself instead uttering a laugh that seemed somehow to come from elsewhere.

"And she is not my daughter," he pronounced softly. "She is my sister."

"That's impossible!" I said angrily.

"There are many impossible things in the world," he said. "All of them real…"

"I'm leaving. I've had enough of madness. I am going to the police."

"Wait," he said. I turned back and saw an old man in need of the confessional. "If you go you will never know the truth."

I took the seat opposite him. The room was lit by gas from the wall-hangings, but darkness separated us like a black river. His voice was a croak, as if his throat protested against the tale he told.

"Before you were born – some half century ago now – when my sister and I were approaching our twentieth year, our father provided us with the means to travel. It was his belief that we should see something of the world, as he had done as a sailor before making his fortune. Alba was a spirited, rebellious child, and I was the quiet, studious one. My thoughts were for a career in the priesthood, hers only for excitement and laughter. You see me trembling? It is because I have not heard that laughter for fifty years! Please…" Prelati fidgeted in his seat, head nodding like a bird towards the side table. "Please, light the hookah. There are substances within to ease my pain."

I did as I was asked, rapidly, impatient for him to return to his history. He took a deep inhalation of foul, pea-green smoke and spoke with slow modulation:

"In Alexandria, I became incapacitated with severe sunstroke, and was confined to bed. Alba was not a good nurse, and I told her to travel onward, that I would meet her in Ushpur. My fever became worse and I was delayed much longer than I thought – and when I was strong enough to lift a newspaper, I was horrified to find that Khudi brigands, religious fanatics, a devilish horde, had invaded Ushpur, and that all Europeans, together with thousands of innocent women and children, had been flung into the vile pits of Ushpur prison.

"In a state of panic, I accompanied a contingent of English troops, only to find the city in a state of siege.

"It was four months before the Khudi were routed by the massed armies of our allies. We found the prison in a condition far beyond our worst nightmares of human degradation. Hundreds upon hundreds of people had been confined in utter darkness – and left to starve. I helped clear the many dead bodies. I sorted the living from the dead. I touched living and dead hands. Black and white. I dug through near-skeletons in the dark. Many had been mutilated as if by pestilential vermin. As for the living – their pitiful eyes looked up at me, but my only thought was for Alba.

"I found her, a withered shadow of her former self, a tiny stick-puppet cowering in the dank dungeons of Ushpur amongst the slime of faeces and decomposition that surrounded her like a bog of inhumanity. She could neither speak nor move.

"I returned with my sister to our home in Paris. She was nursed to health. Or, more correctly, what I believed to be health. It became clear to her family that her mind would never be the same. She stared out of the window, took no joy in the scent of flowers or beautiful music. She ate little, to begin with; then ate nothing. And yet she was no longer losing weight. In fact, she began to show a glow in her cheeks that the Alba before Ushpur never had.

"She slept erratically. More than once I woke from my own fitful slumber to hear an unfamiliar voice echoing throughout our family home – a voice neither Ushpuri nor Khudish, indeed approximating no tongue I had ever heard before. A voice racked with the anguish of sheer physical torment, the voice of a lost soul howling in the dark. One night, I was so agitated I went to her room; but the bed was empty, the bedclothes strewn around, the window open. I found her a street away, walking blindly. When I called her name, she stopped, and, suddenly aware of where she was, began weeping. I carried her home.

"I became curious as to the cause, purpose, or intent of her somnambulation. Perhaps, like the doctor and nurse observing Lady Macbeth, I could perceive some answer to her peculiar malady by a nocturnal vigil. This I decided to do.

"I entered her room, fully dressed, and sat in a corner far from her bed, an oil lamp at my side. For an hour nothing happened. Even the streets were chillingly quiet: no Parisian chatter, no far-off music, no dogs. Just the silent eye of the moon. Finally, my sister began to toss and turn. Her long fingers clutched at the sheets, pawed at her belly and throat; then she rose from the bed and slowly, like a wispish phantasm, drifted to the door and out, into the night.

"I followed.

"She descended the cobbled path towards Montparnasse cemetery, and I watched her scale the locked iron gates like a cat. Once inside, she became ever more like a stalking animal. Her eyes, glazed in half-sleep, fastened upon a small marble tomb in the corner of the graveyard reserved for poets. With a quiet intensity she set to the door, which, even though split, must have been incredibly heavy. Nevertheless the urgency of her task imbued her with supernatural strength, and the slabs were cast aside as if they were cardboard. I…"

Gaetano Prelati took another long suck on the hookah pipe before he could master his emotions. "You can have no idea, no man can have *any* idea – what I beheld when I looked into that – that *ravaged* sepulchre. She stood over the open coffin with the hideous substances of the grave staining her chin and breast. The inhabitant of the long box was naked, a man, decomposed, or mutilated, half lifted out, and his head tilted back, his sagging jaw dropped almost to his chest, no eyes in those dark orbits. Alba had his arm lifted in what I first took to be the act of kissing – of running kisses up the corpse's festering arm. But the sounds…the sounds, you see! The sounds, they were of crunching, they were of breaking, they were of gnawing, chewing, *swallowing*…"

My heart was in my throat. I could not believe what I was hearing.

Prelati waited. He moved his eyes in arcs around the room, as if moving us through time – as if passing over the years of pain, murmuring the names of other cemeteries in the city. "Pere Lachaise, Ivry… Paris was in the grip of a defiler of tombs. The staunchest efforts of the police could not apprehend the evil-doer, who seemed to roam with impunity, like a theatre-goer choosing an entertainment. Countless graves – their contents scattered – shrouds torn to the wind…

"There were no vermin in the dungeons of Ushpur," he

intoned with insufferable melancholy. "Or if there were it had two legs, two arms, and the face of a beautiful woman."

I tried to comprehend the horror he was trying to force on to me. My mouth gaped, unable to respond. His mind seemed to wander uncontrollably.

"In the age of Plutarch, the daughters of King Orcommenu of Boetia were imprisoned in his palace. Soon they were overcome, unable to resist an insatiable urge, falling upon the young Ippasus and devouring him. You look dumb! Do you still not see? Do you still not know?

"Perhaps you have read the *Arabian Nights*? The 'Story of Sidi-Nouman' in the 'Encounters of Haroun-Al-Raschid on the bridge of Baghdad'?" I shook my head. "Amina, the wife of Sidi-Nouman, nightly deserted the marital bed to feed upon the dead!" Gaetano Prelati looked to the book-lined shelves. "Each of these books contains the legend! Hoffmann told the same tale to his Serapion Club in the form of 'Aurelia: Vampirismus'. Same story. Same creature. It comes from the Slavic word *ogoljen,* you know – meaning 'mortal remains'."

I stared at him, dumbfounded and more perplexed by the minute. He saw the mystification in my face, and leaned forward.

"Ghoul," he said precisely. "Eater of the Dead! Vessel of Demons! Being of the Night! You see? You understand? In the dungeons of Ushpur, those who survived did so by one means alone – by *cannibalism.*

"I see your visage grow pale. I am beyond the horror now. But I have learned, to my pain, that such a thing is not beyond human endeavour – or taste. The Scythians and Bretons devoured their dead. The Carthaginians, ancient Gauls, and Sioux Indians of North America consumed the blood and flesh of their enemies as a way of assimilating their courage into their own bodies. The Brahmins and Estonians began the practice of draining blood from meat before eating it. In hot countries this became the norm, until final vindication came from the voice of the Hebrew God: 'Be sure that thou eat not the blood: for the blood is the life...' In Ushpuri legend, a cannibal in life will become a ghoul in death – and be condemned to eternal purgatory on Earth. You see! I have done a lot of reading! I have learned many things!"

I decided to humour the old man.

"What happened after you found your sister in the cemetery?"

"I need not tell you the thoughts that raced through my mind as I followed the – *necrophage* that was my sibling back to our home. I did not sleep, but in the morning resolved that my family would not be made to endure further horrors. The bespoilings of the graveyards were already public knowledge, and for them to be linked to our noble house would destroy my parents, I was sure.

"Instead, I said I wanted to take over a wine importing enterprise in England, and I wanted to take Alba with me. I imprisoned her here, this was to be her tomb – and mine. For the first years, I was dominant and she was the prisoner, but then gradually as I became older, she began to inflict her horrifying will. I began to see her waste away with apparent consumption, and, unable to withstand that, I began to give her offerings – God help me, *I* became the grave robber!

"But she demanded more and more. It became like the addiction of a drug. Alba could derive pleasure from nothing but the consumption of human flesh. The Demon within her tormented me as it did her. I felt that I might lose my sanity unless I found her some escape. I read, I read... Filippo Raimondi's *Dissertazione,* Horapollon's *Magie,* Dom Calmet, *De Daemonialitate et Incubis et Succubis* of Liseux, Juan de Lobkowitz Garaamuel's *Teologia Fondamentale* – everything; searching, desperately, in some old grimoire, in some folk-tale, for any recipe to rid me of my hideous tyrant.

"I found it in Stefan Hock's *Die Vampyr sage und ihre Verwertung in der deutchen Litteratur:* the destruction of the *ogoljen,* the ghoul. And the instructions therein were precisely those which I specified to you in such detail – to be administered whilst the monster was in satiated slumber. For the ghoul, like the vampire of legend, once it has outgrown normal human age and attained its preternatural maturity, reverses the biology of life, sleeping during the day and hunting, scavenging by night..." He took again to the hookah, and its copious smoke enveloped him like a ghastly fog of unreason.

"There is a question I must ask," I said. "If you believe all this..."

"Believe? What is there to believe? I believe in nothing without the evidence of my own two eyes. And I have it. The evidence of my own two eyes!"

"Yes, I know," I said, hesitating. "But – why did you come to me to begin with? Why could you not carry out the instructions yourself?"

Prelati sat back in his chair so far I thought he might melt into the shadows. From the dark I heard a whining laugh that had no humour in it. It stopped as abruptly as it started. He said: "Oh but I did. I did. I took the equipment in hand, I visited her bed. I stood over her. I took the needle towards her eyes. I hesitated, you see, and I was lost. I could never do it again. She made sure of that."

I felt a lump in my throat. "She – made sure of that?" I queried in a whisper, almost too afraid to hear his reply.

He lifted his arms from beneath the shawl that covered his knees, and I saw that they ended in blunted knobs, severed at the wrists. The glove-stands were not glove-stands, but wooden hands.

"Yes," he breathed. "She *ate my hands.*"

I ran from the house with the madman's insane and pitiful cries in my ears. He implored me to stay, not to leave him, but I ran without looking back, like a child running from a haunted house.

My conviction that Gaetano Prelati was quite mad did not diminish with the passing of time. My conclusion was that I had been cruelly duped by a sadistic creature who wished to exact an awful torment – of being both *disfigured* and *buried alive* – upon his innocent sister. The thought of having been a pawn in such a bizarre and insidious game filled me with self-loathing, not least because it made me see in myself aspects of personality more odious than I would have imagined I possessed. Whether I would recover from having been a participant in such a horrifying enterprise, I did not know.

But I did tear up the man's cheque, and burn it. Financial stability is not worth the price of one's humanity – or soul.

However, within the week, I was visited by Sergeant Opie. It was not unusual for our paths to cross, since the constabulary are often amongst the first on the scene of a death. But the body that he delivered to the Chapel of Rest that day was more of a surprise.

"Suicide," said Sergeant Opie before I turned back the sheet. "We received a letter telling us when and where to find the body. Poison, it was, Dr Frith says. Some exotic stuff. In a room with a locked door. Locked windows, too. Don't make much sense. And he had a letter on the table addressed to you, in person."

The body was Gaetano Prelati, and the face, remarkably

unaltered, showed an expression of aching peace.

When Sergeant Opie had gone, I opened the letter to find that it contained a note with three words written upon it: BURY ME DEEP. I stared at the cadaver in stunned, wordless dialogue. Prelati's tale went through my head – that mad tale – and I listened to his voice and those final, pleading screams as I had run away. Pleading with me to finish my uncompleted task.

I set about cosmeticising the body, without delay.

With my thumbs I forced his staring blue eyes closed. I combed his cotton-hair. I used mortician's putty to fill the sunken cheeks, and fixed the jaw closed. With foundation, rouge, and cochineal I worked to give his pale visage a mask of health it never had in life.

The funeral was arranged for Monday, and I was pleased to be able to give his body three days' solace in the Chapel of Rest before going to its final resting place. Each morning and evening I visited it and paid my own respects, and gave my own prayers, to a man who, I now believed, was not mad after all.

The funeral was attended only by me, and a boy apprentice I had taken on the week before. He was the son of my new partner. Now there were two names above the door, and the debtors were on the retreat. Why did I not feel more at ease with the world?

Walking back from the cemetery, the boy seemed concerned that we had been the only ones to pay respects. I mumbled an explanation, not too far from the truth: that Mr Prelati was a foreigner, and as such had no friends here, and that he shouldn't worry on such account.

"Was he never married?" said the boy.

"Not that I know of," I replied.

"Then who was the woman?" said the boy.

"Woman?" said I.

"The woman who came yesterday. She was all in black, and skinny. I thought she must be a relative, in her widow's weeds and that. She didn't say nothing, even when I asked, like she was a dumb tit, but I supposed she'd come to pay respects. You were out, so I showed her into the Chapel of Rest. I stayed and waited, because she was strange. She just stood there, didn't pray or nothing. Just stood as still as anything, never saying a word. Then she raised her veil to kiss the body on the cheek and…"

The boy paused, blushed.

"I know I shouldn't have looked, sir, but... She dropped her veil when she saw me staring. But I couldn't *help* staring, sir. Then she went. Turned her back and was gone. But I saw it. Her mouth and eye, sir, all stitched up closed, sir, and this one eye, sir, staring. Just one eye, sir – and it was weeping..."

The Fall Children

I have come to deny Hippocrates, and the notion that case-histories are scientifically accurate only if purely objective. The rule, which may work perfectly adequately in the realm of medical conditions, cannot be applied to my own exploration of, admittedly, less physical phenomena. In the universe of psychical investigation, the subject, that is the experiencer, is the crux of the matter; the person who sees the ghost is indivisible from the ghost itself.

I have never been more sure of this than I was at the culmination of the following events, which, though one would have expected the passage of time to dull them, remain as vivid as if I had experienced them yesterday.

I had spent some weeks of the summer chasing an elusive pike around Loch Ken, north of Castle Douglas, as the guest of John Muir, passionate antiquarian and walker, author of *The Ferrytoon o' Cree,* and a fearsome expert on the works of local hero Sir Walter Scott. It was Muir, to his credit, who introduced me to some of the best beats of the Esk, Nith, and Bladnoch – though I think only as a device to enable him to tell me about the twenty-pound Leviathan he landed the year before, and which now swam startled and spread-eagled in mid-air over his mantelpiece in Newton Stewart.

Muir was a newspaperman and a successful one, though had never foregone the printer's-ink thumbs and pencil-behind-the-ear of a born editor. It was a Wednesday evening, and I was planning a visit to Galloway Forest for the following weekend, when Muir took an unexpected break from the comfort of his pipe-tobacco, and beckoned me over.

"Take a look at these, Venables," he said, and took from an envelope some small brown-stained rectangles and some small semi-transparent plates which I recognised to be photographic negatives. "What do you think?"

I held them under the light. The photographs were similar, but not identical. They appeared to have been taken in the corner of a rudimentary kitchen or scullery with a scrubbed stone floor. A window was present, but the blackness outside indicated that the pictures had been taken at night by magnesium flare. I recognised a mop and bucket, and little else except a construction like a small well-hole, surrounded by shadow.

I shrugged and was about to hand them back to Muir when he said, "Look closer." It was then that I could clearly perceive in the slant of shadow under the lip of the well, a small, indistinct object – one I could not avoid concluding resembled a diminutive figure, huddled like a baby animal, and yet – and it was this that had drawn my attention first of all – which had tiny white buttons for eyes.

"What is it?" I laughed. "Your tabbycat?"

"Fill your pipe, and I'll tell you," said Muir without a glimmer of humour. I did so and he refilled his own.

He told me that he had received the photographs in his editor's office earlier in the week. He then took out a pale blue sheet of writing paper, which he unfolded and read aloud in his melodious Edinburgh English:

'Dear Mr Muir, We are writing to you with these photographs which we took in our house of the elfs [*sic*] which live under groon [*sic*]. Please put them in your paper to prove that we are not making things up and there is such things in the World.
Signed,
Dorcas and Emma Fall,
Carnsalloch House, Monreith.'

"Now," said Muir before I could give an opinion, 'I see two things in front of me: I see the imaginings of two little girls and I see a dashed good story. One side of me says, stuff and nonsense, fakery and wish-wash and the children deserve a good spanking. The other side remembers the hoo-hah about the Cottingley Fairies and Arthur Conan Doyle believing in it all, and how that blew up into a wonderful little circulation-getter for somebody – and why should I pass over this when somebody round the corner might easily get the same letter and say, publish and be damned?'

I let out a sigh. "The question is, to print or not to print?"

"Precisely."

"You can't seriously believe there is any truth in this?"

Muir grunted. "Truth and newspapers are entirely different things. Having said that, I'm not sure I want to create a modern myth if it's going to be repudiated or flattened in five minutes flat!" He sucked on his pipe thoughtfully. "So that's the situation. What would you do?"

"Well, my interest would be this: why do the children want to create such a fantastical story in the first place? Clearly not monetary gain. Children don't think in that way…"

"That doesn't answer my question."

"My answer is to forget it."

"Not so easily done."

"I know."

"This could be a big story, and if I pass up this opportunity…"

"Then keep the evidence but don't print. Not just yet. You know I can't condone anything that will deliberately give false credence to this sort of story, and I'll go out of my way to deny it, but I suppose that won't matter in the least."

"Quite right," he replied. "It won't."

"Listen," I said, leaning closer to him. "I'd tell you to just run it as an expose. You know the sort of thing. Publish the story one week and tell the real story the next week…"

"Except we don't *know* the real story."

"Then let me find out more," I said, as unaware as he was that the remark would usher me into one of the strangest of mysteries, one on which I now look back from the still uneasy comfort of middle-age.

Muir nodded and the gong sounded ominously for dinner.

After the lush glories of the Galloway Forest, the road via Carsegown and Bladnoch reveals the progressively more bleak landscape of the Machars, flattened and made barren by the constant onslaught of winds from Luce Bay and the Irish Sea, and one that leads to a community of fishing villages each coldly isolated but warmly hospitable to the stranger.

Monreith itself is hardly even a village, but a roadside appendage consisting of a sprinkling of buildings – smithy, mason, joiner, post office, school – and an Inn which seemed in a perpetual state of Hogmanay. The landlord of The Earl of Galloway, through an almost impenetrably thick dialect, gave me precise directions to Carnsalloch House, which he told me had been a Laird's retreat and had lain in ruins until comparatively recently. It stood, he said, beyond a crannog (lake village) and earthworks to the northeast, and as it was accessible by road only from the far side, would necessitate my traversing a number of fields and a thick gorse wood. He assured me that the young bullocks I might encounter were not dangerous.

I set out after a sterling breakfast, in walking boots and well-prepared for the changeable weather that the greyness of the cloud cover hinted at. The wind was bracing and briny, the soil full of dips and hollows in the stone and clay – the views were sweeping but chill, trees seeming to cluster together as if for warmth or company, but the sun was strong and pleasant and the two-mile walk an easy one.

I first caught sight of Carnsalloch House from the peak of the dolmen. It was every inch the Laird's retreat the landlord had implied – a considerable building in its own fortified but tastefully arranged grounds, with a few out-houses from which I could spy a number of hens and geese – but most noticeably, with an impressive round turret extending to three storeys, immaculately restored from its medieval grandeur. I could not help but associate it with memories of *Redgauntlet* and the Raiders' Trail, of clan feuds and cattle-rustling – and ghosts.

Picking my way through the chickens, I approached the castle-door and wrenched the rusted bell-pull. I could not hear it ring, but it was soon answered by a polite and bird-like woman, well-preserved in middle-age and with slightly deep-set though benevolent eyes. She looked me up and down with more interest than suspicion as I told her I had come from Mr Muir in response to a letter sent to his newspaper. She ushered me into the large, long dining-room which abutted the spiral stone staircase of the tower, and while she left the room, I took the opportunity to observe my surroundings, the decoration of which was uniformly severe yet pleasing – completely unostentatious and simple, yet gently comforting for all that. The kitchen and dining area were as one, the black iron stove in full view of the long refectory table upon whose polished surface stood two candlesticks. The floor was stone, and slowly my eyes fastened with a tingle of recognition upon the well set into one corner, some two feet or so off the floor.

A voice made me look up. Instinctively, I stood, and found myself shaking hands with a tall, frail, elegant woman with a lilac-coloured dress tightly buttoned to the chin, and her brown, grey-etched hair drawn back from her face in a bun. She announced herself as Devergilla Fall, and asked me my business.

I said I would prefer to discuss it with both herself and Mr Fall, if that might be convenient. She said without emotion that unfortunately it was not – that her husband had passed away some three years ago. I offered my sympathies, which she accepted with a gracious wave of the hand and a flicker of a smile, which for a second betrayed a martyred beauty in her features.

After a few introductory words, I wasted little time in getting to the point. I told her that her daughters had written a letter to Muir's newspaper, and read her it, word for word. As I did so, she first rose to shut the door, then returned, pale, to the chair at the dining table and sat with her head propped wearily by her forearm, thumb and forefinger spanning her temples. I passed her the photographs. Her expression became increasingly anguished as she stared at the images with wide, uncomprehending eyes.

"Those...those devilish children!" she whispered tremulously, hardly able to form words, though they were more of pity and worry than anger.

"I detect you are not entirely surprised," I volunteered carefully.

"Surprised!" she bleated. "I never thought it would go this far, of course not! That camera of their father's – they are always taking it into the woods and out to play. Lord knows what they've been up to when I'm not around. And that Arbiglogan woman..."

She looked across and saw that I raised a querying eyebrow. She took a deep breath, shaking her head with concern once again.

I said, "Let me assure you that as far as I know, Mr Muir has no intention of publishing the letter or the story. It is his concern for the children that prompted him to ask me to come along here today. He was, unfortunately, otherwise engaged, and I am a friend spending the summer here – and I was, and am, eager to do anything to help."

"Thank you," she said.

I fetched her a glass of water, which she sipped delicately. "Would you like to tell me what you know about this affair?" She was silent. "When did it all begin? I get the clear impression this has been going on for some time."

"That's correct," she said. There was a sound upstairs, a light footfall. She looked round, and then back to me. "May we walk? I shouldn't like us to be heard by..." Her sentence did not need completion.

We took a wide circuit of the land adjoining Carnsalloch, and after a few minutes of silence invigorated by the breeze, Mrs Fall began to feel more at ease. In fact, very soon I began to feel in the position of a father confessor, for she began to pour out not merely the sequence of recent events, but the larger tapestry of her life and the guilts and responsibilities entwined around it. Here was clearly a woman – perhaps a family – isolated and turned in on itself. Devorgilla Fall was a woman sorely lonely, sadly bereaved, and tortured by the fecklessness of children who resented her presence and secretly – she imagined – blamed her for their father's untimely death.

Alexander Fall had owned a shipping company in Stranraer, and had been married happily to Mary Kirkinnear, who had in time borne him his two children, Emma and Dorcas. It was the birth of the younger, Emma, which took a fatally heavy toll upon Mary Fall's health – she was weak, unable to suckle, some internal disorder or infection developed, and within a month she had gone to an early grave. Devorgilla was the daughter of Fall's partner, William Garlie, and offered friendly solace to the cruelly bereaved widower. Naturally, as a close friend of the family, she was already close to Dorcas and became, in time, a frequently visiting 'aunt' to Carnsalloch. Affection blossomed, and in less than twelve months after Mary's death, Alexander Fall was wed a second time. One might be forgiven for wishing that the family's misfortune would end abruptly there, but this was not the case. Alexander was not a young man – he had fathered his first child at the age of fifty, and in the first, harsh winter of his second marriage he contracted pneumonia and passed away.

Now, Emma was five and Dorcas eight years of age. The former was, as her stepmother described her, angelic and unable to perpetrate any wrong without the incitement of her elder sister, who continually baited her. Dorcas, more affected by her parents' deaths, was solemn, sullen, introverted of temperament, quick to anger and to find fault, physically aggressive and – Devorgilla felt – harbouring a deep-seated hatred of the woman whom it now fell upon to raise the girls as her own.

"It is not unnatural, is it," she asked me rhetorically as we circled a copse and came back in sight of the grey tower, "for children to create invisible friends, figments of their imagination that they claim to be real?"

"Not at all," I said. "But it is rather singular for them to be photographed."

She sighed. "I don't remember when or how it began. The girls had always been secretive, whispering in corners about this and that, and then going silent when they saw me watching; though how long they have been concocting *this,* Heaven only knows!

"I think the first I really noticed – that is, the first they actually mentioned this nonsense to me – was a Sunday night about two months ago. I was upstairs, doing the accounts and paying the wages for the week – we have two men to work the farm, by the way – and when I came down I saw that instead of being tucked up nicely in bed, Dorcas and Emma lay on the kitchen floor in their nightgowns, peering excitedly in the direction of the well. At the side of the well I noticed a saucer of milk. 'What on earth is going on?' I asked them. Emma sat up smartly, looking bashful, but Dorcas just lay there on her stomach, chin on hands, feet crossed in the air. She said, 'Shshshsh! You'll scare them away!' I began to get angry and told them how naughty they were – what did they think they were doing? Attracting mice or rats or cats – whatever was the case, I didn't want *any* of them in *my* kitchen! I took them off to bed at once. Emma tried to protest but I would hear nothing of it, the candle was out and I shut the door. However – and this is something I took no notice of at first – when I returned to the kitchen the saucer was empty. I was sure at the time I had knocked it over in the hurry to get them to bed, but thinking back, I am positive that only a drop or two of milk lay on the kitchen floor."

"Go on," I urged her, making shorthand notes in my pocketbook while she spoke.

"I thought nothing of it. It had been a game, nothing more. But the following Sunday the same thing happened. The saucer of milk was there, the children raptly watching it. I was in no mood for a repetition of the previous week, and immediately emptied the saucer into the sink. Instantly, Dorcas went into a screaming fit, crying, 'You mustn't! You mustn't! They'll come out and – No! No! Poor babies...lost!' This, you understand, in a torrent of tears and unimaginable screeching – the intensity and suddenness of which froze me rigid, the more so because no sooner had Dorcas started than Emma took her up. The din was deafening, uncontrollable. All I could do to pacify them was re-fill the saucer with milk and place it beside the well. They became instantly calm, and went to bed quietly. I came down on Monday morning and the children were already at breakfast. As I appeared they sprung up and Emma brought me the empty saucer, smiling. 'See, they came, they *did* come! They drank it all up! All up!'

"There is not much more to tell. Just that now, every Sunday, I have to leave a saucer of milk at the mouth of the kitchen well, and in the morning it is gone. But like the glass of sherry left for Father Christmas, I cannot believe there is a very supernatural reason for its disappearance."

We paused before entering the house. "Have they ever offered an explanation for their actions?"

"Not in the least."

"Have you not asked them outright?"

"I will be honest with you," she admitted. "Until now I saw it as trivial enough – a little harmless play-acting that they will grow out of – just like Father Christmas or Guy Fawkes. I wasn't sure it would do any good to puncture their illusion. That might do them more harm than good. Children cease to be children all too soon. If their dream world gives them pleasure, lets them live their child-life a little longer – who am I to take it away?"

As I heard her words I looked up to see two round and innocent young faces looking out from the curved window of the Laird's tower. They registered no expression, and on seeing my gaze upturned, let the heavy drape fall back. I offered to carry in some logs for the stove, as I felt sure the wind had suddenly turned colder.

I examined the well, as best I could. It was entirely disused and emitted a slightly stagnant but not overpowering smell. When the hatch was lifted one could see a tiny inkling of light playing on the moving surface of black water some fifty or a hundred feet below. I shone a light down, but it revealed nothing but a fibrous chimney of cobweb, a well within the well, like a gossamer, ghostly throat. There was no sound but that of lightly-running water – Mrs Fall informed me that there were many underground streams in the area, veining the countryside like a subterranean labyrinth. I leaned down inside as far as I could safely venture, to discover only that the stone fabric of the well seemed sound and very ancient, though some slivers of rock had fallen away and some bricks seemed dislocated by the encroachment of pernicious weeds. I asked my hostess about the likelihood of rats. She said only that none had been reported.

I stacked and ignited the fire for the evening, and it roared magnificently within minutes of taking a match, the black-lead furnace gradually imbuing the long room with considerable warmth. Mrs Fall had insisted I stay and meet the children, which I was glad to do, but they eyed me with suspicion over the beef broth. I realised later they may have thought me to be a suitor and prospective new stepfather, which given their late fast-changing circumstances was understandable.

I observed the girls carefully – avoiding any direct questions initially, meandering the conversation around to books that they liked and activities they enjoyed. I have to say that in all respects they seemed, if it is not a contradiction in terms, exceptionally normal. There were none of the peculiarities Devorgilla had prepared me for. Emma seemed indeed angelic, and exchanged many a smile with me over the dinner table. Her sister was more adult, a little shy, but not abnormally so – and I found her equally pleasant. Neither showed any wayward streak, aberrant personality defect, or unnatural predilection for fantasy.

Fortuitously, the evening was a Sunday, and before going to bed the children – without a word of explanation – busied themselves in preparing the now ritualistic saucer of milk, and placed it carefully in its usual position. Mrs Fall took them to bed and I accompanied her, offering to read them a bedtime story, which I did, paraphrasing a piece of Gaelic folklore from the dim recesses of my memory. Thus they became relaxed in my presence, and after the story, in their state of near-sleep, ideally prepared to answer some gentle questions pertaining to the real purpose of my visit.

As I tucked the bedclothes around the dozing Emma, I said, "I didn't know you had a pussycat."

"Pussycat...?" she repeated. Her sister was already fast asleep.

"Yes. I saw you leave her a saucer of milk." I waited a long while for her to respond.

"That's not for the pussycat," she said very definitely. "There isn't any pussycat, silly."

"Oh," I said. "Who's it for then?"

She sighed. "The *babies*," she said, with the sort of emphasis that meant I should know such things.

"The babies? What babies?"

She sighed again, rubbed her tired eyes. "The Devil's babies. The Devil's babies who live down the well."

"Why do they live down the well?"

She said, with the logic only children have: "That's where they live. Under the earth. Down below. Deep. With him. With their Daddy."

"Why do you leave out the milk?"

"Ask her, she knows. I'm tired."

"Who?"

Emma snored a deep, deep breath.

"Who told you about the babies, Emma?"

"Mrs Arbiglogan told us."

I let her drift in her dreams for a moment. Then I spoke very quietly. "What did Mrs Arbiglogan tell you, Emma?"

"She said that the Devil who was thrown out of Heaven lives under the earth, right down below. And he doesn't have a wife because he's so nasty. He had a wife once whose name was Lilith, who was in the Garden of Eden, but she was bad, so God sent her to Hell. She was the Mummy of the babies and the Devil was the Daddy – but they were bad babies, they never stopped crying and wanting to be fed. Then God forgave Lilith and took her back to Heaven. So now the Devil needed a new wife to look after the babies who were crying all the time.

"So one Sunday he came to the church at Monreith because he wanted a good Christian woman and good mother, and he lurked around the churchyard waiting for the congregation to leave. He was dressed as a handsome soldier and he took the prettiest girl but as he raced her quickly back to Hell, he threw a shoe and had to stop at the smithy. But the smithy recognised the Devil with his hoofs and shod him with two nails in the shape of the cross – and the Devil went hopping off and dived down into the well of Carnsalloch.

"The blacksmith married the pretty maid and the Devil still has the shoe in the shape of the cross which is why he's so angry. And his babies still need a mother, and you can hear them crying at night for their mother's milk.

"So you don't leave some milk for them every Sunday, they'll take the nearest young lady down to hell to be the Devil's wife forever and ever."

"Is that true?" I whispered.

"Mrs Arbiglogan says..." she answered.

Suddenly Dorcas sat up in bed – not from a dream, but as if suddenly aware she should be awake. She looked at me with piercing eyes, then glared at her sister accusingly. She gave the clear impression that these things were not to be talked about.

"Go to sleep," she said firmly, and curled over into her blanket. I took the lamp and the halo of light it carried from the small bedroom and down the spiral staircase back to Devorgilla Fall. But before I left the room I gently prised from Emma's grip a tiny figure – furry and with tiny, button eyes that sparkled in the light.

I laid the furry bear in the shadows by the well and asked Mrs Fall to compare what she saw to the photographs. I think she was so eager to have an explanation, she sighed with relief before she even looked up. Then she began to laugh – a long, desperately sad and quiet laugh. I told her the legend that Emma had told me, and her housekeeper, the bird-like Mrs Arbiglogan, was summarily called for. Of course, she was unable to deny it, only confirming her guilt by saying it was a "proper tale from round here" and "not made up" and "only for fun". She seemed not in the least upset to be relieved of her services at the house, and packed her bags and was gone inside the hour. I told Mrs Fall she need look no further for an explanation of the missing milk – Mrs Arbiglogan was first up and about every day, so clearly it was she who removed the milk in an attempt to play along with the children's deception, for whatever reasons of her own.

At each revelation, Mrs Fall seemed ever more relieved. In the space of hours she transformed from a pale, frail widow to a picture, if not of strength and beauty, then one from whose shoulders the weight of the world had been lifted.

I recommended that in future she place the saucer of milk in the requisite place, indulging fully in the girls' wishes, only to pour it away later for them to find empty in the morning. I was sure that, no longer fuelled by the housekeeper's tongue, the story would soon be forgotten in favour of pressed flowers, butterfly-collecting, horses, and the other passions of little girls.

I could not have been more wrong.

*

Mrs Dinwiddie's testimony ran thus:

"I had known Mrs Fall for some years, my late husband and my brother both being employees of the late Mr Fall in Stranraer, so when I heard that Mrs Arbiglogan had been dismissed – or left, at least, was what I was informed – then I suggested myself for the position, loving children like I do and loving to have them round and things.

"Well, that first week was all very right and the house work quite reasonable for what I had been used to – pubs and that sort of thing being much harder. The girls themselves were always very good to me, very good and quiet and never anything out of place and always polite and things.

"It was Sunday afternoon when Mrs Fall and I sat and had our afternoon tea that she laughed and said, 'Listen, I have to tell you this. It is an embarrassment but it's as well you know, for I have it on advice to carry on the deception for a while,' and she told me about the visitor, Mr Venables, sent by Mr Muir, and the photographs taken by her girls and the tale that that evil Mrs Arbiglogan put into the heads of those poor mites. So she told me, 'Put down the saucer but empty it before lights out so they'll find it gone in the morning and it'll all be fine.' Which is what I did. I do what I'm told and things.

"That night I didn't sleep too well: I don't know whether it was the strange house or what. The wind was up, the windows banging – like all Hell was let loose. I could hear the horses whinnying from the stables, the barn door clattering, and the trees – awful night it was, or so it seemed to me, though nobody else reported it, so maybe it was my fancy. All in my head, so to speak – halfway between waking and sleeping, perhaps.

"At around four o'clock – I saw by the top landing clock, by the way – the wind had gone, fallen altogether. The house was still and peaceful. Peaceful as the grave, one might say. Strangely, it was the sudden quiet I think that woke me, as opposed to the din. I sat straight up in bed, and I could hear a most peculiar sound.

"If there was a new-born babe in the house, or two, or more than that, the thing would have been solved at once – but there was not. If the house had possessed a tomcat, or cats, whining and moaning their love life at all hours, that too would have offered me an explanation – but Mrs Fall was allergic to them and came out in a vicious rash, so none were allowed in the house. The only conclusion I could come to was that some strays had been attracted to the house from the surrounding countryside and were doing battle over the leftovers in the outside bin – although for the life of me, the sounds seemed to be coming directly from below me, that is to say, inside the house.

"I put on my dressing-gown and lit my lamp and went out onto the landing, only to find Mrs Fall already at the top of the stairs.

" 'Damnable cats at the refuse, ma'am,' I said. Her hair was plaited, her face white. She waved me back to my room. 'It's all right, Mrs Dinwiddie,' said she, 'I'll see to this. You get your sleep.'

" 'Thank you very much, ma'am,' says I, and returned to my bed.

"I was on the point of extinguishing my lamp, when the caterwauling, which had grown quiet, suddenly erupted with a ferocity that made me think, "Lord have mercy! They're in this very room next to me!" My heart leapt up in my throat, but my first and only thought was for my mistress.

"I hurried downstairs as fast as my legs could carry me – the lamplight flickered, caught in all those draughts from the windows – I cupped my hand over the funnel, praying it would not give out. I think I jumped the last few steps and fell more than ran into the long dining-room and kitchen from which the desperate, horrible mewling was emanating, howling round me louder and louder like a frenzy as I came down.

"Now I must first say that I screamed, and it may have been the breath of my scream that extinguished the light. However, I feel sure it was a gust of cold, some tangible icy aura that doused the flame in almost the same second that I arrived.

"I cannot swear here today that I was not mistaken, and that every impression my perception received is infallible. It was night. I was tired. I was frightened. But I can swear, and do swear, that this is my true and honest opinion, which I give in the full knowledge of the ridicule that has been, and will be, heaped upon me for doing so.

"In that fraction of a moment before the light went out, when I had only its orange glow and the low light of the quarter-moon to aid me, I saw Mrs Fall struggling and writhing as if caught in an invisible trap, as if gripped by a strangler from behind, doubling and kicking as if to shake someone off... and then I saw – the black shapes, yes, the size of small cats but without tails – with the eyes of cats but hairless, *skinless*; pink and livid like a paunched hare, dripping with a pungent saliva from every pore, climbing up her body just like hungry kittens, pawing with tiny almost-human hands, one fastened hideously to her bosom...

"And then they were gone. All vanished. Mrs Fall had disappeared along with the creatures that were attacking her. Somehow the floodgates of terror held back my emotions a minute longer, for I remember having time to walk to the well, and to look down it, and to see one tiny, pestilential *thing* submerging in the gloom.

"I then fainted to the floor, where one of the farm labourers, Mr Andrew Tanoltry, found me and revived me the following morning."

Ironically, the children had slept through the lot, entirely un-roused by the violence below. This in itself cast doubt upon Mrs Dinwiddie's testimony – giving rise to the rumour that she (perhaps with Mr Tanoltry as accomplice) had done away with Mrs Fall – but to every detail of her evidence, even under extensive questioning by the coroner, the housekeeper strictly adhered.

Dumfries had not played host to a legend since Robert the Bruce's spider, and my friend Muir, amongst many others, contributed heartily to this one – though, to his credit, he abstained from the usual ghoulish speculation, rife in baser publications.

What were the rational theories propounded at the time? Many simply believed that part of Mrs Dinwiddie's story which ascribed the sounds to cats. Others insisted that a colony of large and, presumably, carnivorous rats had bred in the bowels of the well.

Someone writing to *The Times* suggested that Mrs Fall had deliberately deserted her children and left the country and was now living under the name of Bayliss in Cockermouth. Still another elaborated eloquently upon the possibility that she had committed suicide – possibly drowning herself in the well (but not necessarily, as the well was dragged and no body found), and leaving a suicide note pleading with (or blackmailing) her housekeeper into hiding the facts. This theory fails to account for why someone would substitute the stigma of a suicide with a story as wildly improbable as that implied by the key witness.

Mrs Fall was never found, alive or dead. I would hope and pray that wherever she may be, she is in a happier life than the one she had on earth.

I hope she will find her way, rapidly and without pain, to her God.

The Supernatural is often a force for justice, for righting the wrongs of life, for upturning the inadequacies of our feeble physical world – or redressing the balance. There are, however, dark forces, mirrored in mythologies all across our world, that tell of entities intent on causing harm to the good, in clawing and tugging at the fabric that keeps the Universe in a state of Righteousness. They seek their victims in the frail and weak, and will take them when they can.

Dorcas and Emma Fall travelled to America to live with their godfather, Mr Emil Plant of New York City. They have since married and hence, gratefully perhaps, changed their names. Emma has married a high-ranking official in the mayor's office, and Dorcas an engineer. They both now have children of their own.

Carnsalloch House has had only one owner since, and whether by dint of superstition, the weight of recent publicity, or the wish not to tempt fate, I can vouch for the fact that a saucer of milk is placed on the sill of the kitchen well every Sunday evening before dark...*without fail.*

A Pair of Pince-Nez

Whilst on a skiing holiday in the French Alps, Hugh, Lord Albany met and fell headlong in love with the Boston heiress, Amarylla Frue – headlong, that is, in the most literal possible sense. Their collision was physical as well as emotional, though luckily neither hearts nor bones were broken. They shared identical interests, made a fine couple to behold, and most important of all in this day and age, she equalled him in forthright speech, indomitable strength of character, intelligence, and good humour. After one short week, they married in Geneva and honeymooned, blissfully, in Malta.

The time came all too soon to kiss goodbye to warmer climes and return to the inevitably damp English summer. However, Amarylla, as the new Lady Albany, looked forward with indescribable excitement to the prospect of her new home, and when their carriage first arrived at Puget Hall in Hampshire and she entered the immense white portico, the Stone Gallery, and suite of damask drawing-rooms, she could not help but shed tears of delight. She was – they were – in short, immensely and completely happy.

But, as in all things, this was not to last uninterruptedly for long. Awaiting Lord Hugh on his return from what had admittedly been a longer than anticipated stay abroad, was a desk-ful of correspondence, much of it legal, and legal of the most unpleasant yet unavoidable kind. Much of it concerned his brother's contesting the will of their late father, and was upsettingly threatening in tone. The rest, soberingly, were nothing but bills from the long-overdue upkeep of the estate. To begin with, Hugh kept most of the worry on his own shoulders, but there was no concealing from his bride that he was stricken by a considerable misery which he stubbornly refused to divulge.

By and by, a servant was lost here, a field or out-house was sold there, certain valuable items or furniture or much-beloved oil-paintings were parted with, and so inevitably Amarylla put two and two together. They were in dire financial straits. Hugh's brother had bled them dry, and it was only by the income from their farm-land that Puget Hall was keeping its head above water.

In spite of all this, they had, at least, each other. The crisis, if anything, made them closer still – which is a peculiarity, yet true.

Amarylla did not mind the loss of some of the more ornate trappings of aristocracy, though she was clearly used to them. She would be happy in a cave living on a crust of stale bread, as long as she had her husband. However, he was laden with a certain guilt over their hard times.

The house was virtually empty of servants, though they retained a cook and housekeeper, and Mr Evans came periodically to take care of any repairs. By the time evening fell, then, the newly-weds were alone in the vast house and habitually sat together in the library or chapel parlour—fret-panelled Strawberry Hill Gothick but with a notable Javanese settee – enjoying a quiet drink and conversation before bed.

The night was warm and Lord Albany, after a tiring day in London trying to drum up investment that might bail him once and for all out of his money troubles, felt his eyelids drooping heavy with the soporific smoke of the pine log fire and tick-tick of the long-case walnut clock. In the end, grunting awake as his chin touched his waistcoat, he decided to call it an early night. 'I'm sorry, my dear. I simply can't keep my eyes open.'

'There was a time when you couldn't keep your eyes off me,' teased his young wife. Her smile was contagious. He took her hand and kissed it. 'You go on up,' she said. 'I shan't be very much longer, but I've reached an exciting part of my book. You don't mind if I just read to the end of the chapter?'

Her husband said of course he didn't. They kissed goodnight, and he left the chapel parlour as Amarylla gently turned up the lamp.

She was an avid reader. She loved Walpole and Radcliffe, penny-shockers that annoyed her husband, who insisted anything after Dante was 'modem drivel.' But she *enjoyed* reading more than he, and gorged on books voraciously whatever their literary pretension – or lack of it.

Tonight, though, her own concentration was sagging. Perhaps it was the smoke, but her eyes had difficulty focusing on the tiny print. She held the book nearer, then further, but it only aggravated the problem. She persisted in reading for another fifteen minutes, then was gradually aware of a splitting headache. Her eyes were simply swimming over the page. It was impossible.

Her husband – and before him, her father – had persistently begged, cajoled, demanded that she buy spectacles. She knew he meant well and she knew she needed them – but only for reading, for goodness' sake. It seemed hardly worth it for an hour or so a day. The truth was, vanity stood in the way. Eyeglasses were worn by spinsters and old maids and made pretty faces look owlish, bemused, lopsided – or so she imagined. However, when she desperately needed a remedy, as now, for her acute short-sightedness, she was prone to borrow her father's lenses, if they were lying around – and he was never any the wiser.

But what now? Father was not here. She had never seen her husband wear glasses – but that may not mean he had none. If he did, then they would be here in this room surely – or in the library? Yes, the library.

She went through into the adjoining room and scuttled round it like a thief, pulling out drawers and looking under sheaves of papers. She found blotters, books, papers, ink, old letters (resisting the chronic temptation to read them). And then, in a sliding drawer noticeably, quite noticeably, more stiff to open than the rest, she found an old yellowing portfolio of manuscripts, so brittle they almost broke at the mere touch of her fingers, and secreted under -- no, amongst – them, a pair of gold-rimmed pince-nez.

'Ah,' thought Amarylla. As she held them up to the light of the lamp she had brought with her, a flame reflected peculiarly in an intense oval, with the colours of the rainbow like many-coloured eyes looking back at her for an instant – then were gone. They were of course the reflection of her own eyes – what else?

A draught from the door tickled goose-pimples up her bare arm.

She curled up in the red leather porter's chair like a baby in the womb, the book – incidentally nothing more remarkable than *The Old Curiosity Shop* – on her lap. She placed the pince-nez delicately on the bridge of her nose and looked down.

Perfect! She saw with wonderful clarity, and read with amazing alacrity the next few pages, surprised and delighted at her find – and that they should be quite so *remarkably* right for her eyesight. Her headache lifted almost immediately. She read not one chapter, but two, and would have read more, I am sure, if not for what I am about to relate.

She looked up from the pince-nez to find the room in darkness for a moment. She raised the small lenses to her eyes, and peered through them and it was lit again – but strangely. But where was the bust of Shakespeare, usually on the plinth in that corner? Where was the plinth itself? Of course, Hugh must have moved it elsewhere. But she was sure – well, if not sure then *almost* sure – it had been there when she entered the room. In any case, it was not *so* peculiar. So she began to read again.

She read half a page, and in that manner most of us will recognise, realised she had read it without taking in a single word.

She looked up again, through the glinting glass of the pince-nez.

Where was her oil-lamp?

Hello – the door was gently opening. A figure entered slowly. She began to smile, because for some reason her heart fluttered nervously now in her chest, she could not understand why, and it must by Hugh, dear Hugh. Her smile fastened unattractively, the eyes behind the intense clear lenses widened until the pupils stood out, as round as carpet-tacks. It was not Hugh who entered, but a round-shouldered old man whom Amarylla recognised beyond the shadow of a doubt.

She shrieked, tore off the spectacles, slammed them inside the pages of Dickens, and ran from the room. Roused by the noise, her husband met her, agitatedly tying his dressing-gown cord, on the stairs as she ran upwards and embraced him tightly.

She told him nothing of her experience that night, and by the time she undressed she was convinced – or almost-convinced – the apparition had been the product of the mature stilton that had rounded off their supper. To quote one of her current author's tales, 'There was more of *gravy* than the grave' about her ghost.

As I say, of this she was almost-convinced.

The next morning they enjoyed their normal light breakfast of toast and tea. As a modern woman, Amarylla diligently kept her figure in check, although Hugh occasionally indulged in a kipper fillet or boiled egg. He invariable read *The Times,* from which he rarely emerged except to replenish his tea-cup. He took little notice of their idle conversation at the time:

"Dear, it's so curious. Did you know your eye-glasses are perfect for me? It's quite astonishing really. I suppose that we're so alike in so many other ways."

Hugh emerged slowly and silently from the paper. "Eye-glasses?"

"Yes. I had no idea."

"No idea of what?"

"That you wore eye-glasses. Reading glasses."

He grunted. "Not I."

"Come along!"

"I don't know what you mean, I have perfect eyesight. Always have had. I can read the spine of that book on the mantelpiece from here – it's Thomas Langley's *Treasury of Designs* – how's that! Whatever made you think that I…"

"But…" his wife began, then stopped. "Nothing," she added quietly.

At various times during the day, she tried to summon the courage to tell her husband what she saw, or thought she saw (it makes little difference) in the library the previous night, but it was dusk, and they were walking back from the village through the conifer avenue that dissected their ornate baroque garden, before she did. "Last night in the library I must have been drowsing, nodding off I think, for I had a dream, or half-dream, although it seemed horrifically real at the time. I haven't wanted to tell you this before, my love, in case it upsets you terribly, but I swear I had the strangest sort of vision. I imagined, but with total clarity – as vividly as I see you now – that I saw your father, entering the room. Exactly as he looked in the photograph you showed me. Please don't be angry. Try to understand how I feel. It was all so real and terrifying!"

Her husband made no remark for some moments. He then ventured that she was tired, that perhaps – yes, there was a painting of his father in the room – perhaps it had somehow been reflected in the glass of the French windows? Yes, that of course was the explanation. He laughed eagerly.

Amarylla did nothing to argue with this hypothesis; nor did she ask him if his father had had a limp in his left leg, as she saw him yesterday. She was, frankly, afraid that he would answer – as she knew he must – in the affirmative.

They returned to the house in silence. Amarylla was cold.

That night Hugh again retired early and his wife, again – though now with a mixture of trepidation and curiosity – ventured back into the library.

She found the bust of Shakespeare where it had always been –

in the same corner, on the same plinth. She sat in her chair and opened *The Old Curiosity Shop* where the pair of golden pince-nez acted as a bulky bookmark, put them on, and began to read.

At first, she was more convinced than ever that her experience the night before had been some severe and unaccountable aberration. She read calmly and happily page after page, gradually becoming re-immersed in the delights of the story – for a while forgetting the chilling encounter entirely.

Then the door slowly opened.

A figure stepped inside and said, "Will you be long?"

She smiled at her husband, removing the pince-nez. "Not long."

"Where did you find those?" He had noticed the pince-nez.

"In the drawer. Whose are they?"

Her husband was perplexed. "I haven't the faintest idea. Not my father's. His eyes were as good as mine, if not better. Uncle Billy wore a monocle, but he's not around any more. Curious – very curious! Well, goodnight for now." She listened to the long echoes of his footsteps on the stone staircase leading to the bedroom above.

She returned to her book and read some more, until she began to be distracted by the flickering yellowness of light from her oil-lamp. Irritated, she reached over to turn up the wick, and her fingers inexplicably touched the horrid texture of warm wax. Recoiling, she saw that where her lamp had stood on the rose-table now stood an elaborate candelabrum, lit and glowing, the large candles dribbling molten wax.

She was frozen with horror, and gradually her over-excited sensations told her that the room she knew was somehow, remarkably, different. Regency colours replaced her Arts and Craft print wallpaper; the delicate Victorian drapery was now rich and heavy, red and gold. She watched aghast as, slowly like paint daubed on a black canvas, events were enacted before her very eyes in the manner of a play upon a stage. First, two figures emerged, one tall and dressed in black with a high wing-collar and frock-coat, and another in a leather waistcoat – both faces were like beaten bronze, weathered and ugly like diseased apples, but it may have been the overall shimmering of colour over the entire tableau that produced this gruesome effect. The villains, for villains they clearly were, skulked around the room with no regard for Amarylla's presence. It was exactly as if she were invisible. They instead directed their whole attention upon a cabinet which, it appeared, was full of gold and silver cups, chalices and ornaments of the most staggering financial worth. The taller one produced a key and opened the cabinet, while the other held open a sack into which the first greedily deposited the contents – while throwing furtive glances this way and that. At one point a floorboard squealed upstairs and the little one snatched out a flintlock pistol, cocked and ready to blow out the brains of anyone who stood in their way. Once their thievery was done, they opened the French windows and Amarylla rose from her chair to watch them run with their ill-gotten gains across the flat lawns where once – where now – stood the elaborate gardens of Puget Hall.

A hand fell on her shoulder. 'My dear,' said the voice of her husband.

Nearly fainting with relief she turned to throw her arms round him. And gazed into the pustular and plague-ridden face of a man emaciated with disease, a mere skeleton puffed up with boils and ruptured skin. And as the inhuman, foetid stench reached her nostrils she fell unconscious to the floor of the empty library.

She did not enter that room again for some weeks, and when she did it was in total daylight, and in the company of her husband. The pince-nez had remained in their drawer for this period – and there, it was intended, they would remain. However, as Amarylla had her secrets so did Hugh, and once more monetary ruin reared its ugly head. Unbeknownst to her, he had invested in certain commodities unwisely and had lost far more than he had gained in the past few months. Debtors were on the point of hammering on the door – it was for the purpose of this unwelcome discussion Hugh had suggested they retire to the library – and he confessed to her, almost weeping, that if not for her, he would commit suicide. Needless to say, she comforted him as best she could, administering brandy and ignoring his suggestions that she should leave him, that he was a good-for-nothing, et cetera. Finally she accompanied him to bed.

She could not sleep.

Their financial worries were now overwhelming and catastrophic. Nothing could possibly save them now, but some miraculous injection of cash, some fortune, some treasure. The word came back into her mind again and again. Treasure.

She sat up in bed. The brandy had at least helped her husband to a sound sleep. She rose and threw on her dressing-gown, quietly left the room, and padded downstairs and into the shadowy library. It seemed that night like a vile Inner Sanctum, protective of its secrets – its rows of books stretching skyward like a thousand sentinels. The lamp made nothing but an oval halo in the inky blackness. She had dreaded ever setting foot there again, let alone at night, but now there was a strength of purpose behind her actions.

She went to the drawer and opened it. Inside, on the stained and empty manuscript pages, lay the gold-rimmed pince-nez. It took every ounce of her bravery – and the love of her husband – for her to pick up the contraption and place it, now like a frightening torture-device, on the bridge of her nose. In the same moment, though in some ways she knew it would make no difference, she found herself praying.

Fine lines of light like arrows and tiny comets flickered in the penumbra of the half-lenses, then blackness drained like an ink-spot over her vision. She blinked uncontrollably. The flashing light seemed to be coming from the chapel parlour next door, and she moved to look in, as if impelled beyond her conscious control.

The chapel parlour was unrecognisable. It seemed at first like an old-fashioned apothecary's, the upper gallery over-laden with bulbous phials and glass jars of noxious-looking liquids labelled with chemical symbols. The upper rose-window was transparent, and touching it was a vast prism, six feet across, which separated light by refraction onto other lenses and reflecting-blocks, some black-polished marble or blindingly polished mirrors. The path of sunlight zigzagged around this huge, complex apparatus like a gigantic diagram of the human eye.

Amongst it, as if entrapped within its convolutions, sat a man who reminded Amarylla in dress and poise of Samuel Pepys, except his coat was threadbare and his wig lank and full of holes. His face was daubed with huge beauty spots to cover plague-marks, and his rheumy eyes seemed deeply misanthropic and unhealthy, as he peered fixedly into a water-trough where a strange optical halo was directed.

"*Pituita, sanguis, cholera…*" the man was muttering through cracked lips. "*Hyerarchia Suprema… Oriens, Meridies, Occidens, Septendrio… Lux mereata…*"

Then the eyes like those of a butcher's-shop sow looked up at her. *"Theologo-Philosophicus in Librostres distributus quorum: I. de VITA... II. de MORTE... III. de RESURRECTIONE..."* His glance passed right through her.

The image faded completely and she turned back to the library, her heart thumping within her chest. Her hand went to the pince-nez and she was tempted to toss them aside, when a smokiness clouded her perception.

The library was dark as pitch again. She was now closer to the glass cabinet and could watch in terrified detail the process, once again, by which the burglars emptied the precious objects from its shelves. Again, the smaller one drew his gun. Again – precisely as before – they backed to the French windows and ran out across the closely-cropped lawns.

This time, Amarylla followed. Gone were the conservatories she knew so well, gone the weigela and winter jasmine, anemone and forsythia – instead a knot garden of raised beds, clipped shrubs, box, and mulberry bushes, gillyflowers and lavender. They approached the lake, altogether different in shape from the one she knew, and without the willow-pattern bridge, or reeds and lilies in such abundance. The water seemed gentle and clear, unlike the swampish, mossy consistency it was in reality. Or was *this* reality?

Half-hypnotised by the glassy water, Amarylla hardly noticed the foul argument that had materialised between the thieves. The sack was dropped to the floor, and one flung a punch at the other. The words they used were so thickly archaic that to ears which found even English in England hard to understand, they were incomprehensible. Suddenly the smallish man had his pistol out. The taller man laughed mockingly. The trigger was pulled and a red hole opened in the centre of his forehead. He fell to the ground, stone dead.

Amarylla suppressed a scream, even as she knew that no one would hear her. In moments the large house was in uproar – the hounds were baying, and in several windows candles were lit. With astonishing speed the small man tied the corpse to the sack and kicked him over the slope into the lake – body and deadweight fell almost soundlessly into the depths, making hardly a bubble.

She watched, still in a state of shock, as the small murderer ran back to the house. Halfway he was met by the head butler, and proffered his lies about the event. Now Amarylla deciphered the gist: he said he had heard noises downstairs – seen Jackson the footman stealing the jewels, had pursued him, and had let fly a bullet, but the bounder had got away, treasure and all. The evil young stable-boy, for that was what he was, had turned his murderous attempt at stealing around so that he became the hero.

So that was where the treasure was: the lake! Amarylla laughed. If only, if only she could be sure they would find it there! It would be the end to all their problems! Oh, please, she begged as she turned homewards.

Light flickered in Amarylla's eyes, and the house faded away completely. The landscape was bare, the grassy slopes shrivelling and fading before her eyes.

She stood rooted to the spot. Her bare feet felt the grass die under them, then the earth shrink and dry into cracked, parched mud. She heard the buzz of insects, and felt them touching her and crawling on her skin. The stench was like the odour of a slaughter-house mingled with the pungency of seaweed and water-gases.

Perspiring with fear, she tried to remove the pince-nez, but somehow they seemed fastened to her face. What was happening? She felt suddenly shackled in time and space, unable to move or think − trapped by the devilish callipers that clung to her eyes. Tears fell down and round the icy gold frames.

She was suddenly sure that she had slipped into some other world, some invisible dimension, the world of the mad Satanist whom she had seen poring over his diabolical work. She had stepped, she was sure, right into Dante's Hell − the hellish stench, the heat, the horror − it could be nowhere else on earth!

She stared into the sickly gloom. She had lost all sense of direction. The weeping willow which was there in reality but not in this feverish dream, now had bloomed a thousand-fold in berserk recompense − the lake, now a bone-dry cavern, was surrounded by a wild forest, lit crimson by the huge eye of a dying sun.

She screamed, but her scream was echoed by a million creatures of the night, squawking and gibbering hungrily. She beat through the undergrowth, weak with horror. A wall of blackness opened its cat-like eye the size of a dinner plate and rose, awakening, like a crane, lifting ten, fifteen, twenty feet in the air. The yellow slit-eyes glared down, and a massive mouth with white dagger-sized teeth opened and roared. She ran, blindly and instinctively.

The giant demon gave chase, swishing its leathery tail, its

huge feet shaking the very ground under her like a charging elephant. She imagined its vast hulk rolling after her, but could not bear to look. She felt its dank breath on the back of her neck, saw its lumbering, horned shadow and monstrous gait bobbing in front of her, growing frighteningly larger as the hideous thing became closer.

The screeching of the wild gargoyle was still in her ears as she hit the rain-dappled French windows and sprawled onto the carpet of the library, and the pince-nez spun off her nose, landing with a gentle tinkle on the parquet flooring near the hearth.

I had known Wisley Lloyd for some years. He was a publisher of impetuous renown and had made a nuisance of himself time and again by trying to goad me into publishing some of my many case-histories – stories, call them what you will – to no avail. Nevertheless we had become close friends, and it is through Lloyd, who was in turn a friend of Lord Hugh Albany, that I came across the tale I have just told, in words as close as possible to those used by Lady Amarylla, from whose lips I heard it.

We sat in the smoking-room, Lady Albany having long since securely locked the library, and over some very good wine were related the entire sequence of events. Her husband by now knew the facts, and throughout sat near his wife, their hands touching. She, it should be stated, showed immense composure and recollection, and I never once doubted or suspected any fraction of what she told us.

She showed me the pair of pince-nez, and at the outset they seemed no different than any other. Afterwards, when his wife apologised, saying she felt weak from talking, and excused herself to her room, I was astonished that Lord Albany confessed his worry to be that his wife had suffered some severe mental lapse – that she was in dire medical need, probably caused by the financial straits they were in. I told him, without mincing words, that I had found it foolish in my work to jump to conclusions – and that if what she experienced had even a semblance of truth, she would be insane to react in any way *other* than the emotional state she clearly exhibited.

He sat quietly like a scolded schoolboy. "Then what shall we do, Mr Venables?" he begged of me.

"Believe her," I said firmly. "You must remember she put herself in extreme psychic danger for your sake. I beg you not to repay that with suspicion. First, I would ask that you allow me to stay here and explore your library fully – I am sure there is much to be revealed there, and from the look of the dust many of the tomes have not been opened since the year dot. Secondly, you must direct everything in your power to draining the lake. I know this is a lot to ask, but please understand..." My host nodded without my finishing the sentence. "Finally," I added, "you must tell me anything at all which you think might be relevant to our understanding of your wife's experience."

He shook his head and said there was nothing.

"Good," I said.

"Good?" he repeated incredulously. "What can be *good* about this matter, when my wife finds herself in some nether world in the grip of some – some demonological entity? Is that what you are saying?"

I said that I wasn't entirely sure.

Next day I wasted no time in acquainting myself with the library index, and set to work on the five thousand volumes, somewhere in the pages of which I knew the answer – if there was to be an answer – lay. There I imprisoned myself for day after day, breaking only for sleep and meals – and, to ease a bibliophile's hunched back, several walks in the splendid landscaped gardens, occasionally pausing to gaze into the dark mirror-surface of the lake.

The work commenced slowly, like the chipping of marble in a sculptor's studio, hours of incessant study causing only a minor indentation in the vast supply of knowledge in that enviable store. At times I looked up to see the pumping equipment and barges and workmen crowded on the surface of the lake, as gradually the pumping of the lake became a reality as slow and steady and murky as my plumbing the depths of Janus Gruter, Cornelius Agrippa's *Chiromancy,* the enigmatic *Quatrains* of Michel de Nostradame, Joachim Frizius's *Summum Bonum,* the *Philosophical Key* and *Declaratio Brevis* of Robert Fludd, and Pierre Gassendi's *Epistolica exercitatio.*

I happened, at last, upon a glimmer in the darkness, from the most unlikely of sources: a journal of Isaac Durelle, violin-teacher to the children of Lord Albany in 1820 (and one time acquaintance of George Gordon, Lord Byron, or so he alleged). Durelle's text was for the most part uninteresting, although in the most beautiful hand – but suddenly a reference caught my eye. A careful reading of the subsequent paragraphs proved more than a little rewarding. In the September of that year Puget Hall had suffered a burglary. The perpetrators were never apprehended, and had been presumed to have fled to the Continent. A stable-boy named David Hand had given chase, to no avail. Ironically, his heroism gained him great favour in the household, and he eventually married the youngest of the then Lord Albany's daughters, Mary. However, soon after the marriage he died of pneumonia; and obviously the secret location of the stolen goods, plus the whereabouts of his accomplice's corpse, died with him.

I rushed to the conservatory and eagerly imparted my knowledge to Lady Albany: the vital corroboration of her 'dream'. She implored her husband to hasten the work on the lake, and returned with me to the library, somehow imbued with renewed vitality, asking rapid-fire questions. "But what of the man? The plague-ridden face? The Satanist, if Satanist he was? What have you found?" I said I had found precious little – but was barely through a single bookcase as yet.

"Have you examined the papers?" She clearly meant the papers she had found with the pince-nez, and I said I had looked at them but they were blank. She opened the draw and unrolled them on the table, weighting the edges with ink-stands and blotters. They were as virgin as when I had looked at them last.

"There must be something in this. Something!" she muttered to herself.

Slowly, she picked up the pince-nez.

"No," I said. "You mustn't!"

But by the time I reached out to stop her, she already had put them on. She reeled back a moment, taking a breath.

"What do you see?" I breathed.

She squinted down at the papers. "Letters. Letters and numbers."

I passed her pen and paper. "Please, Lady Albany. Write them out, clearly, here."

She did so, carefully and unhesitatingly.

FLU trasec 1112
KEPastIII.345
FITphi334

GOUresl21
MOSete9
BRYieh224

It took a moment to realise that these were directions via the library index, to certain works which I prayed were still in the possession of the family. I flicked urgently through the pages of reference, noting the works, as I presumed, coded by author, manuscript, then folio number, thus:

FLUDD, *Tractatus Secundus* 1631, page 1112
KEPLER's *Astronomy,* Vol. III, page 345
FITZER Win., *Philosophiae Et Alchemiae,* page 334
GOUDA, Peter Rammazen, *Responsum Ad Hoplocrisma* 1638, page 121
MOSE, Henri, *Eternal Sentience,* 1659, page 9
BRY, Jan Theodore, *Iehova Lux* 1605, page 224

These page references, however, proved maddeningly inadequate – there was nothing on them to segregate them from the rest, either in content or meaning.

We pored over these codes for hours, reversing the letters, substituting alphabetical letters in an attempt to illicit a new reason behind them – but nothing worked. The only clue, emphatically, was in the library index and its six seemingly mystifying book-references.

It was Lady Amarylla who solved the riddle, and in the simplest possible manner. She merely took the first letter of each of the relevant pages. Together they spelled:

OPTIKA

I looked up the title in the index. The entry read: '*OPTIKA, or, Lapis Lucidium Angularis et Ignis Mundi, the representation of Dyonysian dark and Apollonian light according to the Ptolemaic Universe, also the Nature of the Monochord or Chain of Mortal Being in Time* by Hermes Tetragrammaton, ? –1666.' I took the book from the shelves and laid it on the desk in front of us. It was a large, hand-written tome, in English but in mirror-writing, in the manner of the alchemists who feared that their esoteric knowledge might be misinterpreted as witchcraft – hence our author had decided to conceal his work as thoroughly as possible against any but the most stubborn seeker.

The treatise was full of expected references to Rosicrucianism, Joachim de Flore's earlier mysticism, chemical weddings, the Microcosm and Macrocosm, and the Hebraic cosmology beloved of the occultists of the era. Much of it echoed Fludd's Mosiacall Philosophy: 'Touching the explication of the Profound, namely the Cabbalistic Riddle of God, ruling all things Spirituall and physic with balance, being both participating in Good and Badness (Equal and Opposite to Lucifuge)...this being the divine mystery.'

Further reading explained that 'Hermes Tetragrammaton' was the pseudonym of Christopher Albany, ancestor of the present Lord at the time of the Plague Year, and the man who built the first Puget Hall in 1654.

> 'It behoveth the sereous Student of these Arts to open such Causes in such that these opposites might reveal themselves and Magnify, as two contrarities of discord, proceeding from one Unity or Unison, namely the power of Light and Darkness is born of one essence and which Power impels the World as a machine, turning as a Wheel in Time, the Entire Harmonious Unity of Existence being by that divine Law – *Lux Imperator...*'

Albany was hugely well-versed in the hidden knowledge of the Ancients, as well as the Absolute and Hermetic sciences. He became afflicted by the Black Death and, realising his incurable illness, secreted himself in Puget Hall to die, horribly and alone. His knowledge was his only hope of salvation, but the ravages of the sickness had affected his brain. He began to believe that Light powered the Laws of the Universe, and that sight and perception were the key to the nature of Time. He constructed huge and insane apparati in an attempt to understand the 'dissonancy' he imagined around him.

> 'In the lens I see infinite lights and darknesses, the insecyts of our inception and destruction, spiritual light and the regions of the Lost. The Possession of the Abyss is essential. What I can

see, can therefore be. If I can be as *lux imperator* and travel thus, imperceptible to senses, on that wonderful concavity between the spheres of the Primum Mobile, defying world-mass, moon and Man – I can escape this Pit where the sole Philosopheers be Rattes. I would choose the Empyrean Heaven else...'

The 'Empyrean Heaven else' is, sadly all he did achieve, for he died that year and was buried in a plague-pit at Bishop's Waltham. His great knowledge of occultism and optics did not save him from the pest that decimated Europe. His curious lenses and theories did not save him, and his theory that he could travel in time was, like so much alchemy, an illusory quest.

I closed the book heavily and picked up the pince-nez, wondering how they had come to be – from that strange misguided man's experiments? Or were they merely a kind of looking-glass, amplified by the remaining sentience of a still-convinced ghost?

I was roused by shouting from outside, and went hastily to the group of workmen by the lake, leaving Lady Albany in the library, staring thoughtfully into space.

I was not wholly surprised that they found plates and shields in gold and silver buried in the silt and frogspawn, tarnished with weed but surely priceless. Nor that amongst them were bones. Lord Albany was quite stunned, but the atmosphere was one of men who had unearthed buried treasure – which, in a way, they had. High spirits abounded and Lord Hugh laughed and hooted. The men splashed in the awful water like children. He called out delightedly for his wife.

I walked back to the library and found her sitting where I had left her. She was staring at the wood-fire, where the pince-nez lay amongst the logs, cracked glass melting and blackened metal bending. I watched, and in minutes it was completely gone. Only then did she look up at me.

I could say nothing.

I left shortly before dinner, making my apologies, and have seen neither of them since. I understand the estate is fluid now – I hope the Puget Hall Treasure enabled them to remain happy for the rest of their lives, but of that one can never be certain.

When the lake was drained, however, it revealed more treasure than mere gold and silver. In the rock-bed layer for so long covered in water, Lord Hugh found interesting geological strata and the fossils of certain shells. Archaeologists from the University of London and the British Museum visited the site and termed it of unsurpassed interest. Three years later, after an extensive dig, they found the fossilised footprint which they identified as belonging to a giant reptile many millions of years extinct on these islands, or for that matter anywhere else on earth. The footprint spanned some five feet across and the animal – the *saurian,* or giant lizard – was estimated to stand twenty feet in height, a carnivore of the Jurassic period.

Indicator

In all my memories of my father, I cannot remember him once telling me a story. There were few books in the house: sports magazines collected in binders, the odd political memoir, a few non-fiction books about aviation, an unopened, unwanted gift or two, and newspapers, always newspapers, but hardly any books. I think he was probably rather like the accountant overheard by John Mortimer on a holiday beach who couldn't see the point in reading anything that wasn't true.

There are many possible stories. Even now, I am not sure which this is to be. There is the story of my father's life. Of course, that has been told, and will be told, ad infinitum, in some cheaply printed paperback by some tabloid gnome, or in tiresomely creative television documentaries. Close up, the exhaust with the pipe running from it. Close up, the fumes filling the car. Close up, a bulky, indistinguishable actor slumped over the wheel.

Then there is my story, meagre though it is for any kind of drama, which I am presently negotiating with a publisher friend of Dad's. My brother has got a damn good advance from HarperCollins, and I confidently expect a few k more than that. After all, he is a bachelor, and I have a wife and kids. Added interest. We've been in *Hello* magazine, for Christ's sake.

Then there is the story of the abominable trial. Everyone seems to tell that one differently. According to the judge I'm innocent. According to the man in the street, "He got away with it, didn't he?" The poor old man in the street who can just about understand his bank balance or his betting slip.

Today we heard the verdict. Perhaps that's why I'm in this kind of mood. We came out to face the phalanx of lenses, the massed ranks of BBC and ITN, chattering like baboons in a cage. I took my wife's hand in mine, tightly, giving them time to frame up and focus on it. Then I delivered my statement. Handwritten.

"The last five years have been a protracted hell not only for myself and my brother, but for those around us, completely uninvolved parties nevertheless affected by the relentless and malicious pressure of media accusation. Also those accusations were perniciously directed at my father in his role as Treasurer of the Inner London Development Council and the man directly and personally responsible for those funds." I faintly emphasised the word *personally*. "He, sadly, tragically, is no longer with us to answer to those charges in a court of law." A quaver came to my voice. The requisite flashes strobed. "I am glad and feel vindicated at last that the judge has said categorically that my brother and I at no time acted unlawfully. Were we naive not to ask where the funds came from which our father invested in our construction companies? Yes. Was there nepotism? Arguably. Were there back-handers? No. Was there any sort of criminal collusion? No. Did I believe my father? Yes. Did I trust my father? Yes. Was my father a difficult man to say no to? Absolutely.

"I do not believe however that he had any selfish interest at heart. I do believe, on the contrary, he was doing what he thought best to rescue an impossibly difficult financial situation. Sadly he is not here to defend his reputation. I however have defended mine. I am not a crook. I am not a liar. I am innocent."

Simon is waiting for the car with Dougal McRae in the back seat. We get in and he says, so much for the press release. I say, it's much better from the horse's mouth. The Daimler snails along Fleet Street and turns at Ludgate Circus, its indicator ticking like a metronome.

"Are you all right?" says Dougal. His starched collar cuts into his red shaving-raw neck.

"Fine," I say.

"You look wrecked."

"I'm meant to be," I say. I flip the drinks cabinet open and take out one of the two Monte Cristos. "I didn't shave or wash my hair this morning. Does it look all right?"

"They'd never let you in the bloody Garrick."

As we drive across Blackfriar's Bridge, there is a white van in front with "CLEAN ME" finger-written in the dirt. I look out at the happy throng and their simple lives. The cigar smoke slowly fills the car, like burned earth, like ashes, like Christmas. The interior of the car is muggy again after the sobering chill of the pavement. I run my words through my head, editing them this way and that for *News at Ten*. I am reasonably satisfied that they can't do too much of a hatchet job, but I am inured to that now.

When the car stops again, I look behind to see that my brother is still there in his BMW, alone. I ask Dougal what Kenneth is doing tonight. Dougal says he is booked on a flight to Goa. Booked? That took more optimism than I gave him credit for. On his own, I ask? He says he doesn't know.

Arabella, whose short, tight dress is riding up her stockings, says, "Are you coming to the country?"

I say, "No, I don't think so. There are a few things to see to. I promised Ronnie Philp a celebratory binge at Wheeler's. I'll stay in the flat tonight. I'll be down first thing tomorrow."

She looks out of the car window. She tucks a strand of ash blonde hair behind each ear.

"Do you want Simon?"

"You take Simon. I'll come down in the XJ. Helps me unwind, the XJ."

"Call me," she says. "Won't you?"

The cigar smoke prickles my eyes. I remember how I used to sneak one from Dad's cigar box and suck it, unlit, trying it for size. Somehow the smell was always the smell of his breath, his goodnight kiss.

You know you're famous when people make up jokes about you. There's a joke going round about Dad.

- Did you know that Geoffrey Cush has invented a new car?

- Oh really? How many gears has it got?

- Four. First, second, third, and (teller of joke lapses into a coughing fit).

Boom boom. There are plenty of others. Then there are plenty who don't find the jokes funny. I don't suppose the rate payers down in the docklands who feel that my family took the Christmas stuffing out of their mouths think they're very funny either.

I arrive at Butler's Wharf alone and the flat seems more than usually empty. I rattle round my privacy, the air around me suddenly empty of manic, slanging or sycophantic voices. I have only the sound of my own voice. I almost expect accusations from the furniture, a haranguing from the wall coverings. The silence is like someone who knows, but won't say.

I turn on the telly and pour myself a small Calvados. I recognise the figures of Bogart and Bacall in *To Have and Have Not*, an ironically appropriate title. As Donald Trump said when he owed 600 million, that bum on the street is better off than me – he's just skint. But the truth is, whether Donald Trump has 600 million or owes 600 million, the same number of bankers follow him round by his shirt tails and laugh at his jokes. And I daresay he eats at the same restaurants.

I phone the direct line to Nina Hopkins' office.

"Did you watch the news?"

"How are you?"

"Great."

"Congratulations."

"I'll catch it on the six o clock," I say. "How did I come across?"

"Tired. Relieved. On the edge of tears," then after a pause, the word I most want to hear: "Honest." She must hear the tinkle of ice cubes against my teeth, because she says: "Are you on your own?"

"I am."

"I'll come round."

I hang up. I immediately ring the office. I've received a bundle of faxes, mostly well wishers. I tell Siobhan to bin the rest, and fire off some three line thankyous, apart from two which would need to be personal.

I roll up my tie in a ball. It is unbelievable to think that it is all over. On the first day, when I came into the light, I raised my hand, palm outwards, to shield the sun, and that was the image that greeted me, cropped, blown up, doctored, from every broadsheet and tabloid front page the following morning. I was panned, zoomed, freeze framed, exploded into pixels and whizzed into a box, parrot-like, over the shoulder of Trevor McDonald.

Of course, they said in the beginning, "He must have known." As I'm sure they said as the Daimler sped away, "The bugger must've known. How could the sons not know?"

I telephone Philip and wriggle out of dinner. I say the emotion of the day has taken it out of me, just feel completely drained. He understands. Get an early night, old boy. I shall, I say. Well done, he signs off, uncertainly stumbling over each word, great relief to us all.

"Bless you," I say in a hushed tone, immediately aware it is my father speaking. His smile stays on my lips till I wipe it away. I'd seen him hang up the phone so many times with a blown kiss like that. But what did I expect? I learned at the knee of the master.

Now, I realise, the master is me.

I almost always, in my hour of need, over the past five years, have heard my father's voice in my ear. That trout-tickling basso profundo that so often accompanied his monolithic rise over the boardroom table, usually before his hand-kissing charm turned like a knife into a weltering verbal demolition. "Power was the only thing in the world that stopped him feeling useless." This I found myself saying to ITN the day after my father's suicide. Kenneth, my brother, as became habitual, kept a low profile. (As a result, the research poll we commissioned privately found that whilst the public "despised" me, it merely "felt sorry" for him.) The newspapers said that the Cush brothers seemed "remarkably composed" that day. I don't know. I once read that when a person falls from a great height they look to all intents and purposes unharmed, but when they do the autopsy, every organ is ruptured, every bone shattered, inside they're a complete write-off. That's what it felt like to me.

Dad was alive when my mother found him in the car. When my brother and I were informed, he was already being hurtled in an ambulance to a place in West London where they train deep sea divers. The policeman explained to me that, apparently, the only way to treat carbon monoxide poisoning is to de-pressurise the body, and this was the closest place they could do it. So we arrived at this grotty industrial estate protected by Rottweilers, at this ramshackle Nissen hut in Southall, with a colourful mural of a deep sea diver surrounded by fish over the walls. The place was padlocked and the lights were out. We became suddenly optimistic: obviously he had recovered and they'd taken him to the nearest hospital to recuperate. We were wrong. Dad had never recovered. He'd died in that concrete shed surrounded by badly painted fishes. By the time we'd reached the hospital, he was in the morgue. The nurse we collared used a wonderful euphemism, 'Rose Cottage.' "He's been taken to Rose Cottage," she said to the policeman. Not to me.

Dad was a Quaker, and if you've ever been to a Quaker funeral, it's a peculiar business. It begins in absolute silence, and there are spoken contributions from anyone and everyone who wishes to speak. In this day and age, to sit in "silent reflection" for any period of time is shamefully agonising. As the seconds tick by, one finds oneself thinking not of the deceased, but of whether one has set the car alarm, or whether one's mobile phone has any messages. I loved my father, but I found myself examining with immense scrutiny the polished toe-cap of my shoe rather than thinking of him. The Meeting House was foetid with macs and morning coats and stillness. Most disconcerting of all, I found my eyes wandering to an object on a desk to one side of the room, marked with a Sellotaped label reading boldly "OUT TRAY".

Several people spoke ministries. Outside a *Sun* reporter's mobile rang, and crates of bottles were being delivered to the Bunch of Grapes. Someone afterwards told me that that was the origin of the term Quaker: that people would quake with fear before standing up and speaking at a meeting. Ever since, I've thought it curious that a whole faith should be based on stage fright.

At the graveside – the family only now – one of Dad's jokes came back to me. "Dead centre of town," he'd say, expecting us to look puzzled. "Graveyard," came the punchline as he tapped the car window, followed by his over-loud, ghost train laugh. My brother and I came to anticipate this joke every time we drove down the Holt Road. He used to tell it anyway, and it would invariably be capped by his own laughter. Eventually, it had a kind of comfort attached to it: the joke that is no longer funny.

I could see him, driving, smiling.

Mum always said that if Dad saw one of his cronies and waved when he passed them in Market Street, he'd still be grinning like a fool ten minutes later when we got to Trowbridge Road. That was the public Geoffrey Cush that everyone knew and loved, not his private face. To the outside world he was always "a hell of a nice feller, Geoff." I often saw his arm around the shoulders of a councillor or a mate, but never around his wife's. He kissed her only at times when it could clearly be seen by others. I suppose my mother came to make the most of these sparse shows of affection when she could. It was never a particular priority to him.

One priority he did have, always, was winning. Six years old, he never allowed us to score goals. When we played Monopoly he was always the Banker and he always cheated, sneaking money from the box whilst our eyes were misdirected elsewhere. It was "All part of the fun." Once when I got fed up with him and upset the board and made Kenny cry, my father said, "You have to grow up and learn to be a good loser."

Nina Hopkins arrives at four thirty. She lets herself in with her own key. The straggling residue of the hack pack outside think she's another resident of the block, they ignore her. I am already undressed. She seems harassed to begin with, or she is uptight on my behalf. I have a Scotch ready for her and I ask how her day was. She says "Shitty." She works as a feature writer for *The Guardian*, small and Welsh, well-muscled and squat like a female scrum half, dressed like a social worker in Camden Town baggies and rattling Bombay jewellery. She takes off her clothes and jumps into bed. Her skin is cold and her lips taste of whisky. Her Peter Pan hair is bleached blond, and her pubic hair black as seaweed in a Chinese restaurant.

"You've started without me," she says, finding my erection under the sheets.

"Almost," I say.

She pulls back my foreskin and I'm like a rock. It pleasantly surprises me.

"You're excited," she says. "I thought I might have my work cut out this afternoon.

"Fuck 'em," I say, rolling on top of her. "Fuck the lot of them." Her vagina is loose and wet. I wonder if she masturbated in the ladies at *The Guardian* before she got in a cab. It's a mad fiction, I know. I run it through my mind like a film clip, behind my closed eyes, and I'm there in the cubicle with her when I come – it's ridiculous.

As we lie in the bath, later, I hear the music of the six o'clock news to the smell of Angels on Bare Skin, from Lush. Hopkins drops her cigarette in the toilet bowl and reaches out to pull the flush. The long hairs in her armpit fan and then close. Her attention is focused on a blackhead on my knee, which she anoints with soapy water.

"Daniel and Kenneth Cush have today been acquitted of all charges of fraud. They had been living with the threat of criminal proceedings since the suicide of their father Sir Geoffrey Cush and the scandal surrounding the alleged misappropriation of Inner London Development Council funds..." I climb out of the water and drip into the bedroom, turning up the volume on the remote control. "...Daniel said he regretted the huge investment of time and money by the SFO in their bid to convict him..." A pink nosed reporter outside the Law Courts. "It felt close to madness, he said, when everything you do and say is construed only as deception, and it particularly offended him that his father had been branded a liar, a cheat, and some kind of despotic monster..."

I see Dad's face up on the screen. No, it isn't Dad in the blue shirt and white collar behind the desk: it is me, the docklands outside the office window. My lips are moving.

"The whole idea that the public, if we are to believe the media, had in their head, that there was this grand conspiracy to divert funds to the son's companies, that my father was somehow skimming off the cream to line our collective pockets..." Mixed bloody metaphor. A touch of humanity. Not bad. "...It's simply repugnant. It's simply, terrifyingly untrue. This notion that rate payers' money which was supposed to be helping amenities, housing in the inner city, getting the homeless off the street, keeping pensioners warm, et cetera, was finding its way into my father's cheque book, is errant nonsense."

Hopkins lays down a bath towel and sits naked on the bed beside me. She lights a Marlboro Light. I can smell the bath-water on her. With one hand she manipulates my penis, and she puts her open mouth to my shoulder and blows. I think it is meant to arouse me. Almost immediately after coming, I realise, I wanted to be alone. Even while I was still inside her, I wanted her not to be there.

My close up says: "Dad made a foolish...a series of foolish, bad decisions, but he was doing his job, as he saw it, to manage the funds at his disposal, so that a potential disaster could be overcome. He was guilty of bad judgement, bad practice, hubris – and if I was guilty of anything at all, I was guilty of not standing up to him and saying, what is going on, Dad? But nobody, including myself, was able to say to Sir Geoffrey Cush, are you sure this is not a mistake? That was simply a foreign language to him."

Interviewer: "Do you wish that you could turn the clock back?"

Me: "Of course."

Interviewer: "Would you have done things differently?"

Me: "Of course. Of course I would. My father is dead. Of course I would. Hundreds of millions of pounds were lost, and many, many people suffered considerable loss and hardship as a result. Of course I would."

I reach to the bedside table and put on my watch.

Hopkins stands on the other side of the room, catching herself unwillingly in a full-length mirror. She picks up her own watch and looks at it, then dries herself and pulls on her knickers and leggings. Her knickers have seen better days. Without asking, it's a ritual now, she calls the usual number from my phone's memory and within a few minutes I hear a black cab purring up outside.

"Give me a call," she says.

She understands the situation and she is happy with it.

We have discussed it many times.

Unexpectedly, she moves to the bed where I lie naked. She pulls at my flaccid penis as a person tweaks the rubber of a balloon. Then she kisses my cheek, pulls on her various layers of outer covering, Eskimo like, and leaves.

Dad's picture comes up. The beetle brow, the broken veins in his cheeks, the big pancake roll fingers. If Dad had been in that court, he'd have had the SFO for breakfast. Crook, liar, double-crosser – to his face? I don't think so. Never in a million years. That's the great, deep, shifty cowardice of it all.

He was worth ten times any of them, and they knew it. He'd been through more than they could even contemplate. He'd been one of the first soldiers to step through the gates of Belsen. I don't remember him ever talking about it. I first knew when I was fifteen, from my mother. All the times we'd been watching *633 Squadron* or *Colditz* and he'd say "Rubbish" or "Shut up" and switch channels suddenly made sense. My mother told me he'd had a nervous breakdown shortly afterwards and got invalided out of the army. Once, I asked him why he didn't like watching war films, and his answer was typically evasive, but precise. "The actors," he said, "It's the *acting*."

Within thirty-six hours of him dying, surprise surprise, the SFO suddenly thought they had a case. My brother and I sat through seventy days of prosecution evidence. I was shaking by the end of it. I was white. It was like a witch hunt. The pressure was on them for someone to pay. I stuck to the facts: that every action taken by us was a legitimate and legal action. But I never lost sight of the possibility I could be in jail by Christmas, and neither did my wife or my children that they could have their husband and Dad taken away from them.

The BBC Nine O'Clock News: "Daniel and Kenneth Cush have been cleared of conspiracy to defraud over 100 million pounds of ratepayers' money from regional council funds..."

I remember the way Arabella threw her arms around me earlier today, so tight I thought that she might literally break my neck.

"I love you," she said.

"...The Cush brothers will not face further prosecutions. The Judge said that subsequent charges would be unjustified and a flagrant abuse of power..."

I decide to go to Hamley's tomorrow and get Kit and Zoe a pre-Christmas treat, and something for Arabella. A perfume a little less exotic perhaps. Arabella says the children are spoiled. She's hard on them, being with them all day, every day, she's always the one to blow her top. And Daddy comes in as the big softie to wipe the tears. It makes her so mad sometimes, that their Dad can do no wrong.

In my dressing gown now, I look out of the picture window across the black of the Thames at Alderman's Stairs, at the lights of the Tower Hotel and St Katherine's Wharf, and Wapping. Beyond my grey reflection, I think of the black-and-white PR photos of Dad, shirt sleeves rolled up, hairy arms, gorilla like, meaty knuckles pressing down the conference table. A Neanderthal baby, more built for a donkey jacket than a Saville Row suit.

As I raise the telephone receiver to my face and listen to the ringing tone I can smell the spermicide from Nina Hopkins' cap on my fingers.

"Hi. Did I wake the kids?"

"No, they're watching a video." Down to earth Arabella, cleverly avoiding them watching TV. Kit had already been in punch-ups in the playground with yobs who called his Dad a swindler and a crook who murdered old age pensioners who couldn't pay their heating bills.

"What are they watching?"

"*Childsplay 3*" she jokes.

A breath goes through my nose, a kind of laugh.

"You didn't ask if you woke me."

"Did I?"

"No."

"Listen," I say. "...I'll be down tonight."

"Are you sure?"

"It'll be an easier drive. The roads'll be deserted."

"How was dinner?"

"Oh, Philp chickened out. I was quite relieved. Ended up sleeping for about six hours, spark out."

"Poor sweet, you must be shattered. Will you be OK to drive?"

"I'll be perfect. I'm wide awake now."

"Shall I wait up? When will you be here?"

I looked at my watch. It was getting on for ten. "About midnight. Don't worry if you're asleep. I'll try not to wake you." I have an image of slipping out of my clothes, leaving them in a pile in the dark, and squeezing into the creaky cottage bed with its clean sheets.

I am driving down the M4 with the needle fidgetting under 70, aware that the Calvados is still in my system, though I don't feel it. I feel a kind of out-of-body remoteness now. The car doesn't seem to exist, the dark of it melding into the surrounding night, the only thing hinging it to reality being the lights of the dashboard, like the points in a dot-to-dot puzzle not yet completed.

The road is empty. I do not have the radio on, the tarmac under me providing a rumbling, abstract melody. I watch cars loom up in my rear view mirror, indicating, and overtaking, tail lights disappearing into the dark.

It's remarkable. When we used to go for a run in my grandfather's Hillman Hunter, we used to think we were speeding at 35.

I used to have one of those toy steering wheels when my father had his first car. It was yellow. You'd stick it to the dashboard with spit and pretend it was you who was driving. "Sterling Moss," he called me. With my free hand I'd make up arbitrary gear changes. And I remember, when *Goldfinger* came out we'd all want stick on bullet holes for the car windows, except Dad wouldn't let us have those. Or a nodding Boxer dog in the back window, like my cousin had.

A Volvo overtakes me. Its indicator seems bright and insistent, a warning, an asterisk, an accusation.

It's funny how things come back when you least expect them. The memory comes up like a fish out of water, a flash at first, then so clear I can touch it.

I was eight. I must have been eight, because we were on our way to Bradford hospital and the only reason I can think for going to Bradford hospital was when my brother was born, and he's eight years younger than me. My mother was in the car, so she must've been pregnant with Kenny at the time. I presume she was going for a check-up.

Stephen Volk

I remember Dad asking me if I'd like to give the baby its middle name. I'm pleased as punch. I ask for him to be called Gregory, because Gregory Follows was my best friend in school. (I fell out with Gregory that summer, and I never saw him again once I left primary school. So Kenny was landed with a stupid middle name nobody liked, including me. It was the name of a friend I didn't have any more.)

On this day, we are driving to Bradford hospital in Dad's first car, the green Morris Minor. It is sunny. Dad is smiling. Perhaps he's seen one of his cronies ten minutes ago, I don't remember, but he has one of those grins which was nothing to do with my mother in the passenger seat or me in the back.

I say I feel really happy and I can't remember why. Dad laughs and says it's because I'm going to have a baby brother. I say, oh yes. But I think to myself the real reason is that I've got an afternoon off school.

We are going down the Winsley Road and come up to the T-junction with the Bath Road, and stop at the broken white lines. I am asking Mum if Gregory can come round for tea and play Scalextric and my Dad looks right and left and pulls out to turn left and suddenly *smash*. A van has gone right into the side of us, or for a second it seems as though it has. In fact it has clipped the driver's side wing and bumper, crunching and sprinkling the glass from the headlight all over the road. It makes a sharp bang and my mother, of a nervous disposition at the best of times, shrieks and holds her arms stiffly against the dashboard. "Oh, hell!" she says, her voice drawing it out musically like an opera singer. I am sure she is going to faint.

I, on the other hand, feel calm. I quickly realise that the worst is already over. My mother's fear and panic is retro-active, almost as if re-living the anticipatory graph of horror she has missed by the suddenness of the crash.

"Are you all right, Mum?"

"Of course she's bloody all right," says Dad.

"Daniel?" says my Mum, her voice rising shrilly. She turns and reaches out her hands to me. I am not sure whether she is going to comfort me, or me her.

"Sit down," says Dad. I am standing up in the gap between the driver's and the passenger seat. I see his face from a three-quarters angle from behind. A redness begins to seep from his collar upwards, his lips are pulled tight, and I can tell from the crow's feet vanished from his cheeks that he isn't smiling any more. He asserts a kind of terrifying calm over himself and methodically moves the gear stick into neutral and switches off the engine, completely oblivious to my mother's stifled sobbing. My mother's emotionality was never a serious consideration. Beyond him, I can see the van framed in the Cinemascope of the dusty windscreen, sunlit, a hefty vehicle pock-holed with rust, the automotive equivalent of the kind of boys in school who my Mum tells me not to play with.

"Quiet," my Dad says.

"Oh Geoff. What happened, love...?" My mother's voice flirts with tears. There's a suggestion of blame in her sympathetic tone. My father doesn't ask if she was hurt, or comfort her in any way. He doesn't even look at her. His unblinking eyes are on the van door as it opens and creakily slams shut.

"Leave this to me."

He opens the car door and my mother says, "Now don't start anything, Geoff, for goodness sake. Please, promise me you won't." She reaches out towards him, her fingers not quite touching the sleeve of his royal blue blazer in the second before there is emptiness behind the steering wheel and the door is slammed in our faces.

"Who's the bloody idiot, then, eh?" I can hear my father booming dully outside our car. Mum cringes.

He stands with his hands on his hips, his trilby on head, shirt tight across his pot belly and his cricket club tie, a maroon squiggle, dancing in the wind. The man from the van, a good six inches shorter and thin as a whippet, is a builder of some sort. He has overalls caked in white limey residue, cement or plaster, which salt his face and sticky-up Stan Laurel hair. The lines in his face seem to all point to his powder blue eyes. Some plastic twine ties his overalls together at the hip, where a button is missing.

"Is anybody hurt?" says the man, quietly spoken, and obviously shaken and trying to peer into our car. He hunches down, catches sight of Mum and me and looks concerned.

"No thanks to you there isn't," says my Dad. Dad has his back to us.

The man looks at him now. "What? What are you talking about?" He sounds genuinely baffled. He sounds like somebody picked on for something they didn't do. "What are you on about?"

"On about!"

"You're in the wrong, pal, not me," the small man says, a slight tremor in his voice. Not somebody used to or relishing confrontation, this chap. He shifts from foot to foot as if trying to avoid it. "You want to read your Highway Code."

"You what?"

"Well. Coming out into a main road without looking. Christ. Who the hell's fault do you think it is?"

"You must be bloody joking!"

"Me? I'm not joking, no. You're the joker."

"I've got a pregnant woman in that car!" says my Dad with an expressive gesture in our direction.

"What, I suppose that's my fault too, is it?" says the man. "I wouldn't be surprised."

"Oi. You watch it!" My Dad shuffles closer to him, making the most of his height advantage to intimidate. "You watch what you're saying, you. That's my wife in there, that is."

"God, God alive..." breathes my mother against the car window. She has turned her head away from the confrontation, only to be faced by two passersby, a woman a shopping trolley and another with a pram, transfixed as the altercation gets more and more heated. My Mum closes her eyes. "Geoff. No. Please. Don't..." she prays under her breath, in vain. But she knows her husband of old and since she can't prevent it, what she really wants is for this to be over as soon as possible. Please. Please.

Outside the car, his stubby index finger is stabbing at the small man's chest.

"Hey. Don't point that finger at me, pal."

"What?"

"I said don't point that bloody finger at me, *all right?*"

"I'll do what I want with my finger. It's my bloody finger. If I want to point it at you I'll bloody *point* it at you. Who are you to tell me what to do with my finger!"

The small man does the only thing he can do. He laughs, and turns away, shaking his head. My father goes after him as if to grab him by the arm or the throat. The man turns, unexpectedly. Disarmed, my father backs up a step, a coward, his neck as maroon as his cricket club tie. His chin is in the air, Mussolini-like now, hands on hips, a big strutting cock.

My eight year old mind races with the question: *Is this what Dads do?*

This is not a hero and baddie, like in the pictures. This is not John Wayne and Sitting Bull, this isn't even Ernest Borgnine and Richard Widmark – this is something I recognise all too well, just a big blow-up version of a scrap in the playground. I think: this is how it is. This is how it will be, then. The playground just gets bigger.

Mum dabs her nose with a hankie and puts it back up the sleeve of her cardigan. She sniffs.

I say, "I'm all right," quietly – not to her, but as a statement of fact, to myself, to convince me.

Outside the mute chorus of onlookers is growing, none of them with the slight intention to either arbitrate or interfere. They are like cows in a field.

It seems like we have been there for hours but it is probably less than five minutes. My Dad is putting on a laboured tone of voice now, as if talking to a congenital idiot:

"You were coming down that road, let's face it. And you indicated to turn left. *I saw you.* A hundred yards away. Your left indicator was merrily flashing away, I saw it! *That's why I pulled out.* Because *you* were indicating to turn left. *Except you didn't, did you?* Oh no. You changed your mind and you just…you just came along straight and went straight into the blinking side of me!" He is becalmed now, more considered, so *blinking* replaces the involuntary *bloody*. "Didn't you? Pal. Pally…" A touch of mockery now. Victory in sight, he can smell it. "Go on. Admit it! Didn't you?"

Silence.

The small man whispers something beginning with F under his breath, a bad word I haven't heard a grown-up say before. He looks up and, seeing the wild triumphant gleam in my father's eyes, he says, "You're half cracked, you are."

"Am I? Oh, yes," says my father, showing his teeth. "You would say that, wouldn't you?"

"So I indicated I was turning left?"

My Dad laughs incredulously. "You *know* you did!"

"Bollocks did I…"

"Are you telling me I don't know what I can see with my own two eyes?" says my father.

Stephen Volk

"Your bloody eyes need seeing to, mate, if that's what you saw. I'm on my way to the A4. Why the hell would I be taking a turning to go through Winsley?"

"Well, we only have *your* word for that, don't we? We don't know *where* you're travelling. You could be travelling to *Timbuctoo* for all we know!" The man doesn't move. There is a flicker in my father's face that he might have overstepped the mark. "I – I don't know, do I? For – For all I know you might have flicked the indicator on by accident. All I know is, *that indicator was bloody on!*"

"I didn't do anything by *accident*. Look. Look at my van, look at the front." He moves to his vehicle but my father doesn't follow. "Look. Is the indicator on? No."

"Not *now*, no! Obviously!"

The skinny man looks at the big man. Not yet the elephant seal who will go to Buckingham Palace to collect his knighthood for services to charity. Not yet the chairman of one of the top five banks. Now, back then, a Co-op man, selling insurance and picking up small change from old ladies in terraced houses once a week, invited in for tea and digestives and to listen to their troubles by the heat of a two-bar electric fire, while his two little sons do their homework.

"You don't believe me. Fair enough. No, fair enough!" says my father, straightening his tie. "We'll ask the boy."

I feel a coldness like tapwater run down my back and suddenly I want to go to the toilet. I'm sure I haven't heard correctly. I could't have heard correctly.

"The boy was watching," my father is saying in some distant world. "He saw what happened. Exactly what happened. Didn't you son?" The voice grows louder as it grows closer.

My father's face is up to the window beside me, his enormous palms flattened against the glass. His bushy eyebrows cast caterpillar shadows over his eyes. I see the small black dots of bristle on his top lip, cartoon clear. Behind him, more indistinct, I see the builder looking at the sky, folding his arms, moving his weight from one foot to the other, saying, "Listen, pal..."

"No no. No no," insists my father, holding up a hand. The builder puts his hands deep in his pockets and looks at the clouds, squinting.

My Dad's face fills the window. All of a sudden, I can't see anything else. He's filling my eyes and my head. "Now, Dan. You know I want you to tell the truth, don't you?"

I can smell the warm leather of the seats.

I nod.

My father says, "You know that, whatever happened just now, you must say the truth. Never mind what you think your Dad wants you to say. Your Dad – listen to me, son – " I look into his big chocolate coloured eyes. "Your Dad wants you to tell the truth, that's all." I can see every pore in the tip of his nose. I am closer to him now than when he tucks me into bed and turns out the light. I watch his lips form the words. "…That's all that matters, all right?"

"Wait a minute," says the builder, behind.

Dad straightens up. All I see now is the maroon tie and an expanse of shirt filling the window.

"What's the matter?"

"Come off it..."

"What?" my father sounds pained. Affronted. Hurt. "Are you saying – what? That my boy, that – come on, out with it. If you've got something to say, say it!"

"This is bloody ridiculous and you know it is."

"Is it?" Now my father addresses the pram lady and the four people standing at the bus stop, who have listened to everything. He is playing to the stalls. "*Is it* ridiculous?" He walks over to the bus stop and returns, arms outstretched.

Then the builder silently looks my father from head to toe, inwardly summing him up. I don't know what he thinks he sees, apart from not thinking much of him, but he also looks over to me, and he looks in my eyes for quite a long time. Like he feels sorry for me. Then he looks at my Dad, like he thinks even less of him, and folds his arms and says quietly, "All right then. You're the boss. Ask the lad, go on. Ask the lad if he saw the indicator on." He sees my father hesitate slightly and he picks a flake of plaster dust from his sleeve and flicks it away.

"Right then," says my father. He rolls on his heels, nodding at him. "Right then. We'll settle this. Right. We'll settle this once and for all."

He comes closer and wipes the window next to me with his hand, then taps the glass with his hairy knuckles.

"All right, Daniel. You've heard what we're talking about. Have you?"

I nod.

"The truth. Dad won't be angry at you. You won't be in trouble, whatever you say – all right? All I want you to say is what you *know* to be absolutely true, all right?"

I nod.

It is warm and the seat smell is horrible and I want to go for a wee. I don't look at my Mum. My Mum is no part of this now. I forget she is even there.

"The truth, lad, remember," says the builder. "Nobody will blame you for telling the truth, I promise." He looks in a packet of Woodbines for a cigarette but the packet is empty. He drops it into a nearby the gutter, poking it down the drain with his toe. He looks like a nice, kind man. I wonder if he is somebody's Dad, if he is one of those Dads who take their children to the park, to the swings on a Sunday afternoon.

Dad backs away from the car, away from me, hands raised, as if saying, look, no hands, the boy is on his own. He has no expression on his face now but complete, abject innocence, removing himself from the action, from the equation, from the accusation. He steps the same distance from our car as the builder. I feel abandoned. Alone. Empty. Both are bathed in the same dusty sunlight beyond the smeary glass of the Morris.

The smell of the sun on the leather seats is almost making me sick. I try not to breathe too deeply, because I know it will.

"Just the truth, laddo," says the small man softly. "That's all I want. That's all your Dad wants, isn't it?" He looks across at my father, sideways.

I look into my Dad's eyes, but I can't find them. I know they are there, somewhere, but the sun is too bright. "That's all I want, son. All you have to do is answer the question. Was it off or was it on?"

"That's all you have to answer," says the builder. "Was the indicator off or on?"

I open my mouth. I hear my breath come out. Except it isn't my breath, it's a word. And I'm curious as to what word it is that has come out of my mouth, and I say it again so that I can listen to it this time. And I say, "On."

My father cups a hand behind his ear. "What? – What did you say, Danny? Speak up!"

"On," I hear myself say again, then louder: "ON." And in my

mind I see the word on a blackboard and I am trying to rub it out.

"On! Did you hear that?" says my Dad outside, standing in the road, advancing on the man. "Did you hear that, eh? *On!*" The small man's shoulders fall against the side of his van.

My Dad asks for the man's insurance company and it turns out the man doesn't have insurance. He looks ashamed, humiliated. He doesn't have a tax disk on his van either. My Dad says, "Ho." It doesn't take a genius to work out his vehicle isn't fit to be on the road, and he knows it. And that means just one thing we all know now, Dad, my mother, me: that the man is *poor*. And that somehow seals it.

They have more words, but I don't really hear any of it, it is like being underwater, maybe for minutes, I don't know how long – then Dad backs off, flattening his tie against his paunch and buttoning his blazer across it.

The man stands propped against his van, his arms hanging. He looks at me. He looks at me as if everything makes sense, as if he knows everything, more even than I know or would ever know.

I duck down a fraction, hiding my sight line under the frame of the window. And I hear him laughing. I look up again, and he is shaking his head and laughing. Dad says nothing to him after that.

I look the other way, keep my eyes inside the car, on a copy of *Look and Learn* beside me on the back seat, until I hear the van rev and reverse and clatter away with a miner's lung of an engine. And I hear my father get a dust-pan and brush from the boot and sweep up the broken glass from the front of the car, and as he is doing it he is whistling.

Afterwards, he gets in behind the steering wheel and he shows my mother a fan of twenty pound notes. My mother doesn't say anything and neither does he.

As we drive to Bradford hospital, I can see my Dad's big brown eyes in the rear view mirror. It might be the sun, but there are big crow's feet round his eyes and it looks like he is smiling. Without taking his eyes off the road ahead, he says, "Well done, son." I have that feeling again, that I am really happy and I don't know why.

And he has the smile on his face all the way to Bradford hospital, and all the way home. Twenty minutes, because I am counting. One thousand two hundred seconds. That is more than when he sees one of his cronies, even. Much, much more.

Sleepless Nights

Of the many inexplicable and strange occurrences it has been my fortune to come across over the many years I have sought them, those which present – to me – the most lasting interest, are those which hint at the fragile veil that separates this world from another.

One such circumstance came to my attention by way of a letter, postmarked Norfolk, which ran as follows:

Dear Mr Venables,

I understand from a friend of mine who is reliable in such matters, that you are concerned with examining those aspects of our lives which generally come under the heading of 'the supernatural'.

Whilst I cannot attest positively that this is the case, I implore you to study, if you will, the testimony of a regular patient of mine. This would be best done first-hand, and I have her permission to invite you to Burnham Overy as her guest. She is also prepared to reimburse you the train fare and any other expenses you may incur.

I urge and beg your involvement in this matter, as from a medical point of view the patient is suffering atrociously, and I have had to submit to evidence that this business is far from the normal jurisdiction of a humble general practitioner.

Yours in urgent anticipation,

Joseph Densham, M.D.

This was clearly not a correspondence that could easily be ignored. I hastened to answer, and the reply from the good doctor confirmed the arrangements.

I knew Burnham Overy Staithe from my mis-spent childhood gathering shells, paddling and beach-combing under the watchfulness of my Aunt who lived nearby in Wells-next-the-Sea. It is a magical landscape serrated with salt marshes and creeks, shingle-spits like desert mirages at twilight, and rewarding pathways circling still and silent bays. Where the pine woods meets the sea there sometimes rises an unexpected mist, both beautiful and eerie, in the crispness of mid-winter: it is a precious picture in my memory, and for this, if for no other reason, I was eager to return.

Burnham Overy Staithe was little more than I remembered it.

In my experience of travelling the length and breadth of the country, I have a maxim that the longer the name the smaller the village, and Burnham Overy Staithe did not prove me wrong. For nostalgia's sake I felt obliged to pause for a beverage at the Inn next to the church where Lord Nelson's father had been parson – I remember a delightful Midnight Mass one Christmas there when I was nine, and could not resist a short perambulation around the churchyard, followed by a leisurely measure of ale in perhaps the most amicable hostelry in the county.

Suitably revived, I headed coastwards and walked the short distance, following the pencil-map Dr Densham had supplied, to his small consulting-room, in an out-building of the farm he owned off the main road to Brancaster and King's Lynn.

I sat for a few minutes in the waiting-room amongst the sniffy noses and pale faces, and most disconcerting of all the ones with no apparent malaise at all. The queue gradually disappeared and I was ushered in by the nurse, who seemed more fitly dressed for milking than administering a doctor's practice. However she displayed so warm a demeanour she could be forgiven her manner of attire, and almost anything else.

I shook hands with Dr Densham. He was a middle-aged man, a country doctor to the bone who had probably never had another surgery since he left Medical School. His face matched the warmth of his brown tweed suit.

"Now, sir, what seems to be the problem?" he asked.

"I think the problem is yours, doctor," I replied. Startled, he looked up at me from his patient files, and I gave him my name, Venables. "Have you forgotten you sent for me?"

He looked instantly aghast. "Oh my goodness! You must think me such a fool! I had no idea! How was your journey? I thought Nurse West would show you right through when you arrived. What with these..." He gestured helplessly, almost beside himself.

"Don't worry," I said. "I'm here now."

He returned my smile, and we sat down. Various pleasantries were exchanged: he offered me tea, and a tray was brought in. Surgery was over for the afternoon so he could relax a little and (I thought) tell me what all this was about.

We talked, however, about everything *but* the matter in hand. An influenza epidemic in Cley; a boy's broken toe at Hunstead

Farm; the treatment of chronic myopia; and the financial difficulties of a small practice, fascinating though they may be, were of little interest to my line of enquiry and Dr Densham anticipated my impatience in the nick of time. Jumping to his feet, he asked me to accompany him on his rounds.

We muddied out feet from a sickbed of measles to a phlegmatic lung and I was on the point of catching my host's elbow and interrogating him directly upon the matter which had brought me down here, and which he was clearly avoiding. Once again, however, he anticipated me; for our steps had taken us to a large house overlooking the sea-wall. Dr Densham tugged the bell-pull, and presently the door was opened by a servant. We were shown into the hallway, and a moment later the mistress of the house appeared, a plump woman, once handsome but in truth past her prime. She was dressed in black and said little, diligently avoiding my gaze. She and the doctor went into a room off the hall, where they conversed for some minutes. When the doctor returned – alone – I could hear the woman in tears.

Back at the doctor's house I asked him to please waste no further time in introducing me to the person who was the subject of my visit. He told me I had already met her.

"The coastguard's wife?" I exclaimed.

"The coastguard's widow," he corrected me.

"Of course," I replied, remembering her mourning attitude and obvious grief. "I'm sorry."

"*I* am sorry, to lead you such a dance. I had wanted you to hear it all directly from her. First-hand, so to speak. But she was far too upset to go through it. Perhaps this evening."

Tea arrived again and Dr Densham rocked back in his creaky chair.

"Her name is Mrs Elwes, by the way. Poor woman, her husband has just passed on. They buried him only last month. She's taking it badly – which makes me think perhaps…well, they do say sometimes it's all in the mind, wouldn't you say?"

I sipped my tea. "Sometimes."

He pondered a moment and continued. "I knew Maurice Elwes, of course. Knew him very well. Played a hole or two of golf with him over the years – beat me square every time, too. He used to be in the Navy, long time back. 'Captain' they still called him, and he *was* a 'Captain'. Not unpleasantly, not giving orders or that sort of thing, but knew what he wanted, knew what was right, didn't suffer fools gladly – and wouldn't listen to reason, either, if he got an idea in his head. He ran the golf club, by the way. Did I say that? He was fit, too, very fit for a man of sixty-five, wiry, sinewy – no one expected it. Heart attack. Died in his sleep. Tragic, tragic…"

"And Mrs Elwes is having difficulty coping?"

"Yes," he said. "But not with his death."

"Then with what?"

"Quite the opposite," said the doctor. "But let me tell you exactly what happened.

"The first time she came to me I was surprised – she was always in the very bloom of health, and only ever came for something trivial. But this was the day after the funeral, and she was pale and had black rings under her eyes. It was a feeble, embarrassed conversation. I offered my condolences – they seemed pathetically inadequate, you know how it is. And I asked what I could do for her. She confided that she'd been sleeping badly ever since Maurice passed on. She'd had a couple of restless nights and the night before she hadn't had a wink. It didn't take Sherlock Holmes to deduce that by looking at her – her lids were drooping and she was slurring her speech terribly. I told her, frankly, it was more than understandable and that it must be a strain living in the house all alone after what had happened. Could she ask a friend to stay with her? Or was there somewhere else she could go? She said she couldn't do that, and I didn't want to press the point. I wrote her a prescription for a sleeping powder, and she went away happily.

"I didn't see her for the rest of that week; then I happened to pass the tea shop in town. It was almost empty, which was surprising. Through the window I saw Mrs Elwes at one table, looking if anything even worse than before. Sitting there weeping, shaking with exasperation – classic symptoms of over-tiredness. I went in immediately wrote her a prescription for morphine, and asked her what was wrong: did the sleeping powder not work? She said it hadn't and she was afraid to take too much. 'Quite right too,' I said. 'The awful thing is, if your mind's too active, with some people they simply have no effect.' She became very upset at this, desperate to know what to do. I didn't want to give her a heavy dosage of drugs because there's always the risk of becoming dependent on them, and I thought there might be a psychological cure here. I said, 'Please, sleep elsewhere – go away, if only for a

Stephen Volk

week. I guarantee your sleepless nights will disappear.'

"Well, to cut a long story short, they didn't. She went to stay at her son's in Norwich, and returned in better form, but within two days she was back saying she couldn't sleep at all. I was explaining that it had become a vicious circle – her worry about insomnia was stopping her sleeping, and so on – when she suddenly burst into tears, there in the seat in which you're sitting now. I was acutely embarrassed, and not sure what to do. Finally I went and told the patients in the waiting room that surgery was cancelled, and came back and tried to console Mrs Elwes as best I could. I'm afraid the old bedside manner was never my *forte*, but there you are." The doctor offered me a cigarette but I declined. He lit one and sucked on it feverishly.

"She said to me, sobbing, 'I know now, doctor, I have to tell you the truth, and I don't care now how insane you may think me. It was Hell not telling my son, but how on earth could I? When I don't even understand it myself – how could I ?...'

"I said, 'Calm down, Mrs Elwes. You're becoming far too agitated. Don't you see this is the cause of your sleepless nights?'

"She laughed, somewhat hysterically, I thought. 'Oh, no, doctor. I'm afraid not. You see, it's not as simple as that. Not as simple as that *at all*.'

" 'Then what's this all about?" I asked.

" 'It's about Maurice."

" 'Maurice?'

" 'Yes. You see, I haven't been in the house *all alone* since Maurice died. I wish I were – I *dearly* wish I were! No, Maurice has been with me. I know it sounds mad. I know I must be mad to confess it, but hear me out, doctor -- I beg you, hear me out!'

'I managed to ask her to continue. She was more at ease now; indeed, *I* was the one whose heart was pounding. She dried her eyes and took a deep breath.

" 'It began the night of the funeral and I thought I was the only person in the house still awake. I was sitting looking into the fire – no good thing, I know, but I could not help it. Suddenly my thoughts were broken by a clang, then a clank, then the sound of footsteps. I remembered I had not fastened the door-bolts – that had always been Maurice's job, at about that time, eleven o'clock – and my first thought was to assume someone had come in. I went into the hall, but to my surprise I found it empty, and saw that the door-bolts had been fastened. I was sure I had not done them; but then it had been a funny sort of day, and perhaps I had done it after all, or one of the servants had remembered.

" 'Anyway, I lit the lamp and went to bed. Naturally, I couldn't think of much except Maurice – the good times we'd had over the years, how happy we had been. It made me feel warm and comfortable at the end of a heart-rending day, and I felt a sort of contentment that things were going to be all right.

" 'Until, that is, I turned over and there was Maurice, sitting on the bed in his pyjamas, looking back at me. I was frozen for a moment; then I ran from the room, not stopping until I found myself in one of the other bedrooms with the door locked behind me. From the other side of the door I heard a low voice – Maurice's voice – saying, 'Lettie, Lettie, what's wrong? Lettie, come back to bed!' This went on for a minute or so; then there was silence, and I began to think I had imagined the whole thing. After a time I unlocked the door and returned to my room, which was empty. As you can imagine, I got little sleep after that, and when morning came and I went downstairs I saw that the door was still locked; although I was more sure than ever I had not locked it.

" 'By the time night returned I had persuaded myself that the whole thing had been the product of my imagination; and so, with a brandy to settle me, I was sure I would drift off as soon as my head touched the pillow.

" 'Halfway through the night, however, something woke me – a familiar sort of sound. I opened my eyes, and of course the room was dark. But I recognised the sound. It was Maurice's snoring. It was horrible. I was too terrified to run this time. I simply crept out of bed, into the corner of the room, where I became gradually aware there was *something* under the sheets. I was determined not to scream; but when it said 'Lettie?' and saw it turn and look at me... well, the next thing I knew I was knocking at the door of Mrs Vorgan, my housekeeper, with some story about wanting a bit of company. I had her stay up with me as long as I decently could, but eventually I had to go back to the bedroom. There was no-one in the bed; both sides were rumpled, as if two people had slept there. I didn't sleep the rest of the night; all the creaks of the house, and sounds from outside, had taken on a double meaning to my shattered senses.

" 'There have been other things, lately. I've found his pipe sitting on the arm of his chair, smoking gently as if he's sitting there. I've even felt him there in the local tea room, sitting next to me. I went a little mad one afternoon because of that. I broke some plates, and shrieked, and sent the customers scurrying away, thinking I was insane. 'Why?' I said, to the gawping apparition. 'Why, Maurice – Why?' But there was no answer from his lips. Perhaps there *is* no answer...

" 'So there you have the story, doctor, or part of it. I cannot sleep in the house – nor can I sleep anywhere else, for all I can think about is his poor lost soul there all alone. I have to do something, but I don't know what. And if I don't do something...well, I think I may as well *be* mad, and you can sign the papers and put me away, because I know what I saw and I know what's there..." And she lapsed into tears again.

"I told her categorically that there was no question of putting her away, and that if she were mad, then countless others who had seen such phantasms through the ages were also mad. Not that I entirely go along with that hypothesis, but I think it was what she wanted to hear. I said I was happy she had told me what was troubling her, and that I would get it resolved if humanly possible – she had my word.

"In truth, I don't have any idea how to resolve it; but I believe in God and the Devil, so I must believe in the supernatural. So I've dragged you out here, Mr Venables – though I don't see what you can do, either, to be honest, now that you're here. I hope you don't think it's a wild goose chase."

"If it is," I said, "it's the most interesting kind of goose I've ever come across."

We agreed the next course of action was to be an attempt to see the phenomenon myself; not that there was any guarantee that I would. With that in mind, we resolved on immediate action, and the doctor took me to the quaint little tea shop frequented by Mrs Elwes, where the doctor assured me she would probably be at this time of day.

We were tentatively greeted by Mrs Elwes, who recognised me from our first meeting. She seemed much more composed and apologised for her behaviour earlier. Dr Densham explained that I now knew as much of the matter as he did, and understood exactly the nature of her experience, although not yet how to remedy it. She looked crestfallen at this news; her chin literally dropped to her chest and she seemed near to tears again, yet she hurried away to call upon a waitress to bring one of the establishment's special cream teas. You will notice this is a story of tea and more tea; but that is as it was, and facts are facts.

When she sat back down, the doctor asked if Mrs Elwes if had anything to add to what we already knew. She shook her head. I then asked her if she had any objections to my spending the night in the house, and she replied that she did not; although she added that I would be completely alone, as she had let the servants go prior to her departure to Norwich, and they had not yet returned: "I am afraid to have them in the house, lest they see or hear anything." The doctor kindly offered to put her up in his spare room for that night; an offer which was gratefully accepted.

We went to her house, where she quickly gathered a few things for the night. After she and the doctor had departed, I went through the ritual of locking the door after them. The house seemed strangely silent, which created a sense of incarceration. I spent some time in the sitting-room, thinking over Mrs Elwes's story, then went to the kitchen and had a late, light snack before retiring to bed. The stairs creaked and groaned under my feet as I ascended; but then I daresay there's not a three-hundred-year-old house anywhere in which that wouldn't be the case.

It was a clear night, with barely a puff of wind. The sky was a deep Prussian blue, and the moon full was visible through the window of Maurice and Lettie Elwes's bedroom. I tugged the curtains together, then laid my case on the chest of drawers and arranged a change of clothes for the morning, hanging my folded trousers on the back of a nearby chair. I took my shaving materials to the bathroom, where I washed. Even this room, which was almost completely white with brilliant pattered tiles and wallpaper, seemed replete with shadows.

I returned to the bedroom, which was lit only by the oil lamp which I had brought from the kitchen, and undressed as far as my vest and trousers, then propped myself up on a couple of pillows on the bed and waited.

It was a quarter to eleven.

I cleaned my spectacles – not wishing to burden my eyes in the gloom – and reached for the books I had brought with me: *Superstitions anciennes et modernes*, 2 volumes, folio, Amsterdam 1733-36; Papageorgiu's *Byzantinische Zeitschrift* and Cesare

Stephen Volk

Lombroso's *After Death, What?* After twenty pages or so of this last, I found my eyes weary and switched to the Papageorgiu.

Outside a wind had risen and made a sound like scampering rats in the large tree beyond the window. I don't know if it was entirely my fancy, but the old beams seemed to groan the more now, as if the whole house with its irregular proportions and ill-plumbed perpendiculars were bedded on foundations of silt. It seemed not only a prison but some dark, childish asylum – Jack's House at a funfair.

The lamplight flickered.

I held my breath in case it should blow out – but it did not.

I looked at my watch. A quarter past eleven. Maurice was late; or perhaps not coming. Perhaps, though, he was here already, and no-one but his dear wife could perceive him.

I looked round the room. Even my clothes and the innocent suitcase cast grotesque shadows on the white-painted walls. The simple picture opposite me seemed malicious – the cherubic face of a child it portrayed somehow deeply disturbing. Even the water-jug and bowl seemed to bloom into a harrowing black beast, with a curved beak ready to plunge. It was all absurd – but the absurd effects of an anxious mind, alone in the dead of night.

I grabbed for my third book, read ten pages and realised I hadn't taken in a single word. The wind was louder in the trees outside, and the shaking of the branches somehow lulling.

My eyes became heavy.

Slowly, my head nodded to my chest.

I slept.

Suddenly with the force of a mule-kick fists pummeled my chest and hard hooks of fingers fastened around my neck. My eyes flew open instantly, to find inches from my own – a *face*; bulging, fish-like, bloated with rage, eyes as runny as the albumin of raw eggs, nose a cave, and mouth a caked and dribbling maw – and a sound coming from that mouth; a moan that seemed to be an amplification of the chill wind and the creaking of the house, through the pit of dead lungs and a rotted throat.

Before I could draw breath, I was hurled – lifted and *hurled* across the room, to land at the foot of the far wall, sprawled helplessly. My spectacles smashed on the floorboards under me.

As I lay in a crumpled heap, I looked up to see the monster advance on me, dust rising from its threadbare pyjamas, skin peeling from its bald pate. Its frame was huge and lanky – so tall that, even bent as it was, its head scraped the beams – and its arms were outstretched, grasping.

"Get back!" I cried, pathetically, terrified beyond rationality, and hardly even awake.

The thing stopped in its tracks, the horrid, black mouth swimming with incomprehension. It growled; then, in a monstrous roar of anger, spittle flecking whatever breath it had, it threw itself forward, the arms lunging at me like pile-drivers.

But I was already scrambling for the door. Terror gave me the strength and speed of ten men, and I was out of that room, slamming the door behind me, and down the stairs in what seemed one jump, passing the sitting-room door before those hands even met the wall – or passed through them.

A few seconds more and I was out in the street – across the street in fact – panting for breath and feeling my heart thundering in my chest. There I waited, looking back at the house.

I only needed a minute before I was certain that whatever I had met was not intent on following me, and that whatever extreme peril I might have been in, the pretty little bedroom was ended, and I was safe.

The next day I related my experiences – the horror of which I severely censored for the sake of Mrs Elwes – to both her and Dr Densham. They were, needless to say, shocked; but I detected a certain degree of relief in the dark-ringed eyes of Mrs Elwes, as if to say, *If I am mad, I am at least not alone.*

"There is some progress," said Dr Densham. "Now at least we can be sure in the knowledge that some supernatural influence was at work. But the question then becomes, what can we do to dispel it? *Is* there a way?"

"I have considered contacting the vicar to perform an exorcism," volunteered Mrs Elwes. "But I'm afraid that he will not take me seriously."

"There is that danger," I said. "Not to mention the danger that, with all due respect, the man may not know how to do it. At best, Church of England exorcism is like setting off a bomb in order to redecorate your house – the cure can cause more problems than the malady. It goes against the grain, you see. The Catholic one is more trustworthy, but I still have deep suspicions of it. I believe the supernatural has its own laws of cause and effect. If we impose ours, it merely throws the balance."

"So what can be done?" asked the doctor. "Anything?"

"Well, let's examine the facts," I suggested.

"The facts are all too clear," said Mrs Elwes with a shiver.

"Are they?" I continued. "Then let me ask you a question. Every human being has purpose, motivation. What is Maurice's purpose? He hasn't harmed you; he seems, according to your evidence, merely to be walking through the usual everyday chores he undertook whilst he was alive."

"But he harmed *you* – or tried to at least," said the doctor.

"Precisely. So let me ask you another question: Why did he harm me?"

They looked perplexed.

"I understand that your husband, Mrs Elwes, was a man who did not enter easily into violence."

"I never saw him do any such thing, not in all the time we were married. He never raised a hand to our children. He was the sweetest gentlemen…"

"Good! But what would he have done, Mrs Elwes, if he had come home one night, gone to his bedroom, and found you, his beloved wife, gone – and a strange man lying on the bed in a state of semi-undress?" Mrs Elwes stared at me for a moment, but said nothing. "He might, mightn't he, have been goaded into anger – might have, on impulse, thrown himself at the intruder, thinking something terrible had happened to you!"

"Why – yes, yes he would, I suppose…"

I took her hand in mine. She seemed so pale and incomprehending. I tried to rub back the warmth. "Don't you see what I'm trying to say?"

"What *are* you trying to say, Mr Venables?" piped up Dr Densham.

"Clearly this, and this alone – that Maurice doesn't *realise* that he is dead. He died in his sleep, is that correct? Well, he never awoke. What's the quotation? 'Death and his brother Sleep' – there's the rub! You see, Maurice's mortal body may have been buried, but his spirit still thinks he is alive, and is going about life as normal: bolting the door, going to bed. It is not you, Mrs Elwes, but your *husband* who is truly suffering from sleeplessness!"

"That's preposterous!" said Dr Densham.

"It fits the facts."

"I simply can't accept it."

"Can you, Mrs Elwes?"

The woman was looking less frightened than I had seen her since I arrived in Burnham Overy Staithe. From her fear had come a pride, a dignity. She said simply, "Yes I'm afraid I can."

'Then there is one way to put an end to this, for the benefit of *all* of us; the living and the dead. But it is not a pleasant one, and Mrs Elwes, you and Dr Densham will both need every ounce of your fortitude and your faith if we are to succeed.'

Dr Densham disagreed violently with the plan at first. He said he found it obscene and vile and would have no part in it – particularly since it could have him struck off. It was not my erudition that persuaded him otherwise but the simple plea of Mrs Elwes, whose health and state of mind depended so completely on returning her husband to peaceful rest.

He finally wrote the exhumation order on the pretext – he insisted it be a realistic one – that he wanted to check some findings revealed by the post-mortem. Mrs Elwes, naturally, gave her permission. Mr Elwes's remains were taken to the doctor's surgery, and under cover of darkness were then surreptitiously removed – and this Densham objected to most of all – to Mrs Elwes's house.

By ten o'clock that evening, the body of Maurice Elwes rested in the bedroom which he had shared with his wife. It resembled a corpse laid out for a wake; but the embalmer's work had faded in the two or three weeks it had spent underground, and it consequently produced a noxious odour so bad we constantly kept handkerchiefs to our faces.

Time went by, and we awaited the phantasm. Dr Densham and I passed it by playing cards, which in retrospect seems bizarre but at the time seemed perfectly normal. Mrs Elwes, who had insisted on accompanying us throughout, sat beside the corpse, exhibiting no sense of discomfort or repulsion whatsoever; which is either touching or chilling, depending on one's opinion.

The clock struck eleven.

Almost immediately afterward, we heard the bolts thrown, downstairs: one, two, three. "He's here," whispered Mrs Elwes.

We began to hear the solid, heavy footsteps on the stairs, and I felt Densham's hand gripping mine, his fingers digging to the bone. The hair prickled on the nape of my neck as I watched the door swing slowly inward.

Mrs Elwes smiled.

"Maurice," she said, sniffing back tears.

The tall, gangling shadow and then the hunched form of the visitor approached the kneeling form of Mrs Elwes, and the casket that lay open in front of her.

"It's all right, Maurice," said Mrs Elwes, weeping. "It's all right now, my love, my sweet love! Look...look! Come here!"

The shambling figure hesitated and shuffled nearer. The face seemed so gentile – not at all the vile thing that had faced me like a waking nightmare only days before. As it looked down upon the almost identical face in the casket, the awful recognition was plain for all to see. The figure's own face assumed a pathetic dignity, and with a moan like the sighing of the wind, drawn from the very depths of its being, it slumped to its knees, racked with anguish and confusion, weeping.

"Do you see now, love?" Mrs Elwes sobbed. "Don't you see?"

But in the same moment the moan seemed to switch, and come from the lips of the corpse. Its eyelids flickered, the body shifted, as if waking for a moment; then it settled down into rest. And its ghostly twin was gone.

Mrs Elwes leaned close and whispered something into the casket; then she gently closed the lid. The doctor and I did not know what to say; but she said all we wanted to hear, in the merest whisper of a voice:

"I think I'd like to get some sleep now, please."

The doctor and I left with the casket.

The following day, the body of Maurice Elwes was summarily returned to the Church Authorities, for re-interment. Dr Densham expressed to the vicar Mrs Elwes' wish that a simple ceremony be performed on the newly-dug plot under the yew tree in the local churchyard, and this was gladly undertaken. I can verify this, for I was present.

In the years since, both Dr Densham, and, on a more regular basis every Sunday, Mrs Elwes, return to that simple grave and place the occasional wreath, or flowers of remembrance, with no message save their thoughts for the deceased, beside the tombstone that reads:

Beloved Husband
MAURICE ELWES
"I am not sleeping, but dead"

Curious Green Colours Sleep Furiously

It began with crocodiles.

If it began at all.

It was Juney late October and the baleful sandstone cliffs bit at my tightened skin. I had just arrived back in Rossini Driftwood West after wrapping up the "Bottle of Ducks" assignment in Ishmaelwick. I was sidling along, watching my bare toes digging through the hot sand as I walked, now and then glancing over to the crabs as they hacked open seagulls, ate them, and flew back to their nests with their bellies full.

The place hadn't changed.

The sea was undecided between ebb and flow, and left a red scum of seaweed when it shuddered back as I passed. I smiled as if to reassure it, but (poor soul) the sea had become very shy. It was one of the many consequences of the Time We Don't Talk About.

Unsuddenly the Eastern sky bubbled as a ruby red speck spluttered up over the horizon. It scanned in front of the sun, dipping as its wings changed gear, the velvet cockpit swinging gently as it turned and steered a zigging zagging course for the beach. It was only a few seconds before it swooped overhead, its shadow sliding over the sand and myself like the ghost of an octopus or two. I shielded my eyes as I watched it gain height, change gear again, and come round for a second recce.

It was a big animal, and a noisy one. Its engine dribbled. This time I caught the slap of heraldry on its haunches, sheep en fess engleur, argent, and the silver ribbons fluttering from its tanks. Fake. Someone incognito as hell had made up their mind to land on the spit just off Zut Alors.

The landway took its weight without a murmur but the shellfish scattered. Slowly the BURRRRRING lowered and levelled to a prrrrr then a chu-chu-chu, shshshshs-ttt. The forecast has said onomatopoeia before lunchtime, so I wasn't that surprised.

The baubled hatch slid back.

"Rehab rehab. My name is Beautiful Words."

A woman's voice, deep as a dugong. A leg at a time, a woman's body followed.

I rattled the ice in my cockatrice and feigned disinterest. A lifetime of trying had made me quite good at it. "You're one of those lean and silver-looking seneschals from Yellow Hill. I know because your eyes are the kind that need corkscrewing."

"Is this Boule Major?"

"You mean Bête Noir?"

"One or the other."

"No," I said.

"That's all I want to know," she said, unzipping the unrevealing part of her overcloak. I checked the channels showing her nipples: nothing I hadn't flipped before, he lied. This ma'm'selle spoke like antique sandpaper, licking the heroin grains from her front teeth between sentences. And she had nostrils but no nose.

"Schwagermund?"

She nodded. "Baroque."

"Good machine."

"It gets me here. Wherever here is." She invaded my personal, taking a sip from my glass. "I'm looking for a man called Malachi Persona."

Raised eyebrow. Giveaway. "You're out of luck, ladykill. Persona is dead."

"So he keeps saying, but I met a twambo on the dirt-track and he told me Persona lived in a grounded sloop, a big creaky sola-galleon like that one, with a rounded golden hull inlaid with fascinations."

I said: "Once Upon a."

Beautiful Words followed me up the hospital bed of the shore, her thin high heels needling the shale, her long sealskin legs twinning like vipers as she walked. Picture: she was brown as a beret, her multipack was gum agaric, her waist a nevermore, and she had the hummingbird eyes of an adulterous excuse. She read from a list typed on the back of her hand:

"He has the eyes of the Pharaohs. He has hair of steel. His suit is of scaled lizard-leather and black. He has a peacock-crest where peacock-crests are forbidden." Describing me to a tee. "I believe that you are him."

I laughed. "Believe? What kind of word is *believe*?"

She said: "You are Persona. Admit it."

"Yes, but I am also a liar."

"You are a liar."

"No." Think about it.

"You are a detective."

"More a detective than a diphthong."

"You perform tasks for payment."

"Occasionally."

"You solved the case of the Anorak Treatise."

"Perhaps."

"And the Umbrella Problem."

"Possibly."

"The Fluoride Scandal. The Etonian Powder. The Genital Crisis. The Liberace Zip. The Eisenstein Layout. The Leninist Waltz. The Oupenska Wave."

I held up my hands. "Mea culpa. You have me. What are you going to do to me, and am I going to enjoy it?" I sat down, cross-legged. "You may as well cut to the chase, because I recognise your tattoo."

"What tattoo?"

"The one you've tried to conceal with powder, below your left kidney. The seal of the soft-traders. They have fingers in every pie, so what are you doing in my kitchen?"

She didn't come clean, but at least she toyed with the soap. "Have you heard of Alto Sax?"

I skimmed a flat stone out into the sea as she sat beside me. It made a thousand hops and cried Mamma. "Alto Sax Zarathustra," I said. "Who hasn't? Premier of the Gas Lands, as is. I sang with his first daughter."

"It is required..."

"Paradox."

"It is required..."

"Paradox. Her name was Paradox. We used to pluck pygmies at a tapas bar called I Trod On The Dog. Do you know the place?" I was grateful to see Gwyneth and Fortune dancing up out of the corner of my eye, haloed by the kicked-up sand. "Ah, here's tea. What colour do you want it?"

"Any way it comes."

"It comes any way it likes."

The sound of walrus-tea being poured in a Ning tea set. A cup is passed to Beautiful Words, who takes it, in the present tense.

I sipped dryly. "Don't take it all at once. Thank you, Fortune, my love."

Beautiful Words opened oysterishly now. "Mr Persona, I take

care of Alto Sax. Prick his lobes, varnish his throne, rouge his foreskin. He is my steam train, my saccharine tube, my nose, my bonsoir." She did a lateral on me. "Do you know the date?"

"Apart from the future?"

"Apart from that." ·

"Who does?"

She inhaled. "It is the last but three. You realise what is happening on the last but one?"

"Cataract Day?"

She nodded. "The day of let's start fairly sanely and get more and more stupid silly fantastic erotic bizarre truly truly and erotic. Last year felt-covered spheres dried up, sang and danced in lace shirts to the Blue Danube tickling pinprick stars. And he was bored. He is a demanding fellow when it comes to entertainment."

"Aren't we all?"

She crossed her vipers moistly. "Pylons for pith helmets. Ha'penny coated ceilings. Nobody turned up who wasn't there. Only the man with the same face as Andre Breton."

"Phoenix Finally Burning. He told me the theme last year was *In Search of Asterisks*. And everybody brought a gift to the great goon. And, if you will permit me to begin two sentences with and, I presume you want to acquire some more-than-averagely impressive artefact to give as a gift to your paramour and boss."

"Not just *any* artefact, but one dazzler I have specifically in mind, which Alto has had his volecules set upon for aeons. I know nothing about it, all I know is that it is called the Fi, and there was a hundred year war over it, and it killed my grandfather. And if you don't get it by the day of the Dance of the Absurd, I will be committing suicide, on that baggie tree over there."

I thought for a minute, drank my drink, and said: "Nothing's absurd, surely? Not any more."

"You accept?"

"I accept everything. These days you can do little else. One even feels obliged sometimes to come out with totally incomprehensible observatories in tarmac."

"You digress."

"Ask the children to remember the world before digression."

"First find the children."

"First find the find."

She was having none of that. She combed the hair-drape from

her eyes. "Your fee, sir?"

"Twenty kilos of Persian, cured, weighed, purified, chopped, and graded. Ten in advance."

"Done." She produced it. She was way ahead of the game, whatever the game was. She even had her own set of balances. This widow came prepared. "Don't take it all at once."

"Why not? Where's the fun in that?"

She stood, limply leftside, right eye closed and vampy, black feather hair blustery, whipping her porcelain cheeks. My DNA did a Sherpa Tensing. The pheromones played Polanski with my heartstrings. Luckily something interrupted the call of copulation. Back behind us, a mile or none away in the snow, the animachine snattered, claw-wheeling its rust-ruddied jowls and gnashing its oily pistons.

I trounced my cup. "Miss Words, your Schwagermund looks restless. It's chewing up the rosaries."

She rose too. "I better broomstick. Alto will be sniffing my hammock. And these things cannot be let out of the bag, like cats."

"Just like Mr Schroedinger said."

"I don't understand."

I kissed her lilaceous hand. "Well pretend to, for Christ's sake."

"I will for ours," she said, her manly sotto making my ventricles go all a-quiver, again. "Goodbye."

"Goodbye."

What a specimen. And she came with her own formaldehyde.

Against the red sun, she clambered in dry silhouette, thin-necked and armed by light, controlling the animal superbly with a hard hand on the throttle-ropes. It shrugged and its paws cuffed the sand as she slid slimly into the socket.

She wanked the ignition and shouted back to be heard over the snarling of the pistoloons. "Where will you start?"

I yelled something back as I folded my parasol, but she didn't hear, and now I think about it, neither did I.

Frustrated Talc was a book-brained elf who lived at the Kentucky Palladian Hospital for Six Children on top of Crepuscular. What he didn't know about entropy wasn't worth knowing. I'd worked with him before, almost once, when the case of the Gay Platypus took me out of orbit, and he was the one who ran Vox Humana through the decoder and so prevented Armageddoon (the Musical). He had brackets round his mouth as if his smile was incidental.

"This Way. Left. How is Gwyneth? Left..."

I said: "Good with migraines, comme d'habitude."

"Left. Oy voy, I remember the night we grew her. Rushing into Amber Greenhouse, hello Mr Greene, trippin' through the old amps, looking for the right bean."

"Two were as easy as one," I recalled. "Come to Daddy."

He minnicked quietly, pampering his key ring.

Two lefts later the corridor got to be bee-like and we crossed the wooden ladder to Bedfordshire Wing. Inside were all sorts of Unpeople. Unpostmen, unpolice, unhousewives, uncats and undogs. But that was an experiment, and one doesn't ask about experiments until they go wrong.

"This way..."

By now the requisite key had grown a foot long and was green and covered in thorns. But it opened the door, and, as my old mentor, Fleshless of York, used to say, that is all that matters.

The Quotus Plant sat with its coily tentacles swimming in the air. It was like a mammoth octopus with a daffodil instead of a head, a great pulsating fleur du mal, commanding the small vault it was housed in, swaying to and fro in the air-conditioned silence, as all the best gurus should.

"Porridge?"

"Untouched," said Frustrated Talc. "It's sulking."

At that moment, from the Quotus came a blippering, whining gabble. Said plant made said sounds for several seconds, then twittered into quietude.

"What did it say ?"

"It said it's *not* sulking. And what does the bugger want?"

I said: "Everything. Doesn't everybody?"

"In the long term. In the short term?"

"Info. On the Fi. Rhymes with sigh, die, shy, lie, pi."

"What's that when it's intangible?"

"I have no idea. But I've got to find it, or shoes will be lost. That's why I'm here."

"Gottit." Frustrated Talc stroked his chin. "Let's listen to the flower..."

He started yanking at its buds like a Slovakian milkmaid at a cream contest. Its increasingly fat stamens twitched and it exuded rentophyll which Frustrated Talc's tightening grip on my arm indicated was a Good Sign. Its great yellow heed swayed from side to side. The veg was pondering. And pondering deeply. We watched, lit by the toady glow the veins pulsed out in time with its rhythmic twitches, which continued for some minutes, gradually rising to a peak, its grinding roots and throbbing shoots shivering as surges of excitement gushed in fits through its swishing form.

Slowly, then, it seemed to recover from its orgasm. Its veins shrank, its pale glow dimmed, and its hysterical throbbing slowed to a tired shiver.

"What did it say?"

"It said: *Fi is If spelt backwards.*"

"Ask it to elaborate."

He shook his head. "That'll only get it confused. Last time it just flared its petals and said, *All the world's the world and everybody on it merely everybody on it.*"

I sighed and did another circumnavigation of Big Leafie. "So that's all you can tell me, megabrain? Next time I'll consult a carrot." I headed for the out-hole. I didn't want to waste any more time with this pod-head.

Frustrated Talc caught up with me. "Listen, Mal, if there's one geezah who might knows about this Fi, its a a bratcatcher in Popopolis my cousin carbon-dates. Wise man. They call him Man of the Moment. Designer of shoe lifts and a tobogganist of the first order."

"It's a lead," I said. "And boy do I need one. Not that you're a boy." If he thought he was getting a rectal massage out of me, he had another thing coming.

I left Frustrated Talc cupping the porridge to one of the petals of the Quotus Plant and headed straight to the nearest gondola rank.

The pilot was a rat in a bowler hat but I had no time to argue about headgear.

Cut to evening and the moon was setting in the North. Icebergs in anything but glass spun past on rollercoaster waves and things that weren't submarines and weren't whales peered up and pointed at us. As we navigated the fjords, washing-up liquid slithered hygienically into the sea. The new horizon was a jawbone and white.

It was my first time in Popopolis. I remembered stories my

unicorn had told me as I sat on its knee, and suddenly I believed them all. Every messy shadow waltzing along the string bridge became a bead of sweat.

The pilot was holding his bargepole aloft as the tide pulled us through St George's window. Ahead of us, the cave opened into the usual tract of intestine. It was roll call time again.

A laughing paddle-steamer.

Dancing stones.

And, peeping round a corner, a cloak looking for somebody to wear.

A library of books reading each other.

Bullfighters fighting bees.

A half-flayed cat up for auction to binary numbers.

"What's the fare?" I asked when we got there.

He read the meter. "A cut lip, a broken rib, and unconsciousness."

I flew a punch at his jaw that sent him spinning, and as he came round again my knee came up into his chest, sending him over backwards. I murmured something to myself about bloody masochists getting everywhere, but who was I to deny him his little bit of pleasure?

The road was called Dried Skin of a Serpent because that was what it was, and it led me into the woods. The cobbled grass disagreed with my feet. The forest itself presented nothing but a wolf with an actor's head and a load of mushrooms playing nine men's morris. Not even the ears pinned to the willow trees could give me a straight answer to where to find the Man of the Moment, and the strait jackets certainly didn't take me seriously.

Then, just as I thought that I could really use a glass of water, a glass of water dewly appeared, singing:

> Minim O Minim, flattering free
> Biting on bamboo beginning with P
> Minim O Minim, an orphan at last
> Bum to the future and nose to the past
> Minim O Minim, now adding TV
> Ticking tantrums with gumbooting glee
>
> Minim O Minim affirming with cats
> Sewing the sick back on castrated bats

> Minim O Minim, sylphosing with fun
> Counting twelve coins with a margarine gun
> Minim O Minim, factotum assured
> Waltzing like wax on a plethora bird

"Man of the Moment," I said.

A big bilious eye beadied out at me. "It's a long time since anyone called me that."

"It's a long time since lots of things, hombre."

It said: "I suppose even you have a name."

I said: "Malachi Persona."

"Eleventh Joe they called him, Malachi Persona, young and beautiful in lizard-skin and perfume, decadent and well-to-do, capital soldier of fortune."

"In that long time after the Time We Don't Talk About."

"With his two little girls without clothes on, Gwyneth and Fortune, not twins but the same age, holding hands, picking spotty blue flowers."

"You know a lot, but do you know enough? I'm looking for the Fi. Some droll pointed me to you. Said that you are a geek of the frankincense persuasion."

The Man of the Moment chuckled and slid his tortoise head back in the folds of his mushroom-grey cowl. "I am not a Wise Man. Any man who claims to be wise is a fool. So only a fool is wise. I am therefore wise not to be wise. I am, consequently, very wise indeed."

"You certainly talk like a wise man. No wonder they died out."

I noticed for the first time a mighty book lay open on the sage's lap.

"What are you reading?"

He showed me the cover. It read:

CATALOGUE OF A BLACK...

He opened his mouth as if to speak, paused, hesitated, then spoke softly: "It's the dot dot dot that worries me."

"Not without reason," I said gravely. And sat on the largest of the flowerpots upturned next to him. "You of all people must be able to tell me what the Fi is and how to get it."

He sucked in a mirthful of the not unpleasant night air. "I have a chiaroscuro from the Douanier Rousseau Memorial Desert which I would rather not part with for its theological values. But there are always buttons. There always will be buttons, as far as I can see."

"Meaning"

"I doubt it. Not without the right saddle. And there aren't any. There are more things in our philosophy, Malachi, than are dreamt of in Heaven and Earth. The Fi is a myth. A figment. It doesn't exist, like anything worth a jot in human history. Having said that, it was created by the League of Lies in the 21st Century, when string theory was rife and dog-collars were tight. So if you have to look, look there."

"The League of Lies?"

But my cup was half empty, not half full. He was gone. I was out of time, but not out of questions.

The 21st Century. That old dump. It meant only one thing. If I was going to crack this case, I had to jump, and I hated jumping ever since that bisexual encounter with Ollie Cromwell turned into serious bad news for the Puritans. But a man's gotta do. Even if it meant the Dangerous Lightwork Circus.

The red and green striped cones were tented as always on the stretch of highway that led to the cliffs. As I got closer I began to hear the baying of the hippos as they were hung out to dry before the matinee performance. Fourteen silver cages were arranged in a semicircle around the bonfire. In the hub was the Ku Klux Klan hat of the helter-skelter.

I scrambled up the stairs inside, to be met at the top by a former acquaintance of mine named Doctor Bosphorus D'Extraordinaire. Like everyone else in the Dangerous Lightwork Circus, he smiled like a block of deserted flats.

"Malachi Persona, you old witch-finder."

"Wag."

"What can the Dangerous Lightwork Circus do for a mercenary who isn't even kosher, I ask myself."

"How are things looking for a jump?"

"Fine. When?"

"Now."

"Now? Ludey Farquaharson! Out of the question!" A white

handkerchief flew out and dabbled with his forehead. "Look, there's no way I can rope you a safe jump at this time of day. It's thirteen over. I've got a headache. There's martyrdom in the fish tank..."

"Now or nihilism, extravert. It's important. And I'll pay twice the going rate. Forty jabs. Time is of the essence, mate."

D'Extraordinaire de-twitched considerably, in the snaky way of a snigger that's just found a face to sit on.

"How far?"

"Twenty-first C. Noiseville. I know."

"Shit."

"So I've heard."

"Damn," he said.

"Problem?"

"It's going to be a bumpy ride."

"So be it."

I put out my cigarillo on his padded shoulder.

"Sit on the mat," he whispered. "We'll see what we can do." He handed me a pair of racing goggles and a gum-shield, and put up a sign saying GONE TO LUNCH.

My buttocks sank into the spongemat and D'Extraordinaire disappeared into the penthouse. I gripped my knees. I'd been attached to them for some time and, call me sentimental, I liked the arrangement.

There was a pause you could cut with a knife, so I did. An ace whittler was another of my talents.

Suddenly I heard the nelch as the levvers were thrown. The workings made a yechy noidling sound, grating its timer heads together. It made a wham-bam as it sent a lazy through the fibrous rectangle under me. In the tower, the consoles twanged on their golden pistons, opening and buzzing and clugging and snapping, and the moment the drip feed fed the Corbusier I felt a yank at my scalp, the spiral sent me like a rocket, and I shot tweedling into the softness of the pulp of yestertime with a wow and a bucket.

Ummadums battered my precognition. A fleet of red crash helmets asked me the way to the cinema. Eyes went pow. All of it very dark. Horses made of glass were making love and shattering in slow lotion, raining splinters into big-busted clouds. Matchsticks spun over voluminous trousers, then I passed a line of organists gluing keyboards back together in frantique unison. Far off testaments were quoting from unlikely sources. Then with a shudder like rain on the back of my neck, my feet hit the ground.

I blinked asleep. Up above, the sound of a crow in a fast food outlet. Mississippi bastard. Too big and too loud for any crow in any dreams I'd ever had. And why is the sky up there made of grass?

Ho ho ho, I said to myself. Twenty-first Cent. ...Or was it?

A voice boomed: "O headless stork, take salad with me!"

A shibboleth ran through me. "Who said that?"

"Very very voicy, my pal, but little else."

I decided to fake continence, and replied with fortinbras: "I am Malachi Persona, bona tide afficionado de la bang-bang ampersand bullfighter supreme: specialities a speciality. Where am I?"

The voice said: "Wouldn't you like to know."

Then I heard the can-clattery sound of a titanic chain lurching out of the durk. A chain that hissed electricity. Electrically hissing chains are not my idea of fun, I thought with sudden but heartfelt conviction.

The cobra slished out of the mist, re-start snappers for head, ten feet tall and mean-looking. Possibly hungry. Possibly dangerous. Possibly lunging towards yours truly with possibly lethal intent. No possibly about it.

My cheek narrowly avoided the loud snip of the pincer blades. I realised just how close they were. And ran. The chainbeast was fast for its bulk but too heavy for its speed. Even so, it was all I could do to anticipate the – CRASH! SWIPE! – deadly swing of its spikey steel head. I had to keep on the move – SWISH, THUD! – light on my feet, footsome, rewind, it had scampered me into an alleyway, big brick fences too high too high, coming up on me, taking its time now. No escape. Corpus tycoon, I thought: this is it.

Rattle, clank. RATTLE, CLANK.

It stopped like a sheep, skivvering me up and down with its dumbry red organ-stops, sadishly. It gave me a second, a pure second, to think of something. That was all I needed. Flooding back came my mahatma degree from Pongo pongo. And just as out of the corner of my eye I saw its big head rise to dive in for the coup de grace, I remembered the de-programming software: "The quick brown fox jumps over the lazy dog. The quick brown fox jumps over the lazy dog. The quick brown fox jumps over the lazy dog and the dog turns round and says, *Can't you see I'm trying to get some fucking sleep?*"

And from out of the dark, a screech, electronic, a clatter of links, and buzz-splintering flashes followed by a crackling explosion of wiring and circuits, dying, dying, dying out to a bubbling, bubbly bub.

The ani-metal lay in a coily mass of debris, spitting dead amps. It was slowly reverting to uncle nines. I'd have liked to have hung around to watch the transformation, but I had other things in my synapses.

This was blatantly *not* the 21st Century. D'Extraordinaire had tricked me. In which case, I think you'll agree, he had some questions to answer.

"You crockulous blitzkreig." I got my claws on his million-dollar lapels and shook him. "You turned the buttons and almost defunct me, you, you stag-tupper! I should never have trusted you after the Osmond Situation. You'd timeshag your own genitals for a centime." I had him up against the Romanian Lullaby Factory. The anger passed, but I didn't let him know that. He blurted something about financial straits. Not easy with a 22 barrel up your nasal cavity. "You assassinatory sewage-drinker, who was it? Who wanted Malachi Persona non grata'd?"

"I'll tell you, I'll tell you!" D'Extraordinaire hung from my rubber-gloved hands, wiping drool from his nether lip. "It was the Dolphin."

"The Dolphin."

"An offer I couldn't."

"And didn't. A water mammal, of sorts." I tightened my digits round the tart's windpipery. "Flashback!"

The doctor blubbered. "He came here and said some bod will come looking for a trip to the Age of Stuff. Make sure he don't return and here's a wodge for your trouble. I didn't know it'd be thee! On my tobacco Indian's wife! I was just doing what comes neutrally..."

I was putting two and two together and making zero. What was the logic of this? The Dolphin stopping me going to find the Fi. Unless the Fi wasn't there at all, and he didn't want me to know that. And why would that be, unless he knew exactly where the Fi was his own good self? In his own greedy palm with silver.

After I decided upon my next course of action, there was the small prob of D'Extraordinaire to deal with. I stroked his greasy lox. "Dear poppet, do you remember you once told me about the time you fell four hundred feet from the Steel-less Stained Zeppod, and the lens-faced little schoolboys put you back together again with one very long very strong piece of yarn?"

"Yep." He swallowed. "Four thousand one hundred and ninety three stitches."

"Four thousand one hundred and ninety three."

"Mm."

I smirked. No charge. "And one little knot. Right. Here."

"Be ... careful, won't you?"

"Me? Your old pal? Careful?"

It was a long trip to the Dolphin's abode in Pangolin, so I caught a kite back to Rossini Driftwood west and set about rigging up my hot air balloon, *The Owl*, for the voyage.

I worked long into the night. The gas machine flamed hard and hot. The trees parted after the dance, whispering about teepees and tortoises. Cola birds mated in the sky. And with the night came the coldness of the sea and the smell of pepper.

By morning *The Owl* was ready to lift. Gwyneth and Fortune had decided to dress in black satin frocks and lace pinafores, giggly imitations of Edwardian parlour maids. They climbed on board in front of me, skipping around the gondola as if they'd never been in it before. I washed my hands in chloroform and followed them up.

The interior of the basket was an altar to the Aesthetic Movement. William Morris wallpaper, William Burges cabinet, and in the centre, blown in the hot air from the valves, illustrations from *Le Morte D'Arthur* Vol.1, with "How Sir Tristram Drank of the Love Drink" in pride of place above the helm.

I spun the wheel to winch the ropes free of the bollards holding it down, and oh-so-gently the orb lifted into the sky...

They say that *The Owl* chugs like a steam train. But it was a long time since the last steam train had been shot and stuffed – people still wander past in bored indifference at the splendid husk now standing in the Clintonian Institute Gardens.

I closed my eyes and drifted away like my airship on the wind. Gwyneth and Fortune were dancing in a ring around me with tulips in their teeth, singing:

167

> "For me, for me, for me
> And it was deeply laden
> With good things for me"

They plotted our course on the abacus, and with a turn on the screw for that little bit of power, by midday we were fubble-bubbling over the churny isthmus of Ballyhoo.

"Aaaaaah!" went the girls, as if they'd just seen Santa Claus undressing. The warm wind of widdershins gusted us towards our destination.

After our customary threesome, I tried to deduce what amazing meaningfulness could reside in this fundrous receptacle known as the Fi? Who were the League of Lies and why did they invent it? Or, *did* they invent it, given they were called the League of Lies? And why was it the most precious thing in existence? Yet nobody knew anything about it. Was it imaginary, real or surreal? All, or none of the above? Thinker or thought? A shrew-like ball of delight? A pyramid of mimes? A toy whale? A dancing hat...?

After I came, I untied some more ballast and we skibberskabbered over some onion trees and a moaning of hypochondriacs. As we peeked over the corn-jagged spur, there is was, separated from us by a negligible few thousand miles of sand and fish. Chateau Pangolin. Residence of his escremancy Westminster du Val, known to fronds and emnities alike as The Dolphin. A tall, black, pokey up-pointing hand of a castle, the fingernails being glass bomber-domes with judder-guns manned by aqualung experts in gold lame Oxford bags. The walls were slinked with angel sleeves and ulnas, greased down by the turpins that slithered up and down them as we watched. The only thing they'd forgotten was a door.

I hove *The Owl* to, with my "Permission To Land" lights flashing. That confused 'em. The judder-guns followed my every stroke, and I knew that one false move and I'd be cheesecake. Cautiously, carefully, I tuned the navigational knobs, letting out the hot air in athsmatic bursts as we descended beside the tower and our shadow cleaned a space for us in the middle of the Ponderosa green swimming pool.

We sank with a whistling gush of air almost as if we had been punctured, and we hit the surface of the water with the splash of a

Japanese print. By the time Fortune and Gwyneth and I had blinked three times, we were bobbing like an emu giving cunnilingus.

Not unexpectedly, the guards were there to meet us. More than I thought. Frantically wiping dead flies from their light-bulb heads, and trying to cover their nerves by nervously cocking and re-cocking their Kieslowski 93s, yelling: "Identify yourself! Identify yourself!"

"I've been trying to do that for twenty-eight years," I geilguded. "Gwyneth, give me a bunk down, there's a good girl. Fortune, dear, go and harness us to that Doric column. I don't want you floating off without me."

"Shut up! State your business!" screamed Mr Guard, mutually-exclusively. He was obviously a homicidal maniac on account of his low wattage, his voice was tinged with an unmistakable envy of the intelligent: you know the type.

I walked across the water and shook my cuffs dry.

"My business, dear pierrepoint, is with the Dolphin. Not one of his single-glazed lackeys."

His filament bristled with rage. He needed switching out. Like all light bulbs he was a moody bastard, who would change just like that, one minute all white and bright and happy, the next cold and dark and evil. There was no halfway with light bulbs.

"That was uncalled for," said a disembodied voice. The same DV that had persecuted me with the chainbeast.

I turned towards it. "It's a man's world."

"Which particular one?"

"Which particular man or which particular world?"

He smiled.

"You are the Dolphin. I can tell from the hole in your long grey head."

"Land-mammal chauvinist pig. And you are Malachi Persona, who should have died several centuries ago."

I shrugged. "Things happen. Then more things."

A gaunt flipper beckoned me, trying its best to be like an index finger. Tough job. I kicked the last drips of water from me and followed him inside, casting a last malicious glance to the Edisonian dimp who returned a glow that meant he wanted to kill me. It was those kind of glares that made life worth living. And probably death worth dying. Everyone should try annoying a light bulb occasionally.

Stephen Volk

For a Great Hall, it wasn't particularly Great. Too Santa Fe Russian gangster for my liking, with a touch of Abyssinian mausoleum. Tables were laid with Tibetan crockery but no food, and trompe l'oeils of *Peanuts* cartoons adorned the walls, hieroglyphics I had no wish to see, much less interpret. What is it they say about money and taste? You can't buy money?

I picked up an apple which scampered at my ankles and bit into it. "No beating. No bushes. I've come for the Fi."

The Dolphin flopped into his bathtub and was promptly deluged by a dozen rhinoceros-clad handmaidens pretending to be Warner Bros dwarves. It appeared that he was ignoring me. Needless to say, I was in no mood to be ignored.

I said, "I know you have it. Hand it over and stop grinning." Which is not the thing to say to a porpoise, though marginally less insulting than calling him a porpoise.

The Dolphin laughed, as dolphins do, after a fashion. A fashion that's long out of date.

"What makes you think I'll hand it over to the likes of you, fetishist?"

"Good question."

"All questions are good. Only answers are bad."

"Well, there's only one thing to do in that casa. Pull up your wickerwork chair, slide back and get yourself oiled. We're going to play poker."

"What if I don't want to play poker?"

I finished touching up my lipstick and slipped my inkstick back into my pocket. "Come on. Dolphins thrive on poker. Look it up in the Encyclopedia Aquaria. Under D. You know how to spell, don't you? You just get the right letters and put them in the right order, and read. Preferably without moving your lips. You know what lips are, don't you?"

The Dolphin grinned. Or at least the grin didn't go away. Fact is, dolphins can very seldom *not* grin. It's a burden they have to live with. But it's also what makes them great poker players, impeccable conmen, and lousy kissers.

"What is it about the Fi?" I asked.

"Wouldn't you like to know," said the Dolphin, for a second time.

*

"I have my own pack,' I said. "Or if you prefer..."

"Deal."

The lights came down, and stood in ranks around the walls of the Great Hall, bosh-guns at the ready. It was a quarter past Vegas and the minds of the weaker-willed were fried on a portable barbeque and served to keep us awake. I was still shuffling.

"Before you pick up your cards," I said, "let's get one thing straight. Winner takes all. I want to see the Fi. Right here, right now. No schmelt, no ox. Divvy?"

The Dolphin stroked his elegant snout. "Agreed. Soldering iron? Fetch."

The nearest forty-watter shot away towards the door in the far corner of the hall. I waited, dodging expressions, but under all that my stomach was cavorting with anticipation. At last I was going to see the most sought-after artefact is Christendom, the object people killed and got killed for (and not necessarily in that order). It had better be good.

"*Voilá*," said the Dolphin, when the Fi was in front of us, relishing my expression of awed blankness.

I looked at it and coughed into my fist. "Forgive my imperceptions, but is what I see no more than a sizable cube? A uniformly boring black box?"

He nodded. "But also a lid. But don't look inside. Never look inside. That's its charm, its magic, its power, its value. Years ago, people used to prize as a delicacy a particular kind of puffer fish, knowing that for one person in a thousand the taste would be a fatal, for it contained a poison a hundred times more lethal than the purest heroin. Yet still it was a delicacy. Same with the Fi. It's the promise, the fear, the mystery."

"If spelt backwards," I said, beginning to understand, a little. "It doesn't look much. My client may be disappointed."

Dolphin was nonplussed. "Take it or leave it. Remember the poe who walked around in rags and a beard. Jutes all thought he was an anticlimax, and he turned out to be the Big Manchego."

"One thing. Something so bland-looking has to be the real thing," I said. "I'll take it."

"First you have to win it."

The servants scuttled away to their drains, leaving us alone: another condition I had insisted on up front. I pilled out, took a deep breath, and placed the stack of triangles mid-table, between us.

Stephen Volk

Hoping my cantaloupe days in Reno didn't let me down.

My opponent was inscrutable as any of his species – bland and comical as ever. Dolphinesque. "There," he gargled as the pictures flipped slumber side up. A wheel, no three wheels and a mouse's eye, was the hand. And the D, vain beast of the ocean, sloshed back in his Jacuzzi nubbling self-satisfiedly like the by-product of some illegal pollution treaty. "Top that, condor."

Through the glaze of hookah-smoke I gave him the mask of nowt he deserved. I up-turned my babies. A spoon, a blank, a blank, and another blank.

"I win."

It went quiet as a sumo.

I rolled a long cigaretti, licking the creamy paper neatly with my tongue. "Mucho thanksgiving." I stretched out to pick up the Fi off the plinth next to us.

"Not so fast, skin-face," snurled the Dolphin. "There are ten judder-guns aimed at the back of your not unattractive head."

Who was I to doubt the word of the second most intelligent species on earth? (Or first, depending on how you look at it.)

I looked down and sighed, then I looked up and way over deep into the Dolphin's ugly mugo in that sorry, little kid look I'd learned from bean tins.

"...and there's a hand-sized jabgun under the card-table pointing right into your soft and shiny underbelly, mein host."

The mammal, professional as he was, barely flinched. "You won't get away with this."

"My dear fish," I said, knowing full well I delivered the ultimate insult. "I already *have*." At my signal, Fortune lit the jet on *The Owl* and it lifted with a roar and a volcanic geyser of turquoise. A rope fell in front of my nose and I grabbed it, as planned.

All of a whoosh the jelly babes and lamia came leatherhelling down the Irish staircases, waving their weps like Badminton bats. I climbed into the steering basket, leveling my jabgun and with a ZIP! ZIP! ZIP! spiked the first three, who fell and tripped up the following nine. By now the Dolphin was flipping out. His impotent click-twittering of anger beat up the air between us. I looked down at him as we floated higher, and I looked and laughed as he got peskier and peskier. As we reached 120 feet Gwyneth gave a skree and I span round to see one of the judderguns was brrrrrring round, lining up a blast at *The Owl's* membrane. I had time enough to ZIP! and – BOOM! – with love and roses. And the aqualung expert folded in on himself with a grand old gulp. The rest of them stuck their hands in their heads.

The panic below made me feel like Wellington with a good eye. The last thing I remember as we sailed away on an Eastwood-cool gust from the desert, was the Dolphin rolling about on his carpet as the liquid conductors poured ice over his piss-angry epidermis obediently. Lot of good obedience, when you've just had the most important possession in the world taken off you. In other words, when, in spite of all the bullets in Babel, you've just been screwed.

Suppertime back at Rossini Driftwood West.

I played Salome Gatt's "Litany for Norman Wisdom" in the background, if one can talk of a background in real life, if one can talk of real life at all. But it was a good life. Real or otherwise.

It's funny thinking about life, you never get anywhere, you either travel in circles or you end up with a paradox, which does nobody any good. Which is part of the trouble with thinking, if you think about it. Which is why, with conscious exceptions, I try to think as little as possible. Which is why, I'm convinced, I have survived fourteen separate deaths and a countless number of minor injuries and extreme mental cruelties.

It seemed a logical conclusion. (I was pretty good at logical conclusions. In an illogical world, that came at a price. Luckily, because it was my career.)

It was Cataract Night and I was preparing my physical self for the Grande Apocalypse of the Spine, otherwise known as Alto Sax's Party, to which I was invited by Beautiful Words as bodyguard to the Fi. After consideration to the tune of "Dirigible Blues" I decided upon a black balaclava, baboon-bronze mask, coloured finger-caps, cape, breastplate du slaque et hunched back, bejewelled, not to mention leather strappings and cloven hoofs a la Yitspark. My steel wand seemed a little overexcited, so I sent it to bed.

A last admiring look in the mirror.

"Mr Dodgson would never approve."

*

Big, big places full of small, small people. The air treated with aerosol hum to make it seem as if everyone loved everyone else as the knives went in. Some talked backwards, some in foreign languages, some in no languages at all. In my mind, I imagined every one of the guests disappearing in a poof of coloured fumes, but alas, nothing happened. Telekinesis come back, all is forgiven. Press the button again, Wilkins.

"Ah, Nefertiti-Nirvana! I must talk to her about her new paper farm. *Do* excuse me. Nefertiti, my desire…!"

I sat on my feet and wallowed in the unmiscarriagable noise of Chopin Liszt and the Cashbacks. This was not the first time by far I had been under the roof of the Dodome at Yellow Hill, and I noticed familiar things had flown. The rigging boas were gone, along with the dried marble babies. The floor was checkered for a change and the vaulting varied from rainbow to rainbow as the sundials struck the hour. At the nave end, Alto Sax sat swathed in ermine, flanked by polar bear cubs dressed as cupids. Cute as sixpence stuck in your throat.

"Malachi Persona! Haven't seen you since…"

"Neither have I," I said.

The hall, which was five times as big as it thought it was, breathed around four or five hundred selected guests drink to punchy drink, trembling to the music. I recognised some of the bodies. Phoenix Finally Burning looked dynamite in his maroon revelations. Bosphorus D'Extraordinaire came as the opposite sex. I was surprised to see him in one piece. And Man of the Moment stood at the bar, being mistaken for one for the road.

"Just love the monkey-mask, kingfisher! Just *love* it!"

Across the room a small group of anarchistic-looking Mid-Atlantics started guffooing. Just beside them, there stood a group of hand-cancelled Hopefuls who had dug their way over from Mandible. I saw Frustrated Talc and I wondered why he avoided eye contact. What did he have to hide?

"There you are. Where is it?" It was Beautiful Words, standing next to me. I winked and turned my back to her, and she took the Fi out of my hunch, wrapped in crimson chamois leather. She hugged it to her ribs, eyes darting to and fro. "Stick close."

I said, "Gladly."

"You know, you're the coolest thing since Fiona Mystery." I liked the second 50% of my fee, but thanks was nice too. And so was the angel doing flamenco in her pupils. Then they changed to worry. "Protect me. It's not over till the man gets his gift."

"You forget," I said out of the corner of my mouth. "Was I not trained in combat by the eligible and entire John Ridiculous Really, a woman with long black hair plucking her roses with hand-shears by the light of the moon?"

"Trouble?"

"No such word. Except I did catch that the Dolphin's still in one piece and freaking with Beleth de Vergerence over in Nowhere Fast."

"Worried?"

"No such word. Except I've spotted a few unusual suspects, and my hand hasn't left my pistol since the canapés came round."

I sniffed at one of the many-coloured, many-odoured cigarettes scattered in the ungravity beams situated periodically about the room. New bloodhound. Old tricks. "Do you think someone might try something?"

"Someone always tries something. Tell me when they don't. I'll hang up my beetle-crushing boots."

She tried to look as if she wasn't the second cousin to a screaming abdab. "Keep vigilant. You've got to do your job, but I'd prefer it if you didn't die."

I wanted to raise a hand and touch her neck. I fantasized that it was as cold and smooth as any skin I had ever touched.

Instead I whispered, "Be cheweck, heart. Elbows like Chang and Eng. Don't hesitate to scream. The kids in miming school used to say I'm the fastest zap in Arcadian spats."

Wart Blazer was snorting penny blacks in a corner by the French windows. The rest of the psychoid mob stood or swam, sat or hopped, rabbiting and tittering from one boring blabbering gang to another. People – if they were people – stood if they stood, crawled if they crawled, over and under, sniffing, sniggering, taking nibs of white powder and insulting the Pavlova, hazing in and out of the fog of opium like so many bad special effects. If any of them were snatch-merchants, I was a bald panther. Which I hadn't been since that dirty weekend in Whitby with Aleupicia, and that's best forgotten.

When my eyes weren't on the partees they were on the parter. Pigtailed mandarin Alto Sax, his lidless eyes rolling Beautiful Words up and down his mental inner thighs as she glid around the dancefloor. And I thought: never trust anything from the brass section.

Meanwhile, every reel or two, someone would approach the dais and present holey moly with an offering. That was the etiquette. Alphabetti spaghetti. I took it all in. After all, I was still being paid, and the Soyuz was going down a treat. First up of those I recognized, Man of the Moment gave him an English Gastropod. Not a lot of imagination in that, for an astral projectionist. Next, Frustrated Talc presented a mullah in a minefield. Phoenix Finally Burning handed over a lapidus scroll and a wooden leg: I thought for a heart-stopping moment it was a bomb, but that was far too inventive for a pubic schoolboy. Seven songs later Bosphorus D'Extraordinaire separated from the crowd and, tugging my Siamese with me, I flipped my saintly catch off. There was something of the tuna about him tonight and I didn't like it one bit. But, lo, his gift was the Nethernetherlands and I backed off. If Alto's face cracked I missed it. He was a hard huckabuck to please.

Then it was "Wish me rationality," and Beautiful Words got up there and I think the multitude had a hair of an idea something was about to break, like news, like waters, like mirrors, because they went quiet as the thirty-third psalm on a week day.

"So to thee, my Lord, Premier of the Gas Lands, Messiah Donna," cried Beautiful Words, addressing the assembled as much as the enthroned. "I reveal, I present, I give to you, with all my love and fluids – the Fi!" And she swished away the silk.

The Fi sat there where she had placed it, at Alto Sax's feet, a heavy spectre-black box, a perfect black cube, nothing more, nothing less. Man of the Moment gasped, closed his eyes and genuinely flected. Frustrated Talc looked down at his fondue set and cursed. Bosphorus D'Extraordinaire bleated and fell to his knees, or maybe someone else's. The rest took the lead like a flock of angle-poise lamps and stark terror, paralytic fear froze them to the spot. And no-one was going to plug them in.

"The Fi!" sang Beautiful Words to the george rafters. "Rhymes with sigh, die, shy, lie, pi! If spelt backwards! The Myth Machine of Legend! All things to all Men!"

"Bulbul ah Bulbul!" they chorused. "Green grow the Russians, O! Una paloma blanca!"

Slowly Alto Sax dropped to his knees, his trembling fingers doing a Van der Graaf generator round the Fi, and it took me a while to realise that the nubileman was overcome by emotion.

Beautiful Words continued. "Is it not the most wondrous of sylphs, the most giant of blasts, the most gushing of colours? Is it not truly the most indefinable ecstasy? The most divine of all gifts? The most laudable of all gestures? Is it not, my lay Alto Sax, soft white one, the Greatest Object in All Creation, ever?" And I realised, idiot, what I should have sprung all along: that she wanted to wed this duke. And half the Western womb would be in her trolley-basket. So was it love, or was it enterprise? And where did that put me?

All eyes turned to Alto Sax.

And Alto Sax gazed.

Alto Sax squinted, pondered.

Then Alto Sax began to weep.

A tear ran down Beautiful Word's cheek. At least, I think that's what they are called.

Then in the blink of an anteater's eye, Alto Sax looked inside.

"NO!" shreemed Beautiful Words, covering her face.

"NO!" screamed The Man of the Moment.

"NO!" screamed I. My gun rose. Or my rose gunned, I can't remember which. Anyway, it was too late. And sometimes guns don't solve problems, housewives. Take that home to your nearest and dearest.

Speechless. Nobody moved, but Beautiful Words was the first. She dived to the feet of her lover, pythoning his shins, wailing like a Rangoon gurkha.

Alto Sax was seething, turning from pink to purple like a rumbling volcano about to erupt. I saw into his eyes, deep into his eyes in that moment, and saw more in them than I want to see in any person's eyes before or since – assuming he was a person, of course. I gave him the benefit of the drought.

Suddenly he stood and kicked her away.

I caught her as she rolled down the steps.

Then, like one of those lanced boils of the surface of Venus you see on the newsreels, he went: "DESTROY IT!"

I caught my breath.

"No," sobbed Beautiful Words.

"DESTROY IT! DESTROY IT!"

On his orders, a hundred werebadgers suddenly swung in on ropes from the clerestory, brandishing sledgehammers and pikes, landing like parachutists on the presentation table, surrounding the Fi and immediately setting into it. If you can imagine a hundred blood-thirsty omnivores let loose on one mild geometrical object, that was it for the next thirty or so seconds. I held Words tight to me. Any excuse. The air was rent with sadistic barking as they let fly at the black box without mercy, beating it to pulp with their hammers, not just destroying it, pulverising it till the air bled. It became a seething mass of black and white and grey fur, twenty feet high, and they kept vulturing it till the ketchup stopped running.

"DESTROY IT!" screamed Alto Sax.

"Stop," I said. "Don't be a bishop. It's dead, for Grimm's sake!"

"DESTROY IT!"

"It's dead," wept Beautiful Words. "Leave it alone! It's done you no harm!"

"HARM? HARM?" roared Alto Sax, gnashed his teeth at her. "I SAID *DESTROY IT!*"

And still the badgers tore and bit, and from the convulsing mound of violent creatures, from the fading carnage, came –– no sound at all, except the one we heard in dreams: the sound of a ghost, dying.

The cell was all wire, like the cage of a battering hen. A single candle lit it, miserably. In one corner was a single-bar electric fire and a pair of Sigmund Freud slippers were arranged neatly, side by side, under the wooden bed. The Wardour showed me in.

Beautiful Words sat cross legged in the fark corner, with a glass ball and chain tied to her ankle, with a butterfly inside. She was plucking at the wire walls like a harpist, and in her eyes I saw the white sadness of madness. O, despair. She didn't look up as I entered.

I said, "Embarrassment insecurity helplessness sympathy apathy empathy pathos..."

She said: "You know, when you talk your hands go all over your body as if it were somebody else's."

"Maybe it is."

I went and sat on the bed. "I hate the painting."

"It's not a painting," she said. "It's called *Donald Rumsfeld's Eyes* and it's not a painting." And she went on canoodling with the walls.

"Suddenly I smell snuff," I said.

"Things happen. Then more things."

"True," I said.

"So?"

I ruminated. "Forget the second 50%."

"What did he see? Why did he have to kill it?"

"Mystery," I said. More business, I thought. Nothing's ever solved. Not really. Because every floorboard you nail down with an answer, another four hundred pop up.

"Took a life, took a life, sad, sad, sad..." She cranked her face down and her long hair hung in front of it like a glittery Punjabi curtain.

"I don't know what to say except almadevoney. Ex ex ex, sigh sigh sigh. Crossing hearts. Finger to lips." I spoke quietly. "What will you do now, Beautiful Words?"

She wiped a fly from her eyelid. "Survive," she said. "When I get out of here, Frustrated Talc said there's a job stitching dragon pockets for the commandos. Long way from Yellow Hill. Down in Skattery Look, if you're passing."

"It's likely."

"Amber?"

"Flashing amber, my love."

"L...?"

"That's right. Love, I said."

"Oh. I thought you said Live. Live would have been nice."

I waited a scratch. "Don't be sad, be mad. Your name is Words after all. Get your insanity back and get out of this place. You know what they say. Schizophrenia lives lives." I smiled because I thought I saw her starting to, but she didn't, at all, and I felt lonely again, stupidly. "Can't linger. My girls expect eye ointment on the hour, every hour."

I stood up and wiped the flakey sane-prison dust from the thighs of my wet suit.

She said: "Bye bye, Malachi Persona. You did your best to save the world, but the world doesn't want saving. That's why it's called the world."

I went to the cage door and rapped it with my knuckles. The ordure came bounding back like a husky and rattled his friedkins in the lock.

"Au revoir, late train," I said, not looking back. "Many foolish kisses."

The door opened and I left. I waited while it closed again, with a clish rather than a clang, and the rods wangled in the keyholes with a bear of finality. Just as I moved away, I heard an ice cream voice saying:

"Many foolish kisses, Malachi..."

The Beach sang to me that night.

My chest was weighty and I needed the dark sea air to clear my nerve endings. I walked ankle-deep in the orange sand, heading East so that I didn't see the spiky towers of Nowadays Jail in the West. I trudged on, hands in rubber pockets, across the beach of Rossini Driftwood West.

The tide tidily washed its hands.

I thought back to the Schwagermund that was parked precariously on the spur not so long ago. I remembered the way she threw her long leg over the pullbar, gently kicked the ignite pedal and how she spun the wheel as the heavy cat shuddered onto its metal feet, padded in the dust, then took to the sky in a wall of exhaust fumes.

I wondered if I would ever see Beautiful Words again. I wondered if I had ever met her at all. I thought about the Myth Machine, the black box, the Fi, and what had happened at the dance. I wondered why nobody felt sick except me.

Curious.

Then I looked down at my scar-dotted forearm and laughed like a flute.

Then, forgetting all about that forever, I turned and made my way back to me wrecked hulk of a ship, where Gwyneth and Fortune were waiting on deck with a tray of green rice tea. And, smiling, I began to consider, with great seriousness and perception, the rapid failure of newly purchased ball-point pens.

Time Capsule

I wake with a full bladder and lie there for several minutes, debating with myself whether to ignore it and try to go back to sleep, at the risk of waking again, desperate, in a few hours; or whether to toddle to the bathroom, at the risk of having difficulty getting back to sleep afterwards, perhaps not sleeping at all, or so erratically it made no difference.

The decision is the only thing occupying my mind. Nothing else can even remotely compete with it. I think of the many mornings, waking, peeing, when I was glad I hadn't stumbled in the dark to relieve myself but just nodded back off quite happily. Then again, the awful, silly dreams where you imagine you are in some Jungian urinal world and wake up, horrified, on the point at which the knot you've tied in it comes undone, the sphincter relaxes, fails you miserably, or maliciously, you feel the hot acid of the liquid spurt and you're sitting up, gulping and cursing, and feeling the warm vinegar stain clinging to the hairs on your thigh.

After several minutes, I sit up and swing my feet out of bed and hoist myself up. The draw strings of my pyjama bottoms are loose and I tug them tight and knot them as my bare feet slide like barges along the carpet. My eyes haven't yet grown accustomed to the dark, so I'm negotiating the bedroom like a blind person. I find the latch of the door and shamble out into the landing, running the flat of my hand along the wallpaper towards the bathroom at the far end.

Still on automatic pilot, between waking and dreaming, I dump my weight on the toilet seat, not even worried about the cold unsentimentality of the plastic. I am too unawake to stand, and anyway the chance of my getting an accurate aim in the bowl for the whole duration of my piss is remote to the point of inconsideration. I sit, letting the WC hold me like an egg in a cup, and tuck my prick into the void.

Urine immediately streams out of me, unrestrained, its smell harsh and glorious. I wait, head lolling forward – I am by no means in control of it now, it is in control of me – and look down at my feet on the cold lino. The broken purple flecks of veins surrounding my ankles, the hard scab of white skin at my heel, broken like a chrysalis and showing new pink skin underneath. The markings, like African body piercing; troughs created along my instep by the pattern of my socks. Ugly toes and ugly toenails, the big one gnarled and black-edged, needing clipping, and well on its way to becoming in-grown. I make a mental note to ring that chiropodist who comes to the market surgery once a week. It needs doing. It's starting to hurt, especially in those black slip-ons. It's agony sometimes, absolute agony.

I stretch my back as my pee becomes a continuous flow. I lift my elbows from my knees, and the rough sandpaper skin leaves an imprinted texture there.

I hear a pop from the vertebrae between my shoulder blades, probably only audible inside my head, telegraphed along the bones. It might be a trapped nerve, it might be age, it might be posture, it might be being overweight. I am always getting twinges, especially in bed, trying to get comfortable; twinges in the extremities, legs, arms, hands, like pins and needles. Bad circulation, I'm sure that's at the bottom of it.

Also, the last few mornings I've woken up with my ears blocked, sometimes the right one and sometimes the left. Not every night, of course. I'll get some drops. Forewarned is fore-armed. I don't fancy that syringing business again, I know that.

Ear wax, circulation, backache, ingrowing toe nails! I'm a mess, aren't I? I'm sitting here cataloguing my aches and pains in the middle of the night. But the fact of the matter is, I'm sixty six years old and I've never had a day in hospital in my life. Not even when I was a child. All my friends broke their legs or arms, fell off swings or whatever. I never did. I wondered at the time what it would feel like to have that excruciating pain. I almost wished it would happen to me, so that I would be like them, but it never did. And I never had a bike to fall off because my Dad said there were too many hills, but all my friends' Dads bought them bikes.

That was a long time ago. What are bicycles now? Two hundred pounds if you're lucky. I saw a bike the other day, ultra modern, and I asked the feller, all togged up in his skin tight shorts, showing all he's got, how much is that, and he said near enough a thousand quid. A thousand pounds for a bike! I nearly had a heart attack.

I pick up the toilet roll and tear off three or four strips and fold them. I delve my fingers between my legs and shake it and, taking it between my finger and thumb, I dab the end of it. It seems, as it does sometimes, like some brown and weathered attachment that belongs somewhere else.

When I used to teach Biology, in the years before comprehensives, there was no real attempt to give children an accurate notion of sex. There was no real wish to, by the parents or by anybody else. Who could be so sadistic as to corrupt the innocence of children by describing what such body parts were actually like? And did the adults teaching them really want to be reminded that, in essence, Burt Lancaster and Deborah Kerr in the surf were disguising a veinous seven-inch erection and a hairy, moist vagina?

It was a different age then. Corny but true.

Nowadays, they think innocence is ignorance. Everything has to be *known*.

Then, Sputnik had just gone up and Kennedy had just pledged to land a man on the moon. There was a sense of hope and adventure about the infinity of space: it was vast, empty and beckoning. It was like being a child whose mother opens the front door for the first time and says, "Yes, all right, you're allowed to play in the street. But only till tea time." Tea time, of course, always seemed a long way off.

I worked in a primary school for fifteen years, before moving to the Grammar. Yuri Gagarin, CCCP on his helmet, was the hero of the day, swiftly replaced by the Americans in crew cuts. A few of the boys in class had crew cuts too. Peter Bennett, from the police houses, was one. And all the boys wore elastic belts, with S-clips like snakes, and wore elastic to keep their grey socks up, except they were always too tight, and made a mark, and they'd peel them down and give themselves a scratch. There was never any lip, and the children called you sir or mister, not out of fear, out of respect, out of decency, because their parents had respect and decency. Nowadays everybody assumes bad of everyone. Nobody assumed bad of anyone in those days. Never.

One day I went into a class and I said, "Right, Standard 4, this week we're going to make a time capsule." If you remember, there was a fashion at the time, of putting a collection of things in a sealed box and burying it, usually with some kind of civic ceremony, to be unearthed at some far flung date in the future of Mankind. So I explained the idea to Stardard 4, and asked them to come in the following day, each with an object to go into the time capsule. They got very excited and they had all sorts of ideas. Hands shot up in the air and they jumped up and down like they wanted to be excused, all jabbering at once.

"Can we, can we put food in, sir?"

"Not if it's going to rot, no. And don't take anything without asking, all right? I don't want your Mum coming down here when we've buried her best set of pearls."

"What about a book, sir?"

"A book's fine, but make it something that means something special about *Now*. Or about You."

"Sir, in the future, if they have a nuclear war and everything's wiped out and these men in flying saucers come down, will they find our time capsule?"

"I doubt that very much, Colin," I said as the bell rang. There was a banging of desk lids. "And remember, whatever you choose, it's supposed to tell people in a hundred years what we were like." They all nodded emphatically, those who were listening. I looked round the walls at the paintings before leaving the room: Yuri Gagarin, CCCP, the Lone Ranger, My Mum and My Dad with long fingers and big hair and the sky a blue, uncomplicated scribble across the top of the grey cartridge paper.

At dinnertime I went down to Evans's Hardware shop in town and bought a cash box. It wasn't very big but I chose one that had brass rivets and a chunky lock, so that it had the impression of solidity, importance, like a safe in a bank.

The following day Standard 4 brought in their goodies, which varied from the inventive to the predictable. Ashley Coombs brought a 45 record of "Telstar", which we all sat and listened to on the school gramophone in the assembly hall. His brother Alan donated a Lucky Bag. We also accumulated a Bazooka Joe, a penny, a sherbet disc, a Bassett's sherbet dip, a holiday photograph of Ruth Taplin and her family down Barry Island, together with an ice lolly stick, and a small book of pressed leaves. Then there was a Stanley Gibbons stamp album, nowhere near full. An empty bottle of nail polish, a spangly Alice band, a cub scout's woggle, and two rings of elastic used for keeping the socks up.

I held these up, looped around the fingers of each hand, and said "Brian Richards. Sock elastic," and the kids all laughed. Brian Richards, a freckly boy with stick-out ears, looked flushed and indignant. I said, "No, very good, Brian. Excellent." Brian poked his tongue out to the boy opposite as if to say *"So there!"* The boy punched his arm. Brian punched him back. I said, "Hey," and gave them the cold beady eye.

The rest of the class came forward to my desk one by one. With most of them I said "Good" or "Excellent" or sometimes "What's this?" (for instance if someone gave in a half-smoked Woodbine ushered by titters). Ronnie Ellis gave a tightly elastic-banded set of his brother's Outer Limits cards, so I told him he'd better give them back or we'd all be in trouble. His brother was in the Sec Mod and fifteen and had already been in trouble with the police. To replace it, he dug out of his pocket a lick-on tattoo of a pirate's face, but seemed reluctant to part with it. Somebody else gave a small plastic Santa out of a cheap Christmas cracker. One little girl had written out all the words to a Beatles song, which I told her to stand up and read aloud to the class. It was a bit strange, this girl of nine talking about love, like Peter Sellers reading "A Hard Days Night" in the style of Laurence Olivier. I led the class giving her a brisk round of applause. She blushed bright pink and I told her not to be silly, she did it very well: "Never be embarrassed by your accomplishments, Rhiannon."

Another girl with, in the desk alongside her, walked to the front of the class. (Where is she now? What was her name? Would I even recognise her face?) She handed me her offering for the time capsule and turned and was walking back before I could say: "What's this, Carol?" or whatever her name was. She had handed me a folded up cutting from the Echo.

She turned back to me. "Sir, it's that girl. The one they can't find. From up the bridge."

I looked at the school photograph which had been reproduced, inadequately, in the newspaper. The girl had neatly combed hair, parted in the wrong place by the photographer. It made you want to reach in and ruffle her fringe, to put it right, to make it natural. The headline read HUNT FOR MISSING GIRL, 7. I felt a hard lump at the back of my throat. Standard 4 was quiet. I gazed around at their faces, their lack of knowing. "What makes you want to put this in, Carol?" I said softly. I was shocked, but I didn't say so. I tried to be matter-of-fact about it.

She shrugged, looking at her feet, one Clarks sandal on top of the other. "I just want to," she mumbled, almost inaudibly, fidgeting at her pullover cuffs. "My Dad said."

Stephen Volk

I folded up the newspaper cutting. On the back somebody was receiving a medal for swimming. The ink rubbed off on the tips of my fingers. "All right. If you want us to. We'll put it in the box. Thank you, Carol. Go and sit down."

When she'd returned to her desk, a boy came up. He had a box and in it was an egg, and on it he'd painted a clown's face, bright and cheerful, in Airfix paints, red, blue and white.

We were going to bury the time capsule the following day, over by the edge of the woods next to the tennis courts, just after morning break time.

That night I was sitting by the electric fire and I was going through the various bits and pieces, the Dinky toy, the parma violets, the love hearts, the drawings, a seagull's feather, a Janet & John badge, a toy compass, an air rifle dart and a target with holes in. The metal box already smelled of Sherbet Dip and liquorice pipes. I opened the press cutting about the missing girl, Annette Bayliss, and I read the article from beginning to end, even though I knew it word for word and I also knew it contained nothing new. It was three weeks since her Mum and Dad had last seen her, and the police were still chasing their tails. The girl had gone to fetch some milk from her Gran's in the next road at about five o'clock on the Sunday, and hadn't been seen since. In fact, she never reached her Gran's. She disappeared between the church and the chest hospital.

I folded it and put it in the bottom of the petty cash tin from Evans's. I decided to add something of my own to the collection, which I took from the inside pocket of my jacket. It was a small fragment of cloth, the sort from the inside of a duffel coat, where children write their name. On it was written in blue Biro: "Annette Bayliss". I took a paperclip from the bureau where I kept my papers and attached the piece of cloth to the cutting from the Echo.

It wasn't like Peter Lorre running away from the mob, with long shadows extending up the walls. It was in the back of my Anglia, smelling of plastic and rain.

I most remember her flat tummy, not a hair or wrinkle on it, with one of those belly buttons like the knot in a birthday party balloon. I held her skirt up, against her neck, just pressing enough to stop her shouting.

I told her, "Look at it. Look at it."

She was frightened but she didn't move. She was a good girl. I felt every pulse of blood in every vein of my penis. I felt I was

186

inside it, I was in the blood stream fighting to get out. Its mouth was wet and popping like the little girl in the Bird's Eye peas advert on the telly. It was the only sound we could hear. I was stabbing myself to death in the groin. I was squeezing myself out of my skin. It was sitting there, I didn't exist. The conversation was between her and it. I was ready to explode, and I took her hand, and I wrapped her fingers around it, under mine. Her hand was so small, so cold. I held the tip to her belly and sperm flooded over her.

Afterwards, I saw there was an Elastoplast on her knee, half peeled off. I tugged it away. They say if you do it quickly it doesn't hurt. I rolled it into a ball. The toggle came off her coat and I buried that too, in the same place. If was damned difficult in moonlight, but my eyes gradually became accustomed to the dark. I broke a fingernail, right off. It was excruciating. It was seven o'clock: bath time in our house on a Sunday night, crinkly fingertips and *Sunday Night at the London Palladium*.

She wasn't from my school. I didn't know where she was from.

Everyone used to say I was a good teacher. Some of the young ones coming from teacher training, they didn't know how to handle a class, the kids were all over them in two minutes. And these days, it's worse. The kids do what they blinking well like. And if the teacher raises a hand to them, they get suspended, or sued. Or they get assaulted by the Dad.

The police never found Annette's body.

I was a bit of a Mr Chips, I suppose. I moved on, up the Grammar School, then it all went comprehensive, and that's where I stayed. The old Secondary Modern, that's retirement homes now, what does that tell you? I saw the Eleven Plus come and go. I became Head of Science, then Deputy Head – "Deputy Dawg" – mostly organising the timetables, which meant a lot of burning the midnight oil. He was a awkward old cuss, the Head, (Mussolini they used to call him), but everybody knows it was really me running the school all those years, behind the scenes. I was always just pipped at the post. As they say, it's not what you know, it's who you know. I was never one to better my prospects by hob-nobbing with the right people. I suppose that could be construed as a fault.

I had a lot of other interests. Hon Sec to the cricket for years, and the best President the Schoolboys' Football ever had. I retired from it last year and they gave me this slap-up do in Cardiff. I took Viv, though she doesn't usually like to go to those sort of functions with my sporting cronies, but it was in my honour, for all that I'd done for them over the years. They gave me a large cut glass bowl, engraved with my name, and "For Services to Schoolboy Football", it said. It was a bit emotional, to tell you the truth.

I often bump into some feller about forty, when I'm shopping down the precinct or over at Iceland. And he'll say, "Hello, Mr H. Remember me?"; and I'll look at him and think, who the hell? And he'll say his name and I'll go, "Oh, yes." And he'll say, "You used to teach me up the Grammar. God, you used to whack me. I deserved it, though." I'd like to have a pound for every time some feller has said that to me over the years.

I'm awake now, sitting on the toilet, my eyes getting accustomed to the dark.

I know I won't get back to sleep now, so I pull the chain ("flush the toilet" I should say: when did I last see a WC with a *chain*?) and as it echoes, I go downstairs to the kitchen to make myself some hot chocolate. While the milk is warming up in the pan, I look through the back window at the big brick wall outside.

The fields behind, where I used to play, are all gone now, there's just the new estate getting bigger and bigger. More and more houses for the unemployed, I expect. I never see any of them working. They're always fixing their car or having a fag in the garden. And they all have kids by the truck-load.

You wouldn't recognise the town now. People keep talking about a by-pass. That'd really be the kiss of death, that would. No reason for any sod to stop here then.

I'm standing by the cooker with the smell of hot milk in the air when I hear a light creaking on the stairs and Oscar paddles in, in his SuperTed pyjamas, semi-somnambulating, dazed and on the verge of bewildered panic. He hangs on the fridge door handle and mumbles in his little lisp, "What, what, what time is it, Gramp?"

I say, "Three o'clock, sweetheart. It's still night time. Go back to bed. It's dead early, look."

He sees the milk boiling and sees the mug on the table and says, "No, I want to stay with you."

I sigh and he's awake now, or nearly, so I'm saying, "All right. Just for a minute." And he nods obediently and totters forward and I lift him up on the other chair beside me. He props his head on his hands with his elbows on the table. I make us both some hot chocolate, but by the time it's ready his little head is nodding forward. His head is a beautiful shape, a tiny little neck like the children in the Peanuts cartoons. Freckles you can count on one hand, as if they've been put there by a paint brush. An abbreviated face, bristles and bruises and blushes consigned to the distant and unforgiving future.

"I think this little boy is ready for bed," I say, combing his fringe off his forehead with my fingers. He looks at me bleary-eyed, lost and anxious in the unhelpable way only children can be, trying to think of an excuse to stay up, but the other part, the part that wants to sleep, taking over. He doesn't understand even his own body.

"Come on, nibblo," I say and pick him up. He's as light as air and his cheek is warm as toast against the silver hairs at the side of my neck. I used to tell the second years up the Grammar to go home and ask their mothers to get the butcher to give them a couple of bull's eyes. And when they'd come in the next week we'd cut them open, and I'd put a diagram on the blackboard. Aqueous humour, vitreous humour, iris, cornea, retina. And they'd cut into it, surprised how tough it would be, and the liquid would all come out, and they'd find this little perfect jelly-like lens in the middle of it. And I'd explain how it all works.

I go back to sleep.

Almost immediately, it feels like, I'm being shaken awake, and I'm suddenly sharp and alert and frightened for a second. Then I see that it's Oscar again, with eyes like eggs, saying near tears of panic now, "Is it morning, Gramps? Have I missed school?"

I roll over and squint at the clock alarm radio. "No, it's five o'clock. It's a few hours more, darling. Go back to sleep. There's a good boy."

"I can't go back to sleep now," he says, tugging at his pyjamas in illogical places.

"Yes you can. You can if you don't think about it." I hear Viv turn over in the bed next to me and I say, "It's all right, love."

I get out of bed and take him by the hand. We walk quietly to the room that's now the Boys' Room, and I tuck him up into bed, in the lower bunk, careful not to wake Frankie. There are posters of impressive space ships on the wall, saying "the question of whether we are alone in the universe is about to be answered". Sega games litter the floor: Batman, Riddler, Donkey Kong, Sonic the Hedgehog comics, the various limbs and attachments of transformer robots, and Ribena cartons. I tuck the duvet, awash with Disney characters I've never seen, under his chin, and he is almost, already, asleep.

"Where are we going to bury it, sir?" asked Sam Daniels' boy, who always wore long trousers.

"Anywhere you like, as long as it's not under the concrete," I said, taking off my tweedy jacket with the leather patches in the elbows. "Susan Satherly, you decide." I had picked one of the quietest in the class. "Where do you want it to go?"

She said nothing and pointed with a bendy doublejointed finger. I took the spade I'd borrowed from Mr Duggan the caretaker and prodded the earth in an exploratory fashion before clearing the dry leaves and starting to dig. We were on the far side of the tennis courts, on the fringe of the woods. The children stood in a circle around me occasionally chuckling or whispering; perhaps they were bored by now and other things were occupying their minds. Some boys arrived in soccer kit and started to kick about. Eddie Gayne, the PE master at the big school, waved to me a passing hello which was more like a Hitler salute. He wore track suit bottoms and a cricket V-neck sweater. The following year we would be friends.

The hole was two and a half feet deep when I stopped digging and blowed a hoot. "What do you think, then? Do you think that'll do?"

Standard 4 chorused, "YES, SIR!"

"Good." I picked up the cash box from the boy who was holding it sternly in his arms and put it securely in the hole. I demonstrated that the time capsule was locked and looked down at it and said, "Right then. Here we go. Everybody happy?"

It took a good deal less time to fill in the hole than it had taken to dig it. "OK. Gather round. Andrew Jenkins, I'm talking." The boys and girls came closer in dribs and drabs. "All right, Standard 4. Pay attention. I want you to remember." I looked at my watch. "It's eleven o'clock on Wednesday the tenth of May, 1963. The only people that know about this time capsule are me and you. I'm going to send a letter on school notepaper to the council, which they'll keep on file, which tells them where this time capsule is, with a map and the key." I held up the tiny key in the air. "So perhaps in fifty years, perhaps in a hundred years, when you're much much older, or maybe further in the future, when your children are your age or much much older, somebody will come across that bit of paper and think, hello." I put the cash box key in the breast pocket of my shirt. "Maybe the council won't be the council any more, maybe the school won't be the school any more. We don't know. But the point is it's there..."

They looked blank. I picked up the spade and with the flat of it I patted the rough earth that covered the hole, until it was smooth.

"The point is it's there," I said. "To tell people what we were like."

They had RE in five minutes and I walked them back, across the concrete tennis courts, in a crocodile, to school.

The Good Unknown

Her heart beat a little faster. Just a little flutter, but you can't deceive the old ticker, she thought, sitting in the dark. *Not the old ticker, darling.*

If he didn't exactly shout "discovery" he certainly whispered it, which made him even more appealing. He didn't advertise his talent, like an attention-grabbing child from stage school. Instead he sort of defied you to be interested in his ordinariness. And he had two things that she always looked for: number one, he didn't look like an actor, and number two, he knew how to listen.

The Casting Director had trawled through dozens, hundreds, of sixteen-year-olds now. Bit part players from *The Bill* and *Casualty*, the odd junkie or blood-stained joyrider on their CV if she was lucky. Too tall, too squat. Too gauche, too knowing. Too perfect. Not perfect enough. Mugging too much, desperate to be famous. It oozed from their pores, most of them with as much talent as a woodlouse, and half as interesting to watch.

With stolid predictability the reels from the agents stacked up, which she sat and watched dutifully with the Producer and Director, fast-forwarding to a hopeful, a possibility, right type, wrong type, fast-forward, question mark. The Director walking up and down, starting to worry about the script now, maybe it's the dialogue, maybe they should get the writer in for another pass? The Producer metaphorically holding his hand, knowing if they have no boy, they have no movie, and Overseas and Buena Vista have yet to sign the dotted line.

They needed a kid who would sit in a two-shot with a big Hollywood star and not melt into the wallpaper. A new face nobody knew, a blank page, *tabula rasa.* Somebody with a hint of inner turmoil in their looks. Someone you'd care about when he died.

They'd done a trawl of all the drama schools, spreading out to colleges, techs and sixth-forms in the London area, and they were either no good or too showy, too much Shakespeare, Tarantino or *Trainspotting* about them, all of it acquired, none of it real.

"What we need," said the Director, "is a good unknown."

The Producer pushed the book at him across the malamine-topped table but the Director's hand clawed it back. "Don't read the book.

Read the script. The book won't give you any answers. The book is just reality."

Davy Praed was articulate, bright, intelligent, his eye contact varying from the wary to the suddenly intense, but he had a great twitch of a smile when you earned it. He had bee-stung Leonardo di Caprio lips and a little of the asymmetrical unpredictability of a young Christian Slater. The Casting Director had spotted him working as a runner in a post-production house off Berwick Street. He'd dropped out of studying Chemistry at Cambridge and wanted to get into drama school. When he talked about the movies he liked – *Memento*, *Requiem for a Dream* – and said he found theatre "boring," the Director knew it was a slam-dunk.

"Can you swim?" asked the Producer.

The boy said yes, he could. He said he was like Roger Moore, he said that he did all his own stunts and told all his own lies.

The Director smiled, offered him a cigarette, just watching his body language, enjoying the possibilities, putting him in the scenes in his head. The Casting Agent knew LA had rubber-stamped the video audition, and she could see the chemistry was working, so she wanted to wind up the meeting before anybody got any qualms.

"Well, we've asked you loads of questions," she said, looking right and left. "Do you have any questions for us?"

"Yeah..." The boy leaned forward, elbows on knees, looked at the script pages fanned out on the floor between his feet, then looked up. "Yeah... Why did I die?"

Everybody laughed, and looked at each other, and laughed again.

She had a quality of bewilderment and coldness. It seemed to say, come close but not too close. It was her signature, like Harrison Ford's bemused scepticism or Bruce Willis's pursed arrogance. It was what people paid their five dollars to see. The ice blonde with a red hot heart.

When Karen Berg received the screenplay of *Half of Me, Half of You* (only one in twenty got through her agent, and the agent only read those with a play-or-pay deal attached) she liked it, it made her cry, and, more importantly, it was the right career move.

She'd had a bruising downhill run of playing wives and girlfriends (Mrs Gibson, Mrs Pacino, Mrs Hanks) and was sick of the ubiquitous kitchen scene. She wanted to be a female protagonist who drove the action. And here it was, even if Sandra and Sigourney and Meg's fingerprints were all over it. The most important thing was, she noted as she went through with highlighter pen before reading it, her character was there, on every beautiful one of the 113 pages.

The script was good, not great. The fact that it was really a MOW didn't really matter. What was *A Beautiful Mind* and *Iris* if not disease-of-the-week? It depended on the director, and she had approval of that, and an Executive Producer credit offered by the over-eager production company, terrified she might slip through their fingers on a deal-breaker.

At least she wasn't in a skin-tight silver suit in a see-through submarine battling CGI aliens with an octogenarian love interest, or having a back-lit body double cut into her love scenes, which were now sex scenes. It wasn't *trash*. It was *about something*. It would be a publicity tour that she could manage without yawning or throwing up. Or *lying*.

Not that she minded lying. She had done *that* plenty of times before. She was under no illusions. There was scant little sign of Shakespeare or Ibsen or Chekhov on her IMDb web page: just twenty-five pictures in twenty years, from bikini-clad decoration in a white trash chase movie, all the way through chirpy love interest, to the infamous noir-otic thriller where she bared more than any A-list actress in history. After that, she could call the shots, which according to the wisdom of CAA, meant bigger movies, bigger co-stars, bigger money. Which was *fine*.

No regrets. None at all.

If somebody had said when she was flunking High School exams and the teachers were calling her stupid, and worse, could she even dream of the sugar-white Spanish mission that was now her Malibu home? No. The perfect-blue swimming pool? Never.

What did she have to regret? Nothing at all.

The Make-Up Girl told Karen that Barney was eight and Evan was six, and after the shoot they were all going as a family skiing holiday to France. Evan had said he wanted to ski and break his leg, because he wanted on one of those big white plasters that people write their names on. She saw Karen's smile still in the mirror, then changed the subject. Karen poured the last of her Diet Coke from a can, and nothing came out. She shook it, surprised it was empty.

<u>SCENE No's & SETS:</u>
72 Ext. Beach near pier, D/N (D), PG'S 3, Cast No's 1,2.
Beth and Alex argue on beach.
88 Ext. Beach near pier D/N (D), PG'S 3/8, Cast No's 2,3
Dog-walker finds Alex's drowned body on shore.
95 Ext. Beach, D/N (D), PG'S 2/8, Cast 1
Beth walking on beach alone.

NO:	ARTISTE:	CHARACTER:	M/UP:	HAIR:	CSTME:	ON SET:
1	Karen Berg	Beth	07.50	08.20	09.20	09.30
2	Davy Praed	Alex	07.20	08.00	08.15	08.45

<u>SUPPORTING ARTISTS</u> (c/o Dodi Masson)
1 x Dog Walker
2 x Picnic Adults
2 x Picnic Children
4 x Teenage Beach Types
2 x Bikers

She carried her character around with her, literally. She felt it a creative obligation to carry the book around as well as the script, which now, predictably, sported more pink, yellow and blue pages than white. She looked into the eyes of the author's face on the dust jacket, the face that was going to be her. *What must it be like,* she thought, *as a mother, to lose a son?* She had to think about it. It was her job. Didn't it go against the normal rules of nature, to outlive your offspring? It must feel like God has turned against you. It must feel like plunging your head into cold water, being in another medium trying to survive, finding yourself in the wrong place, a place in which you couldn't breathe, but you had to breathe, it was your instinct, everyone's living instinct to survive. How? Why?

She tried to find the answers in her own face looking back at her. It had to be in her own eyes, or not at all. Her movie star face formed in the Winnebago mirror. It gave her a modicum of comfort, but the headache she'd woken with at dawn hadn't gone away.

The girl's soft fingers massaged the thin layer of skin at her temples and she let the dark thoughts float away, for a while. She had worked out a route to the pain and she would use it when required, like the carefully-coached British accent.

She crushed out her cigarette, surprised to see it was her fourth. The ashtray reeked of self-disgust. She'd tried acupuncture in London, two weeks ago, but her heart wasn't in it and the little seeds held to her ears with tiny squares of Band Aid kept falling off, which she took as an omen. She would try again, when she had the willpower.

She thought of the poor prop guy yesterday, lining up his cigarettes of varying lengths along the props table, for continuity's sake, puffing on them like crazy and jumping in and out of shot to replace the one in her fingers. It was like something out of Beckett.

Her agent had said he wasn't *delirious* about her playing the mother of a sixteen-year-old boy. *I'm forty-three,* she'd said. *What do you want me to play? A Prom Queen?*

I'm not talking creative challenge; his hands sculpting an imaginary box on his desk. *I'm talking...I don't know what I'm talking.*

Correct, Karen said, lighting up without asking him. A pure act of rebellion.

Listen, as your manager, I say, wild horses. As a friend I say, go with God. Or he might have said it in reverse, she couldn't remember. He was ex-Disney and had shaving rash and she tended not to listen.

It was a simple story, a neat pitch. *Based on a true story.* Mother discovers her teenage son is obsessed by an older woman, who dumps him. Boy commits suicide. Mother's backstory is that she had an obsessive passion in her youth and attempted suicide too. She separates from her husband, works with kids with psychological problems. Makes a difference. Husband returns. Redemptive character arc. Feel good ending. It was *Ordinary People* meets *In the Bedroom*.

The script had shape. *Art had to have a pattern because life does not,* as a Continuity Girl once told her. It *was* something. Or could be, when she felt her way into understanding Beth, when she committed her work to celluloid. Then it could be real.

The headache had become a migraine and she asked for a Tylenol. Not an actual Tylenol, she hadn't taken an *actual* Tylenol since that nut-case scare in the late eighties: but the word remained in her head. She tugged the ring off a new diet Coke to help knock back two Nurofen Plus. *I haven't had a headache like this since I used to have my period,* she thought, *and that was a while ago.* She felt the pills slowly travel down. *That was a Hell of a while ago. A Hell of a while.*

Her insides had been like a bag full of elastic bands glued together, Marcus Welby had told her. (More Danny Glover, actually.) Lesions, nodules, inflammatory responses: her mind had clouded at that point. She'd thought of TV shows where doctors give bad news. Must be a challenge to make it fresh each week, she mused, in a slightly out-of-body way, looking down at herself. Anyhow, she gave them permission to get in there and remove what they needed to, and if they found more, cut that out too. Which they did. Boy, did they. And afterwards she was free of the crippling pain that had doubled her up, on and off, since she was thirteen years old. *Free.* Terrible word, but nevertheless true, in all sorts of ways. Ovaries or no ovaries, she felt like a million dollars.

She came out of the trailer wearing the handmade jeans that were stipulated as part of her contract. She had lost eleven pounds since her last movie and she wanted to make sure it showed where it mattered. The sun was bright, crisp and strangely Californian, but the cold chill of the sea air and a briny pungency in her nostrils wasn't Californian at all. It was too real and too dirty to have any credibility in LA, but here it was strangely pleasant and weirdly liberating. It went with the Chim Chim Cheree accents and lack of physical vanity of the Brit crew, who by and large, she found, had a disarming lack of interest in film making.

Over by the catering truck, under sea gulls looping and croaking as if auditioning to be extras, the Producer was gently making the Director aware he was eating into the budget with long takes. The Director was looking grim and dogged. He was an ex-model, and ex-dancer and a former music video director but you would never have guessed it, on any of the three counts.

Karen hugged her windbreaker round her and walked down the beach. She was just grateful to be in the hands of someone who could at least spell Kieslowski. She didn't want to interrupt while a skirmish was in progress. She wanted air and quiet in the hope it might clear her muzzy head.

Down the incline of the beach, at a dip in the shingle just a few yards from the lullaby-hush of breaking waves, sat Davy Praed, looking out to sea. He was costumed up for their scene together, the mother-son shouting match, in Nirvana T-shirt, black cotton NYC hat and torn jeans. Her feet sank into the packed stones, making a crinkly sound as she walked over and stood beside him. The piano-fingered waves hushed and disappeared into wetness.

"How're you doin'?"

Doing a double-take, as if she'd interrupted a daydream, he avoided eye contact, with a mumbled "Hi." Then, like a statement of the obvious: "You."

"You sound surprised."

He shrugged. He was throwing stones out into the water, with a whiplash-jerk of his arm, trying to skim them along the surface, without any sign of spectacular success. "Kind of." After one more attempt he rested his elbows on his knees and held one wrist in a loop of his index finger and thumb. "I never could do it."

"Me neither."

"I don't know why I keep trying."

"I think it's something to do with the satisfying plop. What's a sneaky little skim compared to a great big gutsy *ka-plop*? I know which I'd go for."

He almost smiled. He squinted at the sun, as if there was not much else to look at, then played idly stacking a few semi-dry egg-shaped stones.

Karen sat herself down next to him. After a beat, she took out her cigarette packet, shook it and offered him one.

He shook his head and, painfully shy or nervous, still didn't look into her eyes.

"...What's happening?"

She glanced over her shoulder at the sprinkling of crew, ever busy in their organised idleness. "They're lighting for the master."

He was looking at the sea, not at her. He looked concerned. "I don't understand."

"Well, they're doing it while the sky looks pretty. Then they'll do the medium shots, then the close-ups."

"No, I mean, I don't understand *why*."

"Why?"

"Why is this *happening*?"

She frowned. "Why the scene?"

"Why *anything*."

She saw that his hands were shuddering in the cold. Maybe he was on drugs, going cold turkey or something. *My God.* No, she didn't think so. He was shivering with sheer, unadulterated, wet-the-pants *fear*. Stage fright.

"Relax. Hey, relax, kiddo."

"I'm scared." It came out as a tremulous, almost inaudible whisper, like he was afraid even to say it. He shut his eyes tight. "I'm *scared*."

"Come on. We're all scared. That's the natural state of actors, OK? Scared. By definition. I always throw up before the first slate. Been there, done that. Got several T-shirts." She saw that his hands were clasping each other tightly and she sensed he was trying to disguise the spasms knotting his stomach. "Listen, let me tell you something. We can't do it without fear. Fear is what it's all about. Fear produces the energy. You have to channel it, know where to put it. Focus it, that's all."

Still shaking uncontrollably, Davy Praed forced his eyes open, still not looking into hers, and spoke almost inaudibly. "Help me. Help me?"

She laughed. "What do you think I'm going to do, idiot? If you look good, I look good. If you look great, I'll look even better." She hoped her breezy tone might pep him up, but his mood if anything darkened under a passing cloud. "You've got your sides?"

He looked blankly, as if not even listening.

"You know the beats? You know what your character does? Let's talk about it, if you're worried. What's the ultimate goal of your character?" He gave no response. "OK. After our scene together, what do you do next?"

Davy Praed remained chill and vacant, a perplexed little child teetering on the precipice of tears. "I..." He stiffened and took a deep breath, his teeth chattering. "I drown."

"You don't just drown. You take your own life."

"I take my own life..." Davy seemed surprised. "Did I?"

"You did," she said. "So think about what took you to that place. What makes a person go there?"

The boy said, "I don't know."

"Well, think about it. There are possibilities. Maybe he wanted to make everybody suffer. To say to everybody, you'll be sorry when I'm gone. Is that it?"

Stephen Volk

"I don't know." His chin tucked in to his chest, like it was an effort to keep his head upright. "I don't *know*."

He was pale, so pale, and she noticed for the first time, close to, that he had freckles, and she wondered if it was make-up or his real, sunless generic teenage skin.

"*Motivation,*" she said. "Your motivation. What's your *motivation?*"

"Motivation...?"

"Everybody does things for a reason. Even crazy people have a reason. Even Son of Sam. Even Charles Manson. Even Hitler. That's what you've got to play. The internal logic."

He watched a briny sizzle expand over the myriad of egg stones. "And what's my...internal logic?"

"That has to come from you. You have to find it in yourself, or it isn't going to work."

"I want it to work," he shivered. "It *has* to work." A tremulous desperation distorting his thin, frightened voice.

"We'll make it work." She unfurled the pages and read the first two lines of action. "OK, it's the last time they speak. It's the most important scene in the picture. How do you come into the scene? What are your feelings? You're running down the beach..."

He was looking out past the kingdom of waves, his eyes hidden behind puckered squint-lines. "I'm..." He was there, he was feeling it, she could tell. "I'm not even there...not in my mind. It's like underwater. Not even listening to you yelling. I'm in this...black box with these mad ideas pounding round inside it, hitting me. This...weight...grinding me. I don't see the sky, the sea...nothing...it's not there...there's just me, alone, *alone*, and this pain, this awful lonely space in my head, hurting...making me sick...and all I want to do is..."

He stopped dead.

"...is what?" She heard her voice distantly, like a voiceover.

His salt-cracked lip trembled. "*I'm sorry. I'm sorry. I didn't want to hurt you. I didn't want to hurt anybody.*" The fine drizzle of sea mist forming beads on his gull-ivory cheeks. "*I just want to make the pain go away.*"

"Right. All right. Good. So what are you playing? Happy or sad?"

"Sad."

"Why sad if he's making the pain go away? Why not happy?"

200

The boy shook his downcast head. His voice was calm and quiet now, but the shadow of a tremor remained. "No. He's sad because he wants to tell his mum how much it hurts. He wants to tell her, but he can't, because he doesn't want to hurt her even more. But he wants to. So *badly*. He wishes more than anything that he could tell her he loved her and he didn't want to...never wanted to...but...it was just..."

Karen felt a knot in her throat. A knot she never got, except at the movies, never in real life. She smiled. "I knew you loved me. And I loved you. No matter how much I yelled at you. No matter what."

He looked at her for the first time. "Did you?"

Karen kept her smile in place, and her eyes didn't leave his. No way. "I'm your mother."

After a moment she realised that he was sniffing back tears. He rubbed the back of his hand against his nose and wiped the heels of each hand against the orbits of each eye.

"You've got it. You've got it," she said, searching for a paper tissue and finding she didn't have one. She needed one herself, now, stupidly. "See, acting on film isn't about shouting from the rooftops like you're at the Old Vic. It's all about finding that little glow inside you, of soul, of truth, of *whatever*, and once you find it, you hang onto it, kiddo. Because once you have it, you can do anything. *Anything*."

The boy was shivering still, and she pulled off her glove finger by finger and put her small hand on his. She felt her own inner warmth seep out into the icy cold of his flesh. He didn't move, and his hand did not get any warmer. It felt like a tombstone in a winter churchyard. Instead of transferring heat to him, she found a chill creep up from her fingertips, through her tiny blue-veined hand and wrist as if she'd reached into the freezer compartment of a refrigerator.

The boy said, "I'm ready to go now."

She gave a brief glance over her shoulder and saw that the crew were still mired in inactivity, and chuckled. "I think we artisans have to wait a wee while longer, sweetheart."

"No. I'm ready now. It's OK. I'm not scared any more," said the boy.

Karen smiled. "Good."

"No, it's all right, I can *go* now."

Now she was confused. *"Go?"* Now the movie star was the one who didn't understand. Her ears were like ice, the Nurofen was wearing off and the headache was pounding like a barbarian at the gates. Her smile became fixed because she was afraid to let it go, all of a sudden. *Go?*

The boy had a Da Vinci smile on his face, his eyes fixed on the far, glinting, blinking slit-eye of the horizon. And she heard him say, his words:

"Because you've helped me. That's why you came. To help me. To show me the way."

The cold kept moving up across the skin of her arm within her padded sleeve. She could feel the prickly spread of gooseflesh. Her mouth sagged open as she tried to speak and tried to form a smile again, several times, failing every time, endlessly.

"I needed someone to take me," something said, somewhere, now a voice indistinguishable from the curlicues of the waves. "I've been waiting, for someone to take me. To hold my hand." And then his eyes, once blue grey, now black, turned to her in an aeon and an instant, and said: "Take me."

She thought, *I can't. I can't. I can't. I can't. I can't.*

And she knew the answer even before it came. "You can. That's why you're here."

And it was that little glow of truth that she knew was inside her, that little fact, and she clung onto it, not knowing that she was, and not wanting to, but because it was her nature, her talent. And she heard, like a memory of long ago and far away, the sound of the First AD calling *"Positions please for a rehearsal!"* And she thought, what a nice world that must be, she'd like to visit it some time. And the red-haired boy's face ripped like film in the gate of a projector, torn apart by the sprockets and thrown to the sky, sea gulls and clouds, and there was only the blinding white light of the projector bulb, giver of warmth and life and dreams, burning into her mind.

Solon & Wheat Medical Dictionary (OUP, 1999):

*"A **cerebral aneurysm** is a bulge or dilation that develops in a blood vessel (**cerebral artery**) in the brain. The cause is unknown, though it is widely acknowledged that cigarette smoking increases a*

*person's risk. Some do not grow, leak blood, or cause complications. Other aneurysms bleed (**haemorrhage**) or break (**rupture**) in the brain and can cause a stroke or even death, sometimes pre-shadowed by headaches or facial numbness, sometimes without any warning signs at all."*

Davy Praed was standing beside the catering truck having his costume tweaked and drinking coffee as the First AD called "Positions please for a rehearsal!" He was looking down the beach at Karen Berg, who was sitting alone, staring out to sea. He had been trying for ten minutes to pluck up the courage to talk to her, and he was the one to see her fall over, simply keel over from a sitting position to lie immobile on the shingle. He looked over and was surprised to see that the camera wasn't turning over. She wasn't acting. Later, when he was told she was dead, he cried like a baby, in the arms of the Costume Lady, because he realised he would never be able to tell her what he wanted to: how much he loved her work, her movies, all her movies, even the stupid ones. Especially the stupid ones.

No Harm Done

"Hello?"

"*C'est moi*," said the boy with curly hair, his lips to the intercom grille next to the stack of chipped name plates.

"Oh. Oh. Come up," said the Blind Woman's voice.

There was a loud buzz and Pigalle tightened his fist round the knot in the black plastic bag, pushed the door, and stepped in off the Rue de Bièvre, out of the summer scent of sewers and car exhausts. It closed after him with a heavy clang, the tiled floor making the interior into an echo chamber. He rubbed his nose. In spite of the broad daylight outside, the hallway was as dingy, as unwelcoming, as a church. The light bulb above him came on and, far above, a door clicked open and he heard the same voice, made musical by the acoustics of the staircase: "Hello-oh!" He put the black bag over his shoulder like a character from a children's story and loped up the stairs two or three at a time.

It was the top button, the top apartment, the fifth floor. As he came up the stairs he could hear French voices on a dubbed American TV movie. One of them he recognised as the man who dubbed all the tough guys: Kirk Douglas, John Wayne, Jeff Chandler, Clint Eastwood, it was always the same voice, the same guy. The guy must be rich. On a yacht somewhere, he thought. When he reached the half-opened door, he dumped the bag between his feet. After a second, he knocked with his fingertips.

"Come in, said the Blind Woman.

The carpet was white. He scuffed the soles of his running shoes on the landing floor in a little dance before setting foot inside, and as he walked in, looking round, he stuffed his fingers in the front pockets of his jeans and his shoulders hunched an inch closer to his ears. He saw himself in an antique mirror, fringed by mad Rococo flourishes, like a portrait of Napoleon, except it was a portrait of him: a teenage boy in a black Pearl Jam T-shirt and Levi's cut across like mouths at the knees. Beside it was the doorway to the living room, and framed by it, the Blind Woman was standing fringed by an aura of sunlight against the window, filling a jug kettle at the sink. She wore the same baggy purple T-shirt and the Ali Baba style trousers, baggy and tapering in at the ankles: thin as moth wings, in sky blue, moon and star-patterned like night and day rolled into one. "God," she said, laughing. "Five flights of stairs and you're not even puffing."

"Puffing?"

She blew a few times, patting her sun-tanned breast bone. "Puffing. Tired."

"Ah."

"You must be fit. I usually need an oxygen tent." He watched her fingers find the Marlboro Light in an ashtray. As she smoked it she pulled her ash blonde hair back from her face, twice, each side. Her tan was set off by the silver in her hair and the whiteness of her teeth.

Pigalle smiled uncertainly in reply, shifting his weight from foot to foot. *Oxygen tent.* He didn't understand. It didn't matter. She was being friendly.

"So..." She filled the silence on his behalf. "Where exactly – where did you find it, exactly?"

Pigalle picked his way through his English, his thoughts really preoccupied with wondering if she had been crying. "On the what – the sidewalk, no, the – " He stumbled. "*Je ne parle pas bien Anglais...*"

"In the gutter?"

"Gutter. Perhaps. *Oui.*"

"Don't worry. Your English is better than my French," the Blind Woman said, and even when she didn't smile, there was a smile in her voice. Her British accent was a soft, sing-song like the country accents in France, a kind of music. City voices, Pigalle thought, always sounded like dogs fighting for food, or people fighting for attention.

"Stupid," she said.

"*Comment?*"

"Stupid how it happened," she said louder. Her fingers trawled a curtain of hair away from one cheek. "I'm usually not that – stupid. I just put it down beside me for a second. Everybody warns you, don't they? Even on the Metro, about ten minutes before, I heard this announcement: *pickpockets are in operation at this station...*

"*Cela ne fait rien.*"

"What? Sorry..."

"It doesn't matter..."

"No, it doesn't. I know," she said. Her eyes, almond-shaped

and pale blue, were somehow lost in the space between them. "I just don't like to feel stupid. More stupid than I am anyway."

"You are not stupid," he said.

She laughed.

"Oh you say the nicest things. You don't even know me. Still, carry on." The humour was difficult, she realised. "My name's Nina Danelaw."

"Yes." Not the name on the card, he thought. On the business card it read *Patricia Danelaw*.

As if in answer to his thoughts, she said, "The card you found says Patricia, I know. That's my sister's name. It has this address on it. I carry it around. It's handy for taxis. I hand it to them. It saves them trying to decipher my accent."

"Uhuh. Yes." He looked vague.

"I don't know yours. Your name, I mean." She extended a hand, flat and straight, a handshake a wind-up toy would make. He shook it.

"Luc," he lied. The first name that entered his head. Her skin was moist and her hand was small.

"Is that the English spelling or the French spelling?"

"French," he said.

"Ah, short for Lucas. Not the saint then. Or is it? I have no idea."

He didn't reply.

Her eyes sparkled but there was no sign of tears, no bleariness, no red rims to her eyelids. He was disappointed. No, more than disappointed, he felt cheated. It was as if nothing had really happened. How could she be cheerful? What was wrong with her? Perhaps she was mad.

"Do you want some tea? I was just making some."

"No. Thank you."

"No," she said. "Neither do I." She laughed at herself and went and unplugged the kettle. Her step was light and bouncy, like a young girl. He wasn't sure whether it was enchanting or ridiculous.

"Sit down," she called back.

Pigalle looked around the room, noting that there were several framed prints on the walls. All of them were medical illustrations. He wondered what kind of person has these kinds of images on their walls, instead of a nice poster of Le Chat Noir or *Reservoir*

Dogs.

The Blind Woman came back in and he watched her hand smooth along the back of the lemon yellow sofa. "The main thing is, you found it. And you telephoned. There are a million young men out there who wouldn't have bothered. So, thanks. No, really. I really appreciate it." She knelt on the floor and reached out and touched the glass-topped coffee table, feeling for something that wasn't there. She looked puzzled. "Oh. Sorry."

"It is outside," said Pigalle quickly.

"Outside?"

"I leave it by the door..." he said. "You do not understand."

She laughed. "What don't I understand?"

"It is not nice. It..." He struggled for the words and failed again. "I do not know in English. You would not like. Please."

The Woman's forehead creased, but she was still smiling. "I would not like? What do you mean *I would not like?*" Her eyes flickered as if following an imaginary fly.

He went and fetched the black plastic bag. It rustled as he carried it into the room. He placed it on the coffee table and even before he had undone the knot he saw her nostrils quiver and her back straighten like a rod. The plastic rustled louder as he revealed the white open-mouthed handbag inside. As the smell of urine hit her, the Blind Woman gagged and covered her mouth with her hand. From behind the hand he heard her say, "Oh bloody hell," as she stood up and lurched to the kitchen sink.

Pigalle enjoyed hearing her retch loudly and spit out three times. It was some compensation for the fact that she hadn't been weeping. The sun caught the strand of saliva hanging from her lips before she wiped it away with a square of kitchen towel.

"That's disgusting, that is," she said. "That is disgusting."

She returned to the room with one hand following the contours of the wall and furniture. The atmosphere was dominated by the thick, clinging smell of pee. She wrung her hands together and tried to remain unruffled with her chin firmly in the air, but Pigalle could see that the stench turned her stomach. "Gosh, I'm shocked. I'm really shocked. They're supposed to do this sort of thing aren't they? You always hear about it. When they break in and that." She was still for a while. "Oh dear. It's unbelievable, doing that. What's going on in their heads to do that?" She swallowed sourly, her mouth curling. "Will you put it in the kitchen, please? Will you put it – I think I'm going to throw up."

Pigalle wrapped up the Blind Woman's handbag in the plastic bag again and carried it to the kitchen.

"Blimey O'Reilly," she said to herself, forcing herself to inhale the putrid air.

He placed the square Red or Dead handbag in the sink and held it open under the still flowing water. He took out the contents – lipstick, powder compact, a retractable pen, credit card wallet – rinsed them under the hot tap and placed them on the draining board. It was amongst the credit cards that he'd found the business card with the address and phone number on it.

"There's disinfectant under the sink," the Blind Woman said. "Thank you. This is beyond the call of duty, you know?"

"*Comment?*"

"Will it ever be clean, d'you think?"

He found the small bottle and emptied it into the full sink. A caustic odour started to battle the toxic vapour of stale piss that already seemed ingrained in the air. He turned off the taps and washed his hands and wiped them in a towel hanging on the oven rail.

"I think."

On the kitchen table he saw the folded up white cane. Next to it was the half-eaten *baguette mixte - jambon et Emmental -* and the plastic bottle of Badoit that he remembered from the Trocadero.

"I am sorry," he said as he returned to the living room. "I try to speak, no?"

"To say. Yes you did." She had taken out a canister of air freshener from a cupboard, was spraying it liberally around the room.

"I take out the things inside. Lipstick. Ladies things..."

"Lipstick? Don't even talk about lipstick." She spidered her hands for an ashtray and drilled out the Marlboro Light. "What kind of person does that? What kind of person feels the need to do that, eh?"

Pigalle shrugged, though he knew she could not see him. "Animals."

She sucked her cigarette hard. "Kids."

"Kids. Animals. *Oui.*"

"Oui. Wee wee." Another joke he didn't understand. "A golden stream into a stolen handbag. A bit like the pot of gold at the end of the rainbow. Still. What the hell. It's just some – sad lonely pathetic, incontinent…" She trailed away and then said like a pronouncement for posterity: "Content in the knowledge I shall never be that sad or *that* lonely."

"You must check if anything is taken. Perhaps. I don't know. Credit cards?"

She shook her head. "I've phoned up Sentinel and cancelled them all. Sentinel is this company that keeps all your numbers on file. It was the first thing I did. If the bastard tries to use them he's in for a shock. If he hasn't used them already. Anyway, that's the banks' problem now I've reported it. It's their headache, not mine."

"You are very organised."

"You have to be."

He opened another window to let in more fresh air. "I was wrong to do this."

"No, don't be silly."

"To bring this."

"No. Why? What difference does it make?"

"You are upset."

"…A little bit. I'll survive."

The bitter urine clung relentlessly to the air they breathed.

"You are very strong," said Pigalle.

She laughed. "Sometimes," she said.

"I expect – I don't know, maybe you cry. It upsets you, yes, but…"

"Life goes on," she said. "You start to make a big thing out of everything that goes wrong in your life, it doesn't make your life better, it just makes you weaker. Your life isn't made up of the things that go on around you, it's made up of you, inside. Sometimes you have to say to yourself, tomorrow this will be yesterday."

"*Comment?*"

"Tomorrow this will be yesterday. Life goes on."

She took another cigarette and, as an afterthought, held the packet in the air, offering one to the boy as he finished depositing the contents of the handbag into the pedal bin. He took one and lit it, and hers, with a match from the packet on the table, then sat opposite her on the matching lemon sofa.

"Anyway," she said, but never completed the thought. "God the smell is disgusting. Only a man's pee stinks like that. What the hell had the little swine been drinking? That's what I want to know. Lighter bloody fluid? At least I should count myself grateful, at least it wasn't – the full Monty. Solid fuel."

He laughed. "See? You joke."

"Occasionally. It has been known. I have got a sense of humour, although I must say I don't find *Monsieur Hulot's Holiday* that hilarious."

That went over Pigalle's head. "Why you are not angry?"

"Why I am not angry," she repeated. She took one deep breath without the cigarette and one with it. "What's the point in being angry? I'm not going to be angry, because that way they win, don't they? No, I'm not angry. I'm not anything. Anger doesn't get you anywhere." She made another pronouncement. "From one who knows." She sniggered, wanting to undercut her own seriousness. Or, he thought, her hurt.

He sat forward. "The handbag is strong. It is leather. Good leather. The lining can be replaced, no? It will be back to normal."

She laughed. "It's only a bloody handbag."

"It is expensive."

"You're joking."

He watched her cigarette smoke curl in the air above her as she exhaled.

"Where did it happen?"

"You sound like a policeman now."

"No." He sounded insulted.

She played with her Marlboro between fingers like a magic trick. "At the Trocadero. You know. Big bag-snatcher Mecca, they should call it. It was right under my nose. But, what with – there were so many people. Nobody saw anything. That's ironic, isn't it? Considering."

Pigalle stared at her, wondering now if she closed her eyes when she slept, or if like the old man in the Edgar Allan Poe story he had been frightened by as a child, she slept with her eyes wide open.

"Still. Like I say, so what? I'm not living in Bosnia. It's only a handbag. Worse things happen. No harm done," she said. "Would you like a drink? Coffee? Beer? Oh shit, have I asked you that already? Sometimes I think I'm getting Alzheimer's."

He said, "Beer. Oui merci."

The Blind Woman got up, saying, "Stay where you are. I

think I can get all the way to the fridge and back without the aid of a safety net." He watched her negotiate the room carefully but with surprising speed. She returned a few seconds later with a bottle of Amstel and a bottle opener. The mouth of the bottle was so cold it almost stuck to his lips. "*Merci.*" She drank from a bottle herself. He found it a coarse, unbecoming gesture for a woman of such obvious taste and sophistication. It somehow hurt him. He didn't know why.

"How old are you?"

"Nineteen," he lied.

"You sound a lot younger."

"I am a student," he lied.

"Oh? Of what?"

"History. I like history. The costumes, the big houses... you know?" She laughed and he wasn't sure why, but it was like she laughed at him, and then it was gone. "You are English, yes?"

"How did you guess? Sorry, yes."

"You live here alone?"

She shook her head. "I don't live here. I'm just visiting. I live in London. This is my sister's apartment. She's a translator. She does medical work, medical books, doctor's books, that kind of thing. There's a lot of work about, she earns a bob or two." He wondered if there was a sister. It was possible she was a lesbian. Even a lesbian can be blind.

In the kitchen, the handbag sat squat and open-mouthed in the sink, under the creamy meniscus of disinfectant and piss.

She crossed her legs so that one trouser leg rode half way up her shin. He could see clearly the unshaven hairs on her legs. It made him ponder the hairiness of hidden parts of her body. He swallowed more beer and realised he could stare at her, he could stare directly at whatever part of her body he desired. He could hear his heart beat and wondered, before he dismissed it as madness, whether she might be able to hear it too.

"You have a girlfriend?"

"Yes," he lied.

"And have you made love to her?"

He swallowed. "Of course."

He wondered if the Blind Woman imagined his little, darting cock like that of a little dog in the street. It made her smile. Then she felt guilty for teasing him. "I'm sorry. I like embarrassing people. It's a kind of thrill. I can't help it. It's pathetic I know."

He shrugged. "It's daring. It's dangerous."

"Not really. I just like – oh, I don't know, the moment of silence when I have a feeling of power." She curled her foot under her on the lemon yellow sofa, pressing the heel softly into the warm space between her legs.

Pigalle looked at the beer bottle label he had been picking off with his fingers. "If you can't see the reaction on my face, how do you know it is embarrassing?"

She smiled. "That's why it's exciting."

"Silence? Exciting?"

"I said it's pathetic. You're the one who contradicted me."

He turned down the corners of his mouth. "My English is not good."

"Your English is excellent."

She smiled and the ashtray rattled on the glass-topped table as she stubbed out her cigarette.

She could smell nothing from him, even before the handbag and its contents had entered the room. No aftershave, no body odour. Afterwards, when the police, predictably, asked what he smelled like, (perhaps hoping to line up every fragrance in La Samaritaine for an identity parade), she could only say "He smelled like a boy, he smelled of Boy. Not a dirty smell or a sweaty smell, just That Smell." The male officers scratched their heads but a woman officer said, "I know what you mean." It was the smell when boys get too big for your chairs, when they only have to enter a room to make it look as if a bomb has hit it.

"Did you have any money?" Pigalle asked her, as a distraction to the worrying direction of his private thoughts. "In the purse?"

"Three hundred and fifty francs. What's that? Fifty pounds?" She added, "Gosh, you probably would like a reward, that's probably why you're here."

"No, no. Please..."

"I'm so stupid. You must think I'm..."

"Please – no. That is not why I am here," he lied. And then he asked himself, as she crossed the room in front of him, why *was* he there? A little reward, a little cash, it seemed a distant, stupid idea.

She opened a drawer. She was not very attractive, he thought. She was small, like a pixie, and had quite a good figure for someone around fifty. He could imagine what she looked like at nineteen, but her arse had dropped and there was a fattiness on the inside of her upper arms. She was not like the Marg or Jacotte whose nipples stood out like light switches under their T-shirts. But Marg and Jacotte were full of AIDS. The Blind Woman's face was too round like a cat and she had lines pointing to her mouth. He imagined her with a condom in her fingers, rolling it onto a penis close to her face.

She turned back, taking some folding money from inside her passport and handed it to him. "Go on. Go on, take it. Please, I insist."

Her silver hair was cut in a bob, a triangular shape like a wigwam. He wondered who washed it and cut it, and how she knew it was how she wanted it. Perhaps her sister, her so-called sister, cut and styled it. She was entirely in the hands of her sister's tastes. If her sister chose to make her look like an idiot, she would be none the wiser. Pigalle was frightened by the thought of that, of being in someone's hands – of having to trust someone like that.

"Buy books," she said, fluttering the money like a fan.

He took it and squeezed it into his back pocket, saying nothing. She sat down again opposite him.

The window shutters were open, and for a moment the smell of the sewers wafted in and mingled with the pall of urine. Though he knew he was able to stare at her breasts, he found himself unable to do so. No sooner did he focus, but something made him turn away, look up, focus on her face, the unseeing eyes. Not that they looked unseeing. To look at, they were absolutely normal. The only thing that gave them away was the *way* they looked. The way they looked without seeing, that was the only way to describe it. The way they looked like they were seeing *something else*. But of course they were seeing nothing.

It was because of the haircut he had thought she was French when he first saw her at the Trocadero. He had watched her sit and unwrap her *baguette*, fold her white cane, set her handbag next to her on the stone bench in front of the Henry Langlois Museum of Cinema. He played a game when he was bored: guessing the nationalities of the tourists. The Americans with their loud voices and duck-billed hats, the Germans who looked like shaven headed Bratwursts, the English who looked like white-kneed boy scouts. But of course you were wrong as often as you were right. It would not have been a game otherwise. Against the noisy background of shouting teenagers, stealing a handbag from a blind woman was the easiest snatch he had ever made.

Noticing the passport prompted him to say: "It is not difficult for you? Travel?"

"No, not really. Eurostar. I catch a train at Waterloo at lunchtime, and I'm in the Gare du Nord at four o'clock."

"This is a long way from home, for you."

"This? No. I've been a lot further than this." The reflection of the sun in the window panes gave two dots of light to her eyes. "Last year I went to Vietnam. Before that, Indonesia. Australia. Japan. India." She leaned forward and showed him a small necklace with a metal trinket the size of a pen cap dangling from it. "You see this? This is from India. It's a prayer necklace, people put little prayers rolled up inside."

The metal was warm. "What do you have in it?"

She laughed. "Nothing. I don't pray."

"You ought to put something in it," he said.

She sat back, shrugged and tucked the necklace back down the front of her T-shirt. She wore a lot of jewellery: three earrings on one ear and five on the other – holes punched all the way around, like a punk rocker. She was too old for that, he thought, but it suited her. Ethnic rings clicked and shone on her fingers, reflections dancing in the light.

She inhaled. "Do you smell it? It's getting better. Or my nose has given out." She put both feet up on the sofa under her, like a Buddha.

"But I don't understand. Maybe I am rude. You travel. How is this? I am sorry. Where do you go? What – what do you do?"

"You mean, what do I *see*? Nothing." She smiled. The smile sat easily on her face, as if it belonged there, like the shine in her eyes. "I went to the Louvre yesterday. It was fascinating. The Egyptian apartments. Absolutely *wonderful.*"

"You..." he hesitated. "You went to the Louvre? But – why..."

"I listen to voices. I may not see the Caravaggio or the Leonardo or the busts of the Roman Emperors or the torso of Nefertiti, but I listen, and I hear this voice and that voice. It's like a symphony. Sometimes I don't understand the language, but we enjoy opera in Italian even if we don't understand Italian, don't we? And I hear children, touching something, being told not to touch. Little footsteps, all sorts of footsteps – how old? A child – a girl or a boy? *Mama!* There's a whole picture, a whole masterpiece in a word like that, you see? Or an old voice, how many times has this old man sat in front of that painting? I don't know. It's not important to know. It's important to be there, to experience it all." She suddenly felt shy that she had said so much and cast down her eyes. "At least it's important to me. It's Art, of a sort – to me, anyway. The nearest I'll ever get."

All his life Pigalle had lived in Paris and never once had he stepped inside the Louvre. "You go to places. It's unbelievable. You go across the world..."

"It's in my blood, I think. My Dad was in the army. A Brigadier. We had to follow him all over the world. Germany. Vienna. Middle East. The children got dragged along. Never much time to make friends – but still, we saw a lot of the world. It gave me a sort of wanderlust. I can never sit still very long in the same place. I keep moving. I travel light. I'm not very big on possessions. I never buy anything I can't do without. I think everything I care about can go in two suitcases. Sometimes it has to."

Pigalle thought of his own father, the one who took a knife to him and cut open his belly and gave him a criss-cross pink scar that night he left home for good. And his mother, a junkie. He had not seen either of them for seven years. Almost half his life.

"This is for my old man," the Blind Woman said. She took out a small box containing a lead soldier, meticulously painted. She handed it to him. "It's from a shop just around the corner on the Quai de la Tournelle. Have you seen it? The window's full of all these tiny toy soldiers, all immaculate. He let me touch dozens. I was there all afternoon." Pigalle turned the Napoleonic grenadier round and round in his hands and placed it on the table. "My Dad once said that at Sandhurst they had a lecture about leadership, and this top brass said, we can teach you what we know, but when it comes down to it, if you can explain how a jumped up corporal like Napoleon could take an army that's dead on its feet and take over half the known world – well, nobody can explain that. It's an elusive thing, leadership."

"Maybe we are born with it, inside."

"Maybe we're born with everything inside. Maybe that's why history just plays the same tunes over and over again. Do you want to put some music on?" She waved in the direction of a matt black stereo unit, the kind Pigalle knew from the discount stores in

Montmartre. "Look in there. My sister has got a load of CDs. 'Course they all feel the same to me. My ones at home have got Braille stickers. Put on whichever one takes your fancy.

He put his beer bottle on the coffee table and stood up, restless now. "I – er, have to go soon."

"Well, put on one for me, will you? Before you go? Mm?" She smiled a smile for him, but it missed him completely. She was not so good a shot. "Anything except Sting, OK? I could never get on with the idea of a blond bloke from Newcastle singing like a black man." She hunted with her hands for the air freshener and sprayed a jasmin-scented cloud around her head. "My sister's going to think I had a tribe of tom cats in here."

He took the first CD out of the cabinet and put it into the tray, without looking at the cover. It played Steve Reich's *Different Trains*. She went "Ah, good choice. For someone studying history." If it was a joke, it was lost on Pigelle. He felt everything he didn't understand was a kind of jibe, an attack. And there were many things in the world he didn't understand.

Masked by the sound of the music, he carefully put four CDs under his T-shirt, then another four. Out of habit, he watched the Blind Woman, but he saw only the back of her head. She didn't turn. She didn't see. How could she?

"Do you know what I did last night?" she said. "I went on one of those Paris By Night tours by boat." Pigalle stopped and stood and listened. "I did it on impulse, I was walking beside the river and I heard the announcement and I could hear all the people, chattering. It was almost eleven o'clock at night and I wondered what was going on. So I bought my ticket and I sat outside, up top at the front, and it was great. The sound of the wash, the commentary hopping and skipping from one language to the other, the movement of the boat, people talking to one another.

"We went from the Port de Montebello right round the Ile St Louis, past the Istitut du Monde Arabe, under the Pont Neuf. As we were coming up to the Pont Neuf, the girl asked us all to make a wish, but we had to kiss the person next to us and everybody laughed. Then there was the bridge where she said the water came up to a man's chin, a statue I mean, I don't remember which bridge it was. Then everybody got excited because they could see the Eiffel Tower and they all took pictures. I could hear all this clicking, like insects. This Japanese couple, they asked a French

216

guy in broken English to take their picture, but by the time he had we were under the bridge and they missed it and started arguing again in Japanese. At least I think it was Japanese. Oriental, anyway.

"It started to rain then – just little warm droplets, and the atmosphere changed, it felt lighter all of a sudden, and the boat turned round, and we passed the Musee D'Orsay again on the way back.

"And this man took me by the arm and helped me off the boat and said *Bonsoir, madam.*" Her voice trailed away to a whisper. "He was an American, a writer, with his wife. He was writing a book of stories called *Films That Alfred Hitchcock Never Made.* I told him I thought it was a brilliant title. His wife said, 'Don't tell him that.' They walked me home, past all the restaurants in the Rue de la Buchiere, with all the different smells. We had a Calvados somewhere. It was a lovely evening. Beautiful. A perfect way to see Paris."

She arched her head back and he could see her almond shaped eyes and her smile.

Though she would never know, one week later, Pigalle would take the boat trip from the Port de Montebello, as the Blind Woman had done. He would sit at the front, on top, and he would sit with his eyes closed for the entire hour of the journey. He would listen to the lapping water and the strained commentary, to the snatches of conversation and the texture of the noises from the shore. And even when his friends would yell his name and clink bottles from the riverbank, he still would not open his eyes.

"I must go now," he said.

She stood up and smoothed her thighs with her hands, an affectation from wearing a dress. "Of course. Where are you studying?"

"I am not studying today."

He led the way to the door and she followed, only slightly bumping into the arm of a chair. Her teeth were very white against her sun tan, he thought, but she was an old woman. The telephone rang. She said, "Bugger."

He said, "Answer it."

"Do you mind?"

"I go now. Please. Answer it."

"All right. Goodbye, Luc, and thank you."

217

She turned and felt her way to the living room, prodding the door wide. The minimal music was still playing its repetitive bars and loops of voice track.

Pigalle said "Au 'voir," as the Blind Woman was picking up the phone. He slammed the door without going through it, remaining in the narrow hall next to the antique mirror, quite still.

"Oh hi, you. Fine... Oh, I've had a disaster of a day. You wouldn't believe it... I've just had a toy boy in the flat... Just this second, yes..."

After a few seconds, he stepped quietly forward, though really he had no need – *Different Trains* was covering every move he made.

"Yes. That's what I thought, but he got away..."

He stood framed in the doorway watching the Blind Woman coiling the telephone cable in her fingers as she said:

"Listen. Long story. I'll tell you tonight... Pasta – not very exciting... Out? Why not? OK, anything but the pig's ears. Don't mention the pig's ears... See you then, sweetheart. Seven? OK. 'Bye."

Pigalle watched her hang up the phone and feel her way across the cabinet top to the CD player. She turned the volume down a little, but not much. He thought of the blind beggars up around Sacre Coeur who sold fridge magnets, and how he hated the cheap sentimentality they preyed on. He watched the Blind Woman confidently circumnavigate the room with a straight back and a *smile*, collecting his almost-finished bottle of Amstel from the coffee table. She stuck the bottle in her mouth and downed the final half inch of his beer like a man and he found it peculiarly erotic to watch her neck spasm as she swallowed.

He realised he was in the rare, almost occult position, of being in a room after one has in fact left it: observing his *having been there* as objectively as a camera. It was like watching some shameful and discarded part of himself. Like an out-of-body experience, something contrary to the normal laws of nature. He felt a pull like gravity telling him not to be there, but a stronger one rooting him to the spot.

He watched as she sprayed the room with air freshener, like a housewife from a TV commercial.

Almost immediately, the taste of flowers and springtime from the fragrance was defeated by the urine.

He found it didn't offend him any more. How could it? It was his own, after all.

He watched her move around the room. He stayed absolutely still. He knew the slightest rustling of his jeans or his denim jacket might alert her attention. He became like the idiot living statues that performed to tourists in Montmartre, every breath had to be as shallow as a shaman's, every movement as smooth as a robot's. Even the wetting of his lips with his tongue was a task to be undertaken like a man defusing a bomb in an old black and white movie.

For ten minutes he didn't move a muscle.

The Blind Woman drifted in and out of the kitchen and finished her *baguette* on her lap. Afterwards she gathered the crumbs in the folded kitchen towel covering her knees.

He watched as she went back to the kitchen and picked up the small pedal bin in which Pigalle had dumped the defiled contents of the handbag – the lipstick which, unknown to her, he had put up his anus – and the black plastic bin liner in which he had carried it all in. She shuffled with it between her knees to the door of the apartment. Now, she almost brushed past Pigalle, so close that he smelled the Amstel on her breath. The back of his head pressed to the wall and he felt the air frozen and dry in the pocket of his mouth. He thought for a moment she had detected his presence, but she had not.

He watched her put the pedal bin outside the door, come back in, close the door and bolt it, and put on the security chain.

Fifteen minutes had gone by.

He watched her go to her packet of Marlboro Lights and shake it, finding it empty. "Shit," she said out loud. Pigalle smiled. He thought for a moment of fantasy that this is how it would be, that he could be an invisible partner to her, forever, a ghost. That she could do everything but see, and that he could see, *only see*, but do nothing. It was both horrible and romantic in its perfection. The only problem was breathing. Breath would be his only betrayer.

Thirty-five minutes. The time came when *Different Trains* ended.

Holding his breath, Pigalle watched her flick her fingers and sniff at them reluctantly. She pulled a face and wiped them in her T-shirt in the silence, as if she had caught some infection from the pedal bin. He tried to constrict his throat, to hold the air in his lungs, but he felt a feathery tickle in his chest. He felt as if he were underwater. His eyes were fastened on her. In a quick movement, she slipped off her T-shirt over her head, exposing breasts much larger than he imagined, blue veins like electrical wires under ice.

She walked to the bathroom and Pigalle could watch easily from where he stood. She bent over the bath and parts of her anatomy shook or jiggled as she turned on the creaking taps. He could see the red marks on her back where a bra strap had cut in, and the unshaven hair of her armpit. He could see every pimple and mole and hair, every dot of goose flesh. As soon as the water started to gush the silence was broken again and he could breathe.

She slipped out of her Ali Baba trousers, the elastic easing round her stretch-marked thighs, then knees, then ankles as she stepped out of them. She wore bikini panties that had seen better days. She slipped them off and dropped them on the floor and the prayer necklace fell on top of them. Completely naked, she leaned over the bath to add bath oil – the scent of pine – and swill it into the water, and Pigalle saw everything.

As Pigalle watched, she turned off the taps and stepped in. The sound of the rushing water stopped but the plumbing was still noisy as the tank was refilling. Pigalle knew that once the tank was full, he could expect a return to the dull, empty silence he feared.

The soporific heat from the bath radiated out towards him and he felt uncontrollably claustrophobic. He blinked away the beads of perspiration but he realised that his eyes refused to close. They were fixed on the bathroom and on the Blind Woman, and everything about the Blind Woman. There was nothing else.

He could see her nipples sharply delineated against the porcelain of the tub, the rim of her bottom lip just touching the surface of the water. Her hair was wet now and pulled back behind her ears and her mouth half open and her eyes closed.

Within minutes he was sure that she was sleeping, it seemed, although gently moving sufficiently for the water to lap at the head and foot of the bath, ebbing and flowing over her toes and her seaweed hair.

He could hear her breathing but not his own.

He wasn't breathing.

Hers was steady, a long exhale and then a sharper inhale. Her head turned, dipping first one cheek in the bath water, then the other. Beads clung to her lashes and she occasionally brushed a curl of hair from her eyes. Both knees were arched out of the water, wide apart. He observed everything, like a naturalist. Occasionally one hand or the other would cup a soapy wave up her body or wipe a shining breast under the bright, narrow spotlights.

Minutes passed, like hours at the seashore watching the lapping waves and the unchanging scenery. Even the scent of soap and bubble-bath was like bladder-wrack and brine.

Pigalle tried to swallow and he could not. Above somewhere the tank was filling. His time was running out. His breath was running out. He had minutes, perhaps seconds. And what would happen then? In that terrible moment of silence in which he had to *breathe*?

The splashing was more like a rhythm now. He heard a sound from the Blind Woman. Her mouth was making an 0, her chin jutting in the air. At first it seemed like a cry of pain, but as it came again, and again, a quiet moan, a hushed breath, in a kind of melody of breaths, Pigalle stepped silently towards the bathroom door.

The sounds continued and one leg hooked out of the bath, water running down it and forming a spreading puddle on the checkerboard tiled floor.

She was smiling. He, unbreathing, could see that now, both her and the reflection of her, and the reflection of the reflection of her. The lapping of the water wasn't coming from either end of the bath, where the water was still, but a little maelstrom halfway down her body.

As he grew closer, still not breathing, he saw more of her body lying in the green bath, stretched out under the semi-transparent water. She lay half under the green scum of bubbles, her mouth half open. She was squeezing the island of one breast like a toy, the fingers of the other hand buried in the glistening soapy swamp of her vagina, moving steadily and rhythmically, in and out of the pink underwater lips. The look on her face of totally unreachable, private and sufficient pleasure.

And before the tank's silence threatened to drag a sob from his throat, and before he was compelled to do what he had to do to her, Pigalle could not breathe, he could not move – the only thing he could do was look. All he *was* now was that *look*.

He had thought that the Blind Woman was trapped. That's what he had thought, but she wasn't at all. He realised that now. The one who was trapped was him.

Little H

BLANK SCREEN

A little boy's voice in darkness:

> FRED (V.O.)
> Burly Rose... Royal Kidney...

FADE IN:

CLOSE UP – A FRAMED PICTURE ON A WALL

A Victorian St Francis of Assisi, his arms outstretched, with birds on his arms and circling his head.

> FRED (O.S.)
> Sharp's Express... British Queen...

BACK ROOM – GREENGROCER'S SHOP – LEYTONSTONE, EAST LONDON – EVENING (1906)

FRED, a decidedly chubby little boy (aged seven) sits at a plain kitchen table, his hands flat, his chin resting on them. He is frowning with deep concentration.

> FRED
> Northern Star... Evergood... Eightyfold...

WHITE GLOVED HANDS take away one potato from the table top and replace it with a different kind.

> FRED (CONT'D)
> Up To Date...
> (another)
> King Edward...
> (another)
> Red Duke of York...

FRED'S MOTHER (Victorian-prim, early 40's) smiles. Offers her empty hands, no more left. Ten out of ten. She gives a silent, regal mime of applause. Fred beams bashfully.

> FRED (CONT'D)
> Onions. Test me on the onions, now, Mother. Please. I know them all.

> FRED'S MOTHER
> (Irish accent)
> Back home they say onions are a great cure for The Baldness.
> Rub the scalp with a spoonful of onion sap, it'd put hair on a duck's egg.

She ruffles Fred's hair. He laughs. At the sound of the back door closing, the private moment is broken.

FRED'S FATHER (mid-40's) comes in. A stern man with a handlebar moustache, like Kipling's. He takes off his flat cap and hangs it up next to a crucifix on the wall.

He washes his dirt-engrimed hands under the tap at the Belfast sink. The water runs black down the plug hole.

> FRED'S FATHER
> (East End accent; not turning)
> Is the boy ready?

> FRED'S MOTHER
> He is.

Fred's Father turns off the tap, tight – turns, drying his hands in a tea towel.

> FRED'S FATHER
> Right then.

> FRED'S MOTHER
> (under her breath)
> Name o' God, Bill, he's…

FRED'S FATHER
Name o' God nothing...

FRED'S MOTHER
Let him have his tea first. Boy's got to have his tea inside him.

FRED'S FATHER
Fred, put your coat on, son.

Fred's Father rolls down his sleeves, buttons his cuffs.

His Mother fetches Fred's little jacket, and puts it on him. The little boy is excited.

She crouches next to him, tucks his shirt in, meticulously adjusts his little tie. Tries to mask the anxiety she feels with a smile.

FRED
Where are we going?

FRED'S MOTHER
You're going with your father.

She wraps a woolly scarf round his neck.

FRED'S FATHER
Don't mollycoddle him, Em. Leave him.

His Father takes a different hat – a black Bowler – from the hat hooks next to the crucifix.

Fred's Mother gives the boy a big, tight hug, then a kiss on the cheek. She rubs the lipstick off with her thumb.

FRED'S MOTHER
I'm going to make a great big steak and kidney pie. That's what you like, a nice big steak and kidney pie, isn't it? That's your favourite.

Fred nods enthusiastically.

Fred's Father puts his Bowler on and walks towards the front of the shop, pausing to cock his head. Fred follows him, smiling, skipping excitedly.

Fred's Mother sits back at the table, near to tears. When she hears the front door close – the shop bell tinkle – she clutches her rosary beads, closes her eyes.

EXT. GREENGROCER'S SHOP – EVENING

Fred and his Father emerge from the dark, cases of fruit and veg either side of them on the pavement. Fred's Father flexes a hand. Fred takes it. They go.

EXT. ROW OF TERRACED HOUSES – EVENING

Pigeons scatter ahead of them. Two pairs of feet. Fred's socks. His father's big boots.

      FRED
Are we going to the sweet shop? ...Are we?

The feet turn and walk, in step. CAMERA PANS with them, past a cart horse's legs, cart wheels, along the pavement.

      FRED (CONT'D)
Can I have some toffee? A big bit? The sort you break with a hammer?

Fred's hand in his Father's.

      FRED (CONT'D)
...like grown-ups get?

      FRED'S FATHER
We'll see.

Fred looks up at his Father eagerly.

      FRED
Can I?

Stephen Volk

> FRED'S FATHER

We'll see.

Fred level with his Father's watch on a chain as his Father takes it out, looks at it and puts it away.

EXT. RAILINGS AND STEPS – EVENING

They go along some iron railings. Past some "WANTED" posters. Up some stone steps into a door under a blue lamp which reads: "POLICE."

INT. POLICE STATION – EVENING

Fred's Father enters with Fred, sits him on a plain wooden bench.

He walks to a large desk behind which stands a POLICEMAN with a sergeant's V's on the sleeves of his uniform. He has an even bigger and darker moustache than Dad's, and a razor-sharp centre parting. Sergeant-major, Lord Kitchener type. The men's heads go together and they WHISPER.

Fred looks down at his dangling feet.

Sees a game of OXO in ink on his knee. Licks his finger and rubs it off.

He looks up, at a figure across the room.

Sitting on another bench, opposite Fred, is a DISHEVELLED WOMAN. At first glance she seems like a very drunk, very rough prostitute in heavy make-up. But as Fred looks closer he can see blue-grey STUBBLE under the pan-stick. And the hand that lifts a cheap cigarette to her lips is a hairy-backed MAN'S HAND.

He hears a "Ahem…" cough O.S. from the Policeman.

When he looks up his Father and the Policeman are looking at him. His Father gives him a "come here" jerk of the head.

Fred walks obediently to the desk.

POLICEMAN
This is him, is it?

The Policeman finishes what he is writing with a sharp dot. He comes round the desk. The handcuffs on his "snake" belt are level with Fred's face. He extends a big hand.

Fred looks at his Dad.

His Dad nods.

Fred takes the Policeman's hand. The Policeman leads him off.

INT. CORRIDOR – POLICE STATION – EVENING

Fred goes with him down a dark corridor lined with doors. He slowly realises his Father isn't at his side.

He looks back, over one shoulder, then the other.

FRED'S POV – BACK ALONG CORRIDOR

His father isn't going with them – he stands there, his palm raised, waving it slowly like a wind-up toy.

BACK ON FRED – SCARED NOW

He tries to prise his fingers out of the Policeman's hand. He is terrified. His heart is thumping.

FRED'S POV – BACK ALONG CORRIDOR

His Father is gone. Nowhere to be seen. The police station behind them is empty.

FRED
Father? Father?

INT. CELL – POLICE STATION – EVENING

Fred is pulled by the ear into the deep darkness of a small, grimy cell. His ear is let go and as he nurses it, as he hears a reverberating CLANG!

The heavy door has closed behind him. The keys rattle as they turn in the lock. Fred runs to the door.

> FRED
> Father! FATHER!

CLOSE UP – THE PEEP HOLE SHRIEKS OPEN

The beady eye of the policeman peers in.

REVERSE ON FRED

with a fright, he backs away into the room.

> POLICEMAN
> Now then, now then. I thought you were supposed to be a Well-Behaved Little Boy.

Fred goes quiet. The peep-hole scrapes icily shut. He can hear the echoing of his squeaky-military footsteps, the key ring chinking on the Policeman's hip.

Fred backs up further, until he sits on the creaky bed.

He looks at the long black shadows of bars cast on the floor. The big, grim door facing him. The four filthy walls.

Another door slams, LOUD, startling him, and he starts to cry.

INT. CORRIDOR – POLICE STATION – EVENING

The empty corridor.

> FRED (V.O.)
> Father! Father! FATHER!

INT. CELL – NIGHT – ANGLE – THE WINDOW (LATER)

We can hear O.S., Fred still weeping quietly to himself. A gas lamp outside the window is lit. It casts a dull glow inside the cell. The lamp-lighter's footsteps fade away.

ANGLE – FRED

He pulls up a moth-eaten blanket over his cold, bare knees. It has a hole in it. It also smells of something. Fred sniffs it and his face is punched by the rank whiff of stale urine.

He hears echoing footsteps approaching. He sits up.

> FRED
Father… Father?

> POLICEMAN (V.O.)
I'm not your father. Do you want to speak to your father?

> FRED
Yes, please.

> POLICEMAN (V.O.)
Well he's not here, is he?

Fred's face creases up, he starts weeping hopelessly again.

> POLICEMAN (V.O.) (CONT'D)
Oi, oi! Stop that snivelling! Gor blimey! Take it on the chin. Take it like a man, for Gawd's sake!

Fred tries to force himself quieter. He can't.

> FRED
Sorry.

> POLICEMAN (V.O.)
Sorry what?

Stephen Volk

                FRED
Sorry sir.

                POLICEMAN (V.O.)
That's better.

INT. CORRIDOR – POLICE STATION – NIGHT

The Policeman locks a different door, comes back.

                FRED (V.O.)
                (quietly)
Sir, when's he coming back?

                POLICEMAN
Who says he's coming back?

INT. CELL – POLICE STATION – NIGHT

Fred goes to the door, sits with his back against it.

                FRED
He's got to come back. He's got to take me home. For tea.

                POLICEMAN (V.O.)
Oh, he has, has he?

                FRED
Why am I here?

                POLICEMAN
Why d'you think, laddie?

                FRED
I haven't done anything wrong.

                POLICEMAN (V.O.)
Haven't you?

                FRED
No.

230

> POLICEMAN (V.O.)

What? *Never* done anything wrong? Not ever?

> FRED

No.

> POLICEMAN (V.O.)

Little lamb whose fleece is white as snow, are we? That's what your Mother calls you, isn't it?

> FRED

Yes.

INT. CORRIDOR – POLICE STATION – NIGHT

The policeman puts his face up close to the heavy door.

> POLICEMAN

Well – how come you're in here, then, eh?

INT. CELL – POLICE STATION – NIGHT

Fred doesn't have an answer to that.

> FRED

What did I do? What?

> POLICEMAN

You thought nobody was watching, but they were. Everybody was watching. Everybody.

> FRED

It wasn't me. There's been a mistake.

> POLICEMAN (V.O.)

That's what they all say. Criminals.

> FRED

I'm not a criminal. I'm a little boy.

The Policeman laughs. It echoes horribly, like a voice from a drain.

Fred covers his ears. Listens to the footsteps go.

EXT. CELL WINDOW – LATER THAT NIGHT

Fred's head pokes up, barely opening his eyes as he jumps up to try and catch hold of the bars. He does. Peering about.

INT. CELL – POLICE STATION – NIGHT

Fred's feet dangle. He drops back. Standing on the bed now, wiping away tears with the heel of his hand.

He sees five-bar gate scratches gouged into the wall. Lots of them. It makes his lip quiver all the more as he sinks into a ball in the corner, tucking his knees under his chin.

> FRED
> (sobbing to himself)
It wasn't me… It wasn't me!

INT. DESK – POLICE STATION – NIGHT

The policeman stirs his cup of tea. He's trying to read his newspaper, which is spread flat on the desk. He's seemingly deaf to Fred's endless sobbing.

After a while, irritated, takes off his half moon glasses, folds his paper. Arches his aching back. Walks to the door to the corridor leading off.

INT. CORRIDOR – POLICE STATION – NIGHT

The Policeman walks down to the door to Fred's cell.

> POLICEMAN
Blimey, what a racket! What have we got in here? A girl? Eh? 'Cause that's what it sounds like, from out there. A scared little girlie!

INT. CELL – POLICE STATION – NIGHT

Fred is lying flat on the smelly, skeletal bed. Staring through red-rimmed eyes, cheeks tear-streaked, shoulders still heaving gently.

> FRED
> I'm hungry, sir. I'm starving…

> POLICEMAN (V.O.)
> You should've thought of that, matey, shouldn't you?... No steak and kidney pie in here. No plum duff, I can tell you…

INT. CORRIDOR – POLICE STATION – NIGHT

The Policeman's face is stony, Boris Karloff-like in semi-shadow.

> POLICEMAN
> No bread and butter pudding with nice thick custard in here, son. Just bread and water if you're lucky.

INT. CELL – POLICE STATION – NIGHT (INTERCUT)

> POLICEMAN
> …if the rats don't get it first, that is.

Fred sniffs afresh. Quickly lifts his feet off the floor.

> POLICEMAN (CONT'D)
> No toys… No books… No Mum to tuck you in…

> FRED
> Mother'll come. Mother'll come and get me. I know she will…

> POLICEMAN
> Bit of a Mummy's boy, are we?

> FRED
> No.

Stephen Volk

POLICEMAN
Stay at home with your Mummy instead of playing with the rough boys in the streets, do you?

FRED
No.

POLICEMAN
What do you do then?

FRED
Lots of things. Play.

POLICEMAN
Play? Who with?

FRED
Friends.

POLICEMAN
What "friends?" A little bird tells me you haven't got any friends.

FRED
I do. Lots.

POLICEMAN
What do you do then? Football? Cycling? Athletics? Yer, I can see that. You. Very athletic.

FRED
I go. I do go. And, and watch.

POLICEMAN
And what do you do up in your room for hours on end? All on your own, eh?

FRED
Nothing. Read books. Puzzles. Maps. That's all.

POLICEMAN
Books? What kind of books?

FRED

Stories… And train timetables. I like timetables better than stories, even. Facts, numbers, times. I've traveled on every tram in London.

POLICEMAN

A real trolley-jolly!

FRED

Trains, boats, everything. I love it. I've taken the river steamer to Gravesend. I've made a chart on my wall at home showing the positions of every British ship afloat. I chart their courses and check them in the newspapers every day…

POLICEMAN

Trains, boats. That kind of information would be very valuable if it fell into the wrong hands.

FRED

What?

POLICEMAN

You know the type of person who charts shipping lines on his bedroom wall?

FRED

No.

POLICEMAN

The type of person who watches people, watches them and observes them…

FRED

No.

POLICEMAN

I'll tell you what sort of person. A spy. That's what sort of person.

FRED

I'm not a spy.

POLICEMAN
Who would suspect?

FRED
I'm not a spy! I didn't do *anything*!

POLICEMAN
Don't come the innocent with me, Sonny Jim.

FRED
But I *am* innocent.

POLICEMAN
No you're not. You're as guilty as Sin. It's written all over you.

FRED
I'm not guilty. Ask my Mother.

POLICEMAN
Everybody's guilty of something. Even Adam and Eve were guilty
of *something*, weren't they?

FRED
I don't know.

POLICEMAN
What?

FRED
I don't know.

POLICEMAN
I can't hear you.

FRED
I DON'T KNOW!

POLICEMAN
You don't know very much, do you?

Fred bows his head, stares at the floor.

POLICEMAN (CONT'D)
See, there's such a thing as crime and punishment. Even
in the Garden of Eden. Crime. Punishment.

FRED
Punishment for what?

POLICEMAN
For being bad.
(beat)
See, you commit a crime, you don't just let down your Mother and
Father, who brought you into this world, you let down God. And
you know what happens when you let down God?...

Fred nods uncertainly. The disembodied VOICE echoes sibilantly
in the air.

POLICEMAN (CONT'D)
You go down. Down, down, down... You know what I mean by
"down?"

FRED
Yes.

POLICEMAN
That's where you are now. Down. Down in the dark. With the nasty
people. The slugs and snails who don't wash behind their ears.
Ever.

INT. CORRIDOR – POLICE STATION – NIGHT

A mischievous expression is on the policeman's face. He opens the
peep hole and puts his mouth to it.

POLICEMAN
You know who's in the next cell?
(with relish)
Jack the Ripper.

Stephen Volk

INT. CELL – POLICE STATION – NIGHT

Fred stiffens. Eyes white and wide. Terrified.

> POLICEMAN (V.O.)
> Yer… You know who Jack the Ripper is, I take it?... How many women did he top? And just round the corner from here? Not so long ago? Never caught him, did they? So you'd better pipe down or he'll have your giblets for garters like he did them tarts.
> (beat; considers)
> You know what a tart is, Fred boy?

> FRED
> Yes.

> POLICEMAN (V.O.)
> What is it?

> FRED
> It's a little piece of pastry with some jam in the middle.

The policeman laughs horribly, O.S.

> POLICEMAN (V.O.)
> That's right. A little piece of pastry with some jam in the middle. That's what Jack says – don't you, Jack? Jack's having a little chuckle at that, old Jack is.

Fred hugs his blanket to him.

> POLICEMAN (V.O.) (CONT'D)
> Maybe if you ask nicely he'll tuck you in at night, instead of your dear old Mum.

INT. CORRIDOR – POLICE STATION – NIGHT

> POLICEMAN
> That's who we've got in here, see. Murderers who cut you up in tiny pieces. Thieves who steal your money. Spies who watch you when they shouldn't ought to.

INT. CELL – POLICE STATION – NIGHT

Fred is getting more and more terrified and upset now.

> POLICEMAN (V.O.)
> People who have dirty thoughts. 'Cause dirty thoughts don't
> wash away with soap and water, do they, eh?

Fred shakes his head, sobbing heartily now. Pouring tears.

> POLICEMAN (V.O.) (CONT'D)
> Because this is Hell, Fred. That's what it is. Prison is a little taster
> of Hell, for people who see too much or say too little, people who
> haven't got any friends, or whose eyes are too big for their
> bellies...that's what prison is.

Fred is weeping – uncontrollably now. Like a baby. Mumbling
"Mother...mother...mother..." almost silently. Shivering, shaking
with fear.

> FRED
> Mother'll come. Mother'll come and explain. Mother'll come and
> get me. I know she will...

> POLICEMAN (V.O.)
> Will she?

> FRED
> She loves me.

> POLICEMAN (V.O.)
> Does she? Oh, I don't think so. Not any more. Not after this. Not
> after her darling boy done this.
> (beat)
> Nothing can save you now... Not your Dad, not your Mum. Not
> God. Nobody.

> FRED
> I want to go home. Please. Please. Please, let me go home...

POLICEMAN (V.O.)
This is your home. You'd better get used to it, Freddy boy. This is your home now. For the rest of your born days.

Fred is beyond weeping. Shuddering, pouring tears.

INT. CORRIDOR – POLICE STATION – NIGHT

The Policeman turns and walks away. Fred continues weeping uncontrollably. He switches off the light.

POLICEMAN
Nighty-night. By the way, tuck them toes in, the rats get a bit peckish in the wee small hours.

The Policeman goes into the station and shuts a heavy door after him, taking the picture to:

BLACKNESS

FADE IN:

INT. CELL – MORNING LIGHT – BREAKING THROUGH THE BARS

Sunlight falls on the bed, the shadows of bars across the huddled shape of Fred under the grubby blanket. His grey socks sticking out from under it. A key rattles in the lock. Fred wakes, hair tousled. He sits up on the creaky bed. Still half sleep.

The Policeman opens the door.

POLICEMAN
All right, Jack the Ripper. Let's be having you.

INT. DESK – POLICE STATION – MORNING

The Policeman takes Fred by the hand, out into the station desk room.

Fred's Father is sitting on the bench the boy sat on. He wears his flat cap and a greengrocer's apron.

FRED'S FATHER
Behaved himself, I hope.

POLICEMAN
I think he's learned his lesson.

Fred's Father puts a box of fruit and veg on the desk. The Policeman takes it, puts it on the floor behind the desk. Rubs an apple on his chest and munches it.

Fred's face is bleary from a night of weeping. Traumatized.

FRED'S FATHER
(to Fred)
Now you know what happens to naughty little boys.

Fred sniffles. Nods.

Fred's Father holds out his hand. Fred takes it. He looks up at the Policeman.

Who puts his pencil in a desk sharpener, grinds it, blows at the point.

He watches Fred and his Father walk out into the sunlight. Gets back to his newspaper.

EXT. STREET OUTSIDE POLICE STATION – MORNING

Pigeons scatter again. Fred's Father and Fred walk away from the police station, up the pavement. The city is starting to wake. A passing WORKMAN doffs his hat.

WORKMAN
Good morning, Mr. Hitchcock.
(then to Fred)
'Morning, Alfred.

Stephen Volk

Fred flickers a smile hello. The workman walks by. Fred's Father pauses before crossing the road.

Without letting go of his Father's hand, the chubby-faced little boy looks back in the direction of the police station.

FREEZE FRAME

ROLL END CREDITS

FADE OUT

Afterword

Stephen Volk

I remember vividly the first adult book I bought with my own pocket money, in Gould's newsagent's in Pontypridd, at the tail-end of a misspent childhood immersed in *Fantasic Four* comics, Marvel classics, and *Famous Monsters of Filmland*.

Its cover depicted a man in an electric chair, with a hood over his head, against a lurid green background. It looked like a photograph. Maybe it *was* a photograph. It was emblazoned with the no-nonsense title *Torture Garden*, a collection of stories by Robert Bloch, published to coincide with the release of the film of the same name. Dredging up the memory of that long lost paperback still brings a weird, pathetic frisson. It probably cost two shillings: it was only big fat paperbacks cost half a crown in those days. But it was my inauguration to the pleasure dome of horror stories.

The movie itself I remember far less clearly. IMDb tells me it came out in 1967, one of those Amicus portmanteau films post-*Tales from the Crypt* (or post-*Dead of Night*, in fact) produced and sometimes written by horror aficionado Milton Subotsky. Wonderfully enjoyable as they were, and are, those movies blur together after a while, and all I now recall about this one in particular was the marvellous Jack Palance as an insane Poe fanatic and Burgess Meredith (The Penguin of TV series *Batman*) playing The Devil.

But the book was another matter.

The first story was 'Enoch' and it was about someone hearing voices. It was about someone who was mad. It was horror, not outside in the world of special effects or make-up, but in someone's head. And I was never the same again.

What got me about Robert Bloch wasn't just that he was famous for *Psycho* (which I hadn't yet seen, but was already notorious), but that he wrote stories, *and* films. And horror! And *Star Trek*, for God's sake!

This was who I wanted to be. I wanted to be Robert Bloch. No question.

My first screenplay was written in school, when I didn't even know how to *type* a screenplay, and had barely mastered the typewriter. I sent it to Milton Subotsky, in the heady days when producers even deigned to *read* unsolicited manuscripts – and he did. He even wrote back to say it had potential, and gave me notes. I got my first producer's notes and I was still in sixth form. I couldn't believe it!

There the fairy tale ends. Of course the film was never to be. And I know now what I didn't know then: that a producer showing interest only means you have a one-in-a-million chance of a film being made, as opposed to one-in-several-countless-billions.

But some stories in my illusory Amicus portmanteau film weren't bad. One, about astral projection, I used twenty-odd years later in the BBC anthology series *Ghosts*, as 'I'll Be Watching You'. Another, about a Dracula ventriloquist doll who gets a taste for blood, I still think could be fun, very much in the Subotsky/Bloch mould.

Fast forward to now. By no means comparing myself to the master, but in as far as a Grammar school boy from the Valleys can turn into Robert Bloch, I have. Or as near as my talent and perseverance have allowed. Which is astonishing, not least to me.

I've written enough Hollywood studio films to earn a nice living, though I've never written anything purely for the money. Some were made, some not. Some I'm pleased with, some not. I've worked with Oscar winning directors like Ken Russell and William Friedkin. Both were an experience. I've shocked the nation, albeit briefly, with the BBC TV Halloween hoax *Ghostwatch*, and had my own supernatural drama series, *Afterlife*, recently air on ITV to pretty good critical and audience acclaim.

I've also, from time to time, written short stories. Which Mr Bloch showed me is not impossible, either. Thank you, Mr Bloch.

And here they are, collected under one cover for the first time.

But I can't pretend otherwise: screenwriting is my day job. In fact you could say I'm married to it, and my occasional forays into prose fiction are akin to an illicit affair on the side.

However, though I love the craft and art of writing for films and television, with all screenwriters there is inevitably a sense, a knowledge that, however good, one's work on the page is a means to an end, not the end itself. And it's natural, sooner or later, bruised and battered by the tortures and vagaries of the Biz, to seek solace in a world where we feel at least we have 'Director's Cut:' i.e. creative control.

That is, the world of prose fiction.

Alluring as it is, the two disciplines require of the storyteller the development of very different creative muscles, as well as a different toolbox of skills.

The novelist, most notably, is at liberty to describe (and describe *only*, if she or he wishes) the internal voice of a character. The screenwriter, on the other hand, can't. He or she has to convey thought and character by action and dialogue alone. I think of it as alternate sides of the eyeball. The novelist looks in towards the brain and thought, with all the freedom that implies, and the screenwriter is limited to pointing the other direction; seeing and hearing external scenes on the far side of the pupil.

I don't know which is the most difficult, but I know screenwriting isn't the easy option, and woe betide anyone who thinks so. A script has to be mercilessly concise, and some novelists find this hard to learn – or perhaps, fair enough, don't want to.

The inherent skill of film writing isn't just in the formatting of the dialogue down the middle of the page (any fool can be taught that in five minutes), but a way of imagining – and like all things that look easy, it's a hard thing to do well.

In my experience, novelists' first-time screenplays often make clunking mistakes in the 'Full Ashtray' department. I call it this because they will often write, for example: 'INT. MATERNITY WARD. DAY. Joe (34) is a banker. He has been waiting for six hours.' I say: How can we possibly know he's been waiting six hours? We can't. So we have to cut to the full ashtray (or whatever). For that matter how do we know he is 34 without seeing his birth certificate? 'Mid-thirties' is fine. And how do we know, yet, that he's a banker? And so on.

Sound and pictures. That's the blessing and that's the curse.

Also there's the plain difference of temperament. John le Carre said wisely in an interview, "Novelists don't easily delegate. They don't naturally give away the costumes, the atmosphere, the voices." Screenwriters can do that – indeed, *have* to do that. "Novelists are crabby and possessive about the stuff they imagine."

Newsflash: Screenwriters are too. But suffer in silence. Or bitch about producers over their cappuccinos. As they have done ever since Louis B. Whatever called them "schmucks with Underwoods."

It can be the world of the underdog. True.

So, over the years, in between getting so-called "creative notes" from studios, I've found a welcome liberation in writing short stories. Mainly because they weren't commissioned. Mainly because nobody asked me to. They were simply what I felt like writing, and nobody could stop me. There was a gleeful privacy about it.

They were *mine*.

It was nice to have a total absence of collaborators, and do battle with the blank page, grimly and excitedly alone.

It was nice to challenge myself to write a story that would be *impossible* to film, like 'Curious Green Colours...' (Even if now I wonder what that film might look like.)

It was nice to take an idea, character or *voice* and run with it, without being mindful of film-making constraints or commissioning editors' foibles.

It was nice to play with words knowing that they were your direct, undiluted connection to your audience.

These stories would often be written in between script assignments, as a welcome relief and necessary revivification before returning to the more familiar trenches of warfare in Hollywood or Shepherd's Bush.

In short, the joy in short stories for me was to be designer, cast, director, prop man, sound recordist, editor and producer. And not to have to endure "death by a thousand improvements," for once. To, instead, just listen to a voice and only one voice; the voice of the story.

For those who care about such things (as Russell Banks puts it), here are a few words about the genesis of some of the tales herein:

'31/10' was written in response to a request from a publisher who was planning a book to celebrate the ten-year anniversary of *Ghostwatch* in 2002. On Halloween night, 1992, the BBC had transmitted this TV drama, written by me, which purported to be a "live" broadcast from a haunted house in London. Everything about the show was fictional, however some of the audience clearly didn't think so, and the phone lines were jammed with calls from apoplectic viewers, some scared out of their wits. Headlines hit the Sunday newspapers that "Heads Must Roll at the BBC," questions were raised in Parliament, some people even thought the BBC had "raised demonic forces" by transmitting the programme, and Ghostwatch assumed a kind of cult notoriety for terrifying the nation. (It was even cited in the British Journal of Medicine as being the first television programme to cause Post Traumatic Stress Disorder in children.) The tenth-anniversary book never happened, so I am glad for the opportunity, here, to include the tongue-in-cheek sequel.

'The Best in the Business' was based on an incident that happened to a friend of mine, director Christopher King at his home in Wiltshire. I pretty much only changed the setting to California, the protagonist, which seemed fitting, and added the ending.

'The Anamorph...' was partly inspired by a painting, of similar description to that in the story, bought from a junk shop by Chris's wife Lizzy.

'The Latin Master' came from a visit to the historical Roman Baths in Bath Spa, combined with mixed memories of various teachers in Pontypridd Boys' Grammar School, of my youth.

It was the first of a number of ghost stories I've written in the style of M.R. James, Arthur Conan Doyle, Algernon Blackwood and Seabury Quinn, though an astute reader may detect the flavour of other masters of the genre from the late 19th and early 20th Centuries. These tales mostly appeared in Ash Tree Press anthologies and the magazine of the Ghost Story Society, *All Hallows*. 'The Anamorph...'; 'The Chapel of Unrest'; 'The Fall Children'; 'A Pair of Pince-Nez' and 'Sleepless Nights' all feature, directly or indirectly, an "amateur supernaturalist" named Venables, and I hope I might add more of his adventures to the list in the future.

Like Oliver Onions, who was sceptical of ghosts in reality, I have always found them irresistible as an art form with its own regulations, idiosyncrasies and beauties. After all, one does not have to believe in war to write a war story.

'Three Fingers, One Thumb' began with that Ambrose Bierce-esque title, and the fact that early animators chose to digitally-inhibit their offspring. That, and my deep suspicion of feel-good factories such as theme parks and the cheery characters who populate them.

'The Chapel of Unrest' emerged as I realised I had never read a horror story about an undertaker – which I felt very remiss of the genre.

'Blitzenstein' was born out of my macabre obsession with *Frankenstein* (viz. the BAFTA-winning short film I wrote, *The Deadness of Dad*, and Ken Russell's *Gothic*). It was also informed by my brother Andrew's obsession with building a Guy Fawkes dummy when we were young: figures I always found, and find, vaguely disturbing.

'The Fall Children' was written after my wife and I moved to Wiltshire, to a 17th Century weavers' cottage which had a thirty-foot deep well in the kitchen – though the house we live in has never given any indication of being haunted, other than by us.

'Indicator' is an exploration of how a liar, or criminal, is born. In its second half it describes almost exactly an incident from my own childhood. I transcribed as accurately as I can remember it.

'No Harm Done' grew out of seeing, in Paris, a woman fighting off a teenage pickpocket who had grabbed her handbag. That, and the memory of Poe's tell-tale heart. All hearts tell tales, and sometimes the blackest are the more interesting.

'Curious Green Colours…' was an experiment in fantasy, and language, to see what would happen if you put the most logical profession (private detective) slap-bang in the most illogical world. This story is probably the nearest I could ever come to writing a whodunit. I realised afterwards that Malachi Persona is the illegitimate offspring of Jerry Cornelius and Jason King: two of my great boyhood heroes.

I don't believe monsters can be picked out in a crowd or even at home, and this is the basis of 'Time Capsule'. I explored a similar character/theme in a different way in 'Lower Than Bones', episode two of my TV series *Afterlife*.

'The Good Unknown' was inspired by meeting Madeleine Stowe on the set of a film I wrote, *Octane*. The idea of an anxious American, alone in Europe, on a film set, appealed to me. We earlier sent the script of *Octane* to Sharon Stone: we never heard back, but she, unbeknownst to her, subsequently inspired the ending.

'Little H' is a well-known anecdote about a well-loved director: a traumatic incident from his childhood, which may have set him on the road to great art. It was a true story crying out to be dramatized, I thought. I wrote it as a short film, but realised afterwards it also worked as a short story, keeping the painfully apt script form. Perhaps it will be a short film one day too. Who knows?

If the above account of the stories' various inceptions is obscenely prosaic, it has to be said it's only at best half the story, of course.

Observations, images, thoughts, anecdotes or memories do not always result in stories. Any one of the above elements can sit on the back burner for years. What makes a tale worth telling is a juxtaposition of many things – two at least. The blue touch-paper is lit. Then it becomes a mysterious compulsion, a need, a directive you cannot ignore. And it's not for nothing that often we writers feel that a story 'tells' itself – or knows when it is right.

I'm sure Mr Bloch would understand.

He is one of many writers whose influence is no doubt all too palpable in these pages.

Whether, en masse, these diverse fragments tell you anything about their author, I honestly have no idea. Other than the 'Venables' stories, they all seem quite diverse to me – but that is probably my failing of self-knowledge, and common threads of theme, tone and recurrent obsession are probably there to be discovered to those who wish to look for them.

As the director Nicolas Roeg once said: "What is there but to be continually obsessed?"

Stephen Volk
Bradford-on-Avon, Wiltshire
October 2005

Acknowledgements

The stories in this collection originally appeared as follows:

'The Latin Master' in *Midnight Never Comes*, 1997

'Three Fingers, One Thumb' in *Samhain*, April/May 1998

'The Anamorph of Hans Baldung Grien' in *All Hallows* 21, June 1999

'Blitzenstein' in *Hideous Progeny*, 2000

'The Chapel of Unrest' in *Shadows and Silence*, 2000

'The Fall Children' in *All Hallows 26*, February 2001

'A Pair of Pince-Nez' in *All Hallows 29*, February 2002

'Indicator' in *Crimewave 7: The Last Sunset*, 2003

'Sleepless Nights' in *All Hallows 33*, June 2003

'Curious Green Colours Sleep Furiously' in *Postscripts #3*, November 2004

'Time Capsule' in *Crimewave 8: Cold Harbours*, 2005

'The Good Unknown' in *Poe's Progeny*, 2005

'31/10', 'The Best in the Business', 'No Harm Done' and 'Little H' appear for the first time in this volume.

My heartfelt thanks go to those editors and publishers who have generously shown me an open door into the print world: John Gullidge, Barbara and Christopher Roden, Brian Willis, Darren Floyd, Andy Cox, Maxim Jakubowski, Pete Crowther, and of course (without whom) Gary Fry. Thanks also to Michelle James for her proofreading. Finally, deep gratitude to my friend and mentor Tim Lebbon.

Printed in the United Kingdom
by Lightning Source UK Ltd.
110960UKS00001BA/139-174

9 780955 092237